BREAKING FREE

RISE OF THE DRAGON
VOLUME 1

J.E. Maier

The Prophecy of the Setting Sun
'A dragon of Earth shall rise from the West.'
—circa 1945 September

Breaking Free / J.E. Maier — 1st ed.
ISBN 979-8-9909137-0-7

*It is, in some way, accurate to say I created this book for you.
I wish upon a dandelion seed this tale finds you in your time of
need, and the characters save you just as they saved me.*

*I speak many languages, few through words, and hope my blood,
sweat, and years of anxiety for the future will soothe you in
whatever phase of growth you're in.*

*'Love is and has always been our greatest connection. That which
makes us human.' —Jenilyn Evette Maier*

*"Money. Love. Knowledge.
These are the three powers that rule the world.
And each comes with a price.
Acquiring wealth requires you to sell your soul.
Love requires you to bet your heart.
And wisdom? Well, it simply requires your sanity."*
—J.E. Maier

Contents

One for the Ages

March 16th, 1988

'This is Jaxx Wilder, and you're listening to WNDY—Chicago's number-one radio station! I hope all of you listeners out there are staying dry during this downpour—it's said to be one of the worst in history! Excessive flooding in the northern suburbs means trouble if you're looking to travel. O'Hare airport has been evacuated and stands as an island while the expressways are underwater. Bad news for us, good news for the fish! Over fifteen thousand buildings have been affected by the accumulation in Cook and DuPage counties as people flee our beloved city.'

The air reeked of panic sweat while the crackling announcement from a smooth disc jockey imbued the stuffy cabin. A pregnant woman lay in the backseat, her hand pressed against the foggy back window. With her thighs splayed across the seat, she bore the burden of intense spasms.

"Hang on for a few more minutes." Examining the blood trickling to the floorboards, her husband hunched forward to speak with the cabbie. Despite the natural progression of labor, an invisible power kept the baby in the womb, as if the threads of fortune were holding out for the right time. "The speed limit is thirty; you're doing twenty-five."

Gripping the steering wheel, the driver's knuckles turned white. He glanced at his passengers in the rearview mirror, and a ghost of fret pained his features. "I can't go any faster! Can't we go to a closer hospital? There's one in La Grange."

He studied his wife; her eyelashes fluttered like a gilded butterfly, unable to remain open after enduring hours of contractions. "Get us as close as you can."

"Léna, stay with me..." He positioned a hand over her uterus. "Remember how much you love music? Sing to our baby."

She recited a few lines from her favorite Breakfast Club tune, pushing down again. Bested, she surrendered to the spasms, her skin pallid and cold. "*Our baby?*"

"Our baby." He embraced her with a faulty smile. "You need to stay alive to see her."

"Our baby—" She mumbled with a glint of hopefulness. "She will save the world."

"That's right, she will." He traced her cheekbone, urging her on. "Listen to the radio and try again—"

'Astrologers believe this could be a year for the ages as Saturn, Uranus, and Neptune form a conjunction that hasn't been witnessed since 1307. Natality rates are predicted to peak for the first time since 1964. What is it that's making the world's population grow at such an exceptional rate? To understand the significance of this triple conjunction, we must first analyze the importance of these slow-moving planets. Last observed in the 1820s, the Uranus-Neptune conjunction spawned many well-known geniuses, and parents across the globe are putting high hopes on the shoulders of their children. 1988 also marks the year of the dragon—earth, to be exact—as Asian populations are expected to jump. Whether or not you believe in auspiciousness, let's come together and pray for a better world and hope, much like the conjunction of 1820, we spawn a new generation with big hearts and even bigger aspirations.'

"We need a doctor!" With a flash of fulguration, the man carried his hemorrhaging wife through the hospital. Blood trickled from under her skirt, painting the ivory tile crimson.

From behind a tall admissions desk, a receptionist rose to her feet. Eyeing the pooling blood, she grabbed the phone. "We're on bypass. I'll find a bed for you and notify the Mobile Intensive Care Unit."

Infuriated and exasperated, the man refused to evacuate. "We've tried two already. There's nowhere else for us to go."

The receptionist's attention passed from the couple to the entrance. Outside, a team of aides erected a triage tent, housing those awaiting treatment. Inside, the infirmary was doubled with patients, stretchers lined the examination corridors, and the operation bays were at capacity. Overrun by Chicagoans seeking urgent medical assistance, the conference center and break rooms were outfitted to accommodate the overflow.

Preparing to turn them away, she caught a pudgy trauma nurse scampering through an adjacent hallway, wheeling a cart loaded with supplies. Dashing out from behind the desk, she blocked her. "Mariana, I need you to look at a patient."

Mariana maneuvered the trolley. "Let me get these—"

Running alongside the cart, the receptionist transmitted what little information she knew about the bleeding mother. "She's full term and hemorrhaging."

"*Hemorrhaging?*" Pushing the cart into the emergency bay, Mariana darted back to the lobby, followed by the receptionist. Approaching the couple, she pulled a stethoscope from her collar and fixed the instrument in her ears. "What happened?"

"She went into labor during the evacuation." The man studied his wife. "I tried to deliver, but the baby is stuck—"

"*Stuck?*" Mariana grazed the woman's skin, gasping at the warmth radiating from her. "She's lost a lot of blood."

Untangling the expectant mother's hair, she inspected her pupils. "Can you tell me your name?"

"Léna..." Another wave of agony struck her midsection.

"You're going to be okay. I've alerted the team; they should arrive soon." Mariana reassured her, though she wasn't convinced.

Smelling of antiseptic, a lanky male intern joined the scene. Pulling two chairs together, he blurted an apology for the makeshift delivery room. "This is the best we can do."

The man helped his wife onto a chair, while Mariana positioned her legs on another. Crouching to analyze the half-birthed baby, she choked a diagnosis. "Shoulder dystocia—"

Saturated in blood, the father paced the red-splotched floor while his spouse attracted further practitioners. Continuous beeping from the life-monitoring devices proved erratic, and he knew it couldn't have been normal. Immobilized, his nails dug into his fleshy palms, helpless in the face of his wife's distress.

"You're doing great." Mellowing acute contractions with gas and oxygen, a senior assistant revealed a face of horror.

The young male intern vocalized unrest. "What do we do? The doctors are busy with the train derailment."

"We'll do what we can," answered Mariana, administering a healthy dose of meperidine through an intravenous line.

The husband grew anxious after hearing hushed murmurs from the team. Though each professional assessed the crisis, few acted. "Can someone explain what's happening?"

Pivoting to address him, Mariana placed a hand on his shoulder. "Your wife is experiencing a rare complication causing the baby to become impacted on the mother's pelvis."

Blinking at his wife, his lips quivered into a frown. The heavy droplets of sweat on her forehead were testimony to physical exertion. She was on the verge of giving up. "You can't take some clamps and pull her out?"

"We're taking all necessary precautions to free the baby while keeping your wife's well-being our top priority."

When she returned to the laboring mother, four sets of relatives passed through the double doors. Clamoring in the lobby, they barraged him with rapid-fire questions, each competing for answers. He struggled to keep up. "I don't know."

"Halmoni!" Setting his focus on his grandmother, he enveloped her fragile frame. She stood a few inches above table lamp height, her back curving from the weight of her age. He smoothed her wiry hair. "She's caught on—"

Remembering the remaining elders, he gave a respectful nod to the husbands and addressed the wives by name. "Grandmother Ingrid, Borbala, Achukma."

"We came as soon as we heard—" Smelling of cooked onion and bell pepper, Borbala removed a black and white apron from around her well-fed waist. "How is my granddaughter?"

He bit his lip, eyes fixed on his wife. "She's in pain..."

Achukma, who bore a striking resemblance to the man, stepped forward, wearing traditional garb ornamented with intricate beadwork in shades of blue, red, and yellow. A white and blue lightning sash cinched her waist, signifying her status as a revered elder. "And what of the baby?"

Her deerskin puckered-toe moccasins pointed to her nascent great-granddaughter. "Will the baby survive?"

"They're doing their best..." His head wobbled, unsure where to lay his gaze.

Ingrid clutched her husband's hand. "Being born on such a destructive night? Hundreds of people have died."

Borbala's eyes expanded. "What if we were *wrong*?"

Achukma clicked the roof of her mouth and gave a glare of abhorrence. "It's too late for that. You should've remained in Hungary if you didn't want—"

"You're going to blame *me*?" Borbala flushed with anger, jabbing a thick finger at Ernest. "What of Ingrid and Ernest? He's the one who believed the old coot and sought us out to complete the rule of fours!"

Ernest's jaw clenched, prepared to defend his honor. "The Originator was adamant the prophecy was—"

"The *prophecy*!" Borbala elevated her arms in a melodramatic wave. "How can you be so sure you didn't force a fate on an innocent child?"

Ingrid advanced to guard her husband. "*Force a fate*? Is it so wrong to imagine a peaceful world?"

"Don't patronize me with more buffalo shit about the end of the world. The world will not cease to exist; *humans will*." Achukma's voice intensified, gesturing wildly at the torrent. A volatile fusion of leaves and dirt swirled through the air, desperate to seize the hospital. A tree branch crashed against the glass, causing her to flinch. "This is not how peace is born. Destruction is loud! Creation is calm and quiet. The falling tree makes a sound; the growing seed does not."

Swiveling, Achukma found the nurses positioning Léna on all fours, her agonized cries pervading the room. "Does *that* sound like calm to you?"

"The cord is wrapped around her neck!" Shouting to cover the beeping monitors, Mariana collapsed to her knees, hurling instructions to the adjacent caregivers. The soon-to-be grandparents stood in shock, capturing a glimpse of the baby's head emerging from the parturient canal, pale and tinged with blue. Panicked hands grabbed for water, towels, and surgical shears as the team labored to emancipate the newborn. "Hustle! Before we lose both!"

Running his hands through his sudor-drenched hair, the father-to-be kicked an empty chair. "*Halmoni!* You never said this would happen."

"Pa-Goe—" A thunderbolt struck a shrub outside the hospital, and rolling thunder rattled the walls. His grandmother's jagged silhouette twisted to face the birthing area. "It was always meant to be like this."

"You're wrong, Yu-Chi." Ingrid's nostrils flared, refusing to meet her eyes. "We should have never—"

Yu-Chi stood in the center of the room, her broken squawking echoing down every hall. Arms lifting, her white robes billowed, encircling her ankles. "Be proud of what we've done! We've combined the four corners of humanity."

"No—" Borbala's breath strangled in her throat. "I didn't think this would—"

Yu-Chi's wrinkled features contorted into a sinister leer, revealing a mouth full of crooked teeth. She poked a bony forefinger at Borbala. "After hearing about the Originator, *you* immigrated to this land to prove the predictions wrong!"

"*You!*" She jabbed an appendage at Achukma. "You dreamt of a Sun God who asked you to move from your tribe to this city in exchange for fair weather!"

"And *you!*" She transferred her focus to Ingrid and Ernest, moistening her parched lips with a slavering tongue. "You brought the second piece of the prophecy here! You could have left it in the ashes of war. Instead, you brought a constant reminder of conflict to your home."

"It's not a reminder of war." Ernest swatted her hand away from his face. "It's a prayer for peace."

"There cannot be peace without conflict." Yu-Chi's flowing vestment brushed the blood-splattered tiles as she motioned to the group of elders. All four sets, united with the father and mother, formed a six-pointed star. "Pa-Goe, don't you see? The six points represent the union of heaven and earth. The push and pull of all things. We have done as the forces wanted."

Thunder rumbled overhead. Terrified professionals huddled around the patient, clutching flashlights for a feeble amount of light. Yu-Chi stood with her arms facing the stormy sky through the glass panes. A vivid bolt zapped the sidewalk, illuminating her wicked smirk. "*This* is the moment!"

Achukma snickered at the baleful senior. "You don't seriously believe the prophecy? Surely nobody could predict—"

With each stamp of her worn goosefoot cane, Yu-Chi's snarl cracked the facade of reality. The fluorescent lights, flashing like fireflies in a swirling tempest, established her dominion, and the gasps from the room were an orchestration of her ferocity. "A dragon of earth shall rise from the West!"

"Halmoni, stop!" Pa-Goe seized her arms.

"What's done is done!" She clutched the stick, slamming the base onto the floor. Splinters scattered around her feet as she began to chant. "A dragon of earth *will* rise from the West!"

Conjured by her words, the heart monitors affixed to the laboring mother beeped erratically. Nurses rushed in, toiling to stabilize the exigency. "We need to deliver this baby *now!*"

Amidst the chaos of beeping and shouting, one grandparent roared. "We've come all this way!"

"It's not for us to intervene." Another utterance was suppressed by the staff knocking over equipment in their haste to rescue the baby.

Reaching into her vesture, Yu-Chi extracted a stone dagger. Intricate and hand-carved, the weapon was dappled with imperfections along its slender blade and appeared to be antique, if not ancient. Inspecting the hilt, she cackled, recognizing the power within her family's heirloom. "Pa-Goe, do you remember the significance of this? It's from the Bronze Age—passed down for thirty-five hundred years. Any museum would die to have it, but we kept it for this specific purpose. You see, I had a vision, too. Just as our ancestors have sacrificed for thousands of years, I will make the needed offering."

Gripping the handle, she charged at Borbala. She swung the blade, and Pa-Goe lunged in front of his wife's grandmother. "Halmoni, stop! This isn't how it's supposed to be!"

Invoking the combined strength of their predecessors, she thrust the knife, spewing ramblings as if she were speaking in tongues. "A choice that isn't free!"

He evaded her attacks, though the dance with danger only fueled her aggression. "In blood they are bound!"

Stepping back, Borbala stood in horror as Pa-Goe tried to pacify his grandmother. During the scuffle, an unexpected arc illuminated the room and triggered the lighting to flicker off. From the shadows, the racket of a conflict penetrated the darkness until the backup generators engaged. When the harsh light recrudesced, Pa-Goe stood over Yu-Chi, gripping the bloodied shiv. She lay on the floor with a deep wound to her chest, a well of blood spreading towards their shoes. He released the weapon with a deafening clatter, falling to his knees.

"She's out!" Among the mayhem, life entered the world. Mariana wrapped a pink blanket around the slippery newborn. The clinical staff held their breath, waiting for the infant's cry, and when it came, they rejoiced.

"Just shy of midnight. A few more minutes and she would have been a total eclipse baby." The intern recorded the time. Turning to reveal a successful geniture to the waiting family, he saw the gruesome aftermath of the struggle and released an overwhelming wail. Ichor blanketed the floor, marking a tragic end to what should have been an hour of new beginnings.

Pa-Goe's kneecaps dug into the floor, cradling his grandmother's lifeless body. He swiped at the blood stains on her jowls, only smudging them further. "Halmoni, no! You're not gone—you can't be—why did this..."

"Pa-Goe..." Achukma hoisted the wailing infant into her arms. "She made it."

Elevating his chin, he sneered. "This is *her* fault!"

"Pa-Goe—" Léna hollered for her husband, perspiration blurring her vision. Resting across two chairs, her legs were streaked with a mix of blood and amniotic fluid. Practitioners busied around her, wiping down the birthing area and cleaning bloody tools. "She is your *child*."

"No—" He thrashed his head, pointing a hemic finger at the newborn. "She's an *abomination!*"

Achukma shifted the soft fabric to cover the infant's shoulders. "For a father to say such things makes him not a father. Even if he is the child of my child, he is undeserving of having you carry his name."

Her gaze shifted to the entrance. The squall passed during the delivery, taking countless lives. While holding the newborn against her bosom, a moonbeam illuminated the night, unveiling a small birthmark above the baby's left eyebrow. "Our ancestry runs through the blood of our mothers. Her name will be yours to carry."

Pa-Goe refused to look at the child. "Appo'si, do whatever you want. She is no child of mine."

"And *you* are no grandson of mine." She marched the infant to her mother. "Have you thought of a name?"

"Not yet." Léna inspected her child. With tear-stained cheeks and bright blue eyes, her contours were framed by soft wisps of hair. Emitting a piercing wail, the newborn fell into a peaceful slumber. "She's beyond beautiful."

The hospital doors burst open, and a succession of police officers marched in. Achukma's eyes alighted on a virtuoso songbird spilling an unstoppable waterfall of notes without being discouraged by the passing humans. Beautiful and sorrowful, the bird tweeted a melody, while the footfalls of the officers created rhythmic drumming. A collaboration of humans and earth, she absorbed the vibrations as a sign of the times. An ushering in of a new era.

Scrutinizing each set of grandparents, who were segregated into niche divisions, she grasped why they were chosen. Equivalent to the medicine wheel she relied on, they collectively embodied the best and worst of humanity. The four points of everything, from start to finish.

BIRTH. YOUTH. ADULT. DEATH.
SPRING. SUMMER. FALL. WINTER.
SPIRITUAL. EMOTIONAL. INTELLECTUAL. PHYSICAL.
FIRE. AIR. WATER. EARTH.
RAVEN. BEAR. WOLF. BUFFALO.
DRAGON. TIGER. TORTOISE. PHOENIX.

With the room covered in blood, medical equipment, and chunks of afterbirth, it was difficult to differentiate where the conflict originated. Parturition or extermination—the polarities converged to create an overall disturbing tableau of life.

Achukma stared at the scion, replete with love transcending generations. "She is the anticipated outcome of our dynasties—the daughter of the Emperor, King, Minko, and Monarch. The heavens are coming together in mourning and praise."

She sealed her eyes and consecrated the child.

Walking the sacred passage is not easy. You will endure many hardships, suffer through the vast darkness, and transcend beyond what others seek. To discover worlds unknown, do not follow the paved road. Guided by the Earth Mother and grounded by the Great Spirit, you must never forget, little one, that destiny has chosen you. Do not fear the great

fire of fate but become the flames and burn your way
through this existence.

"Wren!" Léna pointed to the tweeting chick just beyond the egress. "Wouldn't that make a beautiful name?"

"Wren," Achukma repeated. "A secretive breed who offers complex songs. Touted as kings, they are applauded in the same way they are hunted."

Léna caressed the child's hand. "What does it mean?"

"Chickasaw—much like the raven, the wren symbolizes good tidings and is a curious messenger from the spirit world." She locked eyes with her grandson, who pleaded self-defense. "Other tribes believe them to be family guardians, warding off negative energy."

"A messenger from the spirit world?" Léna rubbed her thumb over the baby's puffy cheek.

"Although—" Tearing her gaze from Pa-Goe, Achukma exhaled. "The Pueblo tribes considered the wren a fowl of war, thought to boost a warrior's courage upon sight."

"A totemic leader? How fitting for such an eventful birth."

Achukma stared over the scarlet resolution of misfortune, a mosaic holding the imprint of a life gone. "It would be best if the child didn't know the tragedies of this day."

<u>CHAPTER TWO</u>

A Coincidental Meeting

Fall 2021

His eyes danced over the audience as the cheers of forty thousand fans echoed through the stadium. From the front of the house to the back, rolling support crashed into him in one enormous wave. Basking in the glory of admiration, the pulsating energy pumped through his veins, electrifying each nerve. He was where he thrived, surrounded by ardent spectators.

'Black-mir-ror! Black-mir-ror!'

Fear filled his heart, a reminder he performed for forty thousand pairs of eyes. Forty thousand people with forty thousand opinions. Forty thousand phones with cameras to capture forty thousand mistakes. He dwelled on every error. Missed cues. Voice cracks. Failed steps. Wardrobe malfunctions.

While the rhythm swelled, he was lost in the moment, but before and after, his mind throbbed with a mix of euphoria and agony. A rollercoaster of emotions he tried to suppress, they always resurfaced. After six long years, he couldn't deny the impressions were a permanent fixture in his life.

Standing center stage, spotlights beat on his sweat-soaked skin. Designer clothes covered his body, yet he couldn't shake the haunting feeling of being exposed. His greatest solace was that he wasn't alone; he was with his four bandmates.

The loyal companions who stood by his side in times of victory and defeat. They fought with the same ferocity as family, cooperated like colleagues, and shared a deep understanding of one another. They were more than bandmates; they were a brotherhood bound by bonds of loyalty and trust.

He bent forward to admire his teammates as each made an end-of-concert speech. As head of the limerick, he was proud of the growth every member had shown throughout their career. Watching them display love for their fandom—the Enantiomorphs, or Anti for short—made his heart plume with pride.

Whistling, one of the mates garnered his interest. "*Rem!*"

Breaking his concentration, he raised his black crystal-encrusted microphone. "I told myself I wouldn't cry..."

He savored the lingering warmth of the spotlight, the hushed anticipation of the crowd, and the deep breaths of satisfaction filling his lungs. "The past two years have been hard. Standing here, looking at your faces, it now feels a world away. I can't tell you how many nights I laid awake praying for a night like this."

"We missed you, and we love you more than you will ever know." He buried his blushing face in his elbow but regained composure with a smile. Yelling into the mic, he tipped his head back far enough to lose his balance. "Thank you, Anti!"

As the stadium emptied, the musicians returned backstage. The leader isolated to the side of the confetti-coated platform. While his bandmates collected their belongings, his sight drifted to the empty seats. Watching the droves of fans leave the arena, waving their eungwonbongs in support of the band, he squeezed the last remaining drops of dopamine from the hall.

If someone had asked him six years earlier where he envisioned himself in half a decade, he wouldn't have said standing on stage. When he was a budding artist with hopes bigger than his brains, Blackmirror had hardly more than a handful of members. They didn't have a concept, let alone a name, and their fandom light stick had yet to be created. He remembered when the agency summoned them into the boardroom to develop their own cheerstick. While working with his bandmates to craft Blackmirror's wand, he became aware the group would succeed—only groups with sizable followings had their own branded commercial goods.

The Galabong, as it was known to the Enantiomorphs, featured a black handle and a clear, chubby crescent moon, with a ring around the thickest part of the celestial body. Bluetooth-compatible, the design featured three phase buttons to turn the device on, off, and enable pairing. Equipped with glow-emitting diodes, the wand produced a spectrum of colors. Dangling from the waning moon was a Blackmirror charm.

"You did well, Hanjun." A loftier man spoke from behind.

Hanjun held a drained expression, focusing on the group's longtime manager. "Thanks, Ha-Rin."

Ha-Rin patted his back. "Time doesn't wait for anyone."

"Certainly not us." Grumbling a solemn retort, Hanjun turned his back on the dimming lights. Leaving the hall in a beyond-tired state, he settled in the back of a cramped bus. Dark with a chilly interior, it was the same bus he sat on during the ride to each venue. Resting his forehead on the cold window frame, he peered out the tint. Fans were returning to their cars with their light sticks, and he was happy to offer them a small slice of joy, if only for a night.

"Three, four, five—" The last to enter the bus, Ha-Rin conducted a head count. "It's a five-hour drive to Chicago. You performed well. Be sure to rest up for tomorrow's gig!"

★⁺₊★☾★⁺₊★

It had been a night so inexplicably dull that it made her question her life choices. Fluorescent lighting flickered overhead, casting a warm tinge over thc rows of stocked shelves. The register sat on the counter, displaying the wrong date.

Without a customer for hours, she sat alone, surrounded by a plethora of purchasable snacks, watching a trending series on Netflix. The wooden stool creaked as she shifted, the smooth surface providing little comfort for her fatigued body. Her stomach ached, yet staring at dozens of snack options made her hunger diminish, knowing the offerings would taste like plastic and disappointment. The only thing satisfying her was the occasional sip of lukewarm tea.

Bored senseless, she paused the show and went to the restroom. Leaning into the mirror, she found her eyeliner smudging under her eyes. Her box blonde hair, frizzy and limp from a long day, cascaded down her upper back. Clicking her tongue, she tampered with unruly flyaways.

It was her day off, and she should have been spending it on a duo date with her best friend, but due to unforeseen circumstances, the plans fell through. Instead, she chose to pick up the shift for a few extra dollars.

Tugging at her clothing to adjust the seams, she possessed a feminine physique analogous to a classical guitar; shapely breasts were held up by a cinched waist, further accentuating her curves. Her bottom was heart-shaped, even in her stretched-out jeans.

Worried her outfit was unkempt, she untied a black and white flannel from around her waist. Pulling the well-worn fabric on over a white top, she sighed. "You only have another half hour, Jen. You can do this."

★⁺₊★☾★⁺₊★

Hanjun woke to quick, sporadic movements vibrating the windows. The air was musty and stale, carrying the scent of old sweat and spilled cola, and as the bus shuddered, an odor of exhaust fumes seeped in. Grasping for the seat in front of him, he called out to the manager. "What's going on?"

"We're experiencing engine difficulties." Ha-Rin slapped a palm on the dashboard. Annoyed, he signaled out the smudged windshield, asking the driver to make it as far as he could despite the smoke rolling off the motor. The operator took the next exit off the interstate, a ramp lined with slumbering truckers, leading to the middle of nowhere, Indiana.

Hanjun lowered his focus to the vast expanse of empty fields, barren and devoid of life. Scattered across the land was farming equipment, some rusted and stagnant, others bearing corn and silage. Aside from the massive amount of machinery, there were few establishments, and the land was underdeveloped.

"There's nothing around!" Ha-Rin complained as the bus pulled onto the main road running through a series of trucker attractions. Through the murky fog, he was able to make out a green accommodations sign, proudly boasting the only shelter within a thirty-mile radius: a single campground with a primitive black logo of an animated squirrel. "Imagination Acreage? I *imagine* it'll have to do."

Jen finished stocking the four-door fridge when blinding lights pulled in front of the store. Having already turned off a row of overhead fluorescents, her lips curled into a frown. "Last-minute shoppers; the absolute worst kind."

Within moments of the high beams stinging her eyes, a grouping of five men trotted into the establishment, each dragging baggage. Without acknowledging her, they bickered about the pungent smoke wafting in behind them. Following the train of young men, one last man arrived, tucking a pair of sunglasses into his suit pocket. With black hair and a somewhat hostile aura, he projected subtle command of the gang.

"Can I help you?" She stood on her tiptoes to get a better look at him.

Tall, mature, and of clear East Asian descent, he sauntered to the desk, offering out a hand. "Ha-Rin. Our vehicle broke down; I'm hoping you may have somewhere we can stay for the night."

She kept a straight face, but in her mind, she questioned how the bus load of travelers accessed the park to begin with. The private grounds were situated off a major interstate, and there was a gate system with security who monitored incoming traffic. Or at least they were supposed to.

"We should have something available," she answered with the last bit of pep she could squeeze out at the end of her double shift. "Let me find out for you."

Picking up the phone to call the reservation office, a glance proved the five young men had collapsed on the floor. One lay on the others, flopping his arms and legs over his friends, while another walked around the shop, retrieving random objects and calling for the others to look at the oddities he found.

"We have three luxury rentals and three standards. The premium units are equipped with linens—" She hung up the landline and prepared for an unfavorable reaction from the worn-out travelers. "The regulars are not. You'll also need to visit the reservation office to make payment. It's the small building you passed on the way in."

"Okay." One of the men groaned from the floor.

"I guess that's fine." The manager emitted a subdued chuckle while she marked a map with each unit's location. Stretching for the highlighted chart, he discerned that the accommoda-tions were scattered amidst the hundred-acre park. "I hate to ask another favor, but can you take them to the rooms? It's been a long night."

"I close in five minutes." She pointed to a clock hanging above her head.

He turned to the young men, gesturing to the purchasables. "Do you want any snacks before the kind girl closes?"

Girl. She laughed to herself. She was in her early thirties, far from a girl, although she presented younger. New hires as-sumed she was in her mid-twenties, and she didn't bother to correct them. She didn't hide her age, but she also didn't dis-close information. She held onto secrets that had the potential to cause chaos if revealed.

Rising from the tiled floor, the loftiest of the five young men followed the others around the shop, explaining what the items were. Though they conversed in an unfamiliar language, they riddled each other with English phrases, spouting off high-pitched squeals at sporadic intervals.

While they shopped, another man marched in. He looked like he had lived on a reservation his entire life, with rugged characteristics and a sturdy, wheatish-skinned body. With black hair sweeping to his abs, a glimpse of his torso could be seen through a white button-up. Virile, with sharp angles and defined muscles, he must have been carved from marble.

Hanjun gave him a side-eye, heeding the man's interaction with the cashier. As the member of the band most fluent in English, it was hard for him not to eavesdrop.

He greeted her with an amiable wave. "Jen!"

"Toshi!" Gentle and melodic, she chimed back. "What are you doing here? I thought we agreed to meet up tomorrow."

"I'm leaving." His voice wavered with regret. "Someone at work got into an accident; I have to go in tomorrow."

"Oh..." Her voice held a note of disappointment, but her shrug was a quiet resignation. "There seems to be a lot of that tonight."

Fiddling with point-of-sale items, he shook his head. "I was looking forward to seeing you."

She manufactured a smile. "Perhaps another time."

"Yeah." Breaking his trance from her, he spotted a gang of unfamiliar men walking among the narrow aisles. "Do you know them?"

"I don't." Eyes lingering, she noticed their clothes were tailored to perfection. "They're here for the night."

"Nice meeting you!" His voice echoed like a creature in search of its pack. "I'm Tisho!"

"Not very friendly," he grumbled after they mumbled hellos.

Her eyes crinkled in amusement. "Give them a break. I'm pretty sure they're foreigners."

"I see." He cocked his head, persuading her to walk around the counter. While wrapping his hefty arms around her back, the most impressive of the five men gave him a glare of annoyance, and he hugged her tighter.

After having the air squeezed from her lungs, she stepped back from their embrace. "Text me when you get home."

"I was going to give this to you at dinner." His hand emerged from his pocket, clutching a glinting brooch. Brushing a lock of hair from her shoulder, he pinned the item to her shirt. "My mother was elated to hear of your consideration. This is a gift from her."

The charm featured a beaded raven with green eyes sitting at the apex of a totem pole, with each spiritual animal representing her closest relatives. A talisman of her identity, woven with the threads of her heritage and the symbols of her kin, it was a breathtaking expression of her soul. "Your mother crafts the most beautiful jewelry. Please tell her thank you."

Wearing a telltale grin, he leaned forward to whisper without whispering. "Maybe you shouldn't agree to go on a date with me just yet. The tall one's checking you out."

She pivoted to find the tallest of the five staring in their direction, only for him to glance away. Tittering, she nudged him towards the door. "Time to go."

Returning to her place behind the desk, snacks and drinks were piled high enough to tumble off the surface. Water, chips, and cups of instant ramen noodles—there was enough for five hungry, exhausted men. As she packed each bag, the consumers grabbed their purchases and retreated to the floor. The sounds of crinkling snack packages shrouded today's jams emanating from the speakers of a vintage five-disc shelf stereo.

Biting her lip to hide a smile, she thought they were cute with how they compared snacks. Popping open one bag at a time, they passed around the goodies. They may have been grown, but they were boys at heart.

Looking as if he stepped off a plane from the Netherlands with his Eurocentric attire, the leggiest young man approached the desk, laughing and shaking his head at his friends. "They act like they haven't eaten in days! How much do we owe?"

Standing across from her, he grinned. Her facial attributes were striking: positive canthal tilted blue-green eyes, upward eyebrows, and an almost diamond-shaped face. Despite the angles of her jawline, she retained chubby, childlike cheeks. Her bottom lip was fuller than her top, giving her a natural pout, and her skin looked to be of pure porcelain, reminding him of the moon jar displayed in his recording studio. Wearing a small amount of makeup, a beauty mark near her left eyebrow could be glimpsed, hidden behind a curtain bang.

"$134.89." Meeting his gaze, a gasp caught in her lungs.

He was the color of honeyed sable and held an air of earth and lemon. Unique-looking, his cordiform face matched well-manicured eyebrows. He flaunted soft cheekbones and a solid jaw when he smiled. His lips were full, and his hair looked to be between blonde and silver, as if the previous color were fading out. His dark brown eyes were distinct in shape. Heavy and hooded with sharp edges, he possessed the eyes of a dragon. He stood tall and brawny, towering over her five-foot-four build. Holding his shoulders back, he knew how to intimidate others. The most surprising thing about him was how properly he spoke. He carried an accent yet strained his pronunciation, reminiscent of how a teenager would talk to his date's dad.

"Boyfriend?" Handing over a glossy international credit card, his voice rattled deep.

"Huh?" She swiped the plastic on an outdated reader.

"*Toshi? Tisho?*" His lip twitched into a curious smirk. "Is he your boyfriend?"

"Toshi?" Pinpointing the moment her face turned pink, she fixated on the credit machine. "We're friends."

"*Friends?* Not interested in him?"

"Um—" She hesitated, thinking of a way to explain her relationship with Tisho. "We've known each other since we were children, and our families are close."

"Didn't hit it off?"

The simple monetary transaction wouldn't be long enough to explain the convoluted relationship. Tisho, whom she called Toshi because his name reminded her too much of her ancestors, was named after the greatest and last Minko of their tribe. And she was one of the last descendants of the late chief. And she was one of the last within the Shawi' clan, and Toshi, from the Nashoba' clan, was one of the last full-blooded among the tribe. And both spoke a language on the brink of extinction.

With fewer than sixty people in the world fluently speaking the mother tongue and the majority elderly, they were two of the last who could carry on the language. As the great-granddaughter of one of the nation's last alikchi's—a God-chosen healer—immense pressure was imposed on her to fan the fire of their endangered culture. While the remaining clans would prefer her to bear children with one of the last full-blooded, they would have been happy if she procreated at all, as the bloodline was matriarchal. "It's complicated."

"Most things are." He caught passing glances at her when she wasn't looking, only to smile and avoid eye contact. Fidgety, he fiddled with knickknacks on the displays. Knocking a box of overpriced candy onto the floor, he muttered under his breath. "Jesus Christ, why are you like this?"

She smiled at his clumsiness, and her chubby cheeks emerged. "This thing is so slow."

"It'll take as long as it takes." Rising from the floor to replace the candy, he shot her a lopsided smirk, and a handsome dimple formed on his cheek. "I'm Hanjun, by the way."

Gaining confidence, he held a peace symbol over his right eye. "I also go by Rem."

And just like that, she knew exactly who he was. Who *they* were. Perhaps it was the late hour, but she hadn't connected the dots. Five friends who dressed in designer threads, spoke articulate Korean, and were attended to by a manager—how did she *not* recognize them? Controlling her breathing, she focused every fragment of concentration on the credit machine.

Blackmirror were lauded worldwide as a five-piece boy band hailing from Seoul, South Korea. The third-generation group debuted from a small agency in mid-2015 and, after a rocky start, began dominating the charts in late 2019. With a curated theme touching on topics of the unknown and unexplainable, they reserved their seat as prominent figures amongst the Korean-pop industry. Though their names were splashed on the pages of every publication, they had not become accustomed to their massive fame.

Ryu Hanjun was the spokesperson and supportive rapper, though his bandmates referred to him as Jun or Hanu. His singing voice was a tenor, while his rapping voice ventured closer to baritone, sometimes almost throaty. At the beginning of his career, he didn't choose a pseudonym, later changing it to Rem, a combination of the first initial of his surname and his favorite childhood rapper. During Blackmirror's early years, he was one of the most hated members, often receiving hostility from fans who claimed he didn't fit the strict idol standard. A lyricist by nature, he provided many of the lyrics for the quintet. Contrary to being the 'middle child' of the five, he was thought to be in the Hyung line, a term referring to the eldest.

He smiled at the group as they enjoyed the snacks he had purchased. "I'm kind of like their leader."

"Jenilyn." She tapped a finger on the name tag clipped to her sleeve. Confronting his gaze, she believed his smile was one of his best qualities. "You can call me Jen."

"It's a pleasure to meet you, Jenilyn."

The simple repetition was velvet from the tip of his tongue, and she didn't think something sweeter could exist. Interrupting the encounter, the machine spat out the receipts. She passed him a pen and the receipt to validate and checked the time. "One minute is close enough."

He reached for the pen, and his hand brushed hers. Heart racing, he scribbled the first letter of his name. He considered cracking a joke about the receipt being a roundabout way to ask for an autograph, though he decided the wisecrack would be too cheesy. "It's not often I have to sign one of these."

"This place is stuck twenty years in the past." Receiving the receipt, she positioned the paper under the change drawer and bumped it closed with her hip. "I need to break down my register. You can wait outside."

The musicians funneled out of the store while she closed up shop. Exiting after them with a miniature floral bag strapped to her back, she locked the door and tugged four times. Turning to face them, she spun around to check the door a second time, yanking another four times.

One of the young men burst into laughter. "You're as forgetful as Hanjun!"

"My brain wouldn't let me leave without making sure." Inspecting the luggage hugging their calves, she gestured to her vehicle. "I can't fit all of you in my car. With your bags, I can take two of you at a time."

Shadowing her to the lonely pearl-white Hyundai Elantra in the parking lot, paint chipped from a faulty finish on the model, Hanjun jostled one of the boys on the back. "You want to introduce yourself? It'll be an awkward ride if you don't."

"Deok-Sun." He stepped forward, and a wave of hair fell over his face. His eyes were wide and bright, as if he had drunk an excess of caffeine. Out of all of them, he smelled the best; base notes of vanilla and chocolate surrounded him. He had angelic features, redolent of a young Michael Jackson. His lips featured a prominent cupid's bow and reminded her of her own, though far more symmetrical. As one of the most popular members, he had a certain aesthetic that appealed to the masses.

Ha Deok-Sun, anonym Sunny, was the lead vocalist. Renowned for possessing a golden voice, his stable breathing and powerful vocals made him versatile in most genres. For lack of a better word, he was the most average guy in the band. Identifying as the Maknae—a term given to the youngest—he was deemed to be the 'attractive' one. Although the term appeared to be a compliment, it was more often used as a slur. According to critics, the only thing he had going for him was his physicality. Though he was an ordinary guy with a preference for food and video games, his outstanding appearance and professionalism told a different story.

Sparking recognition, her eyes met his. "Hello, Deok-Sun."

Hanjun rammed another on the back, harder than the first. "You too."

"Honey." He shook the bangs from his vision and stared at her with an unamused glare. He was about an inch shorter than Deok-Sun, and his shaggy fringe was chopped above his eyebrows. His face was rounded, and his eyes were dark and angular, as if he were in a state of constant criticism. For how doubtful his eyes were, his contours were boyish, perhaps delicate in soft lighting. The first thing she recognized was his confidence. Nothing bothered him, and he had no problem looking her in the eye when he gave a saucy attitude.

Yi Soogi chose his professional name, Honey, as the sticky substance was a symbol of wealth and exclusivity in the history of Korea, reserved for the higher class. He was the lead rapper for the group and one of the fastest rappers in the Korean industry. As a descendant of an influential clan during the Joseon dynasty, he had a rich heritage despite growing up poor. A composed guy with a mild temper, he was regarded as the 'father' of the brothers. He enjoyed bringing his friends ice cream to cheer them up and preparing meals during their vacations. He let his bandmates lead the way and was commended for being an advocate for mental health. Though he looked like he could be crowned the youngest, he was the second-eldest.

"Good to meet you, Honey." Opening the car door, she tossed her backpack on the passenger seat and dove inside.

Deok-Sun and Soogi sat in the back, shuffling the overstuffed pillows around to sit more comfortably. Everything in the car was galaxy-themed, from the seat covers to the air freshener swinging from the rearview mirror.

Honey picked up one of the pillows, fluffing it between his calloused hands. While he was the worst at speaking English, he concentrated on his enunciation. "You like stars?"

Pulling the seat belt over her breast, she reversed out of the parking space before answering, her eyes colliding with his in the mirror. "I like galaxies."

"Cool..." Gripping the back of her seat, he fixated on the dashboard. "Bluetooth?"

"I have an adapter. It works the same." She clicked a button to enable pairing. "You should be able to pair."

He connected his phone and played the next track on his list. "Do you like Drake?"

She turned the volume down to avoid the kick snares sending pain through her temples. "I like most music."

"What's your favorite Drake song?"

Deok-Sun mewled. "Can't we listen to Kendrick?"

"The Best I Ever Had." Clamping her jaw, she exhaled a nonverbal groan. Listening to two grown men arguing in her back seat was not on her bingo card for how she thought the evening would end. In an ideal scenario, the night would have concluded with her in silky undergarments, cuddled in a fuzzy blanket, and a hot mug of cinnamon tea in her hand.

"Can I pick the next one?" Deok-Sun leaned forward.

Soogi pinched his arm. "If you wanted to control the music, you should have asked first!"

Traveling along the bumpy road, she was annoyed at the five-mile-per-hour speed limit. "We're almost to Honey's rental. You can listen to a song then."

Less than a minute later, before the tune ended, she parked. While Deok-Sun paired his phone to the transmitter, she exited the car to retrieve Soogi's luggage, having a tiny laugh at the smallish bag situated in the trunk. "You pack light."

Shutting the lid, she passed over the key. "There's extra bedding in the closet."

Soogi stared at her, evincement afflicting his brow. Something about her was familiar. He saw many faces through his profession, and though it was impossible to recall everyone, he was drawn to her. He seldom developed an allure for anyone, but a sensation tugged at his heart—an internal nagging begging to know her. "Can I contact you?"

"I, uh—I'm not a groupie." She thrust the notion out of her mind and apologized. "I'm sorry. I shouldn't have assumed—"

Clutching his phone, he sent her an icy glare. "Just talk."

Bridging the gap, she input her number and returned the device. "Good night, Honey."

Turning his back to her, he gave her a final cold look, his accent manifesting viscous. "It's *Yi Soogi*."

She doubled back to the car. Deok-Sun lay in the backseat, sprawled on the pillows, as if he didn't plan to leave. In the rearview mirror, she caught a glimpse of his smile, bopping along to the song he was impatient to enjoy.

While creeping towards his rental, her phone sat in the cupholder, startling them when it sounded. Having an awkward laugh, she fumbled with the device and rested it face down, hoping he didn't catch on. But he heard the Blackmirror ringtone and continued to sing after the alert ended.

Erected by the catchy tune, he scooted to the middle, flashing a set of pearly teeth in her direction. "You're *a fan?*"

The steering wheel was a lifeline in her grasp. "I am."

"You didn't ask for an autograph." Though his statement appeared accusatory, he was naively curious.

She stationed the vehicle outside his lodging and swung the door open. "I'm not into that kind of thing."

"What do you mean?" Hellbent on furthering the conversation, he exited after her.

"I like to admire from afar." She released the compartment to remove his bags and set them on the gravel. Slamming the lid, she stared at him. He appeared illusory with flawlessly sculpted hair—an intense shade of midnight garnet. Pitch black, if not for the red undertone. "Humans weren't designed to withstand torrents of adoration or criticism. The least I can do is not contribute to an ongoing problem."

Standing open-mouthed, as if he had a million racing thoughts, he reached for her hand. Startled, she glanced down long enough to study his prominent veins bulging. Releasing an uneasy titter, she pulled her hand back and transferred the key. "Goodnight, Deok-Sun."

"Four more to go." Plopping into the driver's seat with the thought of cinnamon tea on her mind, she retreated to the front of the park, where she popped the trunk but didn't bother getting out. At minutes to midnight, she was exhausted, even with the excitement of encountering Blackmirror.

After loading their baggage, Ha-Rin joined her in the front seat, while another bandmate hopped in the back. He sat in the middle, leaning between them. "I'm Hanso!"

He possessed a thick accent and was comparable in height to the others, though noticeably slimmer. His initial impression was his unerring style. With incredible ease, he made high fashion appear casual. He had an elongated face, a defined jawline, and high cheekbones. Like Hanjun, he had dimples when he smiled and an adorable, upturned nose. Beyond his handsome exterior, he was nauseatingly animated.

Tickled by his bubbliness, she wished she could be that person. An introvert by nature, she conserved her energy. It was rare someone didn't drain her, and she believed most people were energy vampires, literally sucking the life from her one pointless compliment or complaint at a time.

Gan Ho-Young, nicknamed Hanso and sometimes referred to as Honsa, was the final rapper of the group and another member who received criticism in Blackmirror's earliest days. A funny guy with a temper, he was easygoing until he was agitated. Once angered, he would speak with ferocity—impossible to understand, unless you were his bandmates, of course. As the eldest, he was Hyung to the brotherhood.

Ha-Rin sat voiceless as Hanso babbled. He was transparent, and within the first few minutes, she knew his favorite apparel brands, food, and color, along with heartwarming stories about his mom and sister. A bit of a jabber jaw, he chatted about a bird inside the terminal when they arrived in the States and how the second youngest's shoulder was violated by the fowl's untimely droppings.

The deep register of his voice provided an autonomous sensory meridian response, and she was nearing the point of asking him to hush. Unable to hold her eyes open, she pulled up to Ha-Rin's rental and reached for the door when he gave the dashboard a gentle tap. "I'll get my bags. You stay here."

Unlocking the trunk, she waited until he entered the accommodation before backing out, only to pull up to Hanso's room, a mere forty feet away. Forcing her body out of the seat, the hope for a cup of tea was evaporating. The only thing she wanted was the embrace of a coma-like sleep.

Opening the luggage compartment confirmed Hanso traveled with more suitcases than his bandmates, which she assumed were filled with fashionable apparel. "Here's the key. There's a button next to the sink; push it fifteen minutes before you need to use the hot water."

Picking up his bags, he turned away for an instant, only to flip back around and make a shaka gesture next to his face. "Phone?"

She laughed louder than she should have. "You're the second to ask."

Offering the phone, he held a baited grin. "Who asked first? Deok-Sun?"

"*Yi Soogi.*" Tapping in her number, she gave a two-word reply and restored the device to his hand.

Gasping, he stowed the mobile in his pocket. "He doesn't even respond to us!"

Her body wanted to collapse, and she had two more customers to go. "Good night, Hanso."

<u>CHAPTER THREE</u>

Heartoo

Jen parked to escort the remaining guests to their accommodations. The final bandmate she hadn't been introduced to dissolved on the concrete, resting a cheek on Hanjun's thigh. When she gestured for them to hop in, the unintroduced mate emitted a squeak. "I'm hungry!"

Releasing a deep exhalation, Hanjun rose from the ground, pausing to dust off his jacket. "U-Jin, you just ate."

"No! *Real food!*" He stomped a foot, and his icy blonde hair waved with the motion. Compared to his teammates, he was petite. He had chubby cheeks yet, as pattern would have it, prominent cheekbones. He was content with his sexuality, and his complaining was mildly charming.

Kim U-Jin, stage name Jin, was the second youngest in the band. Main vocalist—he was a sensitive guy on a quest for attention. In their earliest days, he was alienated when the musicians were pushed towards a bad boy facade. Over time, he allowed his true nature to shine and was greeted with acceptance from his fans. He loved their supporters more than life itself, though he was sometimes the target of smear campaigns. Not by Blackmirror's admirers but by enthusiasts of rival groups, and it was not uncommon for him to receive anonymous threats on his life.

Hanjun expelled an exaggerated groan. "We can eat later."

"I can't sleep if I can't eat!" He stomped his foot again.

"I can get you something." She hesitated to invite two unfamiliar men into her home, but she knew they weren't going to find anything to consume within a reasonable walking distance. Small towns in the heartland of America weren't like the big cities they were accustomed to. There were a few truck stops with questionably edible food open at the hour, but the thought of taking them off-park made her gut churn. The beloved quintet commonly had a swarm of security to protect them, and the idea of her name getting plastered in a tabloid due to incompetence held no appeal.

"That's not necessary—" Hanjun started to reply.

Jin bounced up and down. "What kind?"

Humming, she recalled what was available in her kitchen. "Chips, fruits, and spicy ramen?"

"We don't mean to waste more of your—" Hanjun rebutted to calm Jin, who vibrated at the thought.

"Not a problem. I live up there." She pointed above the shop.

Craning his neck, Hanjun skimmed the sky to find a faint glow at the peak of the log cabin. A gust of wind whispered his name, and swirling leaves surrounded him for a moment.

Jin pouted, employing puppy dog eyes. "Pwease, Hanu?"

Tugging the handle of his suitcase, Hanjun grudgingly agreed. "Long enough to eat, and then we're going."

Motioning for them to follow, Jen walked around the building and up a flight of stairs. Halfway up, she detected Jin struggling with his oversized luggage and volunteered to carry one of his bags. Arriving at the small landing, the bandmates stood awkwardly while she dug in her pocket. Bumping into a tiny bistro table and a barbecue grill, she tried to alleviate the tension. "Your bags are heavy."

"Our lives are in there." Standing at the railing, Hanjun took in the view from the deck. Though it was dark, the moon provided ample illumination for the amenities: spacious in-ground pools, tennis and basketball courts, picnic pavilions, a tug-of-war zone, playgrounds, and what he could only assume was an arcade based on the retro sign. Behind the line of buildings were the sparkling ripples from a lake. Gasping, he almost asked if she'd take him there despite the midnight hour.

"I suppose so." She popped the door open. "Make yourself at home."

Jin barreled through, taking in the aroma of syrupy pancakes. "Were you having breakfast before work?"

She giggled; he floated through the room with his nose, identical to a cartoon character. "It's a candle."

"She's like you, Hanu, except you like incense."

"Yeah." Stepping inside, Hanjun glanced around the apartment. Decorated to suit her demeanor, pretty pastels complemented distressed off-white furnishings.

Jin abandoned his suitcases near the door and kicked off his boots. Opening the fridge, he pulled out produce. *"Strawberries! Blueberries! Peaches!"*

Hanjun gave up trying to stop his bandmate from rummaging through a stranger's kitchen. "I don't know why he's like this."

"If you keep going straight, you'll find the sitting room. The remotes are on the coffee table." Jen gestured to the hallway, slipping her sneakers off at the door.

Thankful for the new pair of socks he wore that morning, Hanjun headed to the couch. Passing an outdated shelf stereo emanating contemporary jazz in the hall, he paused to admire her collection. Blues, Pop, Folk, Indie, Dance, Rock, Alternative, Hip-Hop—she was a melophile.

Continuing to the sofa, he removed the decorative cushions and settled in. He rubbed along the soft fabric; it had been months since he sat on anything remotely satisfying. Living out of a suitcase, the closest he came to comfort were the hotels Blackmirror stayed at between back-to-back performances.

When he left Korea earlier in the year, he didn't expect to be gone for so long. Somehow, the series of gigs their agency planned turned into multiple shows throughout the states. For months, it was him, his bandmates, their manager, and the supportive crew. The same people, the same conversations, day in and day out. The repetition was maddening, and he was one dull conversation away from going criminally insane.

While surveying the room, he spotted a brown box in the corner and ruminated about how long she had lived there. She was too settled in her workplace to be a recruit. There was a die-cut sticker on the side consisting of a dragon and a phoenix. The white phoenix and black dragon were paralleled, maintaining distinct identities, with the heads forming a bow, arched backs rounding the heart, and tails joining to complete the effigy. The phoenix featured wispy feathers, while the dragon boasted jagged lines. Counterbalancing differences in synastry, their wings reached towards the center.

Leaning forward, he spotted a QR code cleverly hidden among the wings. Curious about the representation, he scanned the code to discover a website offering crowd-based dating solutions. The platform, stylized in lowercase as heartoo, was a monthly subscription focusing on casual outings, stress-free communication, and a long-forgotten friends-before-connection approach.

WELCOME TO HEARTOO! WE'RE A CHICAGO-BASED DATING SERVICE PUTTING LIFE BACK INTO YOUR DATING LIFE! OUR OFFICIAL LAUNCH IS THE FIRST OF OCTOBER, AND MEMBERSHIPS ARE OPEN FOR ENROLLMENT.

Slumping, he was jealous that Jen, with her average life, could enroll in such an avenue for companionship. While envy clouded his vision, he tapped in a temporary email to subscribe to updates. Even if he couldn't use such a program, he at least wanted to know what he was missing out on. Opening the correspondence, he was greeted by a welcome letter.

THANKS FOR YOUR INTEREST IN HEARTOO!
ARE YOU TIRED OF CYBER APPS AND FAST FLINGS? FRUSTRATED WITH CATFISH AND PERSONALITY IMPERSONATORS? OR MAYBE YOU PREFER LOGICAL SOCIALIZING IN A TECHNOLOGICAL WORLD? WE'RE OVER MOBILE ROMANCE, AND WE KNOW YOU ARE, TOO!

DATING IS HARD, BUT IT DOESN'T HAVE TO BE. WITH HEARTOO, YOU'LL EXPERIENCE THE BENEFITS OF CASUAL COURTSHIP WITHOUT THE RISK OF HAVING A BAD TIME. IN INVITING, CONTROLLED ENVIRONMENTS, YOU'LL JOIN GROUPS OF LIKE-MINDED SINGLES SANS THE ADDITIONAL PRESSURE.

YOU'RE IN CONTROL! EVERY MONTH, WE'LL OFFER A VARIETY OF GATHERINGS RANGING FROM LAID-BACK TO CHALLENGING—YOU CAN CHOOSE WHICH YOU'D LIKE TO PARTICIPATE IN. THERE'S NO NEED TO STRESS OVER MAKING THE WRONG DECISION BECAUSE THE SOLOISTS IN YOUR CIRCLE WANT TO BE THERE, TOO!

AT HEARTOO, WE BELIEVE LOVE STARTS WITH CONNECTION. WE'VE PARTNERED WITH INDUSTRY PROFESSIONALS TO CREATE EXCITING, DYNAMIC ACTIVITIES THAT MAY CHALLENGE OR SURPRISE YOU. DON'T FRET, THOUGH! THESE JOURNEYS WILL BRING OUT YOUR BEST AND MAKE YOU SHINE LIKE THE DIAMOND YOU ARE!

INTERESTED? CLICK THIS LINK TO FIND OUT MORE.

Following the hyperlink, Hanjun was met with packaging pricing and a calendar of events. Displaying gatherings scheduled weekly from Wednesdays to Saturdays, every date was at capacity with forty singles ready to mingle. The majority of October promoted fall with options of apple picking, winery tours, and haunted attractions. His sights landed on an experience he would attend if given the chance. Robot Night. Clicking on the photo, he found a blurb about the event. Next to the text was a cartoonesque avatar comparable to Jen.

HAVE YOU EVER WONDERED WHAT IT TAKES TO BUILD A ROBOT? ON THIS HEARTOO EXPEDITION, YOU'LL CHOOSE FROM OVER TWENTY VARIETIES AND CUSTOMIZE THE MECHANICAL PAL OF YOUR DREAMS.

His jealousy softened. Her use of the service went beyond socializing; she was launching her own company. One with quite a bit of interest. Shaking his head, he couldn't believe he was uncomfortable over the idea of her dating.

Tucking the phone away, he inspected the room. Her aesthetic was relaxed elegance, with the focal point being a pricy square rattan coffee table in a beautiful French grey. The glow from a strand of lights tucked behind the seating set the mood in an amorous state, and there were ivory candles in abstract holders lining the surfaces. Beside the pillars was an open book earmarked by a heart-shaped paper weight and a finished mug with a teabag hanging from the side. Next to him on the floor was a woven basket with extra throws and a bleached fruit-wood table from the early 1900s.

Though some might have found the apartment eclectic, he recognized the home as a place decorated with things she loved. Rubbing his socks against the tassel shag rug, the ambiance was relaxing without being too showy. There weren't any signs boasting opulence, and she used consumables until they were unusable. The flat screen on the far end of the wall was newish, yet the disk player and sound system stashed in the entertainment center were upwards of ten years old. Even the pillows on the sectional, though grouped in cohesive harmony, were mismatched in varying degrees of wear and repair.

The inspection of her home told him two things: she preferred to have bare areas rather than fill her world with goods she didn't adore. And she was rebuilding, perhaps after a major life change. The domicile appeared much like his when he first moved in, before he filled it with artwork and handcrafted Japanese furniture.

More than anything, it reminded him of his grandmother's home. Nestled into the jagged mountains, her abode was his favorite place to visit. Not only because it was hundreds of kilometers away from the waking world, but because her home told the story of a life well lived. And well loved. Everything she owned served a purpose, consistent with Jen's cow-shaped ceramic kettle on the stove.

Reminiscing about summer days spent with his grandmother, he reached for the remote. Scrolling through the options, it came as no surprise to find prominent streaming services. Deciding on Netflix, her previously watched list paralleled his, though it contained significantly less drama.

Settling in, he covered his legs with a throw from the cushion next to him, taking in the faint aroma of her perfume. Beautiful and warm, rich but not cloying, the scent encased the essence of her. Between the realms of girlhood and womanhood, the blend of juicy raspberry, pomelo, and heliotrope merged with dark amber, musk, and cashmere—too sexy on a young girl and too sex-kittenish on an older woman. It was an undeniable womanly fragrance, and what he imagined nature's candy to smell like.

In the interim, Jen remained in the kitchen, helping Jin locate the utensils. After getting him acquainted with the cupboards, she stopped at the console table to empty her pockets, charge her phone, and replace the finished compact disc. From the hall, she caught Hanjun cuddling with her favorite lounging throw. "I'll be just a moment."

Unsure if they heard or cared, she veered to the right. Closing her bedroom door, she stripped off her blouse and tossed it in the hamper. Rummaging through drawers to find something loose-fitting, though appropriate, she would have preferred to relax as soon as she arrived home. Although comforting to her would be next to naked. Deciding on joggers and a plain white tee, she entered the living room, sitting opposite Hanjun. "Comfy?"

"Yeah." He snuggled in, taking a moment to admire her outfit. The bottoms accentuated her waist, and the shirt slipped up her side when she reached to light a candle, showing subtle hints of skin.

She melted into the cushion. "Jin's having a good time in there."

"I bet he is." He threw her a corner of his blanket, making sure she had enough fabric to wrap her body.

Tugging the material under her breasts, she let her neck fall back. "Thanks."

Just as her eyes began to close, Jin emerged from the kitchen, smiling and rubbing his tummy. "I'm so full."

"Ready to go?" Scooting to the end of the seat, she blew out the candle and turned to Hanjun. "You must be spent."

"Do you mind if I stay?" He ran a nervous palm along the armrest and held a timid smile. "I'm having second thoughts about those noodles."

She popped up and adjusted her shirt to lay flat. "Pans are near the dishwasher. Ramen in the upper cabinet."

"Thanks." Hanjun tipped to the side, watching the duo push Jin's luggage through the threshold.

Jen, although drained from the day, carried a bag and issued a warning. "Be careful. The steps are steeper than you think."

After they left the apartment, Hanjun searched through the cupboards, locating a saucepan. While the water boiled, he opened the rest of the doors to find a plethora of noodle dishes, ranging from Japanese to Taiwanese. He chose the same brand he ate at home, one manufactured in Seoul. Scouring through cabinets above the stove, he found boxes of imported teas and considered making a mug but thought it would be overstepping her hospitality.

Before taking his first bite of prepared noodles, he hunted for the bathroom. Unable to find it off the kitchen or lounge, he tiptoed through her boudoir. Well-organized with generously stuffed pillows on the bed, the room screamed wispy romanticism with light gray bedding and femininely curved dressers. To satisfy his curiosity, he opened the closet to discover an unexpectedly large space for how small the apartment was. Her clothing was fashionable—trendy tees and denim—with an affinity for Adidas and Converse. She had a mild obsession with sweaters, jackets, and cardigans. Closing the doors, it was what he expected based on the little he knew about her.

He located the bathroom next to the closet and stepped in long enough to empty his bladder. Exiting with a paper towel in his hands, he had a clear panorama of her desk across the room. Sauntering over, he eyeballed the screensaver, boasting a quirky photo of The Base Gene. Cracking a smile, he jiggled the mouse, finding a handsome picture of the pop-punk band's lead vocalist, Kyle Richmond, who looked strikingly similar to a young Brendan Fraser.

He didn't expect to find himself, considering he was the black sheep of Blackmirror, but he hoped he was. While it was inevitable for him to have fans, most admired his perceived leadership qualities. He didn't dislike being praised as the captain, but he longed to be applauded as something more.

On the other end of the wall sat a mirrored vanity surrounded by light bulbs. The surface was riddled with cosmetics and powder puffs, and the corner featured two sizeable bottles of perfume, half and three-quarters depleted. Admiring the scents, he resisted the urge to spray his clothing and misted the air near her bed. While he would love her redolence to linger on him, he was afraid she would think he was a pervert.

Leaving the room, he identified a song blaring from her phone in the hall: a catchy Blackmirror tune by the name of 'Onyx.' Picking up the late model, his eyebrow raised at the received text. He shook his head and replaced the device, only for it to begin ringing again. Singing along to the lyrics he constructed years earlier, he retrieved the cooled bowl of ramen at the same time Jen walked through the door.

"Jin is safe." She flipped off the porch light and slipped off her shoes. "Poor thing fell asleep on the drive."

"That happens sometimes." Slurping overcooked noodles, his eyes peered over the dish. "You had a call."

In an instant, she remembered she hadn't lowered the sound. "Oh."

He sucked on the warm broth. "It was Massengill?"

Crossing the hallway, she tossed her keys onto the console table with an excessive amount of force. "My ex-husband."

"Ex, huh? Is he as stupid as his name sounds?" Splashing noodle sauce on his shirt, he licked his finger and rubbed at the mark. "And Soogi texted you. I can't even get him to text me."

"It's a nickname I gave him *after* the divorce." Chuckling, she added Soogi as a contact, then returned the call. "What did you want? What does it matter? I told you to stop calling."

Eyebrows raised, Hanjun perceived the anger in her voice and gestured for the mobile with two fingers. Mid-sentence, she handed it over, giving him a questioning glare. Raising the phone to his ear, he utilized his darkest tone. "She said no."

The deep tremble from the back of his throat sent goosebumps up her arms. Ending the call, he lowered the volume to silent and placed the device face down. "Problem solved."

She glared at him. "Why would you—"

"If he knows you're with a man, he'll leave you alone. For now, anyway." He retreated to the sofa with the noodles. "Not something you could fix?"

"No." She plopped on the cushion, pondering why he chose to sit in the middle.

"Do you want to talk about it?"

"Not really." Refusing to speak about the failed venture sent a wave of rage over her. Shaking her head, she wiped away her tears. "He's the one that's missing out. I'm fucking great."

Mid-bite, he burst into laughter, thinking she was cocky while being intrigued. If she was proud, he wanted to know why. Finishing up the last bits, he held the empty bowl in his lap. "It's been a long night..."

Eyelashes fluttering, she was too sleepy to leave the warmth of her apartment a second time. "You could stay here."

Surprised by the forward proposal, he didn't think sleeping at a stranger's house was a good idea. Especially with how pretty she was with pink cheeks, the way the soft romanticism elevated him as the lead of a soap drama, and how the amorous jazz hummed in the air. "You've done enough."

Tossing the blanket off her legs, she patted the cushion. "I promise it's more comfortable than it looks."

His face reddened, and he could have sworn the temperature sweltered. She didn't want to lull him into her bed like some kind of sea siren. Why would he consider such a notion when he was little more than a customer to her? "If you don't mind."

While he reflected on his assumptions, she left the room. Returning with an oversized duvet, her makeup was rinsed away, and her hair was up in a messy bun. Standing at the end of the sofa, she dropped the bedding next to him and motioned behind her. "Bathroom's off my room if you need it."

He settled in. She was right. The sofa was plush enough to dissolve into, and he imagined she must have slept in front of the television multiple times a month. Before long, he thought about her evenings and which movies she enjoyed. If she reclined in a particular way or if her habits were pure whimsy. He pondered who she watched films with and what that person looked like. She was indisputably attractive, and he wondered what caught the eye of someone like her. Could he?

As every bit of strain in his body vanished, he checked the KakaoTalk group chat on his phone. The popular mobile messaging app was the group's central source of communication.

Honsa: Her car smelled nice.
Jinja: Her apartment smelled nicer!
Soogins: You went to her apartment?!

Jin complained he was hungry.

Jinja: I'm full now!
Honsa: She reminds me of my mom.
Soogins: She likes hip-hop.
Honsa: She likes us.
Sunnie: Onyx is her ringtone!

I can't believe Soogi is responding to us.

Honsa: We should invite her to the show.

We'll ask Ha-Rin in the morning.

Overthrown by boldness, Hanjun sent a selfie of him lying on her sofa. The conversation resurrected, and there was an explosion of notifications as the gang exchanged playful banter and genuine concern.

Honsa: You stayed with her?!?!
Soogins: Omo!
Sunnie: How'd you manage that?
Jinja: We need details, Hanu!
Honsa: Don't do anything too stupid.
Sunnie: I disagree. Get it if you can get it!

Hanjun didn't respond after sending the picture, and if he wasn't so snug, he would have dug out his journal to record the day. For once, it was a day worth remembering. A day with a new person and new conversations. A day replete with new paths and untold stories, where the moon gleamed with the radiance of a first meeting.

Knowing he wouldn't be able to doze off, he rose in search of water. Filling a glass in the kitchen, he peered out the front door. The recreational park was hidden among cornfields and gated off from the world, yet the insides were like a dream. He wondered what her days were like; while he was confined to small spaces and massive stages, she had a private oasis at her fingertips. Swallowing the last gulp, he returned the cup to the sink.

Passing her room, he stole a glimpse of her figure in the blue moonlight. She slept on her stomach with one leg bent. The bottom of her butt hung out of her shorts, accompanied by a portion of the bedspread draped over her lower back.

Standing on the threshold, he wondered if it would be too strange to sleep in her bed. A cool breeze sailed through the drapes, creating the optimal temperature for sleeping. After much self-debating, he climbed between the covers with the thought of withdrawing if she opposed.

The mattress sank and her neck lifted. "Hanjun?"

He placed an arm under his head. "I just wanted to—"

She passed him a pillow. "Do you need another blanket?"

"No. Thank you." He cuddled as close as he thought he could and wanted to be closer. Her perfume slowly faded, and he began fantasizing about never leaving her bed. Or her life. In the morning, he would prepare her a cup of tea and ask her to take him to the sparkling waters of the lake, where they could talk like two people who hadn't experienced misery.

Smoothening his heavy breathing, his eyes narrowed. In his career, everyone knew everything about him without a chance for him to stand on equal terms. Intruders peered into his life with a microscope, and thanks to stalkers eager to sell dirt on him, the world even knew what his home looked like.

To most, he was prestigious. Untouchable. Too famous to mingle with everyday people. But something about Jen was different. She didn't treat him as if he were made of glass, and she invited him into her home, allowing him a deeper dive into her character. Nor did she hide how fatigued she was when she didn't think she could escort him to his lodging.

In his line of work, there were only three kinds of people. The kind who didn't know who he was and ignored his existence. The kind who knew who he was and treated him as a flavor of the month, disregarding him as a human. And the kind who knew who he was and went to extremes to impress him.

She didn't fit the narrow box of social interactions he was attuned to. She knew of Blackmirror and enjoyed the music enough to make it her ringtone. He saw her eyebrow pique when he introduced himself, but she continued to speak with him as if he were any other customer. She tended to each bandmate without bias; while not every fan was so obvious to ogle their favorite member, several signs made it evident. A telltale flush of the cheeks or a gaze lingering a few seconds too long—she displayed nothing of the sort.

When she exited her room without makeup and with her hair in a mound, he was enthralled. For someone to know who he was and still strip down to the bare canvas was unheard of, and he found her imperfections cute—a ripple on her forehead from having chickenpox as a child and a scar under her nose from a dog bite when she was seven.

She was real, and in the short time he had known her, he knew more than just her name. He knew pieces of her beyond the mundane responses he received from most people he encountered, and he wanted to know more. He desired to wake her up and ask about her life, her dreams, and how her marriage ended. He longed to know what made her feel secure, what fears kept her up at night, and what she thought about when she couldn't sleep. What she loved, what she hated, and which beliefs she carried.

But he couldn't. While the breeze caressed her puffy cheeks, the window for asking questions had long been sealed. In a matter of hours, he would be stuffed into another vehicle and on his way to the next concert with the same people he'd been traveling with for months.

CHAPTER FOUR

Same Skies

Hanjun observed Jen while she slept, wishing he could lie with her forever. Despite the familiar ache, he had grown accustomed to fleeting connections. His career left no room for prolonged relationships. The pressure of ambition had him in a chokehold, restricting the intricacies of human bonds. It was a sacrifice he made willingly, but also one that he regretted.

Passing by the console table before the sun rose, he noticed Soogi had sent her another text. Picking up the device, he smirked, surprised that his bandmate tried a second time. A simple good morning was the message he chose to send, and Hanjun understood the anxiety of contacting a possible love interest.

Entering the kitchen, he rinsed his face under the sink to avoid waking Jen. When he crawled out of bed to his beeping alarm, she woke for a millisecond, and he knew she must have been a light sleeper.

Groomed to leave, he cleaned up the mess he had created the previous night and locked the door behind him, dragging his luggage down the staircase. Rounding the A-frame building with designer shades covering his eyes, he was greeted by his bandmates, who not-so-patiently waited for him.

"So?" Deok-Sun simpered, curious to hear of the prior night's festivities.

"Yeah, Hanu! Why were you there *all night?*" Jin giggled, aiming a finger at the apartment's front windows.

"It's not like that." Ignoring his bandmate's speculation, Hanjun looked to the sky; Jen's living room drapes were pulled closed, and he committed the scent of her perfume to memory. Before getting in the rented van, he dug out his journal.

The day was long, and the ride was even longer. Our vehicle broke down on the way to Chicago. We stopped at a campground and met a girl. Pretty. Smart. I slept on her couch and then moved into the bed. I probably won't see her again. Perhaps in another life.

Hanso sat next to him, eyeballing the entry. "She's pretty."

Hanjun chewed on the end of his pen. "So pretty Soogi asked for her number."

Soogi snorted from the back row and pretended to shoot a basketball into a net. "No harm in shooting my shot!"

Hanso covered his face, and Hanjun vented a discouraged laugh. "How many of you do you think she can see at once?"

Deok-Sun leaned between their seats, his cheeks blooming. "She's confident."

Soogi snickered at the youngster's misfortune. "You weren't able to form words around her."

Listening to his friends fight over the girl, Hanjun held a smile. It wasn't unusual for the mates to fawn over beautiful women, but it was uncommon for it to be the same one. It was even more unusual for him to join the tomfoolery. With his bandmates in the picture, he had no hope of impressing her. The stars could align—he could write a thousand poetry lines—and he would never be chosen over his more attractive counterparts. He was aware of what he brought to a relationship, and when it came to women who were doted on by expensive men, his offerings weren't favored.

"I win!" Soogi boasted after Jen responded, showing off the message. "She's made her choice, boys."

⋆⁺₊⋆☾⋆⁺₊⋆

Jen woke to an interesting scent of honey and lemon on her sheets. Moving to the kitchen in the tiny shorts and baby tee she wore to bed, she prepared a morning mug of tea. Taking the first sip, she peered out the sitting room window; the broken-down bus was missing, leaving a puddle of oil in its place. She thought the previous night could have been a fever dream until she glimpsed a note left on the console table.

*Even if we can't be together, we're never too far
apart. If you look up at the moon, we're under the
same stars. —Ryu Hanjun.*

"I met Blackmirror." She smiled at the inscription and glanced at the clean dishes left in the drainer.

Due to the band's popularity, she was never able to secure tickets to any of their concerts. Colliding with them was far better than any concert she could have attended, and she was happy to know they were humble amidst their success.

Hurrying to put on a robe after the doorbell buzzed, she found a bouquet on the landing. She wanted to question the sender before accepting the flowers, but the delivery person was long gone. Returning to the apartment and setting the bundle on the kitchen table, she reached for the card.

Thank you for being so kind. —J&I Entertainment.

For a nanosecond, she thought the arrangement might have been from Hanjun. "You don't even know the guy."

Shaking off the idea, she moved on with her day and while taking her morning shower, reminisced about the previous night. She wished to tell her best friend, Kristen, but the coincidence was so unbelievable, she decided not to. To protect the anonymity of the group, it was a memory she would need to keep private. It would be a fun story to tell her grandkids—that when she was young, she bumped into one of the world's most famous boy bands. The crossing was a real-life fan fiction moment, and she was happy to have had the experience, even if she almost collapsed at two in the morning.

Stepping out of the shower, she heard her phone blaring an unfamiliar melody. She dashed across the apartment to answer it, checking the caller to find a smiling selfie of Hanjun. "Did you add yourself to my contacts?"

"Yeah—" Inside a concert venue, he paced along the raised floor, tracing patterns in the air. His eyes were locked on the empty seats, which would be loaded before the sun set.

The bandmates cackled in the background, and Deok-Sun tried embarrassing him. "Hanjun-Hyung, are you nervous?"

"When in the world did you—" She started to ask.

Hanjun interrupted, a smile in his voice. "We have a show in Chicago tonight. You should come."

She swallowed apprehensively. "I don't have a ticket."

"Not needed. You'll be with me." His Adam's apple bobbed, neck stretching. "With *us*. The concert starts at six. Get here before the streets get busy."

He unexpectedly ended the call, and she gawped at the mobile, wondering if it was normal for people not to say goodbye in Korea. Scanning her notifications, she found another response from Soogi and spotted a text she couldn't recall sending. With a strange number combination at the beginning, she opened the message to find two words and knew it must have been Hanjun in the wee hours of the morning. "What does '*Same Skies*' mean?"

⋆⁺₊⋆☾⋆⁺₊⋆

After an anxious drive to the venue, Jen parked her car in an expensive lot and walked to the loading dock. In a series of long-winded texts, Hanjun advised her to head for the back entry. Passing a series of chain link fences, she required several clearances from the agency before they would permit her in. Each guard she encountered held a walkie-talkie and described her physicality through a two-way radio.

When she reached the final security boss, he cracked a smile and rotated away. "I have a blonde. Blue-green eyes. Fox-like features. Says her name is Jen-ah-lyn."

A husky voice countered a static reply. "Let her in."

Returning the handheld to his belt loop, he walked her to the back passage and pounded on the solid steel. "You must be special. I've never known Blackmirror to have guests, and I've been detailing their concerts for years."

"Never?"

The door clanked open. Meeting her at the threshold with a toothy grin, Hanjun's makeup was only halfway completed, as if he had gotten up in the middle of being styled. Holding an all-access pass, he motioned to the pretzel-shaped satchel strapped to her chest. "I like your bag."

Handing over an ultramarine and black lanyard, he pointed to his own neck. "Keep this with you."

"Thanks." Sliding the nylon material over her head, a sudden throb of apprehension hit her stomach.

Wielding a handsome smile, he gestured for her to step inside. "C'mon, I'll introduce you to the crew."

She shadowed him wearing white chucks, cuffed skinny jeans, and a hot pink sequin tank topped with a black peplum blazer. He rubbed his nose on the back of his hand while naming dozens of handlers by title. "That's Hanuel, the production manager. Beom-Seok leads the lighting team. Dong-Min takes stage photos. Myung heads security and inspects the platform to ensure it's safe."

Dodging a maze of sound personnel and pyrotechnicians, he led her through a labyrinth of hallways riddled with dead cases when they reached the well-stocked dressing room. Sitting in folding director chairs with their pseudonyms displayed on the backs, each vocalist received individual treatment from countless beauticians and stylists. Jin and Deok-Sun were having their makeup done, Hanso was handed his performance outfit, and Soogi was getting his bangs trimmed.

Captivated by the collection of bodies, she was surprised to see everything completed at the same time. "This is cool."

"Hello, Jenilyn." Ha-Rin's voice vibrated from behind her.

She spun to greet him. "Thank you for allowing me here."

"They wouldn't let it go until I agreed." He tilted his head toward the musicians.

"Hey Jen." Deok-Sun smiled, hiding his embarrassment.

"Thanks for the invite." As an avid concertgoer, she attended the exact venue many times in her life, but never anywhere near the backrooms. "I always wondered what was beyond the stage."

"Just don't go *under* the stage," Hanso chuckled. "You don't want to know what's down there."

"Why would you mention that?" Slugging his arm, Hanjun fired a disgusted look.

Facing away from her, Jin raised an elbow to cover his face. "She can't see me like this! I'm not wearing makeup."

She employed her best British accent to coax a smile from him. "You're beautiful, darling."

Without giving her time to object, he pulled her close, wrapping a hand around hers. She ruffled his hair, sticky from styling products. Making a disgusted face, she wiped the goop on her pants while a stylist swooped in to fix his look. "I'm sorry."

Feeling awkward as the musicians stripped to be fitted with their outfits, she walked to Hanjun, who admired her from across the room. "I'm gonna take a walk."

"Where are you going?" Pulling on a slinky pair of denim, he zipped the fly and reached to remove his shirt.

"To see what it looks like empty." Backing away, she gestured to the building. "The bones."

Hanjun ogled her walk. Her shape from behind was a voluptuous hourglass, with a slim waist curving into round hips. She moved with fluid grace, her curves accentuated by the hug of her jeans. Ripping his stare from her, he caught Soogi and Deok-Sun fancying her as well.

"Beautiful?" A primped peacock, Hanso flaunted his coiffed locks, shouting over the deafening purr of a blow-dryer.

Hanjun's face flushed, and his long-standing makeup artist teased him. "You're right. She *is* pretty."

"She's Hyung's type!" Deok-Sun drummed on his thighs.

"You never know," Jin answered, uncaring if he overheard. "Hanu values intelligence over everything."

⋆⁺₊⋆☾⋆⁺₊⋆

Like serenity before a storm, the empty halls were tranquil. With the lanyard hanging around her neck, Jen thanked every staff member she spotted, stopping to have a chat with anyone who wanted to talk.

Though she was far from perfect, she tried to be kind, especially to those in the service industry. She had a deep understanding of the harsh conditions those working with the public were subjected to. When she attended large festivals, she offered to clean the countertops, change the trash, or do any small thing to make the crew's day a little brighter. Her antics annoyed the hell out of her ex, and she did it twice as much out of pure spite. After all, the best revenge is a life well lived.

Pausing to lean against the counter of an unopened food stall, she absorbed her surroundings. Throughout her life, she viewed experiences as if she were taking snapshots, complete with hand motions and shutter sounds.

"Can I help you?" A chubby man questioned her from behind. Low and gruff, he yielded a hint of a southern accent, muted by living in the North.

She removed her back from the edge, fingers trailing the worn surface. "I'm just checking the place out."

His mouth curled in a disobedient smirtle. "We aren't open, but I'd make an exception for you."

She shrugged off the advance and fingered the lanyard around her neck. "I'm visiting Blackmirror."

His retreat was an inhalation of hesitation. "In that case, is there anything I can get for you guys?"

"There's five. Are you sure you want to offer?" He reached for a small pad of paper while she spat off the order, glancing at the limited menu. "Two pretzels, two nachos, and three of the ice cream cups, please."

While he prepped the goodies, she searched her cross-body—she had a love of kitschy carriers. The pretzel-shaped bag featured a yellow mustard packet as the zipper pull, and it was one of her favorites. Much in the way certain scents were a trigger for distinct recollections, specific bags were a reminder of days well spent. The pretzel held the memories of many concerts she had the pleasure of attending.

The attendant positioned the completed order on the counter. "It's on the house."

"Pardon?" One hand deep in her wallet, she was dismayed.

He pushed the platter toward her. "Can I get your Insta?"

Flustered, she added the total. Around eighty dollars. Slapping a crisp hundred-dollar bill in place of the tray, she huffed. "Keep the change."

Escaping the uncomfortable situation, she made it halfway down the hall when he called again. "I take that as a no?"

"This is why I stay home." She knew she was a cute girl, but obvious flirting was a major turn-off. More often than not, men were interested in her physicality, not who she was as a person. Prompted by her conventionally attractive appearance, the gentlemen she admired were often discouraged. Their hesitant footsteps were drowned out by bro dudes who used the same pickup lines she'd heard hundreds of times before.

She initiated conversations with men she found appealing, though she was usually dusted aside. Believed to be too high maintenance at first glance, she understood why her presence was intimidating: love was a game of chance. As with any gamble, it was smarter to make a bet that you had a higher probability of winning. By choosing a woman who wasn't bombarded with affirmation, an ordinary man would have a lower risk of rejection. It was a simplified equation to describe the laws of attraction, and she had always hated math.

An old soul with a strong temperament, she adjusted her appearance to avoid having too much emphasis imposed on her. She didn't partake in casual flings, and the whole 'getting to know someone' period was an annoyance she avoided at all costs. Modern dating was problematic, so she didn't.

The makeup artists were almost finished with the musicians when she returned with the tray of treats. Placing the serving plate on a lounge table, she picked up a pretzel. Biting into the spongy texture, Deok-Sun chomped the other side, while Jin joined in on the third section. From his seat, Hanjun suffered secondhand embarrassment. "They have no shame."

Shrugging, she tore the twist into two pieces and offered them to Deok-Sun and Jin, who flirtatiously fought over a portion of cheesy sauce. "The guy working at the concession stand was kind of aggressive."

Soogi reached for an ice cream from the tray. "Why do you say that?"

"He didn't want me to pay and asked for my Instagram." Massaging her upper arms, she rubbed off the unpleasant sensations creeping up her skin.

"What did you do?" Hanso glanced at Hanjun, whose eyebrows were in a permanent state of alert.

"What any self-respecting woman would do," she expressed with a spot of cheekiness. "I left the money on the counter and told him to keep the tip. And I mean it—he can *keep the tip*."

Though the Hyungs laughed at the innuendo, the Maknaes were confused, and Hanjun did his best to translate. "Keep the tip, like the end of his—"

Bursting into laughter, she apologized. "I'll be more mindful."

"*Oh.*" Jin flashed a mischievous grin. "She means he can keep his *penis!*"

Suddenly, she was caught in a downpour of raucous hysterics—an unexpected deluge of childish humor and creative vulgarity. The room swelled with giggles as the youngest musicians and their accompanying staff brainstormed phrases to describe the end of male genitalia.

Spearhead. Helmet. Cue ball. Globe. Bell end. Lip filler. Knob. Curtain opener. Mushroom. Fishing tip. Turtle shell. Shooting saucer. Beef injector. And her all-time favorite from a member of the sound squad: Black and Decker pecker wrecker.

"Thunder dome!" Deok-Sun shouted.

"You know way more slang than I do. Note taken." Cheeks turning apple-red, she averted her gaze.

Ha-Rin's tone came in stern. "Let's not say anything that will require the girl to sign a non-disclosure agreement."

"Knobin Hood," Jin muttered loud enough for the room to hear. Hanso gave him a tap on the back of the head, and he aimed an accomplished beam at Jen. "Worth it."

As time ticked down, the stylists finalized their outfits by handing off handfuls of jewelry. Once finished, the artists inspected themselves in the mirrors—they were rock star gorgeous—but her gawk fell on Hanjun. He didn't bother looking in the mirror with his hair slicked back to perfection and a ring of heavy chains around his neck.

While snatching a glance at him, he revealed a smile she thought might kill her. He had to know how attractive he was. He *had* to. She caught her eyes lingering on him just as they were asked to vacate the dressing room.

A friendly worker approached her with a folding chair. With the flick of his wrist, he placed it where she could view the production without obstructing the stagehands. "Try to stay put. It gets crazy back here."

Taking a seat, she checked her phone, rolling her eyes at the missed calls from her ex. Her finger slid over the power button, and the device went dark. "He's not ruining tonight."

"One minute!" Clutching a wireless mic in his hand, Hanjun beckoned the artists into a huddle. "Let's do this!"

Each placing their hand in the center of the circle, the bandmates raised their hands in the air before bending towards the floor. "Making the impossible, possible! Blackmirror!"

Heading for the stage, they took their places. The platform was bathed in colorful lights, illuminating the fans. A billow of ultramarine smoke hid their figures until the followspots caught their shimmering costumes. A momentary hush fell over the audience, replaced by gasps as their outlines emerged from the cloud. As the par cans followed the band members, a melody of cheers filled the hall.

Jen had never been to a Blackmirror concert, though she imagined their shows were entertaining, given the enormous budget and star power behind one of the biggest boy bands of the decade. Despite her overactive imagination, she was not primed for how great the performance was. Every aspect, from the choreography to the cutesy turnovers, was planned down to minor details. The musicians gave it everything they had, to the point of exhaustion, and then a little more. With racing hearts and wobbly legs, they crawled off the stage after their synchronized dance routines.

Ha-Rin stood near Jen during the short intervals between tracks when the group prepped for their next appearance. He had overheard the performers mentioning she was an admirer. Following the beat, her body swayed, and her palms tapped her thighs. Her hair, disheveled from the backstage heat, grazed her face as she nodded to the music.

To him, she didn't resemble a devotee—she recognized the effort Blackmirror put in, not necessarily the product they put out. It was the distinct contrast between a fan and a supporter. All supporters were fans, but not all fans were supportive.

The fan-supporter ratio was the baseline the agency trusted when recruiting. While the company preferred to hire enthusiasts, there was an algorithm designed to determine if the prospective recruit was a fly-by-night ally or someone who would continuously uplift the group. A fine balance between passion and practicality—loyalty and longevity—all determined by the calculations of a high-achieving formula developed by the agency's founder and Chief Executive Officer.

"You like them, huh?" Ha-Rin was stifled by the screeching guitars of a live band.

"It's clear they've worked hard!" She mimicked the grace of Jin's movements. "Making something look effortless takes a lot of effort."

"What they do is a full sensory experience." He motioned to the platform, a dazzling array of colors, with swirling spotlights illuminating every alcove. "It's more than melodies and visuals. It's an energy, a bond, and a connection. It's not easy."

Her tongue darted out to wet her parted lips. "Nothing ever is."

⋆⁺₊⋆☾⋆⁺₊⋆

Three hours into the concert, almost through the set list, Honey swiped Sunny's leg from under him during their hit anthem, '*Valiant.*' Deok-Sun crumpled to the stage, his face contorted in agony. He clutched his right ankle, bulging at an unnatural angle. Silence saturated the hall, a stark contrast to the music and cheers that suffused the space moments before.

Without missing a beat, Hanjun draped Deok-Sun's arm around his shoulder, lifting him from the platform. Soogi joined on the other side to distribute his weight. Carrying him offstage, they lowered him to the floor. Jin returned to the audience, apologizing for the inconvenience.

After making two failed attempts to rise, Deok-Sun collapsed, rocking back and forth. The taste of blood lingered on his tongue—further injury from the tumble. "I can't..."

Hanjun crouched, pulling up Deok-Sun's pant leg. Discoloration was visible through his white sock. "This is bad."

Ha-Rin rushed over with a medic to assess the damage. Performing a swift inspection, the medical assistant shook his head. "We need an ambulance."

"I think it's popped out of place." Falling to her knees, Jen kneeled on the opposite side of Rem. She swiped the sweat-matted strands out of Deok-Sun's eyes. "This will hurt. Terribly. But then it won't. Do you understand?"

"Yes." He nodded with a willingness to do anything to stop the pain.

Caressing Deok-Sun's shoulder, she glanced at Hanjun. "He needs to have the bone popped back in."

"I can't do that!" Hanjun backed away.

She grabbed his wrists, grounding his concerns. "I promise you can do this."

She moved out of the way for the attending medic to make his recommendation. Taking a second glimpse, he gaped at her. "I don't know how, but she's right."

Yielding, Hanjun placed his palms on one side of Deok-Sun's ankle, while the medic held the other. Deok-Sun clamped down on the collar of his shirt. Exhaling through his nose, he nodded for them to continue. In one forceful push, the bone snapped into place, producing a popping that caused the team to gasp.

Deok-Sun released a pained howl and then slowed to a controlled whimper. Spitting the polyester from his lips, he tilted his head back. "She was right. It *hurt*."

Jen examined his pupils. "Are you okay?"

"I think so." Puffy-cheeked, he clung to his bent knee.

Her focus shifted to Rem. "How many songs do you have left?"

Biting his lip, he observed the medic administering a brace around Deok-Sun's contusion. "One."

"This will get him through, but you need to take him to the ER. The only thing holding the bone in place is this fabric." The medic secured the straps with a rough tug.

"Can he walk?" Ha-Rin directed the question to the medic, though Deok-Sun answered.

"I'm okay." Attempting to stand, his knees knocked, and he groaned to mask the weakness in his ankle.

"Get him a chair." Ha-Rin beckoned the crew. "Don't let him put pressure on that."

"Let's go, Sunny." Hanjun stooped to pick up Deok-Sun. His grip was strong, and he lifted him up onto his back with ease. Though he was an only child, he spent years carrying his cousins by piggyback.

Relocating the injured bandmate to the platform, the musicians wrapped up without dancing, gathering around Deok-Sun like an a cappella troupe. They lingered under the blinding lights until the confetti cannons were discharged and wished their supporters a wonderful evening. Afterward, they sprinted off stage, stripped out of their outfits, and rushed him to the nearest medical institution.

⋆⁺₊⋆☾⋆⁺₊⋆

Five silhouettes huddled beneath the porte cochère. Clouds loomed overhead, casting a shadow over the hospital. Rain fell in a gentle sprinkle, reflecting dim light from the windows.

Fists clenched, Hanjun's eyes narrowed after witnessing the youngest admitted into the emergency room alone. "Dumbass Covid restrictions."

"He's going to be fine." Hanso patted his back.

Leaning against jagged bricks, Soogi's shoulders slumped. "I kicked him. We've practiced every day, how could I..."

"It was an accident." The odor of ethyl alcohol seeping from the front doors filled Jen's lungs. Resisting the bitter wind, she pulled the thin blazer over her chest while Jin blocked the gusts with his own.

Soogi's eyebrows furrowed. "It should have been me."

Ha-Rin burst through the double doors, pushing Deok-Sun in a wheelchair. Deok-Sun smiled, finding the young men, along with Jen, combating the cold. Crashing the pity party, he balanced on one foot with his opposite ankle encased in a bulky cast. "Did you know I could have had permanent nerve damage if the bone didn't get moved into place right away? Crazy, right?"

Leaving Deok-Sun in the care of his supportive teammates, Ha-Rin pulled the van up to the sidewalk. Hanjun helped lay the youngest in the backseat, ensuring his injured leg remained propped up. Strapping him in, he encouraged the mates to rest. "I'll take a cab."

Ha-Rin's hand fell on Hanjun's shoulder. "Offer the girl a room. We shouldn't allow her to drive home so late at night."

"Will do." Hanjun's gaze chased the vehicle as it drove away, its shiny black exterior glimmering under the moonlight. He then turned his attention to Jen, finding her eyes downcast on the chipped concrete. "Are you alright?"

"He may need physical therapy." Bewildered, she couldn't remember the night's events. Once Deok-Sun was debilitated, she forgot she was at a concert. She forgot that he was famous. She forgot everything.

"He's resilient." Providing a hand, his jacket rustled.

She fixated on his extended arm. Matching his pleasantry, she discovered his hands to be soft, aside from the calluses on his palms. Standing to her full height, she didn't feel short compared to the rest of Blackmirror, but she felt tiny in comparison to him. Her feet were planted on the sidewalk, yet he towered over her by a head. "I hope that's true."

He continued to hold her hand even after he hoisted her up. "You saved Deok-Sun."

The ground was littered with patches of grass—dying earthy colors blending into a disorganized puzzle. She focused on a jagged rock jutting out of the concrete. "It was nothing."

He moved cautiously, contacting her chin in a non-threatening way. "It was *not* nothing."

She swiped at her phone, squinting as the bright screen temporarily blinded her. "I should get home."

He formed a smile that reached his eyes. "Stay with us."

Her mouth parted in quiet concentration. "I wouldn't want to impose—"

"I slept in your apartment. It's the least we can do."

⋆⁺₊⋆☾⋆⁺₊⋆

Home for the night was the entire floor of the swankiest hotel in Chicago. The interior was immaculate, right down to the terrace. Natural light and glimmering chandeliers combined with rich wood, orchestrating prideful luxury.

The lift opened to reveal a hallway decorated with golden accents. Hanjun motioned for Jen to depart first, though a security officer stopped her as soon as she stepped out. "Miss, you're not permitted here."

Exiting after her, Hanjun's face hung tranquil, his eyes serene. "She's with me."

"Yes, sir." The guard stepped back at his command.

She scurried behind him. "Your defense is tight."

He paused his brisk walk five doors from the elevator. "There have been instances of fans breaking into our rooms."

She blinked consecutively. "That's *insanity*."

"That's *reality*."

As soon as they walked into Deok-Sun's room, three of the bandmates rushed to hug her. Soogi and Hanso enveloped her petite frame, creating a warm and comforting trio. When he had the opportunity to embrace her, Jin clung to her side, wrapping an arm around her as if they were childhood friends.

Greetings were shared during the reunion, and following a harsh knock, Hanjun cracked the door. Excusing himself amid the commotion, he reappeared minutes later. "J&I heard about what happened, and they're not happy."

He pointed toward Deok-Sun's cast, which stood out against the dark blue covers. "For obvious reasons."

J&I Entertainment was the agency responsible for creating, managing, and caring for Blackmirror. Finding immense glory through the boy band, the company saw a meteoric rise—a tidal wave of fame and fortune, launching it to the heights of South Korean conglomerates. Hosting a diverse roster of talents ranging from thespians to social media mavens, the organization was a force to be reckoned with.

The whites around her irises grew, noticing the tension in his neck and the sharp set of his jaw. "Am I in trouble?"

"If it wasn't for her, the show would have ended right then!" Deok-Sun blurted without a thought.

"It's not up to us what happens." Hanjun's eyes lowered, avoiding direct eye contact with the room. "They're sending a car for you in the morning."

"I should sleep, then." Turning to the door, her heart plummeted into her guts.

Hanjun followed behind, offering accommodations that were booked by the agency but weren't claimed by staff. Though he offered her a dozen—including a grand suite left unoccupied after a disagreement between the musicians—she chose the first empty room and slipped inside.

Ensuring the door was locked behind her, he returned to his room. He sank into a plush velvet armchair, uneasy over the conversation he had with Ha-Rin. "What do they want with her?"

J&I were known for using scare tactics on anyone who came close to mistreating Blackmirror, though he didn't believe Jen meant harm. She may have overstepped, but she hadn't intended to wrong Deok-Sun, and while the rest of their staff stood unresponsive, she sprang into action.

The tang of resolve drenched his tongue whenever those who threatened the artists faced J&I's team of legal advisors, but he didn't feel Jen deserved discipline. His faith in her innocence remained unshaken by the agency's impending wrath.

Pulling the cell phone from his pocket, he knew his bandmates would be chatting about her. Too bright in the dim room, the frequent dings of messages rolled in.

> **Soogins:** She's so cute!
> **Jinja:** I love her top! Do you think she'd let me borrow it?
> **Honsa:** Ask her.
> **Sunnie:** Did she text you back?
> **Soogins:** She did this morning, but nothing since.

Honsa: She barely used her phone.
Sunnie: What ethnicity is she? American?
Honsa: American isn't an ethnicity. It's a nationality.
Soogins: She has features that make me think no.
Soogins: Pouty lips.
Soogins: Aegyo-sal when she smiles.
Sunnie: Get it, Soogi!
You're lucky this is a private chat.
Soogins: Don't act like you haven't noticed.
Sunnie: She has thick hips and thighs.
Honsa: You can't go calling girls thick.
Sunnie: Hanjun said thick is good, right?
Jinja: You can if they call themselves thick.
Honsa: Your ex-girlfriend was the exception.

Resisting the urge to reply while the chat room turned into a place for locker room gossip, he closed the window and wrote in his journal.

The night harnessed a jagged edge, glimmering with resilience and charm, though he was positive he saw Jen for who she was—an empath. In the face of difficulty, she exhibited understanding without saying a word. Her approach and demeanor were music for the heart, and he craved to know more about her.

Jen was quick to help Deok-Sun. I'm not sure what the management has planned for her, but I hope she will continue to speak with us. I haven't seen my bandmates getting along so well in months.

CHAPTER FIVE

Choose What Kills You

"Are you up?" Hanjun yelled through the door.

"I am now." A bittersweet taste filled Jen's mouth—the remnants of a dream she had. Wrapping a comforter around her body, she opened the door and sidestepped.

"Your escort will be here in an hour." His sharp glare landed on her folded garments on the floor. Crossing the room, he sat on the sofa with his back hunched over, resting his arms on his knees, tapping nervously against a paper coffee cup.

"I'm gonna get ready." Gripping the edge of the blanket, she turned for the bathroom. Spacious, with marble floors and countertops glowing in mood lighting. The stall was a glass-encased sanctuary with multiple jets, and eucalyptus scented the air as she slathered hotel-provided gel over her frame. Her mind was a twisted garden of thorny vines, prickling at her consciousness with the burden of unanswered questions. Why did Blackmirror's agency search her out? Why all the secrecy? And why couldn't it have been a phone call?

She stepped out of the shower and draped a towel around her figure, only to find Hanjun had not moved an inch. She was less bothered than intrigued. "I thought you'd be gone."

"You thought wrong." Casting his phone aside, he didn't say a word. Interweaving his arms, he provided a confident grin while her moistened body dripped on the floor.

She pointed to her clothing. "Can you at least turn around?"

He erected and rotated, allowing her to grab the textiles and sprint back to the washroom. Pulling the sequin tank over her torso, she wore the same outfit from the previous day. She wasn't equipped to stay the night and only had the makeup she carried with her—powder, mascara, and a dab of eyeliner. She tamed her flyaways with a fingertip of lip balm—a modeling secret she discovered years prior. Clearing the bathroom of toiletries, her damp hair glistened under the fluorescent bulbs.

Keeping an eye on her, he smirked. "You look ready."

She strained to detect any flicker of emotion. His features were unreadable, though his dimples remained prominent. They were weapons, and he was aware. Only someone who knew they were instruments of destruction would wield them continually. "As ready as I'll ever be."

Departing the room, they strolled the hall to visit Deok-Sun, each clinging to their side, almost bumping shoulders with the wall. The tension was dense, and she wondered when their interactions became strained. Was it when he called her for the first time, when she laughed at his jokes, or when he stripped down to his briefs at the end of the previous night? In under twenty-four hours, their communication became a chore.

Upon entering the youngest musician's room, they were welcomed by the bandmates. Deok-Sun hadn't slept—his eyes were red, and he solicited an argument with Hanjun. "She didn't do anything wrong. Why are they doing this?"

Hanjun's neck bent at an unnatural angle. "Deok-Sun, we've been over this. I don't make the decisions, you know that."

Stationed near the door, she watched as they squabbled. Acquiring languages as an adult was arduous, and Spanish gave her one hell of a time. She had such an issue with trills that she alternately channeled her energy into sign language and braille as she braved a fear of sudden deaf blindness. Although she didn't feel it was irrational, it was a real thing that happened to real people. While her luck was fortunate, when karma came around to settle her dues, it was always something enormous.

She came back from her musings after hearing Hanjun reach irritation. His once poised face turned taut, his cheekbones jutting out. He held himself in self-possession, demonstrating why he was the commander. Nobody would dare mess with him. "It's not up to us."

"I hate this!" Jin stomped the carpet, muttering profanities.

She told a lie she didn't believe. "I'll be fine."

Tears welled during their goodbyes, and she hugged each bandmate. Deok-Sun cradled her for so long that she worried they might merge. Jin squeezed her so snugly that she thought she would pop. Hanso twirled her around, causing her sniffling to end. Soogi offered a friendly fist bump. Once accepted, he pulled her into a hug before returning to his cool charade.

Waiting near the door, Hanjun received a notification. "Your ride is here."

"Time to go." Ensuring she had her bag, mobile, and insulated bottle, she advanced towards the door.

"We'll miss you!" Jin bawled while the door closed.

Feeling as if she were headed to her execution, she acquired a cupful of ice at the hotel's dispenser. "Might as well hydrate if I'm going to burn in hell."

Standing at her side, Hanjun shattered the reticence, noticing she never went anywhere without the silver tumbler. "Drink a lot of water?"

Replacing the lid, she shrugged. "I cut out soft drinks."

"Did you start for a diet?"

She hesitated at his curious line of questioning. "I did lose weight, but that wasn't the goal. If I'm going to consume empty calories, I want it to be from food, not sugary concoctions."

Guffawing, he patted his well-toned abdomen. "Calories aren't empty if they're packed with joy. Sadly, I stand in front of people all day, so I have to maintain a certain aesthetic."

She wagged her head, tossing off a cheeky simper while he rubbed his tummy in a way she wouldn't have imagined him to. "I don't see myself being thin. It looks great on some people, but I prefer to be curvier."

Her gaze hovered on his chiseled lines, comparable to the delicate curves of a sculpture. "It's better for my mental health. I lose weight when I'm stressed."

In the States, she was midsize—between straight and full-figured—and most of her bulk rested on her bust, posterior, and thighs. In other countries, she would be seen as thick or even chubby.

Blooming in the late 90s—when heroin chic was the only thing in—she went through a phase where she wanted to be slender, yet despite working out and suffering every diet imaginable, skinny wouldn't bless her. She wasn't thin and had more bosom, buttocks, and tummy than her slimmer classmates, but she wasn't quite plus sized. Though she was humiliated less than her plushier counterparts, she experienced a varied fusion of body-shaming from being an in-betweenie. To some, she was too much. To others, she was too little. Receiving criticism from both ends of the spectrum, her formative years were speckled with hellish ridicule.

As a grown woman, she focused on wellness by accepting all bodies—hers just happened to have childbearing hips, adding an extra amount of oomph to her figure. It was an undesirable body type when she was young, but thanks to trendsetting celebrities, her shape was more validated, if not idolized. Nevertheless, she occasionally stumbled into past insecurities.

The pair moved in sync, their arms contacting as they walked. His head wobbled in agreement. "I have a hard time maintaining. There's an eighty percent chance I'll order takeout every night. But I also can't eat when I'm stressed."

"I'm sure it's more stressful for you since any fluctuation will be a topic of conversation."

His teeth sunk into his lip. "Yeah."

Her shoulder connected with his—a calculated jostle that fired a burst of heat through his extremities. "Your value to humanity doesn't increase or decrease with your body mass. We're souls trapped inside meat carcasses."

"What's your ideal type, then?" Accompanying her into the elevator, he ruptured into a smile. "What gets your heart pumping about someone?"

"For a man or woman?" Stretching for the buttons, she pondered why he was asking such things.

His eyes stretched. "Both?"

"I don't have a type; they just need to be taller than me." Wearing a rosy hue, her eyes were cast down. "It's almost impossible not to be."

He glanced at her. She was petite. Although he was accustomed to looming over most in his six-foot body—or meat carcass, as she would call it—he thought her to be the optimal height. Small enough to hold and tall enough to leave smooches on her forehead. Reeling in his runaway thoughts, his face turned red as she rambled about her type. "Communication is important, so they need to speak a language I speak or be patient while I learn theirs. Otherwise, smart and funny. Personable. Creative. Quirky. Someone who is just as happy staying home as they are going out."

His head rocked, a buoy caught in an unexpected wave, when she declared something unanticipated. "Such a person needs to have dreams."

"*Dreams?*" His eyebrows ascended. "Like becoming rich or running for president?"

"Dreams don't have to be grand, but I find those pursuing their dreams to be attractive. There's something intoxicating about sharing a common purpose in partnership." She shook her head, strands of hair sweeping her lips. "Perhaps I'm more in love with fantasy than I am with people."

"Falling in love with dreams isn't bad. Everything worthwhile was forged by someone with dreams."

"True." Dreams were one of the reasons for her divorce. Not the deciding factor, but considerable enough to stick with her as a bothersome inkling in the back of her mind. Her ex not only doubted her potential; he wouldn't grant her the time to pursue her dreams after she worked tirelessly to achieve his. After escaping his clutch, she swore to avoid anyone who tried to crush her ambition and dodge everyone who didn't reciprocate the support she gave.

He poked her shoulder. "And your ideal woman?"

She tittered at his prodding. "That was a joke, but women are remarkable. If Ashley Graham contacts me, I would consider. But I do find myself most often attracted to men."

His cheeks flushed for asking such a private question. Luckily, the doors slid open to the ground floor before he felt too embarrassed. He walked her through the lobby, across the asphalt parking lot, and led her to an Uber. It was misty and breezy—typical weather for Chicago. He spoke to the driver, confirming the destination. Once verified, he opened the door for her.

The surrounding wind grew calm as she placed her bag on the seat. When she turned to face him, he froze in place. "I guess this is goodbye."

Holding a tight-lipped smile, he broke eye contact only to make it again. He remained quiet for what felt like forever until he gathered a puff of courage. "It doesn't have to be."

He employed a non-native drawl, and his natural tone resonated lower than his celebrity voice. Perhaps the man she met the night before was his alter ego. She was charmed, but assumed they were too different to be anything other than acquaintances. What did she know about surviving as a star? What did he know about living as an average person? He knew the cameras, perfectly tailored outfits, and adoring fans clamoring for his interest. She knew office buildings, congestion on the metro, and the unremarkable attire of ordinary people. If her life were a movie, she might seize the opening, but it wasn't.

Even if they had a shot at making it out of the awkward interaction stage, they would be performing a dance of opposites. A kaleidoscope of glitter and gray for the world to see. And to rip apart. "I think we both know it has to be."

Accepting her response, he expanded for a hug. Falling into his arms, his body felt hot in the cold air. "Go well, Jenilyn."

Hopping onto the seat, she rolled down the window to make a final statement. "Perhaps we'll meet again."

His palm yielded a repetitive beat on the roof, expressing an unspoken pact. "I'll look forward to it."

⋆⁺₊⋆☾⋆⁺₊⋆

Settled in the back of the vehicle, the Chicago traffic was unforgiving, and Jen's patience was thinning. Her heart hammered in her chest, and the steady thump of apprehension made her dizzy. Cars honked, and melodies floated in through the driver's window. Disregarding the cacophony, she concentrated on the imminent summit, visualizing every possible discourse.

"Here we are." The driver pulled up to a footpath and engaged his flashers.

She peered out the window, finding a queue of people outside the premises. "Here? It's a restaurant."

Checking the destination, he doubled down. "That's it."

Exiting, she lingered to examine the establishment. Boasting neon lights, a marquee billboard advertised the special of the day; melanzane alla parmigiana. She eyeballed the colossal waitlist lining the sidewalk. She arrived early, but not enough to wait for an eatery's worth of individuals. Scanning her environment, she spotted an elderly couple heading for a vacant door. When they tugged the handle, she spied the reservations-only notice on the glass and hurried over. Venturing into the dark, Italian-inspired anterior, she approached the hostess station. "I'm meeting someone. His name is Ha-Rin."

Pen in hand, the kindly woman peered up from the reservation book. "Jenilyn?"

Following her nod, a waitress motioned for her to shadow. Passing families at oversized tables, they made it to the back corner of the restaurant, where it was unsettlingly quiet and darker than the front. In a date-night setting, it would have been romantic, and she worried it wasn't Blackmirror's agency who wanted to talk with her, but their manager.

She arrived at the table to find Ha-Rin preparing a cup of tea. He gaped at her without expression. No smile. Stern eyes. Motioning for her to sit, he displayed the presence capable of making a room stop in its tracks, such as when a strict father reprimands his offspring in a crowded grocery store.

Taking a seat opposite him, invasive thoughts assaulted her mind. Was she about to be sued by one of the biggest agencies in the world? Concerned for her finances, she tallied her assets, though she didn't have much after the separation. They divided their possessions and were awaiting a buyer for the home they once shared. The sale was the only reason for not blocking him. "I shouldn't have touched Deok-Sun. He was injured, and my brain stopped working."

She wasn't poor. She was broke. Her basic provisions were met, and she didn't fret about trivial purchases, but substantial setbacks, such as costly car repairs and overpriced medical care, would have her checking couch cushions for loose change and eating ramen noodles for weeks.

Her savings were healthy, though she would be devastated to hire a defense attorney. While her main job kept her afloat, side gigs afforded her a sizeable cushion. The hustles didn't amass much individually, but they collectively equated to twice her salary, and it was money she never touched. Ever.

The funds were her backup plan. The previous year, the owner of her organization summoned her to his office and revealed a stack of signed documents. She wasn't sure what they were when he spoke in layman's terms; the business was being sold. As a businessman who toiled his entire life, he was eager to live out the rest of his days in Boca Raton with his bride.

The announcement was a crushing blow. Imagination Acreage saw her at her best and worst. From the heartbreaking split from her former partner to the introduction, marrying, and divorcing of her ex-husband, the stomping grounds were her place of frustration, healing, and discovery.

And she saw it at its best and worst, too. She encountered thousands of families and witnessed the passage of time as the kids aged into adults and the parents became grandparents. Summer flings and first breakups, marriages and divorces—she had the pleasure of watching the rise and collapse of life.

Unable to imagine a job that would suit her better, she had creative influence over the leisure experience. From creating tie-dye shirts with bunches of children to teaching painting classes to the elderly, there was never a dull moment. Every weekend brought new possibilities, and each week was spent preparing for the weekend.

In a perpetual state of innocence where the fun never ended, she was a winged godmother. A staple in her customers' childhoods, she was *Miss Jen*. She was the one who instructed them on how to cross-stitch with jumbo plastic needles and paint with their fingers on canvas. Who organized epic water balloon fights and assisted Santa in the middle of July. Who planned car shows, haunted houses, and dance parties to attract moderate audiences. She was a happiness creator, and her fingerprints were left on everyone she crossed paths with.

It wasn't easy, though. Crafting, planning, and executing activities with a small budget, limited staff, and an unknown number of attendees was, at times, excruciating. Between the weekends of fun were hours of brainstorming, the gathering of supplies, and the creation of gadgetry needed to pull off her over-the-top ideas.

There was a balance of fluidity necessary to perform her duties. Her job was juggling deadlines, securing sponsorships, and trading abilities with professionals, such as when she required functional trap hatches for a haunted house. The kind gentleman who constructed the contraptions was a skilled carpenter, and he asked her to develop a website for his business in exchange for his handiwork.

That's how she conducted her life: by digesting every bit of information and attempting everything. It was something her great-grandfather taught her. He worked at General Motors and South Works for the better part of his life and knew how to do everything. And what he didn't know, he learned. No ability was not good enough, and his tenacity saved his household in times of poverty. Losing a job was less worrisome when there was a menagerie of abilities he could offer.

Adopting her grandfather's advice, she led a fulfilling life and possessed the potential to convert any interest into a money-making venture. Those she bartered with introduced her to friends, and along with a roster of associates, she had a range of contacts to call on.

The instant she heard her unorthodox way of existing would end, she began formulating ideas for the next step. Working a nine-to-five job or ringing up cold beverages wasn't going to cut it. She craved stimulation, eccentric people, and perpetual challenges, not superficial conversations about the weather or what she planned to have for dinner. She would never have an answer, but she knew the percentage of adults who shrieked at clowns or the count of adolescents who were unnervingly accurate at throwing axes into wooden targets.

Her boss, whom she had grown close to, was kind enough to communicate with the new owner on her behalf; she was permitted to inhabit the apartment for twelve months after the finalized deal.

She appreciated the kindness extended to her but refused. As the end of the era ticked down and her colleagues moved on to fresh opportunities, she needed to move on, too. She had an enjoyable life with even better memories, but her separation had been settled for a year. The community ensured her ex-husband couldn't bother her, but she couldn't hide behind security walls forever. There was more to discover.

With her bank accounts thriving, she intended to harness her skills in an improved way. After months of formulating the perfect strategy and getting the tedious details out of the way, she initiated an endeavor catering to those who didn't conform to modern dating. It was something she thought of on the coat-tails of her annulment, though she was arguably at her lowest at the time. While airing the never-ending hurdles in her union, her psychologist asked a question she couldn't answer.

'Do you know why people stay in unfulfilling relationships?'

There were several answers she could have given, and all were correct. For the children. Because so much time was invested. Familiarity. Financial security. Fiscal hardship. Love, or the wish for acceptance. The responses would be different based on the circumstances, but her therapist said something to change her viewpoint.

> *'We're afraid of what's next. Courtship has changed, and with it, the people, the steps, and the interactions. It's become an exhausting process, and we begin to weigh the benefits; if our bad circumstances are better than the rejection we may receive from a society that's desensitized to the vintage notion of love, we may compromise our needs to make an unsalvageable situation work, even if it kills us.'*

It was a painful realization. She *was* anxious for the future. She *was* terrified of never falling in love again. And she *was* frightened of how much the world had changed. Her young coworkers talked about their matches and how rapidly the conversations soured. Between the unsolicited visuals, prying requests, and sexual expectations, there was no way she could use the mainstream practices of courtship. It would be more exhausting than her marriage, which was quite literally killing her.

While she released the last thread of her shame, her counselor suggested an exercise to help her transition into the next chapter: to court herself. After years of overlooking her needs and neglecting her wants, she needed to learn who she was because the girl who lost half of her hair to stress and enough weight to be rail slim wasn't her.

Focusing on self-love and gratitude wasn't effortless, and there was a lot of homework involved. Redetermining her likes, dislikes, and passions. Evaluating her morals and admitting her vulnerabilities. She had to rid herself of the toxicity and recognize her sensibilities by addressing her shortcomings, regardless of what her ex did or didn't do.

She was pushed to exercise, sleep, and eat through severe depression, diverted from gratification-inducing distractions, and curbed escapism. Gorging on a tub of Ben & Jerry's and binge-watching Boy Meets World would have numbed the existential crisis, but her destination was more important.

The day she moved out of her previous residence was the day she reclaimed her life, and she implemented her therapist's proposal. She found the concept far-fetched in the beginning but uncovered the science. She apologized to her mind for years of pain and appreciated everything her meat carcass did for her. She took pride in every mole that identified her body and every muscle used to carry out strenuous tasks.

Thankful she chose to end the partnership before the coronavirus penned the world indoors, the subsequent months were spent befriending herself. She was removed from society for three sennights, and the isolation was healing. There were no arguments or anger. No gaslighting, shame, or interrogations. No weeks of muteness, no begging for the minimum, and no disputes about why she wasn't up for sex on demand.

When the ban was lifted on hospitality services, she returned to work, and her boss disclosed the purchase of the property. The setback was another catastrophic blow to the serene life she was working towards. Uprooting her life, settling in a comfortable apartment, and then being told the job she loved would soon be gone catapulted her into another bout of desolation. Perhaps sad, she adapted to the unknown and rebounded faster than she should have.

While helping an elder with her accommodation, Jen began to see a speckle of hope. The woman, who wore foundation thick enough to spoon off, was newly widowed. Taking one last journey around the globe, she was stranded at the park due to the pandemic.

Sensing a friend of heartache, she gravitated towards Jen. And Jen played along because it was her job to ensure a memorable stay. She found her to be a bit obnoxious with the way she greeted her from across parking lots and shouted before diving into the lake. Brushing aside their differences of character, she eventually warmed up to the peculiar woman. With sickness swirling in the air and most modes of amusement restricted, they scheduled get-togethers. Over milk and biscuits, they exchanged tales, hardships, and cries.

Koroleva was a Russian immigrant with an indistinct accent. Exhibiting the personality of a sarcastic sitcom grandmother, her humorous one-liners were always good for a laugh. She was swift to assert her dominance, yet she was willing to teach those who took the time to listen.

The elder pulled toward Jen because she identified a kindred spirit. As an aspiring actress, she possessed an inquisitive fascination with the world. One country was never enough to hold her down until she fell in love. The entanglement was the talk of the town, but behind locked doors, he was an abusive, nightmare of a man. A child in a mature body, he belittled her, proclaiming his superiority as head of the household. He did what he wanted with little consideration for the family—a tale all too familiar to Jen. And before she assembled the courage to withdraw, he suffered a stroke that disabled him for life.

The woman was built differently. With a wheelchair-bound husband who couldn't bathe or stand on his own, she resigned to become his full-time caretaker for forty long years. Jen even thought she heard the number wrong. *Four. Zero.* A decquad of torment. Disability didn't pacify his fiery temper; it only made it easier for her to avoid direct abuse.

She nurtured him for forty years amid the cruelty, and Jen knew she was a better woman than her. What would she have done if, before separating from her ex-husband, he faced a similar difficulty? She didn't love him two years prior to the split and couldn't envision sticking it out for another four decades.

At eighty years old, Koroleva was living out the rest of her days in liberation. She screamed until her lungs were sore, cackled through side pains, and wrung the last bits of happiness out of life. She didn't mind if people thought she dressed too young or was too old to flatter attractive men; she was focused on making one individual happy. Herself.

She was a superb woman who deserved a better hand at life, and although her external youth departed, she gained the devotion unattainable in her marriage. Or perhaps love found her. While enjoying a coffee with Jen one chilly morning, a distinguished gentleman entered the restaurant, and she issued him a compliment. Charmed, he joined them at the table, and the trio enjoyed stories over the hours.

The affair developed organically, and though they never wed, the couple were indivisible. They sustained an innocent, school-aged adoration—exactly what Koroleva needed after years of abuse. In the final hour, they established a beginning. Not only as lovers but also as caregivers, and they referred to each other as the light of their lives.

Six blissful months later, she departed, and her lover cried more than Jen thought was possible. Despite knowing her for a short time, he mourned her all the same. More than her deceased husband would have. Visiting her grave with the same flowers he'd bought her when she was alive, he lived with honor and respected the woman he had waited his life to find.

Before her passing, Koroleva gave him a letter for Jen, encompassing a slice of advice from someone who embraced life when it was a little too late.

My dearest Jenilyn,

When you smile, the world smiles with you, but when you hurt, you hurt alone. You hide your pain, grit your teeth, and move forward because you know, with time, your bruises will heal. You wait for time to pass when you are just waiting to die.

My girl, you must live like I didn't. Death will come for you, as it does for all of us, but you have the option to choose what kills you. Marriages, jobs, traveling, children, food, alcohol—everything will take a small piece of you. You said you never want to love again, but I don't believe that. It is more accurate to say you never want to hurt again, but shunning love will also take pieces of your life.

Just as death will come for you, so will love. And when the time comes and you're staring love in the eyes once again, do not back down. Do not be afraid of the past or the future. Jump in lips first, strip down to the bones of your soul, and put your heart on the line. Only when you share your secrets will the masks of those you encounter fall off.

May you always remain without wax,
Koroleva.
P.S. If reincarnation exists, I hope to find you as friends or sisters.

With the counsel of her adviser and the wisdom of Koroleva, Jen began spoiling herself. She enjoyed dinner at her favorite restaurants, treasured leisurely walks in beautiful parks, and visited art galleries. She was the person she looked forward to talking to, and it never failed to provoke reactions. Co-workers thought she snapped, couples thought she was pathetic, and the feedback from men was staggering. There was either a potent fascination or complete disgust. While on a solo movie outing, she pondered why a woman dating herself would be intimidating and came up with one single conclusion: humans were fearful of being alone.

Still figuring out the next stage of her life, she studied the way courtship evolved over the decades. Gone were the days of organic meet-cutes, as most individuals were too consumed with social media and content creators. Sex had become disposable, whereas establishing close alliances was daunting.

Stimulated by lust and insecurity, the populace tolerated flimsy links. The dating pool wasn't a reservoir teeming with hopeful singles; it was a swamp infested with deadly creatures prone to devouring anyone in their thirst for popularity, philandry, or supremacy. Since the dawn of matchmaking apps, the game of love was won with detachment, not collaboration.

Delving into the realm of application users, she stumbled upon legitimate grievances, many comparable to her own. Research proved that around half of all Americans who tried connection services complained that the experiences left them more aggravated than before they started. And the chronicle was always the same: what began as a way to participate in the world of romance turned into a soul-draining encumbrance.

Irrespective of how unprocessed a person's photos were, how true their depiction was, or how sincere they responded in text, a virtual profile couldn't illustrate a whole character. Technology was too superficial to capture full personalities.

Matchmaking apps were nothing more than a glorified lottery system. For a small fee, consumers spun the reel to win the lover of their dreams. Unfortunately, only four percent of gamblers won a shot at love, let alone a long-term partner, and the losers inherited self-depreciation, rewarded with the grand possibility of wasting time on people they wouldn't have entertained in the physical dimension.

With a staggering group of individuals dissatisfied, Jen considered her great-grandfather's sage observations.

'Where there is dissatisfaction, there is room for innovation.'

Understanding she wasn't the only one nostalgic for a slower approach to romance, she discovered her next challenge. Using the knowledge from her longtime job, she formulated a strategy prioritizing real-life synergies and began devising a projection for the first year. Enrolled heartoo users would enjoy no-pressure outings with batches of like-minded singles. Each month, teams would attend workshops while learning about themselves. With plans to relocate the operation to Chicago, the company's launch date was set for October.

Facing legal action would destroy the schedule she exhausted hundreds of hours planning, annihilate her savings, and put her back to square one with no employment, no investments, and no hope. Unable to breathe as her livelihood was threatened, she nearly passed out at the table.

Ha-Rin bounced a teabag in the cup. "Tell me, how long have you been a fan of Blackmirror?"

Gulping, her bottom lip tightened. "I've only known of them for about three years."

He stirred the liquid with a small silver spoon. "How did you hear about them?"

She stared at the table. He would never believe the actual way she heard about the ensemble—from an unexpected visitor who wandered into her workplace one late evening. Instead, she went with the second way she caught wind of the group. "My favorite band, The Base Gene, covered one of Blackmirror's songs and later shared a piece by Rem on Insta. Before I knew it, I fell down the rabbit hole and became a fan."

Adding one sweetener packet to his mug, he flicked the package to remove every grain. "Who is your favorite?"

"I won't make comparisons. Precious gemstones are different but are each valuable." Her shaky voice betrayed her.

He clasped his hands together. It was as if he were toying with her like a mouse, fascinating her with scraps of cheese. "Jenilyn, I've summoned you here to offer you an opportunity. I cannot stress enough how significant an opportunity this is. I've never seen them take to someone so rapidly. Why do you think that is?"

Shifting in her seat, she didn't know they took to her in any particular way. "I-I'm not sure."

"Behind the glamour, they're entertainers with hopes and dreams. They can't interact with the public in a natural way." He sipped the brew, returning the cup to the saucer. "Have you ever wanted to be famous?"

Head shaking aggressively, her hair flung in all directions. "Absolutely not. We all have that dream as kids, but as an adult, I value my privacy."

A shallow chuckle escaped his lungs. "Imagine living in a world where you are constantly judged. People whisper, scrutinizing your every move. All while you resist letting a reality nobody knows about crush you."

She had always perceived celebrities the same; what they shared with the public was a treasure, and anything beyond was their private business. She couldn't grasp the idea of treating creators as gods and thought it did a disservice to them as humans. "I watched a recent GOlive where Hanjun talked about his latest works. I swear his eyes sparkled when he discussed the song he created, but looking at the comments was disheartening. Few cared about what he was saying; they just demanded he acknowledge them."

GOlive was a platform established to facilitate communication between artists and fans. Not only could the musicians arrange live streams with their supporters, but admirers could leave proclamations and kudos for the idols. The twisting infinity logo symbolized the waltz of appreciation, with the performers and followers twirling in harmony. Although the application was originally designed to host Blackmirror, it was extended to house every personality under the J&I umbrella.

Releasing a crestfallen sigh, she added to her statement. "That has to be exhausting."

The moment hung suspended when he spoke. "They need someone to confide in. The band relies on Hanjun, though the agency deems it unfair for him to bear the obligation."

She nipped her lip. Hanjun was a genuine captain. He encouraged his teammates to rise and be heard, all while he stood apart for the betterment of the act. He excelled at an unappreciated job and was ridiculed as the artist who didn't deserve a place among Blackmirror. "I'm sure he's under a lot of strain."

"It seems as if he would open up to you." He spoke clearly, each word enunciated with certainty.

"He's striving to survive in an accelerated environment." Reflecting on his solo ventures, a surge of sentiments swept over her. It must have been challenging—belonging to a team loved by everyone and somehow favored by no one.

He tapped a finger on the oak table, leaving behind a faint imprint. "We want you to join our company. A liaison, if you will. Bring their concerns to me, and I will remedy any issue they have."

CHAPTER SIX

A Curious Cypher

"Why?" The jack-in-the-box question sprang out of Jen. "You're their manager, why wouldn't they come to you?"

"My job—" On paper, Ha-Rin's responsibilities included organizing activities, soliciting appearances, and guaranteeing the idols reached where they were required. But the reality transcended management and chauffeuring. He also functioned as a travel agent when the act appeared overseas. And a nutritionist by monitoring their diets. He was a personal shopper when they had requests, and it was he who did the food runs.

During promotions, he had the added work of platform monitoring. He tested their mics and verified each had a proper name tag for interviewers who were unfamiliar with the band. He recorded rehearsals so the agency could evaluate their performances, and when a member was absent, he subbed in to avoid overworking the performers.

But the most demanding—and perhaps most essential—responsibility was a triple threat. He was bodyguard, guardian, and drill sergeant for the young men. Pre-debut, he reared the team in the absence of their parents, ensuring they remained on task and slept well enough to perform. As they reached maturity and gained an expansive audience, his role transformed to that of a defender; he was the first line of security for individuals who adored the ensemble a little too much.

The job didn't pay well, considering he was on call twenty-four-seven. When there was a schedule, he was there. Morning or night. Rain or shine. Accident or injury. And for every hour Blackmirror worked, he slogged as long and then a little more to ensure their itineraries sailed flawlessly.

Because he assisted the agency's highest earners, he was subjected to mistreatment by the directors when something went awry. And the fans were sometimes just as bad as the head honchos. It wasn't rare for him to endure hate mail, death threats, or extortion attempts by those who thought he knew the dirty little secrets of the artists.

Ruminating over the worst aspects of his profession, a guttural growl escaped him. "Have you ever tried to herd five stray cats into a basket?"

"No." She assumed he was reliving a traumatic experience.

"That's what my job is." Profile softening, he mimicked her contagious smirk. "Ensuring they stay on task is difficult."

"Why did you accept it, then?"

"The job grew with their popularity."

"Couldn't you ask to manage another group?"

His hands wrapped around the mug, though he didn't drink. "When you live together, you become closer than friends."

"Right, but you haven't explained why they can't go to you with their concerns."

"When they were young, they were like my little brothers. They came to me with their girl problems, and I'd sneak them in bottles of soju—" Recalling long nights when the superstars couldn't hold their liquor, he chuckled. "Such as the way a boy stops being so honest with his father in pursuit of self, they no longer need to confide in me."

"What makes you think they'll confide in me? They don't even know me." She pouted in consideration.

"I know they will." His finger danced along the tabletop. "So? How about it?"

Pinching her arm, she questioned if Punk'd was still filming, certain Ashton Kutcher would spring out from behind a curtain. "If the agency is based in South Korea, how would that work? Is it something I could do online?"

His mouth twitched. "You misunderstand. We want you to live with them. In their dorm. In Seoul."

She was convinced she heard the declaration wrong. "Huh?"

Entertained by her confusion, he repeated the statement. The proposition hadn't differed; he requested that she relocate half across the globe. He slid a printed agreement to her side of the table. "If you are vaccinated and have a passport, you can leave with us in the morning. The agency will secure your artist visa."

Examining the covenant, her eyebrows piqued. "I am, and I do. I planned to travel at some point..."

He referred to the highlighted sections on the front. "Your contract will end when theirs does, approximately four years, and you will have similar rules to follow."

Focusing her vision, she perused through the article, noting parameters of significance.

NO PUBLIC DATING OF THE MEMBERS.
ASK PERMISSION BEFORE ENTERING A PRIVATE ROOM.
COOKING DUTIES ARE IN ROTATION.
HOUSEHOLD CHORES ARE SHARED.

He poked at the last rule. "They have a maid, but we require them to perform basic upkeep. You don't need to clean for them; however, you will be given tasks to complete."

Turning to the third page, he circled a paragraph prohibiting harmful gossip. "J&I takes aggressive action against slander."

Leafing to the last page, he indicated a section printed in red pigment. "Signing this will give the agency license to use your likeness in material to support Blackmirror."

"A media clause? What *kind* of media?"

"Marketing materials, diversity training, or introduction communications. We may ask you to film how-to videos, demonstrate presentations, or host functions. The waiver opens additional opportunities. As entertainment professionals, we discover and develop talent wherever it is found."

She reviewed the proviso, identifying that it encompassed dual parts. The first segment gave consent to use her image in print, digital, audio, and any communications deemed necessary. Likewise, J&I would retain the right to alter, translate, or outsource. The second excerpt, although cleverly hidden among legal mumbo jumbo, would prevent her from collecting revenue generated from her visuals. No way in hell was she adding her name to that line. "Did you ask them?"

His hands interlocked. "It's a managerial decision."

She shifted in disapproval. "Thank you, but no thank you."

Tongue on teeth, he scowled. "This is a once-in-a-lifetime opportunity. Are you sure you don't want to reconsider?"

Jiggling her head, her hair brushed her cheeks. "I'm not signing anything at their expense."

The gleam in his eyes vanished. "I understand the shock you may be experiencing, but this is how we do—"

"*I said no.*" Snatching her purse, she shimmied out of the booth, though she hesitated at the rumble of his throat.

"Are the boys with you?"

She swiveled to find Hanjun on a virtual call with Ha-Rin. He rotated the camera to reveal Deok-Sun's room, crowded with shopping totes and mementos from their travels. "Yeah."

"Per our discussion earlier, I'm calling to verify the contract." Ha-Rin adjusted the lens toward her while the artists huddled in the frame. "Jenilyn is reluctant to accept."

She leaned in, giving a friendly wave. "I wasn't sure if—"

"Hi!" Hanso thrashed from the rear, gaining her attention.

Hanjun fumbled with the gadget. "This stupid thing—"

Jin mocked him. "Hanjun has butter fingers!"

Ha-Rin exercised an authoritative tone. "Please provide verbal affirmation of Jenilyn's relocation. From this point, you will consider her a noise barrier. What you share with her is confidential, though she is mandated to disclose a general analysis of your collective emotional health biweekly. Her obligations will include acting as manager when I am unavailable and tending to your needs. Once she has completed the agency's placement testing, she will obtain her official title. Are you in agreement with the specifications?"

Jen waited for their reactions. Jin flailed, giddy at the thought. Hanso pumped a fist in the air. Hanjun grinned, exposing both dimples. Deok-Sun nodded, the most he could do with an injured ankle. Soogi remained stoic, his jaw agape.

Terminating the call, Ha-Rin shoved the agreement towards her, circling a figure on the footer. "This is our offer."

Dropping her purse on the chair, she viewed the number. *Twenty thousand dollars.* It was low, considering her Imagination Acreage salary, but excluding rent, which the agency graciously provided, it would be manageable. "Yearly?"

"Quarterly." His response caused her to choke. "Plus benefits, holidays. Of course, you will vacation when they do, and you may be required to vacation with them."

She was too shocked to blink. *Eighty grand a year.* She landed a golden opportunity and felt as if she needed to take the chance, though she hesitated. Her option was someone's dream. Somebody who slaved to make it in the big leagues. Someone who wanted it more. "I can't accept this."

"You can, and you will. I'm not going to lie; those boys are hard to handle." Handing her a pen, he paused to reflect. There were times he had a tough time managing the vocalists, and he had worked with them since they were trainees. They were moody, erratic, and full of attitude on a decent day. Worse under stress.

A trainee was a talented prospect scouted for placement in the entertainment industry, either as a soloist or in a team. Recruited as juveniles, the candidates underwent training in how to sing, dance, and croon. Expected to live within a collection of standards, they were instructed on how to behave, both on and off-stage. Some agencies went as far as fabricating identities for mass marketing.

Staring at the contract, she was conflicted. Moving was risky, and she'd have to abandon her single's start-up. It wouldn't be an entire loss, as she had a few offers to acquire the concept, but it was her biggest investment. She was at a crossroads and imagined what future Jen would want. Future Jen would want to live without regrets.

Gliding black ink across the line, she had a boatload of apprehensions, but pushed them back. When she divorced her husband, she made a promise to never hamper her wishes again. Not for a man. Not for a woman. Not for anyone.

"Welcome to the J&I family." Depositing the agreement in a leather briefcase, Ha-Rin held a firm hand over the table. "You may bring with you anything you can carry."

Thanking and shaking, she wiggled out of the booth and turned to leave when he seized her wrist. "I was lenient with you this time. Do not expect me to be so in the future."

★⁺₊★☾★⁺₊★

Entering Deok-Sun's hotel room, Jen was welcomed by three of her five soon-to-be roommates. Doling out hugs, the weak fragrance of expensive cologne lingered, overpowered by the scent of clean laundry. A clothing line was strung from the bathroom doorknob to the closet, with hand-washed socks clipped to the string.

Waiting for his turn to greet her, Jin twirled her strands, forming loose ringlets around his fingers. "So cute! I want to match!"

She ran her palms through the tresses; her blonde was refreshed with bright red peeking out between bouncy barrel curls. "I stopped at the salon after I met with Ha-Rin. New job. New me."

Soogi's eyes drooped in a peaceful state. "Blood suits you."

Hanjun, who sat next to Deok-Sun, leaned against the headboard. "Ah. Pretty."

Once her new friends finished bombarding her with questions about the meeting, she turned to him. "Did you know they would be offering me a position?"

His smirk revealed a hint of being so much more than he portrayed. "I had an idea."

She nudged him. "You made it seem like we'd never see each other again."

"They asked me not to spoil the surprise."

"Well played." She hiked her bag up on her shoulder. "I have to go home and pack."

Hanjun held out a hand, his fingers trembling. "Let me see your contract."

She passed over a folded copy. "Did you get new versions?"

He inspected the signed document; she refused the second half of the media release—a smart move. "We had to sign agreements for living arrangements. Not much changed beyond the no girls in our room thing."

"I'm surprised it wasn't there before."

"You're the first girl allowed in our condo, except for the maid." A flush crept up Hanso's face, akin to a ripe tomato.

Jin doubled over in laughter. "Look at his face!"

Ignoring their playful teasing, she turned to leave. She only had a small window to empty her apartment if she planned to make it to their concert on time. And Ha-Rin made it clear that he anticipated her attendance. "I need to go."

Sticking to her side, Jin bounced up and down, and she questioned his excitability. "Do you want to come with?"

He nodded, his blonde hair flapping. "Yes!"

"Am I allowed to take you? Don't you have handlers?"

"Not always." Soogi scoffed at her assumption, just shy of baring his teeth. "We can do things on our own."

Hanso squeezed her arm. "Me too."

"Looks like I have two dashing men to escort me."

Trailing behind them, Hanjun didn't feel it was right to unleash both Jin and Hanso on the novitiate. "I'm going to make sure these guys stay in line."

"Make that three."

⋆⁺₊⋆☾⋆⁺₊⋆

During the drive, they took turns playing music and singing carpool karaoke, while the young men gushed about what they thought Jen should experience. The airport. The sea. The parks. The bridges. Hanjun raved about the river and couldn't wait to visit his studio.

They recounted their favorite foods, preferred places, and precious memories. Homesick from months of traveling, each exalted a small token from home: a faded photo from Jin's adolescence, a piece of jewelry from Hanso's parents, and a fan-given postcard from early in Hanjun's career.

Entering her home for the last time, Jen looked at what had been her sanctuary for the prior year. Uprooting her life and moving to a foreign land was scary, but not as frightening as her life before moving into the apartment.

Pushing her worries aside, she stopped by her room to switch outfits, and the mates wandered around the living area, retrieving decor pieces. Hanjun thumbed through her possessions, gathering collectibles from under the television: Funko Pops of Luci from Disenchantment and Baymax from Big Hero 6. Removing the unopened boxes, he spotted others hiding behind them: Shota Aizawa from My Hero Academia, Levi Ackerman from Attack on Titan, and Ryuk from Death Note.

"I tried not to collect those for a long time." Standing in the hallway, she wore fitted jeggings and a tee knotted on the side.

Returning the relics, he retrieved a trinket box with silver mounts. Featuring a truncated pyramid roof, a mosaic of mother-of-pearl scales were pinned to the structure with ball-headed nails. "Where'd you get this? I saw something similar at the Ashmolean Museum."

She smiled at his fascination. "I bought it at an estate sale. The agent said it was valuable, but most were put off by the owner's stipulations."

"Stipulations?" He inspected the foot brackets, finding them to be engraved. Unclasping the square lock plate with caution, the caisson revealed an exquisite teak inside. In the center was an elongated, cream-colored skull. "This is—"

She peeked into the strongbox, ensuring the bone was how she remembered, not that she expected it to change. "The agent told me a beautiful tale of how the raven watched over their family for centuries."

"It's lovely." He noticed the eyes were cast with citrine.

"Everyone I've shown it to thought it was weird."

"Some only see their own inevitable mortality." Closing the lid, he gaped at her. "This is from the late sixteenth century. Have you had it appraised?"

"I acquire trinkets without a purpose." Though she had a mild obsession with Halloween—and Christmas, if she was honest—she procured the curio for preservation. She hoped it would find someone who valued history. "You can keep it."

"Are you sure?" Scrunching his shoulders and holding the coffin in front of his face, he gave off a high-pitched giggle.

"I have a feeling it was meant for you." She returned to the bedroom and pulled out her luggage—a black nesting set with embossed skulls on the sides.

Hanjun followed behind, complimenting the trio of hard-shell bags. "Those are cute."

Propping the largest suitcase open, she stood with her head cocked to the side. "I like creepy things. And cute things. My inner self is at war."

She tossed possessions on the bedspread. Shirts, jeans, sweaters, handbags, and an overwhelming quantity of chic jackets piled high. Staying out of her way, he snatched a vintage Louis Vuitton bag, inspecting the bubblegum pink handles. "I've never seen one like this."

Groaning as she stretched for her favorite pair of shoes, she offered an explanation. "I like to restore outdated things. That one is from the eighties. The Vachetta was worn through. It took hours of bonding and sanding to get it to a usable state."

He traced the stitching. She spent a great deal of time perfecting her craft. The handles were repaired to perfection, and it was something he loved to see; when people enjoyed their hobbies so much, they became masters. He didn't think there was a purpose to doing anything a person didn't love wholly.

She paused to admire him. Fondling the fittings, he behaved in an almost intimate way. "Plus, I'm a broke bitch."

Removing his concentration from the accessory, he scoped her closet, noticing a row of handbags just like the refinished one. A rainbow of colors, one for each day of the week, with matching keychains hanging from the hardware. He pulled a turquoise bag from the shelf. "You *have* to take these."

Admiring her months of hard work, she reminded him of Ha-Rin's comment. "Only what I can carry."

"I'll carry them." Pulling the carryalls from the wardrobe, he arranged the handles on his arms, striking a cheeky pose. "Do they look good on me?"

Everything would be appealing on him. And nothing would be more exceptional. She smiled, chastising her psyche. "I'm not going to answer when you know they do."

Floating to her vanity, she packed only what she couldn't live without. Buxom, Too Faced, Tarte, and Urban Decay—enough cosmetics for a full face. Afterward, she moved on to a wall-mounted jewelry box. Hanjun stood beside her, curious as to what she liked. He was surprised to find she didn't own all that much, and the pieces appeared to be vintage or antique.

Pulling baubles from the black velvet holder, she solved his internal questioning. "Most of these came from my great-grandmother. She left them to me in her will. I was also willed my great-grandfather's helmet from the Second War. They immigrated from Germany not long before."

"You're German?"

"Twenty-five percent. My grandparents on my mom's side were full-blooded German and Hungarian." Studying the armoire, her voice washed with grief. "It's a piece of history I'll never see again."

"What happened to it?"

"After the death of my great-grandparents, one of my disgruntled uncles stole heirlooms and sold them to military collectors." She stalled to show him two valued adornments: a ring crafted from bone-colored stone and a delicate silver necklace. "She was adamant I should be the one to receive these."

He inspected the pendant. Featuring a five-blade flower with three stamens carved into each petal, it was dented from years of wear. He admired the deep scratches embedded in the charm when she handed him the band. "What's in the center?"

"I always thought it looked kind of like a basketball." Packing her grandmother's jewelry into a velvet pouch, she opened a drawer in the bottom of the jewelry box. "My great-grandfather left me letters and insisted I read them. To this day, I still have no idea what this one means."

"May I?" He reached for the folded paper. He had a fascination with confusing mysteries and fancied puzzle-solving. The more mind-bending, the better—even if his peers thought using his brain outside of studies made him a nerd.

Opening the creased parchment, the letter had yellowed from age, and the writing presented itself as that of a madman.

hangul hideout vitim
ashes hermit petronille
afoot earths invasion
drowned likens sweetshop

goof hater randa
efrem owlish wristlet
fawn hosed teaching
asst coffee overladen

eighteenth futons st
behold knife signet
afoot dolly dressiest
cannon fluidity mums

The inscription was some kind of cipher, with notations to the side where Jen attempted to break the code. Discouraged by the incoherent scribbles, he checked the back to find a year scrawled in charcoal. One that was all too familiar.

1945.

He refolded the note and handed it back to her. Sitting on the edge of the bed, he watched as she tucked the riddle in her luggage. "Where was he stationed?"

"Hawaii and eventually Korea. He told me stories, but I have few memories from when I was young. He talked about an elder he met while serving. The man died after Japan surrendered, and it was thought to have been a suicide, but he didn't believe that." Staring at the overhead light, her eyes stung. "His name had Chi in it."

He nodded, understanding she missed her grandparents dearly. "I wish I could visit my grandparents more often."

"Well..." She sat next to him, presenting a comforting smile. "We have a predetermined amount of time with our loved ones. Work is important, but so is family."

He acknowledged her concern. "I'm sorry you lost them."

She sucked on her lips. "They were more than my grandparents. They took me in at my worst."

"Your grandparents raised you? Where were your parents?" Though the questioning was intense, he appreciated hearing about people and their backgrounds. What set their souls on fire and which embers they crossed to become who they were.

She glanced at him, deciding if she should confide in him. Trusting her heart, she loosened her lips. "My parents divorced when I was young. Haven't seen my dad since then. He was tired of providing for a family—his words, not mine. It was an abusive situation. My mom tried for a while. There were times we wouldn't eat for days. She dated and eventually settled, but she had some resentment, and she was vengeful. We were the only thing holding her back. My brother was old enough to escape her wrath, but I wasn't. She stopped coming home eventually. We took side jobs and hustled. Luckily, people think it's cute when a child is 'responsible.'"

Unable to meet her gaze, he formed the only words he could think of. "I'm sorry."

"You had nothing to do with it. So anyway, my grandparents straightened me out when I was older. They had those old-world values, you know?"

He draped an arm around her shoulder. "I didn't, but I can still feel sorry."

"We all have a sad story." Her synthetic smile morphed into a chuckle as she returned to the jewelry box. "The only thing that matters is the present."

Joining her, he pointed to a white gold piece with a tiny cluster of diamonds in the center. "Aren't you taking that one?"

"That was my wedding ring. It can be flushed for all I care."

He cackled at the lack of emotion in her delivery. For a sweet girl, she had a fiery edge. "You're savage."

Closing the case, she moved to the bathroom, grabbing personal items. As she tossed containers on the bed, Hanjun picked them up, curious about which beauty treatments she used. As a celebrity, he spent a great deal of time on his skincare routine. Or at least he did, as far as the agency knew.

"Manufactured in South Korea?" Ranging from European to Asian, she dabbled in a bit of everything. Rice water spray from Japan, blue tansy spot treatment from Morocco, cocoa pod soap from Ghana, moor mud from Hungary, and ginseng renewal balm from South Korea. She had an arsenal of skin-loving ingredients in her cabinets, and he understood why her appearance was flawless.

"I'm high maintenance so I can be low maintenance." She echoed from the bath. "Besides, Korean beauty has gained traction here. I believe you had something to do with that."

His participation in the expansion of culture was minor, but more than none. "I should take better care of my skin, but there are too many steps."

Tossing a vial of serum on the bed, she hung her head out of the doorway. "I mixed my serums together. One and done."

"Are you supposed to do that?" Giving the elixir a shake, he ogled the bottle, wondering if the concept could work.

"*Supposed to?* I'm not so sure about that." Returning to the bedroom, she sat on the bag, struggling to make the sides meet. "Why won't this stupid thing close?"

"Because you crammed it full." Kneeling beside her, he smashed the lid while she zipped. "You could not fit another item if you tried."

She pulled the oversized baggage upright. "Have you ever crammed your entire life into bags you could carry?"

Shaking his head, he held a coltish smile. "Never."

Slapping her palms on her thighs, she combed her bedroom. Her life was condensed into three suitcases, a duffle bag of shoes, and an overfilled cosmetic trunk. "I suppose I'm ready."

"We're going!" Hanjun circled a finger in the air.

"Toshi promised to store the furniture." Setting her key on the kitchen counter, she surveyed the dwelling. Even before she left, the aroma of the candles she burned in the evenings dissipated, leaving only whispers of her time.

The landscape of her future was shrouded in a thick fog, obscuring all comfortable landmarks. There were promising opportunities and uncharted territories waiting to be explored, and the only way to forge a new path was to burn her life to ashes. She had to die to be reborn.

Standing on the landing, Hanjun waited, recognizing her choice to leave was not easy. Every bit of happiness was a piece of regret, and the longing and wondering about the road not traveled would linger. What if she didn't relocate and hard launched heartoo? What if she turned down the offer, negotiated to work from home, or never met Blackmirror at all?

There would never be answers because they weren't the choices she made. In a matter of days, she crossed paths with Blackmirror, caught the attention of their manager, and made the decision to move six thousand miles away. She took a leap of faith and joined forces with five musicians she barely knew.

The thought terrified him. Even when he left Korea to embark on a lengthy tour, he knew the exact return date. He could schedule vacations with his family and dinners with his friends. She couldn't do the same.

Jiggling the knob, she shed the last tear she'd cry over the departure. "Here's to the next four years."

Patting her shoulder, he headed for the stairs, ensuring he would be the one to hit the concrete if she tumbled. He heard the remnants of her sniffles fading, and he wiped away his. Carrying the refurbished bags on his arms, he made a silent promise to ensure she transitioned smoothly.

$$\star^+_{\ \star}\star\mathbb{C}\star^+_{\ \star}\star$$

After making a few speeding violations on the trip back to the venue, they arrived just in time. In between mingling with dozens of crew members, Jen watched the musicians methodically fall in line. Hair, makeup, outfits—she hadn't realized how much of a hand their stylists contributed to their looks. Everything was chosen to boost sales for their numerous brand contracts.

During Blackmirror's opening song, she surveyed their performance from the green room, taking records in a spiral notebook. Deok-Sun babied his injured ankle, as expected, and Soogi favored his arm from a past injury. Harboring a growing concern for their well-being, she wondered how many times they carried on as if nothing were wrong.

Stifling tears through an extended interlude, Hanso held a chair to stand upright. Deok-Sun gasped for air between dance routines, grasping any object to balance his legs. Jin glugged from a plastic bottle and poured the rest on his neck.

Jen stood behind Soogi, who rubbed his right palm above his left elbow hard enough to leave a burn. "Are you okay?"

"Eh." He massaged the area while a beauty specialist maneuvered around his jabbing joint.

"Do you mind if I rub your arm?" She was unsure how comfortable he was with her. Even if she did witness the bandmates getting handsy with each other, she was a stranger.

Meeting her eyes in a frigid stare, he held out his arm. She placed her palms at the top of his bicep, and after a few minutes of kneading, he took his leave. "You can do this."

Before she turned away, Jin flopped into the chair, scrunching his shoulders until she caught on. When she began squeezing his neck, he melted like a bowl of ice cream on a sweltering day. "When's the last time you had a massage?"

Hanjun shrugged, peering around a hairdresser who fixed his bangs. "Who has the time?"

"If it's important, you'll make time."

He cocked his head to the side, shocked by someone giving him the business. After all, he was the leader. J&I offered plenty of equipment for anything that ailed them, but it didn't help when they were abroad. On the road, they relied on heat packs and energy drinks. There was a medic on hand for dire situations, though the bandmates usually shrugged the pain away.

★⁺₊★☾★⁺₊★

Deok-Sun sat alone in his room when there was a knock on the door. "Come in!"

"Hey." Carrying a plastic shopping bag on her arm, Jen entered with the master key Ha-Rin gave her. She found him in bed, remote in hand, as if turning on the television was too much effort. A silk robe sheathed around his waist flashed the bulk of his torso, and a glance proved it was the only thing he wore. "I noticed you couldn't walk after your performance."

"I'm fine." He shook sweat-dried hair out of his eyes.

She marched into the washroom and ran a bath, unpacking the purchases she made on the way to the hotel—aromatherapy salts she thought he might enjoy. Plopping a stack of towels on the side of the tub, she turned to find him standing in the doorway.

He brandished a handsome smirk. "Really?"

"Yes, really." She motioned to the basin. "You need to decompress."

"Do you think my clothes would disappear at your command?" Flaunting a daring grin, he reached for his waist.

Her eyes bulged. "I didn't mean in front of—*don't!*"

Expelling a devious laugh, he pulled the string, revealing underwear barely big enough to cover his privates. Shocked and embarrassed, she covered her eyes. "You're unholy!"

In one swift motion, he shot forward. His warmth quilted her, and his hot breath kissed her cheek. He projected the scent of sugary candy and salty snacks—an intoxicating blend that confused her senses. She sensed him inching nearer until she was certain he would kiss her, and she jerked away when his plump lips came into view under her palm.

He reached behind her to grab the package of crystals. Dumping the scented shards in the tub, he held a wicked grin. "Gonna need more of these."

Sidestepping, she created distance between them and lit a candle. Moving the pillar to the counter, she crept towards the exit. "Stay until the water isn't hot."

She was certain his robe hit the floor before she made it out of the room. In the hall, she knocked on an adjacent door, where she thought Hanjun and Hanso were. Scanning the key, she understood the importance of the cards; they allowed the staff to move unhindered. Likewise, it was easier for the bandmates to congregate without having to open the door every few minutes.

Hanso offered a smile, while Hanjun sounded almost too excited to see her. "*Hi!*"

"Hey." Crossing the room, she slumped in the gap between them on the sofa. "Deok-Sun looked worn out."

Hanso suppressed a frown. "He thinks he needs to do more because he doesn't work as hard as we do, but he overdoes it."

She tugged on the strings of her hoodie, lacing her fingers through the cording. "I'm open to suggestions."

Hanjun nudged her shoulder. "You can do this, remember?"

With an unamused eye roll, she popped up from her seat. If they didn't have ideas, she was on her way to find her own. "I'm going to my room. Call me if you need anything."

"Goodnight, Jenilyn!" Hanjun's reaction came after the door closed, and a swear soiled his tongue.

Hanso laughed at his failed flirting. "You think she's cute, huh?"

★⁺₊★☾★⁺₊★

Jen leaned on the door, coequal to a schoolgirl whose crush spoke to her for the first time.

Unlike anyone she'd met, he was cordial and didn't try to impress her with his status. There weren't any crude pickup lines, rude innuendos, or creepy attractions. He treated her like a person and didn't fawn over her appearance. Every time he said her name, his eyes gleamed, clearly nervous yet relaxed enough to sit on her bed or crack a joke about her overstuffed suitcase.

In his eyes, she saw an innocent. Someone who longed for juvenile love. In the purest form of devotion, youth expected nothing but acceptance. They didn't know to be afraid, and heartbreak was unimaginable until experienced.

She didn't believe in credence and deemed maturity the slayer of innocence. From the moment of her fledging, her face lost its cherub-like features and sharpened into defined angles, matching her skepticism. After witnessing the cruelty humans so callously subjected each other to, she developed a distrust in people. Their words, their lies—she trusted few.

For most of her life, she worshipped from a distance, never too close to feel the painful scattershot of a love gone wrong. The handful of times she chose to believe Cupid wasn't a selfish beast luring the vulnerable with happy endings, she was hurt by her own failures. Loving someone too little or loving someone too much—the results were the same: unavoidable heartbreak that began at first sight. Every sunrise led to twilight, and it had to be that way because nothing would mean anything without an expiry.

The buzzing in her stomach wasn't butterflies, but locusts, warning her of an imminent plague. She prayed he didn't feel the same because if he did, he could devour her. Like an addict who couldn't quit the metal spoon, she was a slave to her emotions, and her body always followed her mind.

★⁺₊★☾★⁺₊★

As Hanjun settled into his luxury room, the stink of cigarettes wafted in from the adjacent balcony. Deok-Sun claimed he didn't smoke and carried a container of breath mints, but everyone knew. Even Jen, who had been working for the agency for a matter of hours, caught the stale stench of tobacco on his clothes.

Lighting incense to cover the odor, Hanjun stared at the match climbing towards his fingertips. Jen's name became a steady presence on his lips. It was as if his mind developed a will of its own, steering him back to her. Knowing he couldn't remove her from his thoughts, he reached for his phone to share the information he learned at her apartment.

Her great-grandfather fought in the Second War.

Sunnie: Really?

She likes at least a little anime.
Also, holidays. Christmas and Halloween.

Honsa: Everyone loves Christmas!

German and Hungarian.
Rough childhood.

Jinja: That's why she's humble.

Soogins: Question.

Soogins: Whose room is she staying in?

Jinja: She can move in with me. You are fighting too much.

Sunnie: I'm not.

We'll make room for her.

Tapping a final message, he set the phone aside and reached for his journal.

Jen gave me a beautiful trinket box. I believe it's priceless. The second concert in Chicago was incredible! I can't wait to go back to Korea.

CHAPTER SEVEN

Lifestyles of the Famous

Hanjun rapped his knuckles on each door, giving his one and only warning. "Hustle! We leave in thirty."

Jen was ready when he knocked on hers. Finding the door ajar, he pushed the barrier open all the way, producing a short squeak. She poked her head out of the bathroom wearing a cozy outfit: a red and white plaid sweater with dark blue jeggings and a velvet navy blazer. A pair of Adidas Superstars waited near the door, along with her packed bags.

Snaking inside, his gaze swept over the spotless room, discovering a notebook on the desk. He flipped through the pages to find scribbles about each personality, documenting the previous night's concert. Leafing through the observations, he fumbled the spiraled pad.

She acknowledged his snooping while he retrieved the fallen book. "You found my notes."

"Yeah, I did." Returning the log, he gave a goofy smirk.

"Anything to add?"

Shaking off the mishap, his dimples surfaced like a ray of sunshine on a cloudy day. "No, you're wonderful."

He spoke English well, but the phrases he used were sometimes odd. She found the quirk endearing and chalked it up to a symptom of speaking multiple languages, many of which were worlds apart. "I'll be back in a bit. I'm selling my car."

He accompanied her through the hotel as if he had nothing better to do while she met a friendly Carvana agent in the parking lot. The man inspected the vehicle and handed her a certified check for the full estimated value.

"I'm gonna miss her." Fuchsia, named after the decor, had never given her an issue beyond chipped paint.

Hanjun sighed. "At least you have a car. I can't drive."

"Why not?"

He shrugged. "No point since the agency forbade it. Soogi went against the company's wishes, though."

She tucked the payment into her bag. "That's strange."

He settled his arms over his torso. "Nobody can accuse us of drinking and driving if we aren't driving."

"Huh." She wondered how much they avoided to survive. Though she had witnessed only a sliver of their existence, what she saw was the exact opposite of the average person's. Mundane things, such as retrieving the mail or stopping for ice cream, were taken care of by the agency's many handlers. The musicians didn't think about what to eat; the food simply showed up, and they ate. Anything they desired would be retrieved, and they hardly had to lift a finger to consider the most daunting errand completed.

While their daily tasks may have been reduced to the minimum, it was for good reason. After practicing, recording, promoting, and hosting concerts, there wasn't enough time left to do anything fun, let alone annoying chores.

★⁺₊★☾★⁺₊★

While power walking through the airport, Jen was instructed to remain with the crew. Mixed among the makeup artists and hair stylists, she wore a Blackmirror-branded tee, a black face mask, and an ultramarine windbreaker over her outfit.

At the front of the line, security guards shielded the celebrities, but it was impossible to keep them hidden from all angles. The majority focused on protecting Deok-Sun and Jin. With the media collapsing on the entourage, each had no less than five of their own defenses. Hanso and Soogi were guarded by a duo of protectors. Hanjun walked unguarded, bowing and waving to the handful of admirers who greeted him.

Shadowing Hanjun, Jen overheard journalists making snide remarks about him. Venomous words enveloped the procession, and he was a lone figure amid a sea of judgment. The clicking of cameras and reporters shouting requests were rooted in sarcasm. An overwhelming scent of sweat and perfume suffocated her, and she detected a whiff of cigarettes. The aromas combined, creating a stench that made her sick to her stomach—but not as disgusting as the allegations.

'Dear God, they're wearing makeup! Why are they wearing makeup?'

'How much do you know about North Korea?'

'Have you ever eaten dog meat?'

'Tell us about your girlfriends!'

'Don't bother photographing Hanjun or Soogi. They're unimportant.'

She hoped Hanjun didn't hear the criticism. Catching the scowl on his brow, Hanso's guard veered off to give him a supportive shoulder pat, leaning to whisper what she could only assume was something uplifting. Nodding, his features lightened, and he turned to meet her eyes with an uneasy glance.

She yielded a simple action—a heart produced with both hands, followed by a thumbs up. He returned the gesture, adding a genuine smile at the end.

As they neared the loading bridge, Jen inhaled a whiff of jet fuel and lemongrass—courtesy of the cleaning crew who prepared the interior. Showcasing J&I's fortune, the aircraft featured multiple zones and customized insides. The front was rigged with overstuffed seats—enough for thirty team members—and the center was designed with the wealthy in mind. Flaunting spacious feasting and conference areas, each was outfitted with monitors for presentations or amusement. In the rear, a master suite with an on-board shower awaited. The baggage compartment was accessible in flight, ensuring the musicians had everything at their fingertips.

Seating assignments for the band were drawn from a fruit basket near the entrance. Jen, who maneuvered to the front, was halted by Ha-Rin upon boarding. "Pick a seat."

Pointing to the collapsing door separating the areas, she scoffed. "Shouldn't I be with the crew?"

Retrieving a slip of paper, he gestured to Hanjun, who twisted to face them. "You're next to Hanjun."

She stepped closer to him. "I guess we're travel buddies."

Removing a bag from the adjacent seat, he dropped it on the floor. "Lucky, huh?"

She eyed the panoramic landscape. Finding more portholes than chairs, her stomach flopped. "Can we switch seats?"

He squinted at her from his aisle chair. "Are you scared?"

"I'm terrified of heights."

Gathering his belongings, he lowered the shades to hide the runway. Snuffing out the natural light, the compartment grew shadowy. "The cabin is one of the quietest on the market. Unless you look, you won't notice takeoff."

"Thanks." She sank into the buttery armchair, pre-warmed to Hanjun's temperature. "Heights and drowning are my biggest fears, though I have irrational fears like going deaf, blind, or choking to death."

"I only have two fears." He collapsed into his window seat. "That Blackmirror makes a crash landing; I know it can't last forever, but I hope we come down easy—and giraffes."

She prattled at the thought. "Really? Giraffes?"

His head jerked. "I don't like things that are taller than me."

"I suppose a fear wouldn't be a fear without a certain degree of irrationality."

Once they were soaring among the clouds, she penned a resignation to her previous employer and apologized for the departure. Her boss knew she was searching for a new career from the moment he told her he was selling the company, and an opportunity at J&I couldn't be refused. As a professional, he would understand her decision was strictly business.

Scrawling her signature along the bottom, she wrote a personal check for the same sum she sold her car for, and Hanjun questioned her. "What are you doing?"

"I was fundraising for updated playground equipment. I can't leave the campaign unfinished." She creased the paper, shoving the donation inside. "Besides, I have a new job. I can afford to be more generous."

"Are you scared?" Pulling a book from his carry-on, he slipped off his shoes. "You left your whole life behind."

"I'd be lying if I said I'm not." She tucked the finished letter into her bag. "But I'm focusing on starting anew."

⋆⁺₊⋆☾⋆⁺₊⋆

Sunlight blinded Jen after hours of darkness. Struggling to grasp the fifteen-hour time change, she couldn't hold her eyes open at what would have been four in the morning. She remembered descending the airstairs and getting into a vehicle, but not much after.

Awoken by Jin, she opened her puffy eyes to find him as happy as an adopted puppy. The air was thick with fading blooms, and a breeze thawed her with a whisper of warmth. Squinting at the sun, her vision focused on the lofty structures—ultramodern buildings dappled her peripherals, and concrete art ornamented the walkways. In the center was a prodigious fountain, with children splashing in the water.

The city was lively, with honking horns, chattering people, and the occasional siren blaring. A taste of exhaust fumes coated her tongue, replaced by the saccharinity of sugary treats from a street vendor.

Rubbing her eyes, she searched for her luggage among the bags. Unable to find the embossed cases, she approached Hanjun. "Have you seen mine?"

He smiled at her tousled hair. "We took yours in already."

"Oh." Blinking the sleep from her eyes, she faced a grand arch displaying the vill's title: Windsor Heights. The pavement beneath her feet was firm, free from imperfections. Prestige surrounded her in a dazzling display of wealth—a glamorous world sparkling with privilege but also holding a guarded underbelly. Where security was of the utmost importance, armed sentries roamed the sidewalks, ready to protect the celebrities who called the place home.

Before she had time to ask questions, Hanso embraced her arm with his. Grasping his hand, she gaped at the sky-scraping condo. Two wardens were posted in front of each building, donning navy blue suits with handcuffs dangling from their belts.

Discerning one of the defenders eyeballing Jen, Soogi halted the officer. "J&I is sending the new tenant contract over."

Patting her sleeve, Hanso tugged her to their building's access. Grand, with ornate concrete decorations adorning the exterior. "We'll get you a security pass as soon as we can."

The journey through the lobby was a tactile spectacle, with white marble flooring gleaming under candelabrums. Moving to the elevator, each door they passed required a swipe from a shiny silver Windsor Heights card. The opulence continued with mirrored surrounds in the lift. Recessed lights hung overhead, and tufted black benches encouraged rest.

She caressed the cushions. "This place is crazy."

Hanso nodded, scanning the hoist. "It's a far cry from the dorm we shared before our debut."

Deok-Sun relaxed on the seating. "There was no aircon and the roof leaked when it rained."

Jin trembled from a horrible memory. "We had to leave our clothes on the balcony, or they would mold in the closets."

Tucking his phone away, Hanjun joined the conversation. "Be thankful for what we had. The agency was bankrupt; our producer sold his home to house us."

The elevator doors revealed a well-lit corridor with a lone entry at the end. Despite the building boasting security at every entryway, the condo was secured by a simple six-digit code.

"Six, four, three, eight, two, zero." Tapping on the keypad, Hanso opened the door and proceeded to take her on a tour.

The inside was grandiose, with windows unveiling stunning views of the Han River. Chandeliers lit the common areas. The two hundred and sixty-five-square-meter abode offered three bedrooms, a chef's kitchen with attached auxiliary, two bathrooms, and enormous rooms with enough furnishings to fill the residence without touching a wall.

Their bedrooms were combined to allow her a private boudoir. Jin and Deok-Sun occupied the biggest bedroom, which featured a pair of walk-in closets. Hanjun and Hanso's room sat opposite Jen's, which had its own shower. Jen's room was situated next to Soogi's, with a guest bath across the way. Following a vote, the bandmates elected to give him the study.

Locating her bags, Jen found a black envelope taped to the door. Breaking the wax seal, she read the note inside.

> *I've taken the liberty of opening an account for you.*
> *There should be enough until you receive your first*
> *salary payment. On behalf of J&I Entertainment, we*
> *look forward to working with you. —Ha-Rin.*

The room was just her style. Romantic, with clean lines and minimalist decor. The walls were painted a soft gray taupe, and the substantial pieces of furniture were creamy ivory, adding a vein of elegance. The bed was the focal point, featuring a tall, tufted headboard and crisp white bedding. "Whoa."

Hanjun envied from the hall. "It looks so different."

"This was yours?"

"We had to give up a room for you."

"You shouldn't have." Mumbling, she noticed a wall-mounted disc player emitting the same jazz from her apartment. Music was something she couldn't live without—a crutch for working and resting. Bebop was her go-to in the evenings, and she enjoyed funk, rock, and blues during the day.

"We've spent six years living together. What's four more?"

"I wonder how he knew I'd like it." She ran a hand along the comforter.

Snickering, he couldn't hide his amusement. "I may have sent photos of your apartment."

Appreciating the view from the wall-sized windows, her eyes fell to the corner where a vanity just like hers sat. She inspected the pleather storage bench and opened the lid to find the compartment filled with her belongings. "Is this mine?"

Scratching his temple, he held a sheepish smile. "I had it loaded on the plane."

"I have no idea how you managed that."

His mouth curled upward. "I contacted Tisho and had the crew retrieve it."

"Toshi? How?" The first thing she pulled from the trunk was a neck support. Battered and lovingly abused, rows of stitching were repaired by hand. "I've had this forever. I named him Circle Cow."

She tossed the stuffie on the bed and drew a larger one. "This one's name is Big Moo."

She retrieved the last cow, a smaller version of the largest. "This is Mini Moo."

He admired her love for the toys. "Adorable."

She snuggled the smallest and positioned it on the comforter. "I had another, Miss Moo. She had hearts on her cheeks, but she fought a terrible war with a washer and lost."

"Utpeuda!" He laughed and frowned at the same time. "It means funny, but sad. Utgida is funny. Seulpeuda means sad."

"Utpeuda." Repeating the slang, she sat on the bed.

He joined her. "Do you like cows?"

She wedged the toy between their thighs. "They're my favorite. They do so much for us and are underappreciated."

"I like kangaroos because they're a lot like humans; lazy and unpredictable when threatened."

Eying the plushie, she sighed. "Thank you for doing this."

He draped an arm around her shoulders, pointing out additional gifts with pride. "It wasn't only me."

Surveying the room, her eyes landed on the thoughtful surprises left by her roommates. Planted in the corner, her vanity from Hanjun. On the dresser, a crate of candles and aromatherapy salts from Deok-Sun. A stack of Coupang money cards from Soogi. Various brands of skincare from Jin. And a folding masseuse table and expensive body oils from Hanso.

Overwhelmed by the warm gestures, she noticed the mates awaiting her invitation outside the door. "You can come in."

Squealing, they clamored through the doorway, eager to point out their gifts. Jin ribbed Hanso about his odd choice. "What exactly do you think she moved here for?"

"To assist us—wait, that's not what I meant!" Hanso's eyes fixed on the folded table angled against the closet. "She was massaging you, so I thought—"

"Is that gift for me or for you?" A puckish glint flashed in her eyes. "You've made me feel welcome in your home."

"Our home." Hanso reached for a hug, and the action morphed into a group embrace.

★⁺₊★☾★⁺₊★

After unpacking and getting acquainted with the resonances of her roommates occupying the adjacent rooms, Jen left her bedroom to explore the home. The hallway boasted a giant chalkboard calendar. In Ha-Rin's neat handwriting, every date had something on the agenda. Live videos, interviews, talk shows, appearances, product shoots, and meetings with their management—their schedules were never less than twelve hours, though they were given Sundays off.

The pictures adorning the corridor featured their smiling faces, dressed in trendy outfits, celebrating their trophies. Frozen in time, the memories came alive with applause from their audience and the rejoicing squeals of the artists. Admiring each photo, she spotted a shift in their expressions—their once vibrant smiles weakened by the weight of their accolades. "Uneasy lies the head that wears a crown."

Like a determined detective, she combed through the condo in search of her roomies. Scattered among the common areas, some were gathered in the parlor while others busied themselves in the kitchen. One roommate was nowhere to be found. "Anyone seen Hanjun?"

"He isn't feeling well." Deok-Sun's response sprung after the clang of fallen silverware. "Nothing happened!"

"He says he's an extrovert but hides in his room." Lounging on the sectional sofa, Jin's lips stretched into a carefree grin. The television blared a lively jingle from a variety show. Pausing the series, he turned his full attention to her. "You should check on him."

⋆⁺₊⋆☽⋆⁺₊⋆

Hanjun lay in bed, gazing at the ceiling. The glow of the bedside lamp cast shadows that danced and swirled, creating the illusion of a starry night. Entire galaxies he could wish upon. If he could ask the stars anything, what would he ask?

Blackmirror's recent shows weighed on him. The barrage of opinions, always present and unrelenting, plagued his mind. Criticism was an incessant buzzing he couldn't outrun—a swarm of bees, stinging and distracting. No matter what he did—whether he held his tongue or gave an honest perspective—he would be deemed wrong.

He was an expert at burying his emotions—he felt a lot of ways about a lot of things, but nobody would know. After being betrayed by those he trusted, he lost faith in connections. Vulnerability would only lead to a broken heart, and his barricades were made of steel. Fearful and faithless, he longed for someone to look past his defenses. Or perhaps teach him to be satisfied with himself.

What even was happiness? Was it doing what you love? Finding someone to love you? Loving someone yourself? The sentiments echoed in his mind, a refrain he couldn't evade.

'You can't love someone until you love yourself.'

But he wondered: if someone loved him with his imperfections, could he learn to accept himself? Maybe he could view his life in a different light.

Despite devoting countless hours to determining his purpose, he was no closer to understanding. The concept was intangible, forever out of reach, though he believed there was no ultimate destination. There was no difference between those who lived short lives or long lives. Both were forgotten.

Life was nothing more than an illusion. People were slaves to money, spending every dollar to enjoy luxuries. But once they died, everything became void. "The sorrow of today cancels the sweetness of yesterday."

His meditations were cut short by a melodic knock, and Jen's form loomed in the crack. "Hanjun, can I come in?"

He shook the unruly strands from his eyes. "Of course."

She urged the door open. The room was smaller than hers; two full-sized beds dominated the floor, creating a narrow walkway. One was immaculate, without a crease in the bedspread, while Hanjun's was a jumbled mess with the covers bunched into a ball. Approaching, she eyed the colorful collection of plush animals surrounding him. There were several versions of his own Multiverse character, Joey, as well as Pokémon plushies. "How are you?"

The Multiverse was an expanse of worlds crafted by the collective mind of Blackmirror. In the universe of characters, Joey stood out with a unique personality: a somber kangaroo carrying a pouch crammed with trinkets. Though he had a fear of losing his prized possessions, he constantly misplaced them. Luckily, Joey had a legion of Multiverse friends ready to lend a helping hand in recovering his treasures.

"I'm good." He was devoid of emotion, as if he were programmed to respond in such a way.

She considered him a master at masking his concerns. His stoic expression and calm demeanor gave nothing away. "I don't want some cookie-cutter pretend-to-be happy answer. I truly want to know. How are you?"

"You really wanna know?" He fiddled with the edges of his phone. It had been a long time since someone asked how he was without expecting him to project an image of perfection. Primal instinct urged him to purge his anxieties. Her contract forbade her from circulating information disclosed to her in secrecy, but he was nervous about what she would think of him. He didn't want her to twist his thoughts into perversion. "It's not all good."

Settling in for a lengthy chat, she patted the Joey stuffy nestled between her thighs. "You can tell me."

He positioned his arms under his head. "I *love* Blackmirror. I *love* being the leader. But I didn't choose this; they chose me. I don't want attention, and I push them into speaking out. Some are shy, and I am too, but I pretend I'm not for them."

Each sentence was gesticulated, his hands moving wildly. "On one hand, I crave recognition for my work. But on the other, I'm drowning in conventions. The more people who know my name, the more I feel trapped and unable to escape—a tug between wanting it all and wishing to disappear."

His gaze flickered at her, searching for a reaction. She kept her eyes trained on him, showing no signs of discomfort or disinterest. "I never imagined becoming this fortunate, but I wonder what lies ahead. Will I ever be seen as anything other than a member of Blackmirror? As I approach my thirties, the uncertainty grows, and yet I feel guilty for considering solo projects. How can I betray all that we've built? But how long can I keep up with this lifestyle?"

A twinge of guilt whelmed her for not being able to offer guidance. He needed advice, but she knew anything she said could make the situation worse. Her job was to listen, document, and report to the agency, not act as his advisor. "As long as the flames of passion continue to burn, it's worth persevering—even if that flame is only kept alive by a single fan."

He matched her gaze with a curious head tilt. "Just one?"

"There's an intimate bond between an artist and admirer—an alliance only they can know. If you knew there was someone relying on you, wouldn't it be enough?"

"It would be." As a musician, he found relief in creating his own melodies, but it was the work of fellow artists that helped him understand new perspectives.

She glanced at her hand, indented as if she were permanently damaged. Branded by a choice made before her brain fully matured, the failure reminded her to be careful who she allowed into her life. "When I was going through it, I was lost. I questioned everything about me and the world. Sometimes the only thing that got me through was music. That's my story. You're the reason someone keeps fighting. That's powerful."

"What if I've peaked?" Calmed by her, he spilled his truth.

She settled a hand on his knee, her fingertips brushing his thigh. "Success isn't linear. How do you define your own?"

He skimmed her hand, his lip curling into a smile. "I want to bring joy to people's hearts. To guide others out of the dark crevices of their minds. I just want to know I helped people."

Recognizing progress, a spark of elation ignited in her eyes. "If one person can hear your words and be moved, you have achieved something wonderful. But you've reached the world—that's beyond success."

"You're right." Jet lag weighed him down, but for once, it was a welcome sensation.

★⁺₊★☾★⁺₊★

Deok-Sun shattered the peaceful atmosphere, beckoning the inhabitants for dinner. "Food's here!"

Jen's eyes snapped open, and she shot out of bed. In her haste, she knocked over the Joey stuffie. Hanjun hopped down to retrieve the toy before it could be kicked underneath the frame. "What's wrong?"

She paced back and forth. "I'm not supposed to be in your room. We broke the contract. I'm going to be fired!"

"Don't worry about it." Grasping her shoulders, he guided her down the hall. "The contract was referring to intimacy."

Eyes widening, she remembered placing a hand on his knee. "I touched you earlier—"

"The kind beyond friendship." A red flush crept up his neck, and he stumbled over his words. "*Sleeping together*, Jen."

She grasped the kitchen table as she sat. Situated under a glimmering chandelier, handcrafted bronzeware refracted light, spraying the room with speckles. There were three crystal glasses at each setting. One tall and slender for water, one short and stout for tea, and one wide-mouthed and frosted for beer. The surface was set with spoons and chopsticks. To her amazement, her napkin held a fork tucked into its fold. "We *were* sleeping together."

The admission caught the mates off guard. Deok-Sun choked on his tea. Food went flying from Soogi's open mouth. Hanso's eyes bulged. Jin clapped and slumped off the bench, melting into a pile of giggles.

Hanjun jumped into action, controlling the damage. "We fell asleep; that's it! We didn't do *that*."

"You meant *sex*..." Teeth sinking into her bottom lip, her cheeks reddened. "Why didn't you *say* that?"

Hanjun's face flushed a bright shade of red, mirroring her uneasiness. "I was trying to be polite."

"I don't think there's any polite way to mention sex." She gazed at the spread. Rather than cooking a meal, Deok-Sun opted for takeout. The selection was diverse, filling the table with savory meats, seasoned vegetables, and steaming rice.

He served her a considerable spoonful of food. "I didn't know what you would like, so I ordered my favorites."

Hanjun situated a wooden bowl in front of her and began to fill it with noodles. "Can you handle spice well?"

Her eyes doubled while her ration overflowed. "Not extremely spicy."

He retrieved a chilled can of brew and poured the liquid into a glass. "You'll be fine."

"I can't do anything that lives in water except popcorn shrimp, and it would need to taste more like cocktail sauce." A zucchini dish melted on her tongue, and she gave a nod of approval.

"How could you eat shrimp? They're the funniest creatures in the ocean!" Toasting, Hanso regaled his friends with a joke. Wagging a finger, he delivered the punchline. "You'd think it would be clown fish, but—"

"I won't touch seafood at all." A wry smile lifted at the corners of Hanjun's mouth, though the mates teased him for his aversion. He shot a pointed scowl at Jen, challenging her to defend him. "Why am I the only one being ridiculed for not wanting to consume our fish friends? She's like me!"

She threw up her hands. "I understand your struggle, but I can't help you."

Pouring his second glass of Carneros Pinot Noir, Jin turned to Jen, inviting her to join. "Do you drink?"

"Rarely and socially."

Hanso discharged a sardonic laugh, as not partaking in alcohol could promote ostracization. "Good luck. J&I loves their drink."

Soogi's eyes flicked between speakers. He stayed on the outskirts of the conversation, but when the topic shifted to drinking, he interjected. "If you don't want to drink, don't."

The room fell silent, except for the rustling of clothing and lips smacking. Sampling the offerings, she tried everything—the bulgogi and kimchi fried rice were favorites. And her plate was magical; for every sample consumed, another manifested, gifted from one of her roommates.

Jin transferred another helping, though she stopped him midway. "Thanks, but if I take another bite, I'm going to pop."

He reclaimed the bean sprouts. "More for me!"

After dinner, the task of cleaning was divided. Deok-Sun was responsible for bussing the table. Jin was expected to separate the scraps. Hanjun wrapped leftovers and arranged them in the fridge. Soogi washed the dinnerware, and Hanso dried them. Jen wiped the countertops, swept the floor, and put the dishes away. The last chore was for her own benefit, as she had no idea where anything was kept.

With full bellies, the six roommates sank into the cushions of the leisure room seating. Jen claimed her seat in the middle, sandwiched between Hanso and Jin. To her left, Hanjun lounged with one leg draped over the armrest. Soogi sat at the other end, his posture straight and proper. Deok-Sun chose to sit on the floor, cross-legged and hugging a cushion. The friends huddled around the communal television, voting on what to watch—unanimously anime.

Before the night ended, Hanjun issued a warning. "Don't stay up too late; we film an episode of Parallels tomorrow."

Blackmirror:Parallels was a captivating docuseries offering a glimpse into the musician's affairs. Fans experienced highs and lows alongside the band, making it a must-see for any devoted supporter. Through displays of personality, unwavering tenacity, and fierce determination, viewers were swept away on a journey to discover innovative games, unknown places, and fascinating people with the beloved members of the band.

⋆⁺₊⋆☾⋆⁺₊⋆

Around midnight, Jen lay in bed, staring at the ceiling. On the bedside table, her phone illuminated with a notification, though the door squeaked before she could read the message.

Tiptoeing to her bed, Hanjun's pajamas created whimsical swooshing. The condo reeked with the stench of five men existing in cramped quarters, but her room was a different realm. "How does your room always smell so amazing?"

"Candles." She returned the mobile to the nightstand. "Is everything alright?"

"When I can't sleep, I walk around until I can. I saw your light on and thought you were awake, too." A melodic jazz fusion imbued the room, and he bopped along, settling onto her bedspread. Holding his arms at his sides, he made a conscious effort to maintain distance. "If you could have any superpower, what would it be?"

Pondering the question, her lips pursed. "The ability to make food from garbage. I could solve two problems at the same time. Pollution and starvation in one sweep."

"Not shrimp, though, right?" Emitting a series of high-pitched squeals, he covered his lips as if he were sealing a secret. "Shh. We aren't supposed to sleep together, remember?"

She nudged his shoulder. "What about you?"

He focused on the ceiling, spotting patterns he didn't notice when the room was his. "I wish I had the power to sense people's aspirations. To see who they'd be without others dragging them down. How many people do you think would succeed if they didn't fear judgment?"

"Flying would be cool, too." Mimicking the graceful movements of a bird, his hand landed next to hers, their fingers almost touching. "What do you want from the life you have?"

She maneuvered her body to face him, contentment reflected in the curve of her lips. "I want a life filled with experiences. I want to experience the pain so I can appreciate the pleasure. I want to love someone who loves me. I don't want a lot of things, just to feel happy and healthy."

"Me too." Inching nearer, his eyes crinkled. "And lots of money."

"Oh stop." Her palm met his arm, creating a moment of silence. Startled by his sudden proximity, the wise words of Koroleva echoed in her mind.

*'When you're staring love in the eyes once again, do
not back down.'*

"Hanjun, I think you should leave."

"Goodnight." Slinking off the bed, the air was hazed with the sweet scent of nostalgia. In the privacy of his room, he sought solace between the pages of his journal.

*I bunked with Hanso so Jen could have a room. I
thought it would be hard to share our dorm with her,
but it isn't. I know I've been wrong before, but I feel I
can trust her.*

Soogi sat alone. His desk and twin bed were cramped between towering bookshelves, but he didn't mind.

Jinja: Jen's nice.

I can smell her candle from my room.

Jinja: What's it smell like?

Almond cake.
It's making me hungry, but it's too late to eat.

Honsa: Does anyone know where Hanu is?

Sunnie: Is he not with you?

Jinja: He must be with Jen!

Sunnie: Jun is perfect for her. He's shy and sensitive.

Sunnie: Jen is perfect for him. She's loving and wise.

Tossing the phone aside, he gave up on sleep and padded to the kitchen in search of relief. Reaching for a bottle of water, he swallowed a tablet of zolpidem. Returning to his room, he veered off before reaching Jen's. He noticed a glow pooling from under her door and heard giggles coming from inside, but it was muffled, and he couldn't tell who was with her.

He pulled the room-darkening curtains together and tied them to create privacy. He longed to slam a proper door, but all he had was the makeshift barrier. Shuffling to his bed, he collapsed and shrouded his ears. "I guess I didn't win after all."

CHAPTER EIGHT

Blackmirror:Parallels

Jen woke up to the sound of the housekeeper vacuuming the lounge. It was disorienting to rise in an unfamiliar home. The noises she typically heard were nonexistent—the rumblings of cars crossing the parking lot, campers utilizing the facilities, and birds tweeting on her windowsill.

The maid yanked open the lace curtains, allowing sunbeams to flood the floor. Standing shorter than Jen, in her mid-fifties, her hair was coiled. Her face showed deep lines, though her eyes were soft. She dusted off the dressers, making quick work of the task. "You must be the new resident. Usually there's nobody here when I arrive."

"Shit, shit, shit." Jen flung the disheveled covers off the bed. "Sorry, I'll fix it."

"It's what I'm paid to do." Ripping the duvet from her hands, the cleaner stood with a hand on her hip. Her beige uniform was ironed to perfection, contrasting Jen's rumpled pajamas. "You should worry about what you're paid to do."

Jen unplugged the phone from its charger. Nibbling her lips, she dialed Hanjun. As soon as his voice came through, she unleashed a torrent of apologies. "I'm sorry. I didn't know—"

"Ha-Rin reminded us you wouldn't be in until you passed the placement test, but you can come if you'd like. I'll text you the address. It's a twenty-minute walk, or you can take a taxi. Look for one that says 'International' on the side."

Jen thanked the maid before choosing an outfit from her closet. After a refreshing shower, she changed into a white button-up tank and sandblasted jeans, settling on a pair of wedges accessible near the foyer.

She advanced out the door, her reflection showing a put-together young woman. Exiting the condominium, she was saluted by a guard, his eyes lowering in respect. Inside Windsor Heights, the air was calm and still, but when leaving the district, motor blares and chatter overpowered the breeze, blending with the decadence of pastries from a local bakery.

Hunting for the specific kind of taxi Hanjun suggested, she searched for a red light displayed in the windshield. He explained it meant the automobile was empty, and though she couldn't read a single letter in Korean, she recognized the characters. The first cluster resembled an upside-down A, a sideways L, and a capital I. The second was more defined, resembling the silhouette of a human with what appeared to be half of an H.

Once she found a suitable cab, she flagged it down. The vehicle stopped, and the driver urged her inside. She plunged into the backseat, inspecting the meter to confirm it was reset.

The cabbie secured his belt and peered at her through the rearview mirror. "And where might you be heading?"

"J&I Entertainment." Her knees bounced, fingers toying with the hem of her jacket. She was nervous enough to vomit. The only thing she knew was that J&I accommodated a diversified roster of performers, from idols with power vocals to actors who brought personalities to life.

★⁺₊★☾★⁺₊★

Stepping out of the vehicle, Jen paused to admire the architecture. Towering over surrounding buildings, the monument was fashioned to be environmentally friendly. A circular layout utilized a double-skin facade and external louvers for sustainability. Nothing short of a spark of ingenuity, the structure was developed to conserve energy, eliminate sky glare, and optimize comfort. Louver blades attached to the sides adjusted automatically according to the sun, offering ventilation to the atrium and maximizing natural light.

And the atrium was a spectacle to behold. Housed on the ground floor and off-limits to the public, the space spanned an impressive five thousand feet. A diverse range of birds found a home in the microclimate, while hydroponic gardens supplied much of the cafeteria's fresh produce.

A section of the basement housed a sewage plant that recycled three-fourths of the building's wastewater, offsetting water consumed by the nurseries. Obscured behind the J&I initials were solar panels, which provided most of the electricity. Rather than air conditioning, the framework adopted chilled beams and circulated ducts to cool the temperature. Traditional floor heating was utilized in the winter.

The glass entrance glimmered in the sunlight, and a throng of bystanders amassed on the sidewalks, vying for a peek inside. Skimming the flock, she noted the sentiments written on their signs. Holding expensive devices high, they waited to snap blog-worthy photos. She hurried by, her face concealed behind a mask, overhearing snippets of dialogue.

Just as she reached the skyscraper, a fan bolted over to warn her she would be banned if she pulled on the handle, though she shrugged the threat away. Halted by security upon entry, she presented her personnel file, providing specifics of her affiliation with the company.

"Artist Liaison contracted to Blackmirror." The well-dressed guard ushered her to the receptionist.

The position involved welcoming guests and ensuring they were accredited to meet the quintet. When there wasn't an event for them to attend, she would act as their assistant, unless Ha-Rin assigned her a different errand. But her most crucial role was to keep up with their demanding schedule.

After completing her employment verification at the front desk, she received a temporary key granting her access to all floors occupied by Blackmirror. The card included a brochure highlighting the benefits of working at J&I. Beyond the salary, the building boasted cafés on each level, complimentary parking in the subterranean car park, employee fitness and relaxation centers, and childcare and educational facilities.

She walked to the elevator, positioned behind the help desk, and the gates opened with a hiss. Tunes by musicians signed to the agency played, and a pleasant, feminine electronic voice boomed from the overhead speakers.

'Please scan key card.'

She scanned the card next to the control panel, and her thumb hung over the buttons, poised as the light swapped from a glaring red to green.

'Welcome, guest number one hundred and twelve.'

A joyful chime tinkled, delivering a disturbing sentiment.

'All five members of Blackmirror are located on film production floor nine.'

The elevator sprang to life. An innocuous item, the plastic key held a troubling truth about the degree of surveillance. "They must track everyone's whereabouts."

The lift opened to an empty hallway, graphite gray. Trudging along the corridor, she heard faint snickers whirling from down the hall. Tracking the giggles, she found the musicians among a zoo of production specialists, with rolls of sheeting carpeting the floor. Maneuvering through the swarm, she caught her roommates drenched in chocolate sauce, gliding over a makeshift slip-and-slide on their bellies.

Hanjun waved an arm, splattering bits of liquid confection in all directions. "I was afraid you might have gotten lost!"

She couldn't hold back her cackle; it seemed as if he were playing a live-action version of Candyland, standing atop Gramma Gooey's Mountain. "The creative directors really outdid themselves."

Jin shook off the topping like a playful pup. "C'mon!"

"Nuh-uh." She tugged at the bottom of her blouse. "This is new."

"A little chocolate won't hurt you!" Hanjun made a beeline straight for her and, despite her attempts to run, encased her shoulders. Engulfing her in syrup, he carried her to his bandmates, kicking and screaming. Each companion, their garments splattered in cocoa, took turns wrapping their arms around her, smearing the substance on her shirt and jeans.

Tilting her head back, she yelped. "Who do you think you are? Pollock?"

Hanso booped her nose with a dab of chocolate. Jin laughed, drawing war stripes on her cheeks. The garnish fused their clothing together, making a suction noise during her struggle.

"I feel like a chocolatey molting snake!" She writhed in a desperate attempt to break free, and the gang of friends tumbled, giggling as they landed in a tangled heap. Appendages and sucrose intertwined as they fell; some collapsed on the slippery sheeting, others hit the floor with a thump.

Ha-Rin kept the cameras rolling. "This is comedic gold."

Jen and Hanjun merged into a knot of limbs, scrambling to find balance. Grasping his forearm, Jen fought to remain upright, her shoes sliding in opposite directions. He used her for stability, and she fumbled, falling hard on her buttocks.

He laughed but quickly apologized. "Are you hurt?"

"Oh, you're asking for it." With a mischievous glint in her eye, she grabbed his wrist, pulling him down with her. He crumbled like a deck of cards, grasping for anything to hold during his descent.

The collision was violent, with his body slamming into hers. He hovered over her, creating a dangerous potential for infatuation. Locked in mutual gaze, she felt every inch of him pressing against her, his breath caressing her mouth. He carried the same aroma he left on the bedding in her old apartment—an intoxicating combination of honey and lemon.

Pulling his eyes from her, he spotted six of the ten lenses aimed at them. "Why are we still filming?"

Uttering a few not-safe-for-film profanities, he jumped to his feet and stormed to the cameramen. "The cameras should have been cut!"

Jen lingered in the goo with her head tilted back, watching him challenge Ha-Rin. Something about the way his arms whipped intrigued her. He was dangerous, and she imagined what it would be like to have those hands wrapped around her waist. Or neck.

Interrupting her runaway fantasies, Soogi offered a hand, his eyes meeting hers in silent understanding. Amid the chaotic flurry, he alone caught their stumble. "I think he has a thing for you."

She took his hand, turning red as she brushed chocolate from her clothing. He stood next to her, observing Hanjun's discussion with the production staff.

Hanjun teemed with annoyance. "You can't keep the footage."

Ha-Rin solidified his decision. "We will cut it, and no one will know she was there. But the rest will stay."

Huffing, Hanjun's stare reeled at Jen. His eyes roamed every curve, taking in the alluring dip of her midriff. The syrup clung to her outfit, injecting an unexpected veil of seduction into her appearance. She was otherworldly, a goddess wreathed in tempting treats.

Shocked by a splash of cold water, he swiveled to discover Jin lurking behind him, holding a dripping bottle. "You're in for it, Jin!"

Jin discharged a squeal and bolted away. "It was a joke!"

Hanjun enacted revenge using a nearby bucket of water, soaking Jin down to his soles. Afterward, the entourage moved to the gym showers, cameras ready to capture their comedic antics. Hilarity echoed through the room as they played, singing along to their own songs.

As expected from soapy surfaces, Hanjun fell a handful of times, making everyone chuckle at his clumsiness. He glared at the camera after every wipeout. "Why am I like this?"

Jen's top adhered to her breasts, drenched from the waterfall showers. Stealing glances, Hanjun admired how the fabric hugged her curves, revealing the color of her supports—hot pink clashing with porcelain skin. The structure was delicate, enhanced with frilly trimmings, and an intricate tattoo peeked out from between the straps.

Rubbing bars of soap over their wet figures, the bandmates' eyes flickered towards her. Maintaining nonchalance, they avoided direct eye contact with each other, but each was aware of the curious glances.

Sensing a roomful of wandering eyes, she held her shirt away from her body. "If I knew we were playing in water, I would have brought a change of clothes."

"Be well rested for tomorrow's viewing." The closing scene was captured, and Ha-Rin rushed to them. Harnessing a proud smile, he draped towels around their necks. Approaching Jen, he patted her back. "You, too."

★⁺₊★☾★⁺₊★

Leaving the office at the end of her shift, Jen wasn't sure how to feel. Her coworkers showered her with compliments, but she was overcome with displacement. Did she even do anything? She showed up late and caused a loss of focus. She should have been chastised, not complimented. J&I might have been the strangest company she had ever worked for.

The studio moved at lightning speed, and she didn't fit in with the unconventional workplace. She was proficient in environments where freedom reigned supreme, but she never experienced a crowd of thirty people ready to offer their aid without expecting a favor. She had grown accustomed to being self-sufficient and was reluctant to seek assistance without an exchange of services.

Stuffed between Jin and Hanjun, she remained quiet, clutching a J&I-monogrammed towel over her bosom. The hum of the car's engine coincided with the sporadic blaring of traffic. In her mind, she still heard the deafening screams of adoring fans as their car glided out of the underground garage.

She preferred independence, but the agency insisted she utilize their escort services when leaving, and their strict regulations made it clear they were not to be disobeyed. Their reasoning was sound; the drivers were trained at chaperoning entertainers to their homes. They knew every hidden escape route and were well-versed in evasive maneuvers. She was grateful for their protection, even if the agency's protective grip was a velvet glove.

Hanjun nudged her shoulder. "Most of the time, we don't know what we're doing until we get to the office."

"Good to know." Adjusting the towel around her torso, her words were absorbed in the movement.

He shrugged off a black agency-branded hoodie. Lacking any amount of grace, he smacked his hand on the roof in the process. Disregarding the mishap, he offered her the article without making a fuss. "They like to record our reactions."

She pulled the sweater over her trembling body, grateful for its warmth. Removing the tank that clung to her like a second skin, she crumpled it into a stained mound. "I have a lot of catching up to do."

★⁺₊★☾★⁺₊★

The clock struck half past eight when they arrived home. Greeted by the delicious aroma of lychee soap and clean laundry, Jin shucked off his shoes and headed straight for the kitchen. The quicker he fed his roommates, the sooner he could unwind. Unfortunately, the exhaustion from a long day of recording stifled any hope of creating a delicious feast. But their growling stomachs demanded something—anything—to quell the ache. Using a bit of creative license, he assembled an assortment of cheeses and proteins.

Placing the prepared charcuterie board on the dining table, he apologized to Jen. "We got home later than I thought we would."

"You know, meat and cheese trays are a staple for many lone women." She slid down the wooden bench and beckoned him to sit.

Harboring a twinge of guilt for serving a subpar meal, he sat beside her and transferred a pile of biscuits to her plate. "I take my apology back, then."

Holding a smile, she watched as Jin stuffed crackers into his mouth. She then assembled her own sandwich in a precise, ritualistic manner. Starting with a sturdy bottom cracker, she added a thin slice of cured salami, followed by a piece of Swiss. Another layer of spicy chorizo and a chunk of Manchego. Squishing the stack, she savored a gratifying bite. "The calendar says you're required at the agency tomorrow."

"Following the wrap, we take an easy day and review the material." Chewing a mouth full of ham, Hanjun glanced at his bandmates. Their faces were familiar, though more cooperative since Jen moved in.

Before her arrival, the dining room would often sit empty, with each person engrossed in their own activities. But as soon as she arrived, the atmosphere shifted; the bare table was lined with plates of food and lively chatter from friends.

The image evoked memories of their youth, when they relied on one another for companionship. Through years of working together, the crew fragmented into cliques, each with their own loyalties. Once indivisible, their unity dissipated, replaced by bias and division.

Unbeknownst to Jen, a pact was made when she agreed to J&I's terms; from that day forward, they would act as an inseparable unit. Five parts of a whole, living and breathing as one entity. They would share meals, collaborate, and thrive in each other's company, bound by the oath they swore. It was a guarded secret, known only to a few key players at J&I: for years, they had lived in isolation, and discussions of disbandment were on the horizon.

On paper, she was the group's emissary—a buffer between the artists and those who were contractually permitted to visit them. But she didn't know she was a cushion for the bandmates as well. She was the last hope they had of sticking together. When Ha-Rin pitched the idea, the general line of thought was elementary; in her presence, the group was more likely to be on their best behavior, such as the first night she attended their concert. The fact that she was an admirer was leveraged as motivation. Her visage served as tangible proof of the group's existence, and they were determined to make a positive impression.

"That's good, right?" Sipping from her J&I-branded water bottle, she replaced the lid, awestruck at how the band pervaded every corner of the establishment. The walls were splashed with their iconic ultramarine hue, and their music could be heard in the elevators. It was as if the agency and Blackmirror were inextricably linked, each relying on the other.

"It's neither good nor bad. Tomorrow, we'll watch what the editors have strung together and discuss future episodes." Hanjun's words were accompanied by a rewarding crunch. "Sometimes we need to scrap the whole thing and start over."

"I thought it was just record, edit, and upload."

He shot her a sidelong glare. "They're particular about image and all that."

"I'm sure they are." She blushed, noticing the way his pronunciation worsened when he was tired. Each syllable was a strenuous effort, and he fought to form coherent sentences.

⋆⁺₊⋆☾⋆⁺₊⋆

The living room exuded coziness, with golden lighting casting a luster over the sofa. Clean dishes were arranged on the drying rack, waiting to be put away. The leftover snack board sat in the fridge, awaiting midnight indulgence.

Squeezed between Hanso and Jin, Jen's body tensed at the vibration of her phone. Her teeth clenched, preparing for the onslaught of hatred accompanying her ex-husband's voice. "What do you want?"

"I have a buyer for the house. You need to sign the paperwork." His tone dripped with derision, every word a sharp jab.

"Great, have the realtor email it to me."

"You can't stop by and sign it?" His smug grin could be visualized through the phone.

She answered the question while her roommates laughed. "No, I literally can't. I'm in Korea."

"What in the hell are you doing in Korea?"

Her hands rested on her lap, fingers interlocked in decorum. There was no fidgeting in her body; she radiated an air of stillness and poise. "I had an opportunity, so I took it."

"What opportunity?"

"It's none of your business. Send me the paperwork." The phone slipped from her hand, landing on her thighs.

Jin's words penetrated the tension, causing a collective intake of breath. "I know why he's an ex."

"He's something." Her response came with an uncovered amount of distaste. "Relationships are brutal. I fear I will never make one work."

"Why couldn't you make it work?" While asking the question, Hanso reached to give Hanjun's shoulder a reassuring squeeze.

Hanjun became aware of his own interest and slumped. "I mean, we all heard that, right?"

Raising her phone in the air, she emphasized the absurdity. "When we were young, we didn't know ourselves or who we'd be. At that moment, we loved each other and thought it was enough. But love isn't enough. You must invest yourself in someone else. Continually. Without fail. Let your demons dance together and pray they become friends. Sometimes they're enemies."

Shaking her head, she recalled a time she didn't care to think about. "You know how in sitcoms there's the bit where there's two people in a room with a bunch of doors? They keep opening doors, only to miss each other. That's how it felt. Just when I thought we had an open line of communication, another door would slam in my face. People can't sustain relationships like that."

Murmurs broke the silence. Certain members of Blackmirror were notorious for their fleeting romances, though the media never knew they juggled one or two to pass the time. A fast-paced lifestyle left little room for commitment; their hearts were fickle, and their attention was easily swayed. Artists were wanderers, never in one place long enough to put down roots. Love was simply a passing distraction from their existence.

With intense concentration, Hanjun sat with his legs folded, taking notes on his phone. Light taps from his thumbs matched the conversation he wasn't participating in.

"Everyone has a soulmate, right?" Jin gave her a hug.

She scoffed and rolled her eyes. "I'm not so sure."

"Not something you believe in?"

A spectrum of reactions afflicted their faces, from curious interest to doubtful skepticism. Some raised their eyebrows, while others crossed their arms in suspicion. She studied their expressions, determined to stick to the promise she made after the separation: to be more honest. Her ideals may be challenged, but they were unapologetically hers. "It's a charming concept, but it's just a feel-good idea that gives people false security. Believing in fate makes lovers lazy. Our great-grandparents didn't stay together because they were soulmates. They put in the *work* to stay together. Also, because divorce wasn't a thing, but that's a different discussion—"

Slumping, she admitted the real issues she saw with modern courtship. "There wasn't as much interference from external sources. Having everything at our fingertips has ruined our ability to create connections. Our world is built on instant gratification—fulfilling our current wants, not cultivating our later needs. Most people who believe in soulmates have a new one every month. I'm no expert, but I doubt that's how it works."

Intrigued, Hanjun's heart fluttered. A flower on the verge of blooming, she was a fragile bud, waiting for the ideal moment to burst forth and reveal her innermost convictions. Ignoring the distractions around them, he kept his attention on her.

"I came across a study about the probability of finding your theoretical match. Research found that if you meet someone embodying at least ninety percent of what you're looking for—your absolute deal breakers—you should hold onto them. Sure, there may be a slightly more compatible option out there, but how much time and effort would it take to find them? You could spend your entire life jumping from one individual to another." The eyes of her roommates bore into hers with unwavering potency. "There isn't a perfect partnership, but if there were, I believe loyalty and adaptability would play a big role. The biggest lesson I learned from my failure was that willingness to forgive imperfections goes a long way, but that doesn't mean we should put our ideal selves to rest. Forgiveness matters as much as accountability."

Catching onto her introspection, Hanjun often found himself misplaced in the depths of his mind, but unlike most, he molded those moments into art. Pondering what other topics she spent her time exploring, he ached to hold her.

Jen laid on her white bedding, curling her legs to her breasts. Her tongue traced the tears lingering on her lips. Hearing her ex's voice invoked rage—the same rage she thought she had healed. The finalized papers should have been the finishing nail in the coffin, yet she was haunted by what she overlooked. She grieved the years wasted; more importantly, she mourned the pieces of herself she gave up. Compromising portions of her personality wasn't on her bucket list, but it was underlined in her long column of mistakes. Bile rose in her throat, a bitter reminder of abandoning herself, when an unexpected knock jarred her thoughts back to reality.

She exhaled and wiped away her streaks, hoping to cover the desperation in her tone. "Who is it?"

"Can I come in?" Without waiting, Hanjun strode into the room. He knelt beside the bed, his forehead pressed against hers. Intertwining his arms with hers, he embraced the clamminess of her palms. "You're going to be okay."

She cried as if he could absorb her pain, cursing for giving in to her miseries. Fingers clutching her chest, she clawed to hold herself together. "Fuck, I feel so stupid."

His head bowed like a heavy stone, weighed down by her agony. Yet his touch was light, as if he were cradling something fragile. "You loved someone, and they neglected you. What you're experiencing is normal, but it's something that will pass. You're fucking great."

"How could I forget?" She removed her remaining tears.

Harnessing a smile, he tumbled over her body, landing on the pillow beside her. "I never noticed before, but the textures on this ceiling look like stars in candlelight."

"How didn't you notice?" Her finger extended to a display of celestial bodies, huddled in an asymmetrical arrangement.

Squeezing her hand, he met her eyes. "Maybe the view looks different next to you."

★⁺₊★☾★⁺₊★

Waking in Jen's tangled sheets, Hanjun roamed the lightless room, eyeing an extinguished candle and stack of books on her nightstand. Retrieving his discarded shirt from the floor, he crept across the hall and sank into the cool embrace of his bed. Before succumbing to sleep, he reached for his mobile and tapped the group chat, scrolling through a stream of messages.

> **Soogins**: Did you see Hanjun?
> **Honsa**: They're similar. It's almost creepy.
> **Jinja**: It's cute!
> **Honsa**: Creepy.
> **Jinja**: Cute!
> **Jinja**: I thought Hanjun's jaw would fall off!
> **Sunnie**: He took notes. ㅋㅋㅋ

Tossing the phone aside, he retrieved the journal from under his pillow. Scratching the pen against paper, his thoughts interspersed with the occasional pause.

> *Jen joined us at the office. While slipping on the slide, I landed on her. My mind told me to kiss her, but I couldn't. She speaks passionately about things she cares about. I asked Ha-Rin not to add the footage to the final cut. Her ex is a jerk.*

He captured her fervid debate on soulmates, adding details of how the heavens twinkled above them in his old bedroom. "I wonder what else looks different next to her."

CHAPTER NINE

Nobody Can Know

Jen received clearance to report to the office two hours late, giving the stylists time to perfect Blackmirror's hair and makeup without her presence. Though it was a contracted day of rest, the performers had a photo shoot on the books before the meeting with their management.

She applied minimal makeup and wrapped strands around an iron for loose, bouncy curls. Running her fingers over the hangers in her closet, she chose a minty cable knit sweater and boot-cut jeans. At the door, she slipped on a pair of gray suede booties and fastened a heart chain through her belt loops, displaying her affinity for late-nineties fashion.

She left the condo with plenty of time to spare, determined to make up for her tardiness. Approaching the front desk, the receptionist passed over an identification badge. Inspecting the holographic key with her name engraved on the plastic, the head shot featured a still from the exact moment she walked in the day before. Making a mental note to be more mindful, she trotted to the elevator.

'Please scan key card.'

Tapping her pass, the panel lit up in brilliant blue. Waiting for the machine to establish a connection with the security system, she examined the card. A faint outline of the Blackmirror trademark was visible in the corner.

Ultramarine with black shadows, the impossible optical illusion portrayed Blackmirror's concept at the time of their debut—otherworldly and best viewed in a spiritual sense. A subtle confession that their curated personalities could not exist in the real world.

The triangle was a symbol of unity, and it accompanied them in their salute. When they introduced themselves in interviews, they held their hands up in the same triangular formation, shouting their motto. 'Making the impossible, possible! Blackmirror!'

'Welcome, Jenilyn. All five members of Blackmirror are located on business floor thirty-six.'

Unlike the former day, the buttons remained blue, and she chose the one she wanted. "I guess I don't need to go to whatever floor they're on."

The doors glided open, unveiling an alluring aroma of sizzling foods. Noisy for a supposed business floor, clinking cutlery could be heard in the distance. She lumbered down the corridor, realizing the only business taking place was food preparation. "Maybe eating is serious business."

Tracing echoes of high-pitched squeals, she reached a grand kitchen, where Soogi and Jin commanded a flat-top grill, their tongs clicking in a cook-off. "Something smells amazing."

Standing near an oversized chef's island, Ha-Rin tossed a medley of fermented vegetables in a ceramic bowl. "Samgyeopsal. The Korean equivalent to bacon."

Hanjun couldn't resist stealing perfectly cooked strips hot off the fire. "After shooting an episode, we have a little celebration. We'll eat and discuss what needs to be improved."

"I can't wait. I'm famished." With fluidity, she signed 'eat.'

His eyebrows soared. "You know sign language?"

Enchanted by the kaleidoscope of veggies in Ha-Rin's dish, she nodded. "It's been a while since I've used it."

"This is one of the only things I know." He fumbled an 'I love you.'

"Let's get started." Ha-Rin breezed past, balancing a platter in each hand.

Hanjun was hungry, but he stopped to ensure Jen wouldn't get lost. On the journey, he talked about the tower's floor plan. "Most decks are divided into five sections, with one large room in the center. This is where all the important meetings are held, so it has a kitchen for catering, surrounded by conference rooms on each wing."

"Interesting." She ventured down a narrow passageway and into the assembly room. The door was embellished with the Blackmirror emblem, and three walls were covered with their discography.

In 2015, Blackmirror released their debut album, 'Syzygy.' The electronic broken beats and catchy lyrics were well received in Korea and Japan, though their second album, 'Solar Flare,' failed to chart. A few mini albums followed with unfavorable results, and their agency was nearing bankruptcy. By 2018, the musicians were exhausted, feeling as if they were defeated. Some of the members had invested ten years of their youth by that time and were ready to call it quits. Their producer, who was also their manager and caretaker, offered them a choice: they could halt promotions and disband, or they could push harder in hopes of recognition.

Ten years was a lot of time to spend on a project without seeing it through, and the bandmates agreed to give it one final go. Their producer sold his home and car to fund the project and spent the next six months couch surfing. Blackmirror trained tirelessly—harder than they had as trainees—and produced 'Galactica.' The release was a chartbuster, winning them over twenty awards and sending them on a world tour. Unfortunately, touring was more exhausting than expected, and the members were growing frustrated with their lack of social lives. The experiences led to the production of 'String Theory' and 'Distraction,' both based on the red thread of marriage.

They toured for both albums, with only a few months of rest in between. The days blurred together. Two weeks, two months, two years—it was all the same. They practiced, performed, and drank in the evenings to forget how miserable they were. They slowly began to despise the thing they once wanted but refused to vocalize their quandaries. It wasn't just each other they'd be letting down; it was their fans.

It was a well-known fact within the fandom: the pandemic gave them time to rest, relax, and enjoy some of the life that passed them by. With more time than ever, they teased their upcoming album release, 'Time Machines and Dreams,' and waited out the pandemic, eager to get back on stage.

Designating a place setting for each attendant, the room sat fourteen. The opposite wall was cloaked in white fabric, and she assumed they'd watch the film on it. Circling the room, she spotted her position, though her eyes were attracted to the luxurious ivory lacquered table, adorned with a striking central slab of blue marble. An array of expensive liquors and sparkling glassware were situated on the stone.

Hanso poured amber-colored whiskey into crystal glasses. "Here's one for Deok-Sun. And Hanjun—"

"Thanks." Hanjun's gaze swept the space, discovering Jen at the far end of the table. Rushing over, he swapped his nameplate with Jin's, securing a seat next to her.

Jin tugged on the armrest of what should have been his seat. "No fair!"

"Let him have it." Hanso handed Jin a chilled glass of wine.

Hanjun fell into the seat, causing Jen's elbow to jerk and spill her water. He recovered and reached for a steaming tray of delectables, filling his mouth with food. "I'm starving."

Describing ingredients in detail, the roommates heaped portions onto her plate. The aromas were enticing, though not what she expected. While Ha-Rin compared the meat to the beloved breakfast food, it lacked the familiar smoky crispiness. Similar to cutlets, the protein was no less delicious.

As the dishes rattled, the film played. Although the material wasn't fully edited, it captured the friends in a lively game of truth or dare. Raucous cackling and animated shouts flew like daggers as they taunted each other to expose their darkest secrets or conquer ludicrous challenges.

The rules of the game were simple: refusing to answer a question would result in chocolate sauce being added to the person who opposed it, along with a sticky trip down the slide. Completing a dare granted them reprieve from sharing their truths. But the ultimate award had yet to be won—a sponsored prize for the player with the least amount of syrup on their clothing at the end of the taping.

On the screen, Deok-Sun's infectious smile widened, turning his interest to Hanjun. "Truth or dare?"

"Truth." Hanjun rolled his eyes, knowing the youngest would find a way to get him into trouble.

"Do you have any special feelings for someone?"

Hanjun transformed into a frolicsome schoolboy, but when he remembered the cameras, he choked. Adopting a stoic expression, he concealed any hint of vulnerability. "I like lots of people: family, Anti, even you, Sunny."

In the next take, Deok-Sun's head bobbed. "You know what I meant, Hanu!"

The tomfoolery carried on, with each bandmate posing questions and giving answers. Soogi and Jin were shockingly candid. Soogi admitted to unleashing a destructive force in the work bathroom—waste potent enough to peel wallpaper. Jin exposed his own battle with digestion, specifically noting the culprit—beans, in any form. Bonding over excrement, they shared remedies to ease their suffering, such as ingesting a spoonful of olive oil or eating bellflower roots dipped in honey.

Reaching the critical moment of Jen's arrival, the cameramen seized every angle as the group pivoted to greet her. All lenses were on Rem, who made a mad dash toward her. The segment panned away at the very last second, avoiding capturing her in the frame.

Following scenes exhibited the mates slipping on the slick slide, their hooting ringing in a symphony. However, it was the final shot that left a lasting impression; the artists rinsed off in the gym showers, their drenched clothes clinging to toned bodies—a calculated move intended to make hearts flutter and solidify their status as heartthrobs.

The credits rolled, and the Parallels theme song blared through the speakers, but Hanjun didn't notice. He charged down the hallway, his voice bouncing off the steel beams. "Ha-Rin!"

Jen's eyes fixated on the table. Was it typical for him to express outrage over an insignificant matter? Or perhaps she misjudged the significance.

Hanjun stormed into the kitchen, fists clenched. "You said you would scrub the shots."

"The footage *was* removed." Ha-Rin nibbled a leftover strip of cooled pork, savoring the earthy flavor.

Hanjun ruffled his coiffed hair. "You shouldn't have left any of it. Antis analyze everything."

Ha-Rin sipped a can of J&I-approved beer, his mouth curling into a sardonic smile. "So they find out about your girlfriend. They've speculated before."

Hanjun slammed his palms on the granite countertop. "*She's not my girlfriend!* Nobody can know she exists!"

Gasps from the bandmates suffocated the moment, followed by a silence that hung like a pendulum. Jen sat speechless, every word a heavy pebble tumbling into the depths of her mind. Excusing herself, she fought back tears threatening to reveal her secrets. "I should go."

Hanso lunged after her, but Jin halted him. They shared a glance of understanding—as much as they wanted to aid her, they had responsibilities. Her job was to assist them, not the other way around. "We're not done."

Hanjun marched back to the boardroom, his fury simmering below the surface. He searched the room for Jen, only to find her empty chair facing the door. "Where'd she go?"

Deok-Sun had never witnessed such an explosion of emotion from Hanjun. "She heard what you said."

"*Everyone* heard what you said." Jin's words carried the silence.

Uttering a growl, Hanjun's chest deflated. "I meant Anti will tear her to pieces if they find out we're living with a girl."

The remaining workmates exchanged nods, their eyes reflecting agreement. Regardless, each had a different interpretation of what was said and what went unsaid.

"Moving on..." The lead camera director addressed the room, offering a detailed critique of the taping. "The cut looked good. As usual, there were profanities we needed to chop. It seems as if you worked together better than the last handful of episodes, especially when Jenilyn arrived."

"We're sure the girl will remain a positive influence." Ha-Rin placed a comforting hand on Hanjun's back. "She's a slippery fish out of water, but she will adjust."

Frustrated by his own conduct, Hanjun squirmed in his seat. Thumbs tapping on his phone, he apologized to Jen through text. With one eye on the presentation and the other glued to the device, he didn't know how to smooth the edges.

"Hanjun-ssi, she's upset. Give her time." Jin caught him typing under the table for the fourth time. He shook his head, disapproving of the behavior, and Hanjun stashed the device away.

⋆⁺₊⋆☾⋆⁺₊⋆

In the solitude of her room, Jen coiled like a violent tempest. She couldn't grasp the source of her discontent, but its intensity was tough to ignore. Laid out on her bed, her mind thrummed with endless cynicism. Did she misinterpret Hanjun's actions on the nights he visited her? Or was he seeking companionship in his loneliness?

Her inner voice berated her for entertaining someone she barely knew. But despite her rationality, her heart refused to let go of the possibility. The words echoed in her head: not to relive past heartbreaks. "You're paid to work with him. Get out of it before you get hurt."

Their interactions were professional, and she warned her crux to keep attachments at bay. "The only way to avoid loss is to avoid falling. You *know* this."

Lying for hours, she pondered her attendance. After arriving late on her first day and strolling away early on the second, she worried the company would view her as a potential liability, even if her official start date had yet to arrive.

While drifting in her misdeeds, she was startled by a sudden knock. She had a feeling it would be Hanjun, and her intuition proved correct when his deep voice penetrated the barrier.

"Jen... I didn't mean—I'd never do anything to harm you."

★⁺₊★☾★⁺₊★

Receiving no response, Hanjun trudged to the lounge, pacing along the floor. "Why do I ruin everything I touch?"

"It's awkward because we don't know her personality." Jin fidgeted with the remote, waiting for the right moment to turn on the television. He wasn't unsympathetic, but after hearing about Hanjun's emotional state on the escort home, he needed a distraction.

Hanso nodded, his attention drawn to Jin's sly maneuver. "We don't know what will piss her off."

Scoffing, Soogi dismissed Hanso's underlying tone. "She's like us, you know. Don't you remember the bickering and disagreements we had when we first moved into the dorm?"

Hanso chuckled, recalling the war zone. "It's been so long. I hardly remember our old apartment."

Hanjun sank into the couch. "What is there to remember? We spent four hours a night there."

"I remember Jin putting empty containers back in the fridge." Deok-Sun erupted into boisterous laughter.

Executing retaliation, Jin singled out Deok-Sun. "That's not as bad as talking through a *whole* movie."

"Yeah, well, Hanjun evaded work! You'd ask him to do something, and he'd crack a joke and walk away. I'd say, 'Hey Hanu, can you separate the garbage? It's your turn.' And he'd say, 'I can, but ask me if I'm going to.'"

Hanjun gestured to Hanso. "What about him? Anytime he had congestion, he spit off the railing."

Struck by a core memory, disgust washed over Deok-Sun. "Gross. He almost hit me when I went to the market."

Hanso shook his head. "How about how cluttered you left our old studio, Hanjun? Huh? Wanna talk about that?"

Soogi beat an entertainment magazine on the coffee table, breaking the cycle of blame. "We agreed to move past that."

Deok-Sun redirected the dialogue back to Jen. "Hopefully she's not someone who stays mad."

Hanso set his comic on the nightstand. "Give her time before you try again."

"Yeah." Deciding the eldest was right, Hanjun shuffled to his room. Standing in the hall, he wished to solve their misunderstanding over constructive prose. Instead, he flopped on his bed and scrolled through the group chat.

> **Soogins**: Jen is upset.
> **Honsa**: Give it a few days.
> **Sunnie**: I don't know. She looked hurt.
> **Jinja**: I'm hurt, and it didn't happen to me.

He reached for a pen, unsure if he was ready to confront his fears. The journal was his companion, but he questioned whether spilling his thoughts would relieve his turmoil.

> *I might have ruined things with Jen. I was angry at*
> *Ha-Rin and didn't think about what I said. I'll do*
> *better in the future. That's all I can do.*

CHAPTER TEN

Manager of Managers

Jen dragged her limp body out of bed, dreading the day ahead. Standing under streaming hot water, she couldn't shake her guilt. Her mind thrummed, unable to believe how she reacted to Hanjun's confrontation with Ha-Rin. What was it about him that turned her into such a mess?

Stepping out of the stall, she was disappointed at her reflection. She looked as tired as she felt, and her usual makeup wouldn't hide the dark circles beneath her eyes. Disheartened, she returned to her room. Changing into a crimson cable knit sweater and distressed jeans, she completed the outfit with a longline overcoat, absentmindedly mirroring Hanjun's European fashion.

Exiting her room with a pair of new shoes dangling from her fingertips, she skidded on a loose object. She recovered and inspected the floor, finding a slip of paper with a handwritten message. Deep indentions blemished the lines, as if the author pressed with vigor, toiling to find the right wording.

Can we talk? —Hanjun.

She considered hurling the missive into the bin, but after further contemplation, she placed it on her desk. When would be the correct time to talk? What phrase would she use to convey her reverence? Would an apology be enough? Should she tell him the reason for her upset? What if he didn't feel the same?

Hurrying out of the building, she fell in step with her roommates and climbed into the backseat of an eight-passenger sport utility vehicle. Fashioned with opaque curtains, the escort was a necessary precaution for the high-profile entertainers.

Hanjun settled next to the driver, his sunglasses perched on his nose. He twisted and flaunted a smile, though she feigned a halfhearted simper.

The tense atmosphere was dissolved by light conversation as her roommates sank into their seats. Starting by discussing their food cravings, they also reminisced about the Koreanovela they watched the night before, speculating about potential plot twists, and planned out their single day off.

After a twenty-minute crawl through morning traffic, the driver whisked them away to the car park, avoiding hordes of devoted supporters assembled along the entrance. Gathered once more in the lobby, the group split into two and hustled toward the elevators. Hanjun raced to catch up with Soogi, Hanso, and Jen just as they slithered through the doors.

'Please scan key card.'

Holographic card in hand, Hanjun approached the scanner. Swiping his identification, the floors he had permission to inhabit were illuminated in blue. With full authorization—except for the top level—he could go wherever he pleased.

*'Welcome, Hanjun. You are expected on business
floor thirty-six in five minutes.'*

Jen squinted at the voice command. The system knew Blackmirror's schedule, which struck her as odd—but not as strange as the mysterious penthouse. "What's on the highest floor?"

"Nobody knows." Hanjun displayed little concern.

"Nobody has been to it?"

"Nobody has *access* to it." Hanso erupted from behind her.

Soogi leaned in from her left. "The only person with clearance is Mr. Yun."

Her throat tightened as the lift revealed the thirty-sixth floor. "Who's Mr. Yun?"

"God, as far as you know."

Dissatisfied with Hanso's response, Hanjun gestured for her to exit. "The founder of the agency."

Hesitant susurration escaped her. "I noticed there were pictures of him hanging in the break room, but I haven't had the pleasure of meeting him."

Hanso's comeback was off-putting. "He's a busy man. The only reason you'd run into him is if something bad was about to happen."

Soogi refused to let him intimidate her. "Or something good. After all, he was the mastermind behind J&I, responsible for discovering each of us, and he drove the creation of Blackmirror."

Meandering down the hallway, Jen entered the assembly room. Like the day before, each seat held a nameplate inscribed with elegant calligraphy. She took her place opposite Hunjun, between Jin and a man whose name she didn't recognize. "Who's Dae-Hyun?"

Jin's eyes fixed on the marker, his speech trembling with an undercurrent of worry. "He's the—"

Dae-Hyun burst through the door, his broad-shouldered frame exuding strength. Every detail of his appearance, from slicked-back hair to his designer suit, spoke of wealth. He was the manager of managers, and he claimed the head of the table as his own. His self-assurance gave the impression that he was not the last to arrive, but the first. He was the frontrunner in everything he did, even if he wasn't. "We're here to discuss Parallels. Hanjun, I understand you have a few concerns."

"I uhm—" Splintering under the limelight, Hanjun stole a glance at Jen. She sat at the table, clicking her pen in a rhythmic pattern. "I asked for some footage to be omitted."

"We edited direct shots of Jenilyn. To the casual observer, there is nothing out of the ordinary." Ha-Rin defended from the opposite end.

Hanjun rubbed a palm along his arm, imagining the relentless harassment she would face if word got out. "Anti will—"

Ha-Rin's hand cut through the air. "Antis speculate. It's what they do. Why would this be any different?"

"It's different because it's *true*. If Anti finds out one of us has a girl—" Hanjun's pitch lowered to mitigate his investment. "If Anti finds out we're *living* with a girl, they'll stop at nothing to make her life miserable."

Fueled by lingering enmity from the previous day, Jen's eyes flashed in defiance. "I can handle myself."

Frustration contorted his brow. "You know that's not what I meant. I don't want you to have to endure the same hardships as us."

Dae-Hyun addressed the mouthy musician. "Would you care to explain?"

"I just mean..." His words spilled into a murmur, tinged with defeat. "Sometimes it feels like we're trapped."

Dae-Hyun's penetrating glare bore into him. "J&I invested millions in your careers, provided housing and training, and you exhibit such ingratitude? Do you not realize the sacrifices made for your success?"

Hanjun clenched his jaw, fighting the urge to quarrel. Biting the inside of his cheek, his tongue felt heavy in his mouth. Ungrateful was a word that could never describe him. His heart overflowed with gratitude for J&I, his team, the crew, and their adoring audience. Yet there was a yearning for something greater—a thirst for true autonomy.

Each member of Blackmirror joined the trainee program when they were teenagers, and they were presented with a code of conduct. From the moment they signed with the agency and for the three years following their debut, they adhered to the rules with unquestionable obedience. Strict regulations dictated every aspect of their personas, making their existence arduous, and for the duration, romantic entanglements were prohibited, all while being fed promises of a fruitful future.

After the era of strict decrees, the assurances materialized. The dating ban was lifted, but their relationships were kept hidden from the public. As Blackmirror's popularity grew, they were held to unattainable standards. The bar of perceived perfection was raised, fostering inadequacy despite raking in billions of won for the company. It was a constant effort to stabilize their lives with the obligations of their professions.

He wasn't demanding to be released from the clutches of his agency, nor was he seeking to forsake his fans; he ached for unbridled artistic freedom. Amid the continual push for global recognition, he longed to uncover his true voice—not the one manufactured by J&I.

"Appreciation would do you good." Hyun turned bitter.

The musicians nodded, their focus trained on the table. Knowing Hanjun often felt like a puppet, Hanso patted his back. He wanted to stick up for his bandmate but knew it would only create a greater disconnect.

Hyun's eyes flicked at his watch, unaffected by the silence. "We'll reconvene next week."

As the associates gathered to leave, Dae-Hyun's hand skimmed Jen's back. He erected, rivaling her small stature, and a wave of freshly applied cologne encircled their surroundings. Adjusting his tie, he left no room for refusal. "I hope I'm not being too forward in asking for your number."

The question incited a collective gasp from everyone present. With his mouth hanging open, Hanjun diverted his concentration to the floor. And the windows. And the ceiling. Anything to distract him from the moment.

Jin jabbed an elbow into Hanso. "Look at the vein bulging in Hanjun's neck."

"Uh—" Jen absorbed their stunned appearances, searching for guidance. Her eyes connected with Hanjun's, pleading for him to save her from the uncomfortable situation. But he avoided her. Incapable of rejecting a man in a boardroom of his underlings, she reached for a pen. "Sure. Okay."

Hanjun stormed out the door. Overhearing swears resonating from the hall, his comrades exchanged worried glances. Meanwhile, Jen scribbled her contact information on a piece of paper. Dae-Hyun tucked the digits into his breast pocket and sauntered out with more vigor than he arrived with.

Wrestling with envy, Hanjun stood in the doorway, waiting for Jen to pull on her coat. "Get a date?"

"He's gonna let me know." She awaited some kind of reaction—perhaps a recoil of jealousy or anger. There was nothing but neutrality, and the realization hit her like a ton of bricks. They were friends. Nothing more.

Forcing a painful smile, a piercing throb gripped his chest. Lungs engorged with unspoken words, his eyes challenged hers. He craved to unleash his sincerity, but he couldn't take the risk at his place of work. Not with his bandmates watching, and definitely not with their superiors swarming.

Even if she emulated a spark of affection for him, succumbing to a relationship would only ignite the flames of critique. The idea of subjecting her to negativity was excruciating, like holding a blazing torch to a rare flower. She was a beauty, and he wouldn't witness her wilt under criticism.

On the journey to their shared home, Jen was regaled with stories about Dae-Hyun. The bandmates painted a picture of a stern leader, all while hinting at his less desirable attributes: an unforgiving nature and absence of humility.

"Aren't you being harsh? Masculinity is a balance of hard and soft. Where a man uses those traits is subjective." She believed men who exacted rigidity in their occupation harbored emotional depth behind the disguise. Even if Dae-Hyun didn't fit the archetype, she made a vow to take more risks. What was life without a few well-placed mistakes?

"Just be careful." Jin slipped off his boots at the door.

It was Deok-Sun's turn to feed the condo, but he had no plans of slaving over a hot oven. Instead, he sauntered to the sofa, scrolling through a never-ending list of local restaurants.

Jen cozied up beside him, positioning a blanket over her legs. The peacefulness was severed by the incessant separation of Deok-Sun's lips. She may have pardoned the screen tapping but couldn't ignore mouth noises. "Don't feel like cooking?"

Jin guffawed. "More like *can't* cook. He hasn't made anything since we moved in!"

"*Yes, I did!* I cooked ramyun for you a few days ago, but you were too stubborn to eat it."

"That wasn't cooking; it was a disgrace! You might as well have trampled on the national flag. The noodles were mushy, and you didn't add seasoning to the water."

"I put the soup base in after. If you add it too early, the aromas escape—"

"No, no. When you add the packet to the water first, the flavors absorb better."

The argument escalated into a North vs. South divide. Unwilling to listen to their bickering after a long day at the office, Jen intervened. "Everyone can cook; it just takes practice. What's something you'd like to eat?"

Deok-Sun's focus pulled away from his phone. "Japchae."

"I don't know what japchae is, but as my great-grandmother always said, 'If you can read, you can cook.'" She rose from her seat and extended a hand, inviting him into the kitchen.

"I have to see this." Hanjun hurried after Deok-Sun. Expecting a spectacular explosion, he envisioned the stove erupting into a fiery inferno as soon as the youngest touched a burner. He was infamous for his culinary talents, and the mention of him in the kitchen struck terror into the hearts of bystanders. His attempts at gastronomy resulted in burned pots, and he had a knack for turning the simplest meal into a disaster. He was much like Hanjun in that way.

The friends shuffled about, hunting for ingredients. Determined to make the perfect sauce, Jin scanned the fridge for soy sauce and puréed garlic. Soogi rummaged through the pantry, fetching brown sugar, sesame oil, black pepper, and toasted sesame seeds. Hanjun and Hanso prepped vegetables. Carrots were sliced into matchsticks. Onions were sectioned into slices, scallions were cut into two-inch pieces, and mushrooms were whittled into strips.

Remembering how he ribbed him for insufficiency, Deok-Sun teased Hunjun, who fumbled with a clump of shrooms. "Looks like you're *still* chopping like a toddler."

"My mother did her best." Hanjun chuckled at himself.

Hanso's finger hovered over the butchered produce. "Our ancestors would be ashamed."

The teasing continued, with each bandmate taking a jab at his lack of skills. He brushed off the jokes, but Jen recognized a shift in his mannerisms. His smile faltered, and his shoulders slumped. It wasn't humorous to him; his efforts were falling short of his expectations.

She made a conscious decision to act upon her great-grandfather's advice. He was a man of unwavering principles and didn't believe in tearing people down. He supported the inherent duty of humans—to demonstrate compassion—declaring it was the only way for humanity to prevail.

In her youthful days, when she was brimming with boundless energy and lack of foresight, he cautioned her not to expose the flaws of others. After all, she was not without fault. While her peers paraded their ridicule as harmless banter, he ensured she understood the significance. Behind a veneer of indifference, cruel words pierced souls. A string of callous remarks lingered long after the giggles, leaving invisible wounds only the shamed knew.

*'It's not a joke when the recipient doesn't laugh gen-
uinely. It's badgering.'*

"Let me show you a better technique." Disguising her objective with calculated flirtation, she plucked the knife from Hanjun's grasp. Coquettishly nudging him aside, she positioned his body behind hers, where he could peer around her frame.

He shifted under the proud gazes of his mates, his limbs boiling as she took ahold of his arms and pulled them over her shoulders. Bodies mashing together, he prayed his arousal wouldn't betray his covert depravity. Creating confidence in their closeness, he rested his chin above her shoulder while she guided his wrists. The pungent aroma of onions filled his senses, overpowered by his palpating heart. The room hushed while he sliced, conducted by her affectionate touch. Jin—known for binge-watching serial dramas—clutched his hands to his chest, afraid to breathe for fear of ruining the moment.

Hanso observed Jen's interaction with Hanjun, a smirk pulling at his lip. But when he turned to Soogi, he detected the jealousy etched on his brow. Catching Hanso's eye, Soogi forced a neutral expression and returned to preparing the coating.

"Have you ever sharpened this?" Experiencing the knife slip one too many times, Jen was exasperated. Holding the blade up to the light, it was as though the instrument had been used for years without a single sharpening.

Deok-Sun paused, his knife stationed halfway through a slab of beef. "You have to sharpen knives?"

"Yes, you do." She gawped, struggling to understand how, despite their intelligence, they lacked basic survival skills. In a zombie apocalypse, they'd be beautifully packaged appetizers.

Wagging her head, she read off the directions from a popular blogger's foolproof recipe while Deok-Sun prepared the meal. He cooked sweet potato vermicelli until translucent, then ran the noodles under the tap to prevent overcooking. Draining the fensi, he dunked the spinach in boiling water. Shocking the leaves and removing the excess liquid, he chopped the greens. He added a small amount of sauce to the noodles, stir-frying until sticky. Waiting for the dish to finish, he sautéed the veggies until softened. Leaving the vegetables crisp, he transferred the mixture to the finished noodles. He drizzled sauce in a pan and dumped in the beef and mushrooms, heating until done. Combining the fusions, he incorporated the remaining sauce and tossed in spinach, mixing with gloved hands. Dotting the fare with sesame seeds, he glanced at Jen for an endorsement. "It looks good enough, right?"

She retrieved a bronze bowl from a nearby cabinet. "You first."

Spooning a portion, he took a timid first slurp, wiping away a spot of sauce dribbling down his chin. "I made this?"

Soogi plunged his chopsticks into the grub. "This reminds me of the japchae we had in Gangneung."

One by one, the roommates tried the medley, savoring every bite with satisfied smacks. Deok-Sun's heart swelled, and he vowed to prepare the meal more often. "Let's turn this into a weekly tradition."

The sun dipped below the horizon, and evening gave way to a velvety night. The clinking of empty bowls and rush of water cleansing dirty dishes were soon covered by rambunctious variety shows to cap off the day.

In her brief time in South Korea, Jen had come to understand one universal truth: the country spared no expense when it came to advertising. Billboards dappled the streets, their bright fonts vying for attention. Promotions blared from radios, competing with the dissonance. Every inch of space was dedicated to promoting something—either new products, popular brands, or cultural events.

And television was no exception. Episodes weren't disrupted in the middle of viewing like in the States, yet a myriad of advertisements were interspersed between shows. From sugarfree Xylitol gum to the Hyundai Casper—the only compact car with a turbo engine in South Korea—the plugs were endless. Samsung watches. LG tankless water purifiers. Shinhan pLay. Cuckoo rice cookers. Bodyfriend massage chairs. Blackyak clothing. Maxim T.O.P espresso. Ikea dining tables. Glasslock storage containers. SK hynix memory chips.

The embedded marketing was the most amusing, and she was tickled by the number of Subway avocado sandwiches ordered by various drama characters, regardless of series.

But it was Yanolja that ensnared her eye—an accommodation platform said to have reinvigorated South Korea's once-dying love hotel industry. While she overheard whispers from her colleagues and spotted a few intriguing signs, she remained unaware of what a love hotel was.

When she questioned the commercial, Jin tiptoed around the concept of pay-per-hour rentals. "Love hotels cater to the needs of couples who live with their parents or in cramped apartments. And people go there to—I'm not sure how to put this—*engage in intimacy?* The walls are soundproof, and there's security to protect the identity of guests."

Soogi basked in amusement at Jin's flushed face. Acting as a loyal friend, he stepped in to help. "You can say it, Jin. *Sex.* She's grown. She knows what sex is."

"Thank you." Accepting Soogi's honesty, Jen caught Hanjun's stare. Whenever she reciprocated, he averted his interest. In a game of cat and mouse, she tested the theory multiple times, confirming her suspicions.

The strategic peek-a-boo was interrupted by a thump at the door. Deok-Sun rushed to answer as if it were his sole responsibility. He was met by a condominium guard holding a dozen flowers—opaline and quartz pink roses wrapped in ruffled layers of white tissue.

The sentry peered around the display, breaking into a wide smile. "These were delivered to the front gate."

Eyeing the tag, Deok-Sun nodded. "Jenilyn?"

Jumping to her feet, Jen stood on her tippytoes. "Who is it?"

Hearing her voice from the lounge, the man passed the arrangement to Deok-Sun. "Have a wonderful evening."

He carried the bouquet inside, placing the florals in her arms. "Looks like you have an admirer."

"I haven't met anyone." Cradling the bundle, she collected a note from the center.

The card radiated luxury: a smooth black surface embossed with a deep diamond pattern. From across the room, Hanjun identified the sender. His lungs seized as his worst nightmare came true; only one person at the agency had such extravagant taste in business cards.

"It's a dinner request from Dae-Hyun." Jen's gape traveled the room, studying their shocked expressions.

"I'm happy for you." Hanjun choked out a reply. He wasn't happy; he was as far away from happy as he could have been.

★⁺₊★☾★⁺₊★

Hanjun collapsed on his pillows, his heart pounding with fury, remorse, and disappointment. Dae-Hyun's audacity knew no bounds. Brazenly pursuing Jen, his shallow intentions were clear; he sought her because she was beautiful. The man had a reputation for short-term international lovers, and Hanjun wondered if he should tell Jen about Dae-Hyun's sexual conquests. It wasn't his place, but he felt as if it were his obligation to warn her.

Despite their own unrequited fondness, his friends encouraged him to confess, but he failed to do so. Suffering great regret, he reached for his phone.

Soogins: Thoughts on Hyun and Jen?
Jinja: No way. Not happening.
Honsa: He cornered her in front of everyone.
Sunnie: Hanjun was crushed.
Soogins: She gave him an opening to speak up.
Sunnie: You know Hanjun. He hides his feelings.
Jinja: Hanu, are you there? Hyun is trying to steal your girl!

Discarding the device, he didn't need his allies to remind him of his mistakes. There were plenty of things he wished he could undo, but there was no use dwelling. What was done was done; he just prayed she didn't fall for him.

> *I'm bothered, but if that's what's in her heart, there's nothing I can do. I wish I said something yesterday. I will continue to do the best I can.*

CHAPTER ELEVEN

Surviving Hoesik

Jen primped for the day, choosing a white blouse and aqua trousers, finished with a loose beige cardigan. She shuffled to the hallway and identified a virtual interview on Blackmirror's agenda. Luckily, the rest of the day was open.

Continuing down the corridor, she breathed easy. Her previous life was a leisurely stroll compared to the demands of her role as liaison. The job was a whirlwind of activity, requiring her to be on the move from the moment her eyes opened. Each working hour was crammed with nonstop broadcasting, filming, back-to-back meetings, and travel.

She woke at four o'clock every morning and tiptoed to the bathroom. Unlike her roommates, she couldn't leave Windsor Heights in comfortable lounge clothes and a bare face. No, she dressed in finesse, wearing a full face of makeup and ensuring every piece of clothing was ironed to perfection.

Assembling at the J&I tower, Blackmirror eased into their schedules—beauty appointments, demo sessions, and wardrobe fittings. At times, they would divide their tasks and work alone, conjoining again only at quitting time.

Jen, on the other hand, was immersed in a multitude of projects. Whether it was running errands or testing recording gadgets, she floated around J&I, completing whatever task Ha-Rin assigned her. On quiet days, she wouldn't cross a single Blackmirror member. Despite being hired as a liaison to the performers, she treasured the occasional day away; when a coworker called in sick, she was gifted with the opportunity to work alongside actors, influencers, and music producers.

Though grateful for her job and the opportunities it presented, she awaited the arrival of sundown. Eighteen hundred had become her favorite time of day—a respite from the demanding schedule. As soon as the big hand struck six in the evening, she shed her professional persona. Unless, of course, her superiors requested her presence at hoesik.

Ingrained in the fabric of Korean business, hoesik was more than a simple after-work gathering. It was a vibrant subculture with unique rules and traditions. Official events, marked by copious amounts of food and liquor, often lasted into the night and spanned numerous venues across the city. From dimly lit dive bars to rowdy karaoke joints, the entourage followed their superior, and the night wasn't over until Ha-Rin declared it so.

It was the most significant change she endured—realizing her boss and associates wanted to watch her act foolishly while under the influence. Treading into the office on the first day was like diving headfirst into a television program in its fifth season. Unfamiliar names, faces, and personalities made it challenging to know who to befriend and who to avoid. Adding indignity to the mix was incomprehensible.

After declining the invitation from Ha-Rin, she turned to Hanjun for guidance. His understanding nature helped her feel at ease, and he explained she was not required to participate, though her reluctance could hinder assimilation. Relying on her outsider status would only go so far before it became an obstacle to acceptance.

He didn't sugarcoat the reality of the situation: attending hoesik was an expected part of working life, with only two acceptable reasons for refusal. The first was if she was dead. The second was if she was at the hospital in such a critical condition that she wished she was dead.

The pressure to partake was intense, though she recognized the gatherings as an important facet of integration. Her intimidation was something she needed to work through if she had the slightest chance of establishing her name within the ranks of J&I.

Her initial nervousness dissipated when Hanjun proposed he attend with her. Although he didn't join Ha-Rin for social gatherings, he attended functions with the agency's founder when the schedule allowed. That was how she survived her first company dinner. Armed with a greater appreciation for the custom, she accepted the second invitation, and with Hanjun's help, she navigated a night of kidney killing with most of her dignity intact.

The first one was the worst. Supplementing a fourteen-hour workday, the team enjoyed an evening of trust-building exercises at a local bowling alley. On location, Ha-Rin and Hanjun administered unlimited shots from green glass bottles, fueling the informal tournament. The twelve lackeys were split into four teams, each vying for the title of champion. Afterward, they cooled off at a traditional restaurant. Thanks to Hanjun's helpful tips, she was equipped with clean socks and stored her footwear in the designated cubbyhole without needing to be reminded. Once seated on the warm floor, they were treated to banchan, and a selection of side dishes covered the table: steamed eggplant, seasoned spinach, and stir-fried zucchini.

Fiery gochu peppers piled high on plates, and Ha-Rin and Hanjun engaged in a vicious eating competition. In the end, it was Hanjun who emerged victorious, though he paid for his gluttony with digestive discomfort the following day. As the night dragged on, they were ushered to a local bar where the floor overflowed with energetic patrons waiting for a screeching rock band. She couldn't recall much of what happened inside the establishment, but there were flashes of memories plastered on Ha-Rin's media accounts the next day.

The night ended with rounds of soju and beer chasers, blurring the edges of their memories. Suffering from a staggering gait, Hanjun escorted her inebriated allies to their homes. The clock chimed three when they reached their condominium. Unable to stand upright in the elevator, they fell on each other, chortling about the themed socks she wore and the inebriated man they found face down in the shrubbery.

Exhaustion from a long night of indulging weighed on her, though she was the center of attention at the water cooler the next morning. Her coequals applauded her for comfortably sitting cross-legged, keeping up with their drinking games, and boldly sampling a range of kimchi without coughing. Just as Hanjun promised, mealtimes were a gateway into the culture, helping her adapt during the adjustment period. The most heartfelt conversations took place over acorn jelly, which was difficult to hold with chopsticks, even for a lifelong user.

Looking back, she harbored one regret: that her use of English fell on deaf ears. As Ha-Rin stood and asked her to say a few words, a wave of panic washed over her; she had forgotten the minuscule amount of Korean she learned at the office.

Thankfully, Hanjun stepped in to translate, saving her from embarrassment, though she longed for the day when she could thank her workmates on her own.

Hanjun didn't entertain subsequent hoesiks, but he assisted her in navigating an overwhelming variety of hangover remedies from local convenience stores. Supplying her with a plethora of products—drinks, gum, tablets, gummies, and frozen treats—he not only provided her with enough to alleviate multiple hangovers but also procured his mother's cherished cure-all: bean sprout soup. The roots were rich in amino acids, reducing the formation of acetaldehyde, or so he said.

As she approached the kitchen threshold, she realized how much he was looking out for her. "I should get him something as a thank you."

Roaring over clinking glassware, Hanjun commanded the room, but there was inherent distress in his tone. "We need to be careful—"

Upon her entry, the room fell silent. "What's wrong?"

Expelling a reluctant sigh, Hanjun presented his phone. "Anti are speculating about our last episode of Parallels."

Cradling the device in her palm, she swiped through the article. A blogger known as Blackmirrorify pieced together a detailed analysis of the series, pointing out anomalies within the recordings. Punctuated by frames to support the hypothesis, the creator must have been a detective in their past life.

'WHO WAS HANJUN RUNNING AT? THERE'S A SCENE MISSING.'

'COUNT THE NUMBER OF SHOES IN THE FRAME WHEN THEY ARE HUGGING. SIX PAIRS. WHO WAS IN THE MIDDLE?'

'ANOTHER CLIP SHOWS ONE OF THE BOYS PUTTING WAR PAINT ON SOMEONE'S FACE WITH THEIR FINGER, BUT NONE OF THE MEMBERS HAD CHOCOLATE ON THEIR FACE.'

'WHEN REM LOOKS UP AT THE CAMERA, YOU CAN SEE HE'S LYING ON SOMETHING. OR SOMEONE.'

The post analyzed every scene, calling attention to a feminine outline. One still image caused a frenzy among admirers, provoking disputes over a possible pink brassier under a white shirt. Other commenters assumed the mysterious figure to be a delegate of the agency. The comments section morphed into a heated debate between those who believed Blackmirror weren't dating and those who held onto hope of their favorite bandmates being romantically involved.

She returned the phone. "They're going crazy."

He gripped her arms, meeting her eyes. "They will ask about this. Stay away from the cameras. Do you understand?"

Experiencing a flutter of anxiety hit her stomach, she took in the seriousness etched on his features; his delivery was one of concern, tinged with protectiveness. "If they don't have proof you're living with—"

Suspiring, he withdrew his hands from her. "They don't need evidence if the majority believes it to be true. You don't want to see what happens when the press gets hold of a scandal. Please, for your safety, stay away from the cameras."

$\star^{+}_{+}\star\mathbb{C}\star^{+}_{+}\star$

The day progressed, and the artists were perfected by skilled stylists. Eye-catching outfits were selected for each personality, adding to the overall aesthetic. Two hours before their interview, they arrived at the rented studio. Modern, with five ivory chairs arranged in a semicircle on mahogany flooring. The walls were outfitted with wavy, textured tiles, contrasting smooth furnishings. Giant stacking cubes of glowing ultramarine lights were placed throughout the room, some outfitted with Blackmirror's logo or pseudonyms.

On the sides of the stage, stands hosted crystal-clear screens, giving optimal views of the celebrities, as if their audience were sitting in the front row at a concert. With only twenty minutes until showtime, the musicians were handed personalized in-ear monitors—small devices serving as a lifeline to their director, guiding them through the performance.

Jen swept the set of stray belongings—discarded water bottles, crumpled snack packaging, and unused hair clips. After examining every prop, she stood with the staff as instructed. Standing shoulder to shoulder with the camera lead, he passed her a slender boom mic. Guiding her into place, he tutored her on the proper way to grip. Just as she began to familiarize herself with the equipment, the recording commenced.

Blackmirror, dressed in their signature edgy styles, lounged on the furniture. Monitors flanked the platform, projecting the friendly face of their interviewer. "Thanks for tuning in! I'm Brycen Woods, and today I have the pleasure of chatting with the astronomically successful boy band, Blackmirror. With the pre-release of their newest album, *'Time Machines and Dreams,'* selling over ten million copies, these talented vocalists need no introduction. But just in case you've been living under a rock—"

Paralleling the prompt, each member made a triangular shape with their hands and introduced themselves in the order in which they joined Blackmirror.

"Honey."
"I go by Rem. And I'm the leader."
"Ho-Young, or Hanso."
"I prefer Deok-Sun, but you can call me Sunny."
"I'm Jin!"

With wild determination, the entertainers shouted their catchphrase. "We're making the impossible, possible!"

Standing off to the side, Jen caught nuances the edited footage would omit, such as when Hanso and Deok-Sun drowned in their thoughts, their expressions distant. Soogi rolled his eyes whenever the questioner brought up a distasteful topic, though the cameramen focused on the speaker to minimize distractions.

The dialog was not scripted, but it was heavily influenced. Whenever a hair fell out of place or their makeup smudged, the chat was halted, and an emissary of the crew rushed to fix the issue. Every detail of the exchange was choreographed to project a pristine image of Blackmirror.

Brycen nodded along to each oration. Glancing at his notes, he dove right in, anxious to unearth a secret. "Let's not waste time; we're sure you've heard the rumors."

Hanjun fidgeted. "Um, yeah, we saw something trending this morning. But I can assure you, there is no female member of Blackmirror, as the rumors suggested. It's wishful thinking."

Voice laced with curiosity, Brycen leaned in. "And what about you, Hanjun? Speculation about your romantic life is all the rage. Is there someone special you'd like to talk about?"

Fingers tapping against his thighs, Soogi hid his unamusement, muttering a retort under his breath. "Nice try."

Hanjun shifted nervously. "Our fans are incredibly special, but to answer your question, no, I'm not in a relationship."

The probing carried on for another half hour, with the host delving into deeper topics. They shared lighthearted stories and playful banter, and as the examination came to an end, the stars talked about their goals, expressing gratitude toward their supporters.

The film ceased rolling, and Hanjun removed his earpieces, shrinking under his manager's gaze. Ha-Rin shook his head, knowing he had failed the artist. "We knew they would pry about your private life. You should have been better prepared."

"I know." Being on the receiving end of dating slander was strange. It wasn't he who had such whispers shadowing him; the popular members were subject to speculation, and anyone they interacted with was put under the microscope. Hanjun, however, was immune to the phenomenon.

Jen released the boom handle, her eyes narrowing at his calm demeanor. "How can you lie like that?"

Ha-Rin chuckled, awarding Hanjun a hearty tap on the shoulder. "He didn't lie. He answered questions by offering information as if it were asked for when it wasn't. No, there isn't a girl in the group because there isn't."

"And I'm not in a relationship." The underlining of his pronunciation hung in the air, thick with irresolution. His dark gaze searched hers for a reaction; her breath hitched, and he knew she was affected. Just as he hoped.

Holding a stoic expression, she went about her job, tidying up the set. But deep inside, a burning ache threatened to consume her. She packed away the staging props, her jaw clenched in a show of conviction. Stifling the pain tearing through her heart, she rejected giving into unrequited love, even if it meant creating distance between her and the source of her heartache.

CHAPTER TWELVE

A Little Movie Magic

It had been two weeks since Jen accepted Dae-Hyun's proposal, and Hanjun had written him off as a threat. Sitting in the lounge, he was fifty-six pages into a best-selling thriller when she emerged, wearing a black cocktail dress with sophisticated needlework. A structured bustier highlighted her contours, while gossamer added hidden sensuality to her slender arms and ample bosom. Preparing to leave, she crouched to adjust the tulle on her Jimmy Choo suede pumps, bringing his gawp to the hosiery gracing her calves.

Performing a ballerina twirl, the hemline swished around her thighs. "How do I look?"

"So beautiful!" Jin took her hand, whirling a second time.

Eyes peering over the binding, Hanso flipped a page in his manga. "Why ask when you know you're pretty?"

Hanjun draped a hand over his mouth, barricading the swears that threatened to spill out. Held captive in the moment, he wished to separate from his persona and be remorselessly Ryu Hanjun. "Anyone would be lucky to date you."

A long list of reasons prohibited him from declaring his disposition. He was imprisoned by his life: potential speculation, the anxiety of losing supporters, and the implications of plummeting stock prices—any misstep could lead to downsizing for J&I. The crew's livelihood depended on Blackmirror. Any hint of a scandal, even something as insignificant as dating, could fracture the carefully constructed bond between artist and fan. Years of dedication could be undone in an instant. If the majority of the fanbase supported the pairing, they would sail through unscathed. But if they didn't...

He couldn't imagine the havoc that would ensue if the rumors were proven true. The band had been relatively unscarred by scandals, but he had witnessed the unraveling of esteemed artists; their once shining reputations tarnished. In the best possible scenario, the performer was booted from their respective group, and the remaining members trucked on without them. But in the worst case, the team disbanded due to negative publicity. The artist's lover, along with their family, friends, and workplace, suffered relentless harassment until the courtship crumbled. And the unrelenting barrage of hostility affected the couple well after the relationship's expiry.

Even if she understood the pitfalls of getting embroiled with him, there was the looming probability of jeopardizing his career. A decade of effort could be erased with one oversight, and he couldn't take the gamble. It was too risky for him to follow his heart, even if it longed for her.

Standing in the middle of the room, Jen felt as if their alliance was unbalanced, with her pining for something more. In the end, she concluded their association was lopsided, and any fondness was imaginary at best. "I'll be home later."

The last syllable hung in the air, relinquishing a deafening stillness in her absence. Though the door slammed, Hanjun pretended to be unfazed. "What was I supposed to do?"

The room idled still, apart from the humming humidifier. His friends sat frozen, each with a unique verdict of what they would have done; some may have acted boldly, others with caution. None of their ideas involved letting her go out with another man without professing their adulation.

Jin's arms coiled around a decorative pillow. "What happened to living beyond regrets?"

"I'm going to my room." Hanjun took off for the hall. Following a resounding slam, the door shook on its hinges. He catapulted into bed, reliving the night's events. The heartache was severe, but her decisions trumped his desires.

Savvy to Dae-Hyun's ways, he tried to drive the rendezvous out of his head; he'd bombard her with gifts, such as the Jimmy Choo pumps, which were coincidentally absent in her apartment at the time of her move. He'd take her to a ritzy diner, where a stunning floral arrangement would await. And at the end of a beautiful evening, she would receive a proposal to stay the night at his penthouse. If the tryst went well, he wouldn't see her again until Dae-Hyun dropped her off at the office.

Gripping his phone, he fought the urge to call her. The thought of having to spend the night wondering what she was up to, followed by the idea of seeing her in the morning, carried a sour taste to his esophagus. Sliding the device into his jeans, he couldn't marinate over Dae-Hyun's motives.

Hurrying out of his room, he removed a coat from the hallway closet, dodging criticism from his mates. Making a beeline for the water, Windsor Heights blurred behind him. He rented a bicycle from a kiosk near the river, praying the crisp air would strip his clouded mind. Touring the waterfront, with its ripples mirroring the streetlights, he blended in as a stranger. Gliding past on two wheels, he was another face in the crowd, unnoticed and unbothered. On a bike, he was free.

As soon as Jen stepped out of the cab, she knew the restaurant was too rich for her blood. Ornate chandeliers and velour furnishings mocked her humble upbringing. Even the clientele was extortionate. The women, donning luxurious dresses and flashy jewels too enormous for their necks, mingled with men in tailored suits and shiny alligator loafers. Affluent customers moved with precision, their gestures curated to maintain prominence. Mechanical and lacking natural fluidity, their fake laughs dwarfed the string trio strumming in the corner.

She examined how the hosts dodged tables as if they were taming savage animals. Their movements were benign, doing anything to conserve the capitalistic food chain. Escorted by a timid hostess, every millisecond brought her closer to a sea of complaints, while overworked servers buzzed about, righting the wrongs. Improperly folded napkins, non-imported wine, tablecloths that didn't brush the floor—the diners nitpicked details instead of appreciating their privilege.

As she approached a white-clothed table, Dae-Hyun elevated to greet her. A breathtaking bouquet of sanguine roses lay waiting. Next to the bundle, ivory pillar candles flickered. A young waiter pulled out a chair, and she hadn't sat for more than a few minutes when she began to feel like Rose from the cult classic blockbuster Titanic.

With every word, Hyun single-handedly lowered the air quality. He peacocked about his lavish house, successful profession, and extravagant possessions. His questions were for show; he didn't give her time to reply before launching into his opinion. The volley of self-importance was only broken by obnoxious slurps of liquor. Lacking depth, he reached the pinnacle of his consciousness; to be wealthy and powerful were his only objectives. And while he had achieved his goals, he lacked drive. His plans were to revere improvident booze, attend swanky parties, and collect an ephemera of women.

Biting her tongue, she toiled to keep her composure. His feats were solely his, and he overlooked the countless individuals he trampled to reach the peak. He was above all others who lived or would ever live. A man blinded by narcissism.

Possessing a condescending vibration that made her gut churn, he took another swig of whiskey. "The only thing I'm missing is a beautiful bride."

She regretted accepting his invitation. Jin cautioned her about him, but nothing could have prepared her for his arrogance. There was no trace of humility, only shallowness masquerading as light. Lost in the blether, her mind strayed to Hanjun; he was a man of passion and kindness, modest and unapologetically human in a world demanding perfection.

She refocused on the present and met Hyun's autocratic glower. "If you could have a superpower, what would it be?"

He suspended his self-praise. "What a stupid question."

"Just answer it." The longer she interacted with him, the more disgusted she was.

Tolerating her questioning, he responded like a tired parent who didn't want to entertain their child's limitless curiosity. He lifted the spirits to his lips, slamming the glass on the table with enough muscle to rattle the plates. "Unending stamina."

She fought the urge to gag when he turned the question on her. "If you could have a superpower, what would it be?"

"To turn trash into food." Anticipating the awkwardness of asking for the check, she surveyed the room, trusting the steward would liberate her from an embarrassing predicament.

"Why? It's trash! Throw it away and buy your food!" His voice heightened in indignation.

She positioned a hand to protect her anonymity. As a foreigner, she would be liable for any mishap. It didn't matter if it was his overreaction inciting a stir; she would bear the brunt of the blame. "Some people can't afford food, and our oceans—"

Employing an air of superiority, he callously censored her. "If someone can't afford food, they don't deserve to eat."

She couldn't believe the words pouring from his mouth. "The right to nourishment is not an allowance to be earned. It's a fundamental right granted to all."

He cemented his conservative philosophy. "Welfare has no place in a well-functioning society."

Though the situation was far from humorous, a chuckle leaked from her. It was the first undisputed statement he uttered since she sat across from him. "In a well-functioning society, assistance wouldn't be needed, but we don't live in a well-functioning society."

Before their food arrived, he broadcast the nastiest thing he could have said. "Perhaps you aren't able to understand why it's better to work hard and make something from nothing."

She made eye contact with an adjacent table, who whispered among themselves. He was a pig. He looked nice, and he smelled nice, but he was soulless. "You know nothing."

Assuming supremacy, he stretched his neck. "Did you know all employee personnel files pass my desk? I bet you didn't."

She froze. He accessed her dossier, which contained specifics of her life. Not only the information listed on her resume but also the verdicts from the mandated tests she had taken the week after her arrival. In addition to fitness evaluations and character examinations, there was one final hurdle before she could officially be assigned to Blackmirror: taking the Global Samsung Aptitude Test, or GSAT. The English version was split into three parts: one measured quantitative problem-solving, another scrutinized logical reasoning, and there was a visualization portion where she had to decode unfolded origami shapes and deduce if the folds were inward or outward.

After completing the first stages of the hiring process, she was marshaled into a dreary room, where she faced a committee of recruiters. They evaluated every language she spoke, right down to her meager knowledge of German. In a whirlwind, she was allotted thirty minutes to prepare a ten-minute PowerPoint presentation, tasked with generating a theoretical idol crew with only basic instructions.

Celestreal—a combination of celestial and real—was the theorem she concocted. The premise of mortal torment was woven into the palette, with shades of black, crimson red, and ghostly grey. The proposed twelve-member ensemble, each between the ages of eighteen and twenty-two, embodied beautiful nightmares from the zodiac. Spurning contemporary interpretation, the illusion orbited the unchecked facets of growth. While the phantasy transmitted spiritual ambience, their followers would be known as the Corporeals, or the Reals.

The anticipated music—which she actualized with the help of an assisting producer—promised a fusion of indie pop utilizing eidolic female vocals. The near excessive use of synth produced a gritty tenor with chromatic mediant chords, layered incantation, deep pads, and atmospheric oceanic sounds. Eerie and unearthly, the melodies mirrored the group's proposed debut album, 'Siren's Song.' Birthed from the idea of life forming from the sea, subsequent albums would feature the troupe evolving into more intelligent lifeforms.

The concept was elaborate, but the design of their official fandom stick remained simple. The blueprint, which parroted Celestreal's logo, featured a sleek black handle. Nestled at the end was a plumb circle with a cross etched through, representing Midheaven—the highest point on the horizon. The emblem honored their audience, who would hold power over their progress, achievements, and societal standing.

Presenting her creation to the board, her hands shuddered. The slides showcased hastily sketched examples of the aesthetic—an integration of amatory goth with archaic detailing. Outlining samples of velvet, voile, corsets, and netted materials in dark colors, carnal formalwear was the spotlight, with ruffles and high slits bleeding cosmic femininity. The troupe's influences could be traced to the Brontë sisters, Edgar Allan Poe, and Shakespeare.

To her amazement, her pitch fascinated the interviewers. Each lifted circular placards—tens from all but one, who rated her a nine because he never gave top rankings. Though he didn't have to justify his decision, he believed no individual could be flawless.

As the interview reached its end, it became apparent that the main goal was to confirm her suitability for the organization. However, she was bewildered when a series of unrelated topics were thrown her way, burrowing into her personal life: influential figures, her role in interpersonal circles, volunteer activities, beloved hobbies, recent reading material, and her first impression of J&I Entertainment.

Unveiling a smug sneer, Dae-Hyun leaned back in his chair. "Your résumé shows your first job was as a nurse, yet you obtained an Accelerated BSN, which implies nursing wasn't your original trajectory. At one time, you worked in both the medical and creative fields before choosing to leave one for the other, though it meant a wage cut. You also signed a Fair Credit Reporting affidavit, permitting J&I to review your lending score. This indicates you've had a stable financial history with no significant debt, foreclosures, or bankruptcies.

"During the device screenings, we learned you have one discreet social profile with few acquaintances. Your phone, which we requested to audit your daily usage, exhibited a minimal level of activity.

"Your written GSAT grade was phenomenal, yet your verbal personality scores were marginal and intentional. This leads me to believe you have a strong focus on your inner world while minding your civil duties. You're calculating about what others know.

"As you stood before the directorates, your reluctance to participate was obvious. In half an hour, you not only satisfied the agency's expectations, but surpassed them. We never anticipate a finished product—only a cluster of ideas to prove you have the drive to fit the industry. Amid the compliments, you attributed your work to luck. You were overprepared, with an eye on every detail, yet you appeared nervous throughout.

"The exemplar you created for Celestreal, which you received exceptional marks for, was dark and innately feminine. You drew inspiration from vintage noir, astrology, and classic literature to devise a sensual world belied by your bubbly exterior. You prioritized fantasy over practicality or religious adherence. This suggests a fascination with ancient beliefs and origins, even if you don't subscribe to any particular faith."

She sat silently, their eyes locked in a silent battle of wills. He peeled back layers of her psyche, and when he thought he had solved the puzzle, he asked her out to examine the subject of his psychological experimentation. "You've made me extremely uncomfortable."

A smirk pulled at his lip, relishing in her distress. "I find you intriguing. It's why I asked you to join me for dinner."

"If I had known you investigated me, I wouldn't have agreed." She stood to leave.

His booming voice echoed through the building, drawing disapproving glares. "You're leaving so suddenly?"

Stripped of her dignity, she apologized to the staff before stumbling out of the front doors, folding onto the cold, unforgiving steps. Her anger simmered, creating a hollowness in her stomach akin to starvation. She pulled her phone from her bag. It was a symbol of comfort and connection with those she held dearest, but in the city of ten million, it only served to remind her of how deserted she was. Her life revolved around Blackmirror, and she had no one else to call.

Distraught, she considered reaching out to Hanjun but decided against the idea. "After everything that's happened, he probably hates me."

★⁺₊★☾★⁺₊★

Soogi lolled in bed, penning lyrics into a notepad. His phone vibrated, and he hesitated to answer, but remembered Jen had left the condo. "Jen?"

She released an emotional vomit of apologies. "Soogi, I hate to do this, but could you come get me? I don't have anyone else to call and—"

Hearing the tremor in her voice, his instincts sharpened. "Did something happen?"

"The people were awful, and Dae-Hyun was worse. He was smug and creepy, and everything you warned me he'd be. I left before the food made it to the table—all I had was water, but it was expensive. I tried running the card Ha-Rin gave me, but it didn't work, and they won't let me leave. I wasn't sure who to call, and I didn't think I could call Hanjun after what happened at the office. Maybe you can call the restaurant. I swear I'll pay you back as soon as—"

"Stop talking." He silenced her rambling before she combusted. "Message me a picture of the building so I can find it."

Dropping the call, he contemplated his next move. Opportunism beckoned, tempting him to rescue her. But he knew if he did, he would become her full-time savior. "She's not a princess to be saved, and you're not the prince to save her."

⋆⁺₊⋆☾⋆⁺₊⋆

Pedaling along the water, frigid air pierced through Hanjun's wool parka. Jen strummed his heartstrings, vibrating every corner of his being. Before meeting her, he thought he had it all—a mildly fulfilling life, awarding accomplishments—but there was always an underlying emptiness. And then she came along, stirring up emotions that terrified him. She wasn't the first girl to capture his heart, but she was the first to do it so rapidly and completely.

A notification interrupted the love ballad blasting through his earbuds. Giving his phone a quick glance, he veered to the side of the path, kicking up a cloud of dust. "Hey."

"Jen just called," Soogi crackled through the speaker. "She wants me to get her."

His brow furrowed. "I swear if Dae-Hyun did something—"

"She walked out on Dae-Hyun." The disdain in Hanjun's voice was indisputable, and Soogi knew calling him was the best course of action. "Her card isn't working, and she can't leave until she pays. I don't mind picking her up, but I thought you might want to."

"Uh, sure." Holding his breath, he wondered why Soogi called him. He had a mushy spot for her and yet assisted his rival.

As if he could read his chaotic mind, Soogi interrupted in a knowing voice. "She's your girl. The whole time. It's been you."

"Send me the address." Hanjun licked his lips, unwilling to let another shot at love slip away. "And Soogi—thank you."

Soogi disregarded the comment, his dark hair swishing over his eyes. "Go get your girl, man."

Hurrying to a drop-off, he was sure the universe had intervened. "Don't fuck it up this time. You can't be as honest as you want, but you can be as honest as you can be."

After returning the bike, he hailed a ride from the curb. The cabbie pulled up, and he climbed inside, spitting out the location for the upscale eatery. The rhythmic fall of raindrops pattering the window accompanied his thoughts as he watched the bullets race. "Should I tell her a joke? Share a story about a time I had a bad date? Shut the hell up and escort her home? Ask if she's eaten and order takeout if she hasn't?"

The seasoned driver peeked at him through the rearview mirror. "Girl troubles?"

"You could say that. I missed an opening to confess, and I think destiny may have given me another opportunity."

The cabbie wove through the city, delivering aged wisdom. "Love isn't an opportunist. It surfaces in its own time, following a divine path. If it's predestined, she'll let you know."

A shred of reassurance stirred in Hanjun's heart. "I hope that's true."

★⁺₊★☾★⁺₊★

Perched on the stairs, Jen identified Hanjun emerging from an orange vehicle. Regardless of the mask obscuring most of his silhouette, his penetrating gaze was unmistakable. "I called Soogi."

"And Soogi called me." Approaching the steps, he found her curled up in a ball, hugging her knees. There was something alluring about the way she was windswept under the dark sky.

"I'm stuck here until I settle my tab." She tucked a stray strand of hair behind her ear. "I tried running my card, but I don't know if it's activated. There's a bit of a speech barrier."

"Don't worry about it." He strode into the facility on her behalf.

Left alone, she scanned the windowpane for signs of his return, uncaring that her once-pristine garment was speckled with dirt. Couples sharing umbrellas scurried by, and she pondered why the disorder felt intimate. From works like The Notebook to Breakfast at Tiffany's, rain was a cinematic staple. Being confined in cramped quarters could certainly turn into a real-life movie moment, but she thought there was more to it. Perhaps an instinctual need for humans to gravitate toward the mist.

A young man, around the same age as Deok-Sun, paused in front of her to skim his phone. Shielded by a black umbrella, he spoke into the receiver. She could only make out a few words, but it seemed he was expecting a friend or girlfriend.

Finishing the call, he adopted an amiable smile. "Are you waiting for someone?"

"Kind of." She used the back of her hand to swipe away her tears, smudging clumps of mascara down her face.

Stepping forward, he rationed his sprinkle-free space. "I can't leave you like this."

"I appreciate you, but that's not necessary."

Though he took her words to heart, his nosiness bubbled. "You'll have to wring out your clothes if you stay out here."

She squeezed water from the hem of her dress. "It's a little late."

"You're brave. I would flee from a date if she showed up looking like a drowned rat."

Spotting Hanjun exiting the restaurant, a playful smile bloomed on her cheeks. Defying usual customs, he held the door for an elderly couple, showing his respects with a bow. Droplets fell from his blueish-grayish strands, and he snapped his neck, forcing his overgrown bangs to the side.

Watching him shake off the water like a dog, she was hit with a strange delight. Most found the rain to be romantic, but for her, it held a special significance. The way untimely torrents made everything disorderly was part of the charm. Unpredictable storms soaked the attire of anyone trapped in their wrath. Rainfalls turned perfect hair into matted messes and makeup into dark streaks. Cloudbursts revealed genuineness under superficiality. "Some say the rain ruins a look, but I think it might just reveal it."

The man's eyes wheeled to Hanjun's drenched muscular physique. "I suppose it does."

Relieved from his unpaid position as doorman, Hanjun descended the stairs, his concern flickering from Jen to the peculiar man. "Do you know each other?"

A grin crinkled the corners of his eyes. "No, no. I'm going."

Stuffing the receipt into his wallet before Jen noticed the charge for the Hanwoo she ordered, Hanjun discovered she hadn't ingested a drop of alcohol. The adjusted ticket, which eliminated the high fees Dae-Hyun racked up in a matter of minutes, only depicted costly, straight-from-the-iceberg water. Judging from the price, he assumed it was the same brand Jesus drank. Or perhaps the leftover water he hadn't turned into wine.

He settled beside her on the stairway, debating whether to inquire about Dae-Hyun. He wanted to know what went wrong so he could avoid making the same mistake. She shifted, tugging at the mesh clasped around her ankles. The freezing rain splattered his skin, and he considered searching for cover but stopped when he spotted the glimmer in her eye. While others hurried to find shelter, she embraced the eruption as if it were a friend. "Do you want me to call for a car? I can have someone from the agency pick us up."

"I want to feel this moment." Determined to acknowledge her poor choices, she reclined on the cement, enjoying the stony surface grating against her skin. He spread out next to her, discomfort forgotten as the heavens freckled his features.

Lying perfectly still while dozens of pedestrians passed, she sprouted from the concrete without warning. "I need to clear my head."

"I'll go." Unwilling to leave her wandering Seoul alone, he dogged behind, doubtful she knew where she was going.

She strolled down a claustrophobic alley, drawn to the brick walls. Her fingertips probed the uneven grooves, a ritual from her childhood—a way for her to tether with materiality when her senses wandered too far.

His footsteps cloaked her in a sense of security. He was armor protecting her from uncertainty. The undefined dynamics of their relationship confused her; she couldn't bear the thought of being partial to someone who didn't reciprocate.

Memories swamped her mind, like how he came to her aid when she called Soogi. Or how he took notes during their conversations. And there were the times he helped her navigate through unfamiliar traditions and nursed her back to health after wild nights of drinking. His curiosity about her and his genuine admiration were also hard to overlook.

She was convinced it wasn't a one-sided affair. There were too many instances highlighting his caring behavior. Perhaps it wasn't love, but there was something more than friendship between them. And everything started with *something*.

Halting her slow walk, she rotated to face him. Her voice trembled, barely audible over the faint rustling of leaves. "Why didn't you say anything?"

Pausing a few feet away, the storm pelted through his jacket. "What are you talking about?"

Her pleading reverberated off the surrounding buildings, amplifying her desperation. "Why did you let me go out with Dae-Hyun?"

"I thought that's what you wanted."

"No." Exhaling, her body slumped against the building. If he had been direct, she wouldn't have consented to Hyun's request in the first place. "It's not what I wanted."

"What did you want?" The words suffocated in his windpipe. "I thought you—"

She laughed, but it wasn't amusement or joy. It was the hollow, hysterical release of someone who felt utterly defeated. "*You*, Jun! I wanted *you*."

"What did you want me to say?" His heart drummed in his rib cage. He couldn't deny his attraction, but despite the enjoyment he found in her presence, his anxiety cautioned against getting involved. "What could I have said?"

"I don't know. Everything. Nothing. Literally anything! Any sliver of emotion would have stopped me." She raised her chin to the star-studded sky. One minute, she experienced a profound longing for him to unveil his innermost revelations; the next, she was overwhelmed by mixed signals. Her eyes dipped to meet his smoldering stare. "Anything, Jun."

Imagining how different their night could have been if he had asked her not to go, he pictured them strolling through the city, hand in hand, chortling over shared secrets and corner store snacks. "If I said not to go, would you have left?"

She stood rigid as he posed another question. "What if I asked you not to leave?"

"What if I said I was afraid you didn't feel the same?" Inching forward, his voice quivered, exposing his vulnerability. The moon's rays filtered through the towering monuments, illuminating their faces in a moment of uncertainty.

"I don't know, but you could have tried! You're asking about hypotheticals I can't answer."

He took another stride. Placing his hands flat on the wall behind her, one on either side of her neck, he leaned in until their foreheads touched. "What if I told you my every thought is consumed by you? From the hour I wake until I close my eyes, there's nothing I desire more than you. Your scent comforts and haunts me."

"I. Don't. Know." His hot breath fanned her cheek. Seeking to restrain her quivering limbs, she focused on regulating her heartbeat. But all attempts to disguise her hunger were futile when he opened his eyes, pinning her with his ferocity. She was helpless under his spell. "Because you never said any of those things."

In a fluid movement, he pushed off the blocks and disengaged, running his fingers through his hair. He peered above the buildings, scanning for surveillance. Thankfully, the area was void of Big Brother's watchful eye. Years of rigorous instruction instilled the importance of maintaining a professional image. Even if he ignored his training, openly expressing his honesty would draw unwanted attention.

Moonbeams cast a subtle aurora, illuminating her messy beauty. He ached to match her chaos, to dive into her energy until he couldn't distinguish his existence from hers. He yearned to redefine idyllic love, paralyzing heartache, and quintessential attraction with her. He wanted to be the one who made her heart skip a beat, who left her breathless, and who was the singular piece of poetry on her lips. And he had a solitary chance to make an impact.

Speaking was a hazard with the possibility of regret, but it was a risk he was willing to take. "When I'm with you, my heart ignites like fireworks, popping and crackling with a force I can't control. You awakened something dormant inside me. Each day is a new adventure, and like a child on Christmas morning, I can't wait to unwrap every layer of you. Once, I dreamed of winning awards, but now all I want is you."

Her mouth fell open; she never expected a confession. She cared for him but wondered about the true depths of his nature, aspiring to unravel his stratified pneuma beyond the facade she was familiar with.

He bounced his leg, unable to predict how she would react to his testimony. Was shock a good thing or a bad thing? He cleared his throat and unleashed wanton ramblings, unsure how bottomless they were. "My life was a perpetual stream, drifting aimlessly without purpose or direction. You came along, and now I'm swimming, sometimes drowning in the intensity. Like a breath underwater, you leave me gasping."

Verbosity saddled his tongue, infused with raw devotion. He knew he was confessing too much, but the words continued to tumble. "I'm drowning in you, and I don't want to be saved."

Her eyes widened, the light catching tiny flecks of the gold halo inside her irises. "Hanjun, you were never alone."

Pandering to recklessness, his body knocked into hers, pinning her against the wall. He seized her wrists and held them above her head, his hungry mouth tracing her jawline. In a fevered whisper, he gasped another avowal. "If I'm going under, I want it to be with you."

Her eyes fell, drunk from the thrill of his warm, pillowy lips on her cool, wet skin. Sticky honey and acidic lemon, once lingering on her sheets, ignited a firestorm of prurience. He compressed her with unyielding strength, detonating shocks through her extremities, while the jagged brick left scratches on her back as a reminder of their unbosoming.

"Junie..." The nickname slipped from her lips—sugary poison laced with seduction. Softened kisses coursed her artery, coaxing moans of pleasure. "Why didn't you say anything?"

His calloused palms confirmed his determination to trap her. They were from different worlds, their paths diverging at every turn. The gap between what the public deemed acceptable and what he desired was vast. "I was scared."

Releasing her wrist, his hand trailed the curves of her frame, propelling a shudder through her column. At the same time, his knee rose between her legs, and a gasp gushed from her as the skirt of her dress drifted upwards, revealing smooth, stockinged thighs.

"We shouldn't do this here." Her exhalation was a desperate plea.

Hooking her waist, his fiery breath warmed her ear. "Do you want me to stop?"

"Never." She bent at the knees, feening for the moment his hands slid under her skirt, but her conscience chimed in. "What if someone sees us?"

"I don't care." A dangerous growl rocked her chest; his voice was unlike anything she had ever heard from him, and it made her knees tremble. Reveling beneath his weight, she knew they wouldn't leave the backstreet without indulging in a handful of delicious sins.

Dappling her with gentle, feather-light kisses, he traveled along her neck, rendering sizzling heat in his wake. His hands breezed up her skirt, resting on the outer edge of her bottom. Pushing his groin into hers, the pressure between her legs sent throbs through her pelvis and into her breasts. She was swathed in the sensation of his hands slipping under the thin fabric of her panties. He unknowingly tugged at the lace of her stockings, contrasting velvety skin with textured palms.

Pulling away, his sight rested on her. Her rosy lips glistened with moisture from pleasured nibbling, and her cheeks were flushed. Giving her hips a squeeze, he nuzzled her jaw, trailing a hand between her thighs. "You can tell me to stop."

"I don't want you to stop." His hand migrated under her dress, and she gave into vulnerability. In that moment, and possibly forever, she was his. Hands whisking inside his coat, she yanked him close enough to consume. She wanted him—all of him—inside of her in every way a person could be inside someone else. She'd erase every fear that kept him up at night and haunt him with something much more stimulating. With enough time to untangle his guises, she would become the embodiment of his wildest fantasies.

The moment his fingers grazed the trim of her panties, she was jarred out of her intense sexual trance. Hearing a resonant voice holler in a language she didn't understand, her eyes flew open, and bursts of flashes flooded her vision with black dots.

Realizing they were ambushed, Hanjun extended his arms to shield her face from the cameras. He hoped to at least blur the photos or spare her from the inevitable humiliation of being plastered on every media feed in the modern world. "Jen, listen to me. Keep your head down and run on three, okay?"

"O-okay." Blinking, she nodded.

"One...two..." The third number left his lungs, and they bolted in the direction they entered, evading the ticking bomb threatening to expose their amorous crimes.

Staggering at a dizzying speed, she gripped his hand. "W-what's happening?"

"Ask questions later!" Tugging her along, he noticed her struggling in the pumps, her violent clicks against the pavement echoing like gunshots. "Leave them behind!"

Releasing his hand, she hopped on one leg, kicking off her shoes in opposite directions. "Those were five hundred dollars! You owe me a new pair!"

"*Only* five hundred?" His laugh mimicked hers. "I can't buy you a new pair. I'll explain why later. How about a handbag?"

"Yes, *only* five hundred. They were thrifted! Do I look like the kind of girl who spends a grand on shoes?"

His eyes swept her figure. "When you're in them, yes!"

The damp air teemed with their infectious giggles as they burst from the alleyway into the street. Hands clasped, they splashed each other with puddles formed in the roads.

"From now on, I'm sewing weights into my dresses!" Running alongside him, she gathered the hem of her dress, preventing it from billowing.

Passing a crosswalk, he peeled off his outerwear and dumped it onto a tree branch, hoping to fool anyone who recognized him. "I'm gonna miss that jacket!"

Interweaving the congested streets, they darted past mom-and-pop shops with colorful window displays. The sidewalks were crowded, forcing them to dodge throngs of pedestrians. Tantalizing fried treats from street carts warmed their bellies amid the chilly weather.

Slowing to a leisurely walk, he gripped her sleeve. "I think we lost them."

"What the hell was that?" Holding a hand over her wildly thumping heart, she couldn't determine what caused her blood to pump faster—the unexpected make-out session in the shadows or their narrow escape.

Shaking water from his clothes, his pitch strained. "It's not common, but we have the occasional stalker."

Weighing the damage their indiscretions could have on his reputation made her feel sick. It wasn't a secret; he was *somebody* in Seoul. She was nobody. "I'm sorry."

"Don't be." He bumped his shoulder into hers, savoring the electricity sparking between them. Laughter fading, he admired her; her hair was flattened, and her visage turned rosy from their frenzied sprint. The moments he spent with his body pressed against hers left a lasting imprint, and he knew he would be chasing the dragon for a long time. "I lost myself in the moment. That's not your fault."

CHAPTER THIRTEEN

Celebrity Stalker Haeseong

Releasing a combined exhalation of pent-up breath, they reached the safety of their complex. Jen's feet were clad in flimsy rubber sandals purchased from a roadside vendor, thanks to a small advance from Hanjun. He volunteered to buy a quality pair, but she declined, determined to make it home before they encountered additional paparazzo.

Drenched from head to toe, they tramped through the relentless storm. Accosted by kind-hearted Windsor Heights guards, they accepted cups of coffee, hand warmers, and blankets to cocoon their shivering bodies. The building provided warmth, though the silence was only broken by the rustling of their clothes as they staggered to opposite sides of the hallway.

As Hanjun fumbled with his passcode, she tugged at his arm. "What if that photographer managed to get a picture of us? What will your bandmates think?"

He stitched together a response. "We'll tell them the truth."

"Tell them what? I don't know what this is. What *are* we?"

A forced smile forsook his angst. "I wish I could give you clarity. All I know is that I like being around you."

"What do you want us to be?" She searched his eyes for an answer.

He stroked her temple, brushing a lock of hair from her cheek. "Whatever we're meant to be."

★⁺₊★☾★⁺₊★

Three of the roommates huddled near the door, watching the love-struck couple through the peephole. They giggled at their gestures, moved by flirtation in its purest form.

Soogi bumped Jin out of the way, narrating in expressive detail. "Jen has puppy-dog eyes. Hanjun's smile is suave but sorrowful. She's shaking her head; there's a hint of sadness."

"No fair!" Jin stomped a foot.

The youngest flattened against a wall, roleplaying the lovers. Embodying Hanjun, he feigned desire, speaking as if there were someone shuddering under his breath. "If anyone discovers our secret, we'll be in grave danger."

"*Danger?*" With a shift of posture, he became Jen, all innocent and demure. Emitting a falsetto scream, he clutched an imaginary string of pearls. "That's so—"

Twirling to embody Hanjun, he ran a finger down the curve of his own cheek. "Sexy?"

"Oh my!" Releasing a squeal, his eyelashes fluttered. Collapsing to his knees, he personified a fainting damsel.

Jin sat on the edge of his seat, watching the performance unfold. Wanting to join the drama, he nabbed two theoretical trophies, small and insignificant, from the console table. "Gentlemen and gentlemen, it is my honor to announce the recipient of two Blue Dragon Awards. The winner for best lead actor and actress goes to... Ha Deok-Sun!"

Bowing and thanking, Deok-Sun accepted the prizes. "I never thought I'd win the two sculptures that have been sitting on the entry table since we moved in. I'd like to thank my parents for believing in me. I'd also like to thank Jenilyn and Hanjun; without them, there would have been no characters to play."

"Wrap it up before they get inside." Soogi sliced through the boisterous cheers of his companions. "They're hugging."

"Let me see!" Jin jostled him out of the way, peering through the hole.

Hanso pulled a comic from the coffee table. "You've had your fun. Leave them alone."

Though he refrained from vocalizing his opinion, he found the blossoming couple endearing. Despite forming a mild crush on Jen after their initial introduction, he was happy for Hanjun. He couldn't deny Hanjun transformed around Jen, contrasting his guarded, egotistical persona. Witnessing innocent Hanjun—before the pressures of fame affected his mental health—make a reappearance engorged him with faith in the future.

But underneath was a gnawing, persistent worry: a successful fling would drive Blackmirror to purgatory until the couple reached a state of heaven or hell. Hanjun, who struggled with artist's block, found influence in Jen. She radiated originality, and he sought her, hoping she would lubricate ideas. And Hanso saw it—the way Hanjun anticipated a boost to his craft.

Hanjun crushed on their liaison—the glue burdened with holding their band together. It might not have been so daunting if they didn't also share a home. Blissful living, working, and dating in close quarters would only last as long as the courtship did. The eventual breakup would bring nothing but confusion to the arrangement.

A seasoned vocalist, Hanso believed artist-muse relationships were catastrophic. Would their dynamic align with the age-old trope—a submissive object of beauty, shaped and controlled by the musician? Or would they take a modern approach, with both visions steering the process? But the thought that filled him with the most dread was the possibility of their roles reversing, with the catalyst reigning over the art, making it impossible for him to create without her.

Jen was anything but passive. Should their attraction develop, their collaboration would either be one of harmony, where their energies aligned seamlessly—or they would find unconventional stimulation by challenging each other's boundaries. No matter how their relationship unfolded, Hanso was certain of one thing: Hanjun would change, for the better or for the worse. He hoped, for Hanjun's sake, it would be for the better.

⋆⁺₊⋆☾⋆⁺₊⋆

Hanjun's arms gathered around Jen, whispering words of comfort in an uncomfortable situation. "It's okay if you don't want to be something more."

"It's not that I don't want to—" Heart aching, she hugged his waist. "I don't want to come between you and your group."

Unspoken but undeniable, she had no intentions of becoming the next Yoko Ono—a scapegoat for the group's eventual disbandment. She recognized the warning signs from a mile away: a dominant pop act and their massive fan base—one of which assumed they were a unit that could only be fragmented by external forces. Their popularity was so overblown that they infiltrated daily life. Their music played on every station. Their faces blessed every magazine. Every interviewer vied to have them on their couch, and every fan clamored for tickets to their sold-out shows. Love them or hate them, everybody knew Blackmirror.

Frustrated at their predicament, he turned for the door. "They have no choice but to accept whatever decision you make."

Chatter emanating from inside the home hushed, tingling Jen's suspicions. "It's way too quiet..."

"Hanjun-Hyung, you're popular!" Popping up from the sofa, Jin presented his phone, displaying a journalist-taken snap. On the screen, Hanjun conjoined a curvaceous woman, their forms entwined in provocative poise. "It's trending on every social platform."

"Yeah, I figured." Hanjun's shoulders slumped; he had let down his team, and the repercussions would be far-reaching. In a matter of hours, the incident would trigger national interest, and the company would have to allocate an army of experts to mitigate the fallout.

Stifling their snickers, Jin and Deok-Sun rose from their seats. Pinning each other to the wall, they exchanged suggestive glances and mockingly gazed into each other's eyes. Soogi clapped, egging them on.

Hanso's eyes remained on his phone, scrolling through a stream of breaking news stories. Discharging a sharp breath, he silenced the giggles. "The paparazzi who tailed Hanjun..."

Gulping, he finished the statement. "Was Haeseong."

Amid the reenactment, Deok-Sun froze. "*Haeseong?*"

Releasing a dam of profanities, a cold wave of terror penetrated Hanjun's heart. "Shit, I didn't know we were followed."

Confused by the cryptic exchange, Jen interjected. "What's going on? Who's Haeseong?"

Soogi offered an explanation when nobody else would. "Haeseong is a stalker. He's named after an anti-ship cruise missile because of his sneaky nature and expertise in repeated attacks. He hunts for controversies, and once he uncovers one, he uses the evidence to destroy the celebrities he obsessively follows."

"Why would he stalk Hanjun?" Deok-Sun's innocent question stirred an offended glare from Hanjun. "I mean, he usually follows me or Jin."

"And it gets worse..." Hanso recounted Haeseong's claims of stumbling upon the jacket Hanjun wore in the scandalous photos, hanging from a branch outside a bistro. He also found Jimmy Choo mesh overlay pumps, size thirty-six, abandoned on the sidewalk.

Jin snatched the phone, reading the article aloud. "The hunt for '*Seoul's Cinderella*' is on—hundreds of women have stepped forward, insisting they're the woman in the photo."

Standing barefoot on the heated floor, Jen vividly remembered ditching her shoes. Rubbing her right foot against her left calf, fire slithered up her body. "What should we do?"

Hanjun shook his head. "There's no one more adept at safeguarding their artist's anonymity than J&I."

Having faced privacy violations twice in the same night, the throbbing ache in her lungs magnified. As a non-artist, she doubted J&I would protect her. "Do you mind if I take a bath? I know it's asking a lot to confiscate an entire bathroom."

Met with several answers, none of which objected, she jetted to the hall. Hanjun shadowed her, sensing her anxiety. "Is there anything I can do?"

"No, I don't think there is." Turning to face him, a thought sparked in her mind. "Actually, can I borrow your wireless speaker? I've been meaning to purchase one."

"Of course." He retrieved the speaker from his room. Their hands brushed during the trade-off, and he experienced a pang of regret. He wanted to apologize for the intrusion and even more so for their intimate moment coming to an end, but he couldn't find the right words. The fire, the passion, and the connection dissolved with the precipitation.

Closing the door, she unzipped her dress. Once elegant, the soaked fabric asphyxiated her body. Stripping off layers of clothing, she was liberated from the heft of her actions. The person in that backstreet was her, although much heavier. Metaphorically and literally. That woman was darker than she'd ever known herself to be. To crave another was terrifyingly addicting, and she would have set the world ablaze if he asked her to.

Perched on the side of the standalone tub, she poured in a handful of the bath salts Deok-Sun had gifted her. Watching the crystals melt into a swirl of pink and purple, she wondered why she was so allured by Hanjun. Fleeting attractions went against everything she knew, but then again, she hadn't been herself since before the divorce. "Maybe *this* is who I am."

Easing into the water, she paired her phone and cued a playlist of 90s slow jams. Feeling betrayed by her urges, she had lost all sense of morality in that alley; she wanted him so badly that she didn't care where they were.

Immersed in the bubbles, she inhaled the intoxicating scent of ylang-ylang. The aroma was sweet, conjuring memories of Hanjun. She sealed her eyes; every sensation from the evening was a monument to him. The dark passage where they solidified their confessions and the rainy streets where they made their getaway. Bright moonlight which drove their affairs and the glow of the streetlights as they dodged crowds. Rough brick drilling into her back and how his hands gripped her thighs. Everything reminded her of him.

Settled on his bed, Hanjun reached for an old notebook, tattered from years of use and abuse. Typically, when it came to songwriting, he would begin with a melody. But that time was different; brilliance flowed from him in the form of gospel.

> *You're a little dark*
> *I'm learning I'm dark, too*
> *Honestly, I could be a little darker*
> *If it meant I could be dark with you*

Eyes lingering on the refrain, a rush of exhilaration shattered the dam suppressing his creativity. After spending a single night with Jen, he felt unmistakable change. Threading the pen through the coil binding, he was transported to a time when emotion oozed from every pore, enabling him to write songs in minutes and albums in weeks.

It was a peculiar thing, success. In the beginning, it drove him to overcome obstacles, tick off lists, and achieve milestones. But as he ascended the ladder of accomplishment, there were fewer mountains to conquer. In such an esteemed stature, there was little room for growth without forging a new path.

His life stretched into the abyss. One monotonous day blending into the next, he trudged through an existence lacking purpose. His responsibilities kept him from quitting, while sustaining a life he despised sapped his will to participate and, in grim times, live. Like all tortured souls, he leveraged his assets to fill the void: booze, stimulants, sex workers—nothing cured his self-destruction. Nothing inspired him like Jen did.

Biting his lip, he considered what she could be to him if he opened his heart; she could be *the one* or the one to break him. She held the potential to be *the last* or the last time he loved again. She could be his savior or his downfall, and neither he nor she knew which she'd be. Ink to page, he wove a novella of uncertainty.

Can you love me in the deep?
In the dark?
Can you love the me who has no heart?
Could you love the real me?

Most can't ignore the fantasy
It's why the only thing I love is art
Will you love me when I'm too much?
When I don't know if I want love?

In the thick of it, it's ridiculous
What about when you find out I'm a lie?
And you won't have anywhere to hide
And when you're sick of it?

My presence may scorch you like the sun
At my best, I'm second to none
Can you love me if I'm bigger than you?
What about when it's too hard to look at me?

When I'm dragged through bad publicity
And they highlight everything wrong with me
What will you see?
Who I am, or who they make me out to be?

"That's why I can't let you see the real me." The rhyme dried, evidence of his internal turmoil. He placed the worn book aside, questioning if the poem captured the scale of his angst when muffled ringing caught his attention. Trekking to the bathroom, he pressed an ear against the door. "Jen? Are you alright?"

★⁺₊★☾★⁺₊★

Jen's phone buzzed, but she paid no mind. Nobody needed her at the late hour. Her roomies were safe in the condo. Her friends back home were sleeping or just waking up for the day. And she certainly wasn't ruining a hot soak for a spam call.

Scented water blanketed her body, and her daydreaming drifted to Hanjun, with his lips on her shoulder and his palms roaming her thighs. She was weak for him—a slave to her desires—and she considered ending the illicit affair, knowing it would end disastrously.

Trickling drops of water over her neck, flashbacks invaded her mind—his tender kisses along her breasts and his hands grazing her hips. Recalling the fragrance of his hair—honey mixed with milky shampoo—her core thrummed. Tracing the dip in her chest, she imagined it was his touch. Instinctively, she descended to her stomach, relishing the heat radiating from within. Eyes closing, she surrendered to the fantasy. Her fingers traveled over her thighs, following the same rhythms he had shown her. A symphony of pleasure swelled, building until she was trembling, the sloshing water driving her toward bliss.

Ascending to her climax, a concerned voice pricked through the barrier, jolting her back to reality. The lust vanished—a cruel souvenir of ecstasy she hadn't experienced. Gasping, she fled from the water, wet hair plastered to her face. Stretching for a towel, she left watery prints on the floor and flung the door open. "Jun!? What the fuck?"

Startled by her nudity, he averted his gaze. "I was worried."

"I'm fine." Yep. Totally fine. It's not like the best orgasm of her life was interrupted by the man who caused it or anything.

Revolving to face away, he broke into a nervous laugh. "I heard splashing. I thought something may have happened."

"It was about to." Huffing, she slipped into pajamas. "You can turn around."

He swiveled to face her. Curled strands fell in front of her eyes, and her breathing remained suspiciously labored. He sent her a smug smirk, knowing exactly what she was up to. "Were you thinking about me?"

A rosy flush crept up her cheeks, provoking a bashful giggle. Breezing past him, she stood at her bedroom door and motioned for him to accompany her. "Come on."

Without a moment's hesitation, he followed her to the bed. "You don't have to tell me twice."

Settling under the covers, she turned her wrists towards him, revealing red imprints. "I noticed this earlier."

He traced the prominent marks, lingering over her veins. "I had no idea I squeezed you so hard. Did I hurt you?"

She coquettishly leaned in to avoid being overheard. "It's a little sore, but it felt good at the time."

"Let me make it better for you." He left a trail of kisses on her carpus, intensifying with gentle suction.

Sexual ferocity returned, and she wondered if he knew the control he had over her. He exploded her inner galaxy into a million cosmic pieces, though she suffered a tinge of forbidden lover's guilt. "I'm sorry for causing you trouble."

Caressing her wrist, he refused the apology. "You aren't the one painting me as a villain."

"I shouldn't have put you in that position."

A wry smirk tweaked his lips. "If I remember correctly, *I* was the one who put *you* in that position."

Her lashes fluttered, hiding her fluster. "If I'm honest, I don't even know who that girl was. It couldn't have been me."

Rubbing her chin with his thumb, he paralleled her anxiety. "The night has a way of making us believe our indiscretions will go unnoticed, doesn't it?"

<u>CHAPTER FOURTEEN</u>

Constancy

The first rays of dawn peeked through the windows of Jen's room, stirring Hanjun awake. Trudging to the kitchen, he started a pot of coffee, and while waiting for the first drip, he backpedaled to his room. He retrieved his phone from the bedside table, finding the group chat extended well into the morning.

> **Jinja:** I'm glad Jen isn't dating Hyun.
> **Soogins:** Me too.
> **Jinja:** A real bro, Soogi.
> **Honsa:** She always had eyes for Jun.
> **Sunnie:** None of you had a chance!

Despite journalists threatening to destroy Blackmirror's reputation, the mates stood by him without judgment. Roosting on the bed, he pulled his journal from the nightstand.

> *Her date was awful. As much as I hate how much it stressed her, I'm happy it was. She asked what we were to each other. I don't know, but I'd like to.*

Jonesing for the moment caffeine hit his veins, he returned to the kitchen and reached for a mug. Pouring a generous serving, he caught a glimpse of Jen in the auxiliary kitchen. Hunched over near the receptacle, she was stuffing something inside a trash bag, and as he approached, he discovered it was the black dress from the previous evening. "You're up early."

Wrestling the poofy garment into the opening, she groaned. "I would rather burn it, but we don't have a fire pit."

Pulling the frock from her hands, he inspected the fabric. "Why are you getting rid of it? It looked pretty on you."

"If I wear it again, people will connect the dots." Fondling the allover lace motif, she felt a prick of guilt. "I would have preferred to donate it, but I'm afraid of what will happen. They already found the shoes I was wearing; imagine if they find the dress, too."

Folding the dress into a neat pile, he placed it under his arm. "You're not getting rid of it. We'll hide it until the press forgets."

Scoffing, she met his cool expression. "What if they don't forget?"

"They always forget." He appeared bare-faced and well-rested. Unwarranted, considering the havoc generated in his name.

Trusting that he knew what he was doing, she yielded. "Aren't you the least bit worried? Haeseong sounds ruthless."

Returning to his coffee at the table, he lifted the porcelain vessel to his lips. "The agency will handle unwanted publicity."

She slumped into a chair. "Let's hope so."

He purposely bumped her shoulder. "J&I knows how to tackle Haeseong."

★⁺₊★☾★⁺₊★

It had become a ritual for the roommates to prepare dinner every night. For the first time, Jen stood front and center with an antsy grin. "I'm making one of my favorites—wonton tacos. They're slightly Asian-inspired—I first tried them at Applebee's, but they were taken off the menu."

She furnished her phone, presenting an enticing image of the purposed meal: delicate, golden wraps packed with tender chunks of tangy chicken, balanced with zesty coleslaw.

Deok-Sun eyeballed the delicacy. "I could eat a dozen."

"We'll make extra." Floating through the kitchen, she separated ingredients into filler and slaw. "I tweaked the recipe, and they are delicious. Way better than the restaurant."

While she cooked the protein and crisped the wrappers into u-shaped shells, the remaining companions whipped up the topping. Adding a wrapper to a pan of hot oil, she wiggled the dough back and forth with a pair of tongs. "The secret to crispy shells is to aerate the dough. The faster you shake, the crispier the texture."

Jin peeled apart the wrappers for her. "Can we use the leftovers to make dumplings?"

"We can make whatever you like." She transferred the crunchy shells to six dishes. "We can also make cinnamon sugar crisps."

Hanjun perked up at the suggestion. "Cinnamon sugar?"

She spooned two tablespoons of meat into the fried shells, dressing each with a sizeable dollop of cabbage. "You cut them into strips, fry until crisp, and toss them in a bowl of cinnamon sugar. They're addictive."

Deok-Sun salivated. "I vote we do that."

Jin stomped a foot. "No fair! If it's anything like cinnamon chips, Hanjun will leave us with crumbs!"

Hanjun feigned offense. "I will not!"

She tittered. "I'll make sure you get your own portion."

"Thanks!" Hanging his tongue out, Jin taunted Hanjun.

Ignoring the ribbing, she doled out plates piled high. "It's okay if you don't like it. I can always make something else."

Deok-Sun and Hanjun were the first to try, although Hanjun was more reluctant. Hanjun and Jin were the pickiest eaters, scrunching their noses at anything unconventional. Deok-Sun and Soogi ate just about anything. Hanso wavered somewhere between picky and adventurous, poking at his food before braving a sample.

Deok-Sun shoveled an entire taco into his mouth, relishing the satisfying crunch and zingy relish. "It's so good!"

Hanjun nibbled a small bite, his sight rolling to the ceiling. "Oh my god."

Deok-Sun jabbed at him. "Be careful around Hanjun. You could lose a finger if he's hungry enough."

Chewing a mouthful, Jin wrapped an arm around Jen's. "Marry me and make this moment last forever."

She swatted his hand. "I'll make it whenever you want, but I won't marry you."

Hanso roared, gesturing to Jin. "That's it! From now on, we must ask Jen to wed us at random."

"Please, no." Hanjun covered his face with his palms; whenever the friends found something to annoy him with, the jesting turned into a daily part of his life.

Deok-Sun chuckled. "Too late! It's been established!"

After dinner, Soogi lounged on the short end of the sofa with Hanso at his side. Deok-Sun sandwiched Jen near the arm. Jin settled onto the floor, nestled between Jen's knees, rolling his head around on her thighs in hopes she'd rub his hair.

Though the television blared, each roommate occupied themselves with personal activities. Hanjun exhausted his free time on various social media platforms. Hanso spent much of his spare time on TikTok, and when he wasn't watching reels, he was immersed in a pile of comics he left on the side table. Soogi was most likely to control the television, though he did more channel surfing than actual watching. Jin usually chatted his way through the evening with a bottle of wine by his side. And Deok-Sun sought out fan-created content, using ghost accounts across multiple platforms.

"Check out this edit." Deok-Sun paraded a recent fan creation: Soogi's head superimposed onto a muscular body.

"That doesn't look anything like me." Scoffing, he swiped the photo out of his face. "Why would someone do that?"

"Art creates fans, and fans create fan art." Jin snickered.

Vaguely listening to a debate on whether delusory artwork was flattering or depreciating, Jen flipped a page of her book. *Ivanhoe* by Sir Walter Scott. She clutched the cover; dusty and dull in a plain binding, the faded insides were a stark contrast to the contemporary narrations crammed on store shelves. There was something alluring about the high drama and elegant prose—modern authors simply couldn't compare.

She vividly remembered the moment she plucked the tome from the highest shelf of one of Seoul's oldest bookstores. Tucked among traditional hanok houses, the exterior remained untouched; clay roof tiles and vintage sliding inlets served as a testament to longevity. Inside, a transformation had taken place, though the gallery-turned-café was renovated to maintain its historic charm.

The signboard proudly displayed the origins of the beloved bookstore; inaugurated during a time when new works were luxuries, the bookshop was renowned for trading old texts. But as the community embraced modernization, the demand for used literature dwindled, and the store's business suffered. After the original owner passed, his bereaved wife kept the shop open, even in times of hardship.

A high-pitched, ten-thousand hertz ringtone penetrated through her reading—one she cherry-picked for her ex. Placing the book face down on her lap, she begrudgingly answered. "What do you want?"

The voice on the other end dripped with jealousy. "Is that you all over Twitter? The mysterious girl in the black dress linked with Ryu Hanjun?"

She maintained composure. "I don't know what you're—"

"Is that the new job you claim to have? Sleeping your way through an Asian boy band?"

Her fury sparked. "Why did you have to say it like that?"

Hanso's eyes darkened. "Her job doesn't involve you."

Dripping in hatred, the man ranted about her supposed poor choices. "You're such a whore!"

Pressing a palm against her temple, she waited for him to end his petty rant. In a customary tirade, he often accused her of promiscuity. The insults didn't sting as much as they once did. Insignificant, he was nothing more than an annoyance.

Hearing the disrespectful term, Hanjun snatched the phone from her hand, barking into the microphone. "From now on, you'll talk to me. Do not talk to, at, or about her. As far as you're concerned, she doesn't exist."

Jin's gaze drifted to the phone, hinting at a solution. "You need a new number."

"I haven't blocked him because our previous residence isn't sold." She ruffled his hair. "I'm sorry you heard that."

From behind a horror manga, Hanso chimed in. "It's not the first time we've encountered blatant xenophobia, Jen."

Deok-Sun's expression twisted into puzzlement. "How did you end up with that guy? He sounds awful."

Hanjun smacked Deok-Sun on the arm. "Can we forget about him?"

Jen shook her head. "I was young and naive, and he was deceiving."

"How did you not know he was a racist piece of shit?" Hanjun physically reprimanded him, but Deok-Sun said his peace. Afterward, he repaid the favor with a rough tap to Hanjun's calf. "It's a legitimate question."

"He seemed interested in different cultures. We connected over anime and frequented Moroccan, Mongolian, and Peruvian diners. We dreamed of traveling, or so I thought—it turns out, he only agreed with the idea and never planned to leave the country." Tsking, she grabbed Jin's hand as if she were apologizing to him. "It wasn't until two years into the union that I saw the truth. He was all too eager to indulge in foreign tradition when it suited his interests, but when it didn't, he was wildly intolerant."

Jin was hesitant to hear more. "How did you know?"

"He attacked my passions and then escalated to personal attacks. I always wanted to visit Japan, but he shut it down. I asked him to learn Chikashshanompa—"

Deok-Sun intervened. "What's chickie-sham-oppa?"

"Chikashshanompa is my great-grandmother's native language. One she taught me as a child." She paused while Deok-Sun replicated the word. Hanjun helped him with each sound cluster. "The spoken word is nearly extinct, and he alleged it was too far gone, which ironically, so was the marriage."

She laughed at her joke and glanced at Jin. "He didn't understand why it meant so much to me. I wasn't close to my English-speaking parents but was to my first generation German and Hungarian grandparents, along with my Chickasaw-speaking grandparents. The words, phrases, and syntax I use are sometimes strange, and I unintentionally flip them. We'd get into the stupidest arguments over pronunciation or verb-subject subject-verb. He was pedantic, revising as if he were a college professor. American English and European English are not the same, but he viewed his as the only correct way and tried to intimidate me."

Jin buried his face in her shoulder. "I'm sorry."

"It's not your fault, Jinnie. The first time I noticed was when he formed contempt for Tisho. After he said something about indigenous people needing to adapt to the American way of life, Tisho refused to speak to him in anything other than the mother tongue. And in Chikashshanompa, Tisho clarified everything wrong with what he said, knowing he couldn't understand a word. How his laughter proved his ignorance, and how schools erected to tutor so-called savages into humans were bordered with the mass graves of our ancestors. How those with guns infiltrated the holy lands with diseases and then blamed us for being the problem. There was rivalry; my ex was resentful that I didn't remove Tisho from my life. But how could I? Eliminating Tisho would erase a part of my heritage, and I refuse to strip him of his dignity. Anyone who thinks he doesn't deserve a place in my life doesn't know me."

Soogi, who remained silent throughout the exchange, offered advice to guide her future interactions. "When you share an unfamiliar culture with outsiders to give the history of the land—the traditions, the dances, the customs—people stumble because they have no ground. Let them fall."

"Hindsight brings clarity." Her smile flickered, fading just as fast. "His intolerance reared its hideous head once again when global artists began dominating the charts. The mere mention of K-pop or J-pop would send him into a frenzy. You won't believe this, but I was given tickets to your earliest gig in Chicago."

Mirages flooded Deok-Sun's mind—a time of grand ambiguity. "That was a rough time."

Before Blackmirror skyrocketed to international fame, they performed in small venues for their limited fandom. Regardless of their talent and undeniable presence, they failed to fill a modest hall. Hysteria ensued as Blackmirror's management, crew, and parents scrambled to hand out wristbands to anyone who would take them. It was a humbling experience overlooked by those who couldn't remember when their songs weren't popular, but for those who were there from the beginning, the hard times were cherished memories.

"You were at our Chicago concert?" Jin tugged at her shirt.

"Sure wasn't. My ex had a certain animosity toward anything mainstream. It was odd since he knew so much about it. I only knew what was on the radio, but somehow he knew about Blackmirror before most of the country."

Hanjun shook his head. "People will find reasons to hate."

Hanso sloped forward. "What happened?"

"When I expressed interest in going, we got into this huge argument where he accused me of having an affair with an Asian man. It was so out of left field; I didn't know what to say.

I shouldn't have to explain why I found entertainment intriguing. Why does anyone like anything? But the hatred he held for people he didn't know—and his sheer disdain harbored for an act I didn't follow—were off-putting, especially since he had a preference for Chinese cam girls."

Reliving difficult days, her larynx trembled. "I didn't think much of his bias. It's not my place to dictate what someone finds appealing or be offended on someone's behalf. But it wasn't long before I discovered the reason behind his hostility: he was attracted to stereotypical innocence, and anytime I asserted autonomy, I was challenging his archetypal perspective. Lotus nor dragon, I defied his moral contagion."

Deok-Sun's voice lowered. "You didn't notice before?"

"I can't excuse not seeing something right in front of my eyes. I was focused on creating a life. The time we had together revolved around his pastimes. Watching movies, playing games, and keeping up with the latest TV shows weren't activities I was familiar with. But for him, they were part of his childhood. The same goes for music. He favored death metal, while I leaned towards hip-hop and pop-punk. However, as two kids who grew up in the 90s and 2000s, we bonded over bands from our youth.

"And I'll be honest—I'm not one to battle for supremacy over trivial things like what music to listen to or what movie to watch. I go with the flow, and some may see me as a pushover, but that couldn't be further from the truth. When it comes to something I feel strongly about, I will fight until the end. And that's why it crumbled—because the moment I started finding who I was, he tried to stop me."

Recording memos on his phone, Hanjun listened to her musings. Intrigued by her love of novelty and thirst for knowledge—something he couldn't tire of—he made a mental note to keep an open eye for what mattered to her. The causes she pursued without prompting—that was where her love lied.

Jin clung to her arm. "Teach me Chicka-shimmy-opa?"

She brushed unruly bangs from his forehead. "Of course. Your first lesson is, 'Chihollo'li.'"

"What does it mean?"

"I love you." Following her answer, the companions repeated the word enough times to rival a native speaker.

Hanjun backtracked; the thought weighed on his mind since she mentioned the concert. "Why didn't you go to the show?"

Smile faltering, she recalled the disappointing turn of events. "The tickets were destroyed in the wash. I left them in my pocket, and he took it upon himself to start a load of laundry. This was a man who barely washed a dish. I swear he believed his clothes magically emerged in the closet, folded and ready to wear."

Jin gasped. "He ruined them *on purpose?*"

"He said he didn't, but he said he didn't do a lot of things he did."

Hanso slowly lowered his comic from eye level. "Wait. There were supposed to be five backstage passes handed out by our parents, but only four showed."

The clues started to fall into place for Deok-Sun. "Jen met our parents! Well, at least one set of our parents."

"It couldn't have been mine," Jin interjected. "They gave theirs to the first people they saw."

Soogi added his opinion. "If you recall, the tickets were for a giveaway, but we didn't have enough people show up, so we distributed them to anyone who would take one."

Jin's eyes dilated. "I remember! The winners had holographic tribars, only visible under black light."

Hanso tapped a staccato rhythm on his chin. "I always wondered what happened to the last VIP. Perhaps the ticket was misplaced or carried off by the wind—"

Jin mirrored Hanso's concern. "Or maybe they didn't want to see us perform."

The words hung heavy—a fear for performers in any era—but Deok-Sun elevated the mood. "We found the fifth!"

Jin giggled, tossing his arms around her neck. "It took years, but we finally found the missing VIP!"

★⁺₊★☾★⁺₊★

Lying in bed, Jen's blood boiled at the hypocrisy surrounding sexuality, courtship, and vagary. How dare he judge her? What two or more consenting adults did behind closed doors shouldn't have been a contentious issue.

"Even if I were entertaining all of them, it's none of his business." Eyes fixed on the ceiling's textured surface, she cracked into a spiteful laugh. "Maybe his next lover will *enjoy* subpar sex and calculated mediocrity."

She wanted to feel scornful, but sympathy nagged at her heart, knowing the woman after her would fail to fulfill his obsession with fantasy. How could anyone compare their lovers to impractical standards and still expect to find happiness? He only desired video girls because they were something he couldn't possess. Pining over virtual women gave him synthetic strength—a facade to hide his insecurities. And while he indulged in a toxic cycle of wish fulfillment, his mate would be carnally starved.

Navigating rejection from a partner who prioritized illusion would inevitably leave the significant other plagued with conceptions of infidelity. A host of complications would arise, including a deep-seated distrust of men. Incessant self-doubt would consume their self-worth, leading them to wonder if it was their lack of attractiveness or if their partner's expectations were irrational.

She knew the torment of being that woman, torn between her contractual obligations and her primal desires. Daydreams assaulted her mind at the height of her unhappiness, and she imagined herself with lovers more than capable of leaving her satisfied. Her evasion of adultery had nothing to do with the vow she made or the love she once had; her prohibition was to protect what was left of her sanity. Her integrity outweighed a fleeting moment of hedonism. Cheating wouldn't solve the problems; it would only make an inevitable split more tumultuous. She didn't want revenge. She didn't want to hurt him. She wanted a permanent division.

A sharp, intrusive ache throbbed in her ribcage; despite wanting to shield the next from his grasp, the suffering was inevitable. His words would lull his next catch into a trap. No obvious warning signs—the kind women were coached to watch out for—would adorn him. And why should they? In his eyes, the sole cause of their divorce was her inability to conform to his dichotomy of the Madonna-whore complex. Because if she wasn't the pure, virgin Madonna, she was the filthy, defiled whore.

In Greek mythology, Persephone was a goddess of immeasurable force. She bestowed generosity, but with a single thought, she could unleash madness, destruction, and death. "Why can't I embrace domesticity *and* pleasure? I also bear the power to bring both light and darkness into the world."

Startled by a knock, she sat up to find Hanjun slinking through the doorway. Carrying a stack of binders against his chest, thick glasses framed his face. Settling next to her, he presented a series of notebooks dating back to when he was in school. "For as long as I could remember, I thought I was ugly. My eyes were different, and my complexion was too dark. I assumed I was what others thought of me. If they said it, it must be true, ya know?"

He passed her one of the logbooks. Doodles decorated the margins, a reflection of his inner turmoil. Small poems and notations were stuck between the pages, concealed treasures waiting to be exhumed. Tracing a particularly harsh scribble, she murmured. "Ugly doesn't exist. Neither does beauty."

He glared at her. Perhaps it was a sad notion, but those inky smudges were what forged his career. The ledger was more than a collection of scrawls; it was his journey through self-discovery. "Why do you say that?"

Moved by noir ideation and romanticism, she imagined him scrawling in a dimly lit room, surrounded by piles of books, scattered papers, and worksheets. His idealistic worldview was likely crushed by cold, uncaring realism shortly after. "They're nothing but creations of our making. We label things we like as attractive, believing anything we don't like is wrong. We see it in everything from music to film—beauty is subjective."

Scoffing, his pitch merged with cynicism. "I wanted to comfort you, and you comforted me."

Studying the records, she acknowledged how his handwriting grew darker over time. Flipping through, she found an eerily secluded poem. Candidly entitled '*Leave*,' the rhyming confession outlined his desire to depart from a hateful world. In poignant detail, the limerick described the challenges of school, the jeers of his peers, and his yearning for something beyond conformity. He was a brilliant mind driven to desperation by a society barring individuality. "Junie—"

"I was furious at the world. I still am, but I'm working on it." Fidgeting under vulnerability, he explained how writing became his outlet—a way to express sentiments he couldn't put into words. Through melody, he found freedom. But even then, there was a separation between the identity on display and the person behind the lyrics. On stage, he was confident and full of bravado, but he struggled with insecurity. "The truth is, I don't know what I'm doing."

Expelling a melancholic sigh, he snapped the notebook shut. "There aren't many things I can control, and the few things I can control, I cling to. Things offering stability and security. Like art. Art never erodes or degrades. Art offers constancy for me when I feel like I'm living too fast."

Looking up at her, he realized it was the first time he shared an introspective fragment of himself with anyone else. She made him feel at ease, as if his soul could relax after enduring years of unrest. Registering how much she knew about him, panic crept into his chest. She was extracting hidden parts without him noticing.

The gentle ripple of her voice pulled him back to the conversation. "Junie, are you alright? You're looking a bit pale."

"I'm okay. Great." Hastened heartbeat, widened eyes, and dry throat—his forced smile felt as if it were made of glass, ready to fracture. Every breath constricted, suffocating under awareness—he was falling crazy, head-over-heels, logic-defying, too-intense-to-put-into-words, in love with her.

Taking a shuddering breath, he willed his racing thoughts to slow. He had to focus—had to find the right words before he revealed too much. "I don't want to be consumed by anger. I don't want anyone else to go through what I did—trapped in a world that wasn't built for them."

Reaching for her hand, he reassured her. "Don't let his words define you. You know who you are."

"I won't." Retracting her arm, she shifted onto a pillow.

Scooping up the journals, he scurried to his room, spilling his reflections in a new entry.

I never want her to speak with him again, and if I
have any say, she won't have to.

CHAPTER FIFTEEN

You're Perfect

On location, Jen wore a sophisticated black and white empire-waisted blouse and raven-colored jeans, rolled at the hems. Wrists lined with spiked bangles, the outfit meshed with combat boots and a matching leather jacket.

A sprawling landscape of dying grass and trees, the filming site was scattered with lighting equipment. Scanning the surroundings, her sights landed on a curious contraption in the center—a bright blue dunk tank. Her initial reaction was one of disbelief; why were they playing in freezing water? But J&I was known for filming media up to a year in advance.

Venturing closer, she identified Blackmirror engaged in some kind of game. They were tasked with answering questions and were rewarded with a chance to dunk their fellow contestants. The incentive? A snack or drink of their choice. And as always, the mates were dressed in white.

As soon as Jin spotted her, he darted over to scrutinize her outfit. A predator circling prey, he examined the fabric, giving an experimental tug on the sleeves. Appeased, he motioned for her to take it off and slipped the frock over his back. Fixing the lapels, he posed and asked her to snap a picture. "You have the best taste in jackets."

"It's cozy because it's been worn with love." Full of laughter, she captured a snapshot. "Now give it back. I'm frozen."

He peeled off the garment and blanketed her shoulders, rotating her body to face Hanjun. Sitting inside the cage, he caught Jin flirting with her and shook his head. Diverging his concentration back to the lens, he taunted Soogi. "Admit it, you want to sink me!"

"You're right." Ammunition in hand, Soogi prepared to throw even before earning the privilege.

The production director loomed behind the camera, a deck of trivia cards in hand. "How many -gu are in Seoul? Bonus points if you can name at least ten."

Standing under an ultramarine tent, Jen prepared cups of hot tea and packages of chips, keeping one eye on the shoot. The -gu suffix was something she learned only a few weeks earlier, and she was astonished at how Parallels not only showcased Blackmirror's antics but also subtly introduced Korean to its viewership. The affix meant district or borough, and she marveled at how much she learned while on the set.

Soogi's eyes coiled, knowing he wouldn't be able to answer. "I'm from South Gyeongsang!"

"Twenty-five." The director chortled, offering a follow-up question. "Which city hosted the Asian Games in 2002?"

"Busan!"

"Correct!" Before the director affirmed, Soogi released the projectile, missing by a broad margin. "Last question. What is the national flower of South Korea?"

Soogi wound up his arm. "Mugunghwa!"

"Come on, that's too easy." Hanjun clenched the enclosure, fixated on the object racing towards him. Hearing the excited cheers of the staff, the ball struck its mark, and the icy pool engulfed him. He thrashed wildly, struggling to break the surface. Cursing, he emerged from the water, his clothes dripping and his pride wounded.

"I told you I'd dunk you." Cradling his arm, Soogi recovered the two balls he had thrown.

Finalizing the luncheon spread for the crew, Jen noticed his malaise and charged over to question him. "Are you alright?"

He forced a thin smile. "I fractured my cubitus a few years ago. It healed, but it still hurts."

"If it hurts, it didn't heal properly." Reaching for his elbow, she pressed the soft tissue. "Soogi, this feels—"

Wincing, he pulled away. "Don't—"

"That's a serious fracture. It needs to be—"

Placing a hand over her mouth, he ushered her away to discuss the condition. "I know, and I plan to fix it eventually."

"How long has it been like that?" Glancing at his arm, she realized the angle was off, and he couldn't straighten the bend.

"Three years." An embarrassing story, he shared with her the tale of how his joint became disfigured. During an award show, Blackmirror were presented with the honor of Top Social Icon. The amphitheater erupted into a frenzy of applause, and glittering streamers rained from the ceiling. After thanking their fans, they returned to their seats, but fate had other plans for Soogi. A deviant piece of confetti caused him to slip and tumble off the platform. Security rushed in to assist, but it was too late—his ulnar bore the brunt of the impact.

Listening to the heartbreaking story, she clicked her tongue, envisioning the torment he experienced. "Why wouldn't—"

Expelling a heavy sigh, he skimmed the area to ensure they were alone. "When it happened, we were in the middle of a promotion. We didn't have the luxury of taking time off; every second mattered. The pandemic hit, and our popularity soared. I couldn't bring myself to step away; Blackmirror was the only reason any of us had hope."

Drawing a breath, she wiped a tear from her eye. "Why aren't you getting it taken care of *now?* You aren't touring—"

"Because I've re-injured it multiple times." Admitting a painful reality, his voice cracked. "*Please.* Don't tell Ha-Rin."

"*Multiple times?*"

He covered her mouth before her shock summoned agency eyes to them. "Six months to a year of recovery, plus physical therapy."

Peeling his hand away, she gasped. "A year?"

"Do you understand why the agency can't know? We've worked too hard to give up."

"Then when?"

"Hanso is due to fulfill his military requirements at the end of next year. I planned to do it then."

★⁺₊★☾★⁺₊★

Arriving home from work, Jen dashed to her room and began setting up the massage table Hanso had gifted her. Maneuvering the legs into place, she flipped the surface upright. "I guess it wasn't a strange gift after all."

Turning to her dresser, she fingered through an expensive gift set of homeopathic lotions, whiffing each scent until she found something suitable. Discovering a divine mixture of tobacco and sandalwood, she thought the fragrance would be well-suited to Soogi. She stuffed the jar into her brassiere, warming the chilled glass against her breast.

Departing her bedroom in search of Soogi, she found him in the lounge, pampering his arm. She led him to her room in secrecy and gestured to the slab. Tugging the towel slung over her shoulder, he signaled for her to turn around. Following his order, a cool breeze swept her back, a product of his shirt being removed. The table squeaked as he climbed on, and she counted to ten before facing him. He lay shirtless with the cloth draped over his chest, as if it were a white flag of surrender.

"Is this position good for you?" Approaching him with slow, deliberate movements, her velvety voice pervaded the room. Nodding, his eyes locked on hers, betraying his inner nervousness. Plunging into her bra, she retrieved the vial of warmed serum, pausing to ask for his permission. "Would you be comfortable with me massaging your elbow?"

Controlling his exhalation, he outstretched his arm. "Yeah."

Trickling drops of salve into her palms, she began kneading above and below his ancon, easing into the section where the breakage occurred. "If you're too stubborn to have the surgery, loosening the ligaments will help with mobility."

His body involuntarily curled. Powering through the discomfort, a lengthened grunt leaked from him. Tapering off, a satisfied groan vibrated from his throat, releasing him from a prison of agony. "*There*. Right there."

"Have you at least visited a therapist?" He didn't need to respond; the tension was evidence he hadn't in a long time.

Invisible, Hanjun stood near the door, monitoring the pair. She listened to his every word, her hands moving with precision. Adjusting compression to his liking, his extracted moans congested the airwaves. Battling a mix of comfort and arousal, he watched her glide over Soogi, rubbing extra oil onto his biceps, forearms, and hands. His heart constricted the moment her fingers intertwined with his, and he had to wrench his gaze away before he burst through the door in a flare of jealousy.

But he knew that's all it was. Jealousy. There weren't any sexual undertones that Hanjun hadn't conjured himself. Factoring in Soogi's extended arm, corporeal contact was minimal, with the remainder of his physique concealed. Soogi remained on his back, eyes closed, and didn't ask for anything other than pressure to relieve the anguish. He didn't request her hands visit other areas, nor did she offer. Open-palmed and professional, she used her thumbs to manipulate the tissues. Never did she squeeze or grope him. Beyond the candles diffusing warmth, there was undeniable decorum embedded in the exchange. It was a therapeutic session, not a raunchy adult film.

Hanjun struggled to find a balance between facing a gnawing, obsessive connection with Jen and allowing her to do her job. She hadn't purposely chosen Soogi; it could have been Hanso, Jin, or Deok-Sun reclining on the workbench.

Finishing the massage, Jen assisted Soogi off the table. His posture relaxed, and he thanked her with sincerity. "If you ever become a masseuse, I'll hire you personally."

Taking his comment as a compliment, she crossed the hall to wash her hands. Returning to her room, she disassembled the table and stashed away the oils. Catching a trace of garlic in the air, she followed her nose to the kitchen, where Hanjun stood near the island, slicing through a jumbo-sized carrot. "You couldn't cut an onion when I arrived."

"I had a great teacher." He pointed the knife at her.

"Is that so?" A devious smile upturned her lips, visualizing the things she could teach him—with or without knives.

He returned the blade to the cutting board, rattling her promiscuous thoughts. "Remember; we have to watch the footage tomorrow."

⋆⁺₊⋆☾⋆⁺₊⋆

Feeling uncomfortably full, Jen collapsed onto her bed. Just as she was about to drift into udon-induced slumber, her phone buzzed. She accepted the video call to find Hanjun propped up on a Joey pillow. "Everything alright?"

"Yeah. Are you tired?"

She drummed her protruding tummy. "I'm on the verge of a food coma. You made the hell out of those noodles."

"I ate too much, too." He patted his own noticeably full stomach. "What's your favorite number?"

"Four. Yours?"

"Hana." He employed the Korean word before switching to its English equivalent. "One. How about your favorite color?"

"You have to be on top, huh? Black, white, and pink. It goes back to the whole thing where I feel split between two sides."

He pushed his face into the stuffie. "I swear I'm not making this up, but same."

"Favorite Pocket Monster?" She threw out her first query.

"I don't know the English word for it." He held his hands next to his face, simulating the triple-headed character. "Sam-samdeurae. The purple one with three heads."

She laughed louder than she should have, causing Soogi to beat on the wall in protest. "Hydreigon?"

"Let me look." Performing a quick search, he flashed a smile. "Yes! Which is your favorite?"

"Did you know the 'drei' portion of Hydreigon is German for three?" Her lips pursed in thought, though she knew the answer. "Pikachu is classic. Who doesn't love Pikachu? I wouldn't trust someone who didn't. But if I had to choose, it would be Jigglypuff. That's pretty much my whole aesthetic."

"Why do you say that?"

Her cheeks blushed, emulating the animation. "I'm short and kind of pink, chubby, like to sing, and cute when angry."

"And big, mesmerizing eyes." He chuckled, imagining her as an adorable puffball. "You're not chubby."

She snubbed his attempt to say what he thought all men were expected to say. "That's sweet, but—"

"You're perfect."

The words were said with such sincerity that her train of thought crashed. "I'm tired."

"Sleep well." Ending the call, he lounged on his bed and scrolled through the group chat.

> **Honsa**: Did anyone ask Jen to marry them today?
> **Sunnie**: I forgot.
> **Jinja**: We need to try harder.

He blackscreened the phone and reached for a pen. The day was a rollercoaster of emotions, soaring to riveting heights and plummeting to shallow lows. But it wasn't boring.

I'm surprised Soogi likes her. I'm not even sure he likes me all that much. Tomorrow is a new day.

CHAPTER SIXTEEN

Unnatural Cages

Jen selected an outfit, opting for a loose marbled gray lace-up sweater, figure-hugging jeans, and crisp white socks. Pulling on her clothes, she paused in front of her window.

Jolted awake by Hanjun in the middle of the night, he brought worrisome news: the country was ravaged by the worst flooding in eighty years, and the havoc could be heard inside Windsor Heights. Narrow roadways were rivers, rushing with waist-high sludge. Sewer drains struggled to keep up, spewing torrents into already-flooded pathways. Tragically, lives were lost in the flood, scattering a trail of devastation.

J&I issued a company-wide stay-in-place order, but even while confined to their home, work beckoned. Higher-ups from the agency were expected to arrive, intent on keeping their schedule on course.

Leaving her room, Jen found the once-quiet abode to be a bustling task center. The lead production director set up in the lounge, while cameras were erected in every room. She couldn't believe how quickly their home transformed into a playground for her coworkers. Overwhelmed by the abrupt burst of activity in their normally peaceful dwelling, she sought refuge on the terrace.

Braving chilly gusts, Hanjun slanted over the railing, taking in picturesque views of the Hangang River. Sidestepping, he gave her an eyeful of Dae-Hyun, who clocked them from inside the condo. "Guess who's here..."

"Does he usually attend these gatherings?" Whispering, she hid behind Hanjun, avoiding Hyun's fearsome gawk.

"No. I have no idea why he came." Hanjun glanced at Hyun, catching him glaring in their direction. "Just ignore him."

★⁺₊★☾★⁺₊★

Throughout the day, Jen was conscious of Dae-Hyun's oppressive eyes on her back like a sniper, though Hanjun went to considerable lengths to shield her.

After indulging in a stomach-bulging feast of traditional Korean barbecue, the roommates gathered in the parlor to review the previous day's footage. Hanjun sat next to Jen, their knees brushing. On the other side of her, Hanso transferred security amidst the unnerving stares of his manager's manager.

Jin curled up on the floor between Jen's legs. She ran her fingers through his hair, causing his eyes to reel. "Marry me?"

Hanso slapped Jin's arm. "Act professional. We're at work."

"Actually." Jin returned the shove. "We're at home."

"We're still working." Hanso flicked his ear.

Dae-Hyun stood in the doorway, analyzing their interactions. What Ha-Rin told him was true; Blackmirror were on their best behavior around Jen. Though they bickered as usual, they operated like they did when they were trainees, overflowing with tenacity and enough drive to satisfy the agency.

His sight turned to Hanjun. Sitting next to Jen, he leaned in to point out inside jokes within the recording. Judging from his smile, something was blossoming between them. The subtle taps and nudges of warmth were impossible to miss. "Enjoy it while it lasts. Tomorrow everything will change."

★⁺₊★☾★⁺₊★

The crew packed up their equipment, and Jen reconvened on the balcony. The biting cold hit her like a slap on the face, but it was a small price for a moment of solitude. Minutes ticked by, and Hanjun joined her, his presence bringing assurance.

"The water is beautiful." She gazed at the ripples, absorbing the metropolis below the towering fortress. Seoul was a city that never slept. Even in the early hours of dawn, cars filled the streets, zooming to their next destination. The people moved with such speed that she wondered if they treated every living moment as a chore, as she sometimes did.

"I'm sorry." Hanjun's temple rested on the frigid concrete.

Cold seeped into her bones, matching the distress in her chest. "It's not something you can control."

"I hate how he ambushed you." Glooming into the darkness, his jaw tightened. "No wonder you fled the restaurant."

He was phishing for what happened on their date, but she stayed voiceless. It wasn't a situation she wanted to think about, nor did she believe there was anything to be done. "I'm the new pet he's toying with."

"Sometimes I feel like a circus animal, paid to entertain." Devoid of emotion, it was as if he detached from existence to surrender the truth. "Only to be shoved back into my cage until I need to dance again."

"Hanjun," she answered in a faint whisper. "We're all trapped in cages. If you weren't doing this, it would be another cage. A different cage, but a cage all the same."

Reaching for his hand, his fingers were freezing and fragile in hers. "Your cage may be small, but it will provide opportunities for the rest of your life. You will have amassed enough wealth to do whatever you desire, even if you want to do nothing at all."

Refusing to let him succumb to disparity, tears stung her eyes. "One day, your cage will open, and you will fly."

The more time she spent with Blackmirror, the more she saw how chained they were. Each step they took was choreographed, and every move was probed by critics. Behind the glitz and glamour was an undercurrent of sacrifice and longing. They disregarded their health for the good of the band, bending limits to sustain their stature. And even when they had a moment of respite, they were never truly free.

In rare moments, they confided in her about craving simple experiences most people took for granted: grabbing a meal at a local eatery or attending a theater show were small joys ruined by journalists. And there were certain things they couldn't do without facing backlash from spectators; maintaining friendships outside their clique was unthinkable without spawning headlines. The forfeitures their reputation demanded were taxing, but they endured with artificial smiles and indebted hearts.

Even Hanjun, who genuinely enjoyed her company, had a hard time being honest. Having to tell a prospective love interest they would be ridiculed in every dark corner of the internet was not an easy task. If anything, it tainted any potential connection.

Despite gracing billboards all over the city, they lived in a bubble-wrapped state of confinement. Their home and the J&I tower were their only safe havens. Even leaving the condo was a complicated process, fraught with the risks of being stalked. Private information was easily accessible to anyone willing to cough up some cash, putting them in danger of exploitation.

Her heart wrenched. Considered mere objects, they were reduced to a fad—the fidget spinners of the entertainment industry. Failing to find soothing words in the face of injustice, she delivered an inexact quote from Maya Angelou. "While the free bird soars through the sky, the caged bird can only open its throat to sing."

"Birds sing to defend their territory and attract a mate."

Watching him gaze over the river he loved yet was unable to enjoy, she was struck by a sudden realization: his music was intimately personal. A melodic plea from his cage, where all he could do was produce noise. "Cages are unnatural creations meant to restrain, not protect. One day, they will be broken."

⁺₊☾*⁺₊*

Hanjun retreated into the warmth of his room. Collapsing onto his bed, he couldn't shake off the idea of inhabiting an unnatural cage. But strangely enough, the idea brought him comfort.

Jen was right. Fame was a synthetic construct. A fickle creature born from a toxic mix of ego, merit, and envy. While he appreciated recognition, he loathed the mania accompanying the spotlight. Like being burned under a magnifying glass, there was a perverted allure in the glorification of superstars; their engagements—not just their personas—played out on a grand stage. Fans and haters alike stood in awe, watching the inevitable downward spiral of souls who were never meant to bear such mental strain. Amid their downfall, celebs were romanticized; a struggling rockstar who popped pills before a concert was revered as deep and tortured. The frail actress, who fueled her inner demons with dangerous cocktails of drugs and stimulants, was hailed as resilient and determined.

But the true cost of achievement remained hidden until one was fully submerged. If a celebrity longed to disappear, paparazzi hounded them to the ends of the earth. It was wiser to let sleeping dogs lie for fear of triggering the Streisand effect. Admiration was an insidious disease; the pressure to maintain relevance and cater to the whims of those with ulterior motives was too much for even the strongest willed.

And yet, there were dangers incomparable to the internal ones. John Lennon—one of history's most iconic musicians—was shot dead by a crazed fan. Despite enjoying his esteem, Lennon's words and actions were scrutinized by millions, and it only took one person to take it all away.

Stardom was a precarious balance between achieving one's dreams and risking everything. A shiny surface masking a dark reality: the machine consumed those who dared to dream.

Civilization could not thrive on popularity alone. Contrary to prevalent beliefs, humans were reliant on each other, naturally forming intricate webs of cooperation and support. When a singular personality was showered with disproportionate importance, it was detrimental to society. The power imbalance created by celebrity worship fed into unrealistic expectations and perpetuated harmful ideals.

Fiddling with his phone, he sighed. "Our goals should be to become comfortably anonymous; to get all the love we need from a modest circle of friends, to fulfill ourselves creatively, and to make a decent living without becoming a headline for people to debate on their lunch hour."

Jinja: Dae-Hyun was acting weird.
Soogins: He wouldn't stop staring at Jen.
Sunnie: What happened on that date?
Jinja: I'm not sure. She refuses to talk about it.

Relieved to know he wasn't the only one growing tired of Dae-Hyun, he scribbled in his journal.

Hyun is a problem. I'm not sure what I can do about it. Talking with Jen calms my mind. She's my own personal brand of therapy.

CHAPTER SEVENTEEN

A Forced Hand

Hanjun strode down the hall, finding Jen's door ajar. She sat at her vanity, swiping eyeshadow over her lids. Glowing bulbs cast a heavenly light around her, rendering her ethereal. With practiced precision, she reached for a tube of mascara and coated her lashes, her expression swaying between concentration and curiosity. Catching him in the reflection, she nearly poked her eye with the wand.

He assessed her outfit—a plain black slouchy tee matched with relaxed denim. A pair of sunglasses rested atop a pile of heatless curls. "Good job at stabbing your eye."

"Stalker much?" Plucking excess tint from the tips of her eyelashes, she studied him from her peripheral. "I make more mistakes when someone's watching me."

"Is it stalking if you like it?" He folded his arms over his chest. "Besides, you're adorable when you're nervous. Your cheeks turn red, and you bite your lip."

"Yes, a rapid heartbeat and paranoia are extremely cute."

Scoffing, he turned to leave. "I'll wait for you in the car."

⋆⁺₊⋆☾⋆⁺₊⋆

Walking into the board room, anxiety shadowed Jen like an angry cloud. Scanning the seating arrangement, she found her nameplate opposite Dae-Hyun's. Angered that she'd have to look at his snide mug, she sank into her seat.

Sitting next to her, Hanso gave her shoulder a supportive squeeze. On the other side of Hanso was Hanjun, who offered Jen a concerned glance before looking to the doors.

Commanding everyone's attention, Dae-Hyun examined the room with a predatory glare. "Today we're discussing a new approach to Parallels. After much deliberation, we've decided to give one of you a girlfriend."

Hanjun slanted over the table, shooting Jen a worried glower. Dae-Hyun picked up on the tension and pressed on. "In promotion of your upcoming music release, we need to create buzz. And what better way than to add a potential love interest?"

He waved a hand toward the eldest. "Hanso, Jenilyn will be your on-screen girlfriend."

The announcement propelled hushed murmurs around the table. Hanso stumbled over his words. "W-why? There's no reason to—"

"So suddenly?" Jin was unable to curb his confusion.

"That doesn't make any sense," Jen blurted.

"You *can't* be serious." Head shaking, Hanjun protested.

"I assure you, I am." Hyun pushed a contract at Hanjun, pointing to Jen's autograph at the bottom. "Section 34b.4 states the signee may be utilized in any, but not limited to, promotions, videos, interviews, communications, film, footage, and any other content for the benefit of Blackmirror or J&I. Within reason, of course."

Hanjun skimmed the paragraph. "Signature or not, you can't do this."

Dae-Hyun lunged forward, resting his elbows on the table. "She will participate or forfeit the contract."

Jen inspected her roommates. Certain clauses prevented her from breaking the agreement. It also forbade her from instigating complications that could lead to an early departure. The job came with many perks, but there was one pesky drawback: if she were to depart before the expiration, she would be responsible for paying back every amenity she received.

J&I's ultramodern holographic identification cards totaled everything granted, used, or consumed at the tower. Meals prepared by trained chefs in the cafeteria. Escorts in luxury vehicles. Bottles of water from the lounge. Candy from the vending machines. Artisan coffee from the cafés. Even her share of their upscale condo would need to be repaid. She would be in more debt than she could dig herself out of in a lifetime.

Hanjun scowled. "You can't make her do this."

Wielding his dominion, Hyun rattled the walls. "Nobody is being forced to do anything. Either comply or the contract will be severed. It's your choice to make."

"Why are you doing this?" Jin lifted his eyes.

"Is this necessary?" Slinking from his chair, Deok-Sun pleaded from his knees. "We've always gone above and beyond. We're your top earners—"

Soogi whispered loud enough for the adjacent room to hear. "This is shit."

"Silence!" Hyun quieted the unfiltered complaints.

"Please." Hanjun's hands remained flat on the table, his fingertips tapping an antsy rhythm. "Don't make her do this."

"No—" Her heart dropped at the defeat in his voice.

"I'll do anything..."

"Anything, you say? Alright, then. *You're* getting a girlfriend." Scratching his chin, Hyun pointed two fingers at him. Relief washed over Hanjun until he finished the statement. "But she will be of my choosing."

"Thank you, Sir." Hanjun clocked Jen, wearing a smile so sad it didn't produce a dimple.

"I'll do it." Her voice rose with her height. Fists clenched, she knew Hyun's challenge would be difficult, if not demeaning, but she couldn't burden Hanjun when she was the target.

"What was that?" Hyun's lips curled into a sinister smirk.

Standing tall, she reiterated. "I'll fake date Hanso."

"Jen—" Hanso swore at her in his mind.

"It seems we have an offer from both of you." He clasped his hands over his gut. "I'm open to negotiations."

"I'll kiss him." Removing her gaze from Hyun, she glanced at Hanso and then Hanjun. "On camera."

Holding a smug smirk, Hyun glared at Hanjun. "Well, isn't that something?"

"I'll even wear whatever you want me to wear." She didn't care what he did to her. Well, she did, but she prayed he wouldn't make her do anything too humiliating. "Within reason."

"Within reason," he mocked. "Why should I accept your proposal when we've made great strides in the acceptance of outlandish—"

Hanjun growled. "Anti's will hate her, but that's what you want, isn't it? That's the whole point of this stupid stunt."

Hyun's grin enlarged, unfazed by Hanjun's hostility. Turning to Jen, he held an arm over the table. "Do we have a deal?"

She ripped her hand away a millisecond after touching his. "Yes."

Ha-Rin walked in carrying a stack of documents in his arms. "The congestion on the expressway was awful. What'd I miss?"

Hyun gestured to Hanso. "We agreed to introduce an on-screen girlfriend."

"*Girlfriend?*" Ha-Rin scoffed, trying to catch up on what transpired in his absence. "Why wasn't I notified?"

"Forced us." Jin intervened. "We were *forced* into giving Hanso a girlfriend."

"You were given a choice. Three choices, actually."

Ha-Rin balanced the papers on the table. "Can I meet this mystery girl? Do we need to train her? Does she know agency protocols? What about placement testing?"

Soogi's eyes flicked at Jen. "You already have."

Ha-Rin snapped between Hanso and Hanjun, their faces mirroring the weight of the ruling. "Sir, I can't advise you to do this. I don't think anyone wants to—"

"She's under contract." Hyun banged a fist on the table.

"The agreement pertains to the members. She's not a member of Blackmirror; therefore, the stipulations do not apply."

"We all do things we don't want to do, and we've already made a deal." Hyun stormed out of the office, allowing the door to slam.

Ha-Rin stood dumbfounded. "I don't know what to say. Something like this has never happened."

Biting her tongue, Jen scooped up her paperwork. "There's nothing to be said."

★⁺₊★☾★⁺₊★

The journey home from the J&I tower was unusually heavy. Jin's tears soaked into Jen's shirt. Oscillating between blubbering and wailing, his apologies were too raw to form coherent sentences.

Hanjun sat next to them, barely registering the passing scenery. Trees blurred, their branches groaning in the wind. The laughter of children walking the streets contrasted with the overwhelming despair in the cabin. Even the stoplights took an eternity to change, but his fury wasn't directed at the trees, children, or traffic lights. Throughout his career, there were instances where he questioned the ethics of the industry. It was certainly one of those times.

Jen couldn't wait to escape the vehicle. As soon as the wheels came to a slow, she leaped out, disregarding Hanso's scolding for opening the door before the tires stopped. With her emotions boiling over, she needed to distance herself from everything related to the agency—the escort she was mandated to take and the musician she was coerced into dating.

Crossing the parking lot—which was normally saturated with people but hadn't been since the flood—cold air needled her face. It was nearing Thanksgiving, and in the foreign country, she was more alone than ever before. It was her first time spending the holidays away from her home—being browbeaten to publicly court someone she had little compatibility with didn't help her homesickness in the least.

"This isn't what I signed up for." Barreling through the door, she kicked off her shoes and headed for the one place where she had some semblance of control. In the hallway, she paused in front of the calendar. Each square highlighted how little authority she had. Looming deadlines and endless tasks bled into her life, suffocating any chance of relaxation. "You made a commitment, Jen. You have to honor it."

Hanjun joined seconds later, pretending to study the schedule. "Have you packed?"

"Not yet." She spotted an odd chunk of time penned with a single word: travel. "Where are we going?"

"The beach. Parallels, a photo shoot, and filming part of a video." His voice faded. "You didn't have to cave to Hyun."

"One of us had to." Following the empty reply, she turned her back on him.

In his room, Hanjun collapsed on his pillows. He was tired of having obstacles wedge him away from her, but she was right. A second scandal pinned on him in such a short time would have catastrophic repercussions, while Hanso had never been embroiled in romantic speculation. When it came to Jen, despite their efforts, the press hadn't discovered her name, making it easier for her to navigate rumors. It had to be her.

Taking a moment to scroll through the group chat, the comments read as sullen as he felt.

> **Honsa**: I don't want to come between them.
> **Soogins**: Hyun is screwing with us.
> **Sunnie**: Why? What purpose does it serve?
> **Jinja**: Hanjun is being targeted.
> **Honsa**: Do you think he considers Hanu a threat?
> **Jinja**: Why else would he be doing it?
> **Sunnie**: Maybe the agency is afraid it's happening again.
> **Honsa**: You mean the shitstorm with his ex-girlfriend?

Tossing the phone aside, he reached for a pen. Dark ink flowed, tattooing an entire page; every word acted as a punch to the agency, emphasizing how much time and energy he had dedicated to the company, only to be treated like dirt. Ruminating over Dae-Hyun's decision, his hatred grew—a strong emotion he tried not to let consume him. Even if Blackmirror's management believed the situation with his former lover was repeating itself, Jen was innocent.

CHAPTER EIGHTEEN

Rise in Love

The drive to the beach was longer than anticipated. They left Windsor Heights over ninety miles earlier, and the winding roads stretched on endlessly. Ha-Rin gave the bandmates strict instructions not to capture Jen directly—all part of a grand plan to let their fan base figure out the fabricated truth about her relationship with Hanso. And they always did.

Soogi twisted in the front seat, omitting her face from the camcorder in his hand. "Marry me?"

Staring out the window at the trees whizzing by, she rolled her eyes hard enough to cause an ache. "You're hilarious."

Regardless of her platonic position, her superiors insisted she act lovingly towards Hanso. She grudgingly played the part by laying her head on his shoulder or caressing his knee. In return, he pecked her hand or left a love tap on her arm.

Seated next to Jen, Hanjun fought to keep his eyes off the spectacle. Witnessing his crush canoodling with his bandmate made his stomach knot. Desperate for a distraction, he jammed his hand between his and Jen's thighs, snapped a smiling selfie, and uploaded it to YOUniverse, accompanied by a quote.

'Believe none of what you hear and half of what you see.'

The virtual world of YOUniverse was Blackmirror's primary tool for connecting with their audience. Operating as a form of social media, the interactive platform strengthened the bond between artist and admirer. From thoughtful comments to one-on-one interactions, YOUniverse created an intimate setting for Blackmirror and their followers.

On the horizon, a charming cabin came into view. Situated right on the beach, it was quaint, with three bunk rooms and a tiny bathroom. The kitchen and lounge areas were combined, boasting exposed beams and rustic charm. Residual pinewood billowed from a wood-burning stove tucked into the corner. Adjacent houses served as accommodations for the personnel.

Suffocated by flashing cameras and overwhelming attention, Jen stole a moment for herself. Fleeing out the back door, she found solace on the landing leading to the beach, where the landscape was unlike any she had seen.

Hanjun joined her, his face obscured with a protective mask. Leaning against the railing, his legs intertwined with hers. "I was wondering where you went."

"I needed to breathe." Impulsively playful, she pulled the cover from his face. "We're alone, you know."

Exposing a sad smile, he untangled the loops. "I'm sorry they made you wear that."

The stylists clad her in a fitted lace bustier, paired with snug jeans and towering heels. To avoid exposure, she threw on a faded jean jacket, though it did little to veil her assets. Tugging at the corset, she whined. "Is Hanso attracted to someone who dresses like this? He strikes me as someone who appreciates effortless style. Femininely casual. Maybe someone who can whip up a delicious meal. Possibly even sporty."

"You're right about that." He poked at the shoes that made her nearly as tall as him. "How can you walk in those?"

"I can't." Being sausaged into an outfit she hated brought back painful childhood memories. "When I was young, I always felt out of place. I matured fast. In the States, you're judged for showing too much skin. You're also judged for not showing enough. At the time, I was the only one coming of age, and I was ridiculed for being a few years ahead."

She plucked dead weeds next to the walkway, tearing them into biodegradable confetti. "I concealed myself in layers, and while it stopped the teasing and comparisons, it didn't stop the interest. Boys would talk to me and never look at my face. They didn't know my eye color without looking. I was reduced to being attractive when I didn't understand attraction."

He squeezed her ankle, fiddling with the pearl accents on the hem of her jeans. "They're bluish green with a gold ring around the center. Depending on the lighting or your makeup, they can sway more blue or green."

Elated by his pure observations, she smiled. "As I aged, I still dressed that way. I didn't want to stand out, but conformity was expected, and deviation fostered ridicule. Boys would try to date me just to see what was under my shirt. The whispers and rumors about my body chipped at my self-esteem. People would befriend me only to betray me. It was like a circus, and I was the main attraction. I was so fearful about using any kind of public facility. I always felt watched."

His head bobbed, reflecting the weight of similar battles. "When everyone thinks they know who you are, you feel numb. You can't have a bad day—at least not one they can see. People hunt for a reason in everything you do. There's no such thing as privacy; everything gets recorded, amplified, and dissected. You pretend to be happy, even if it's the lowest day of your life. People aren't meant to be happy all the time. It's impossible, yet we have to."

Slumping, he fiddled with the holes in her jeans. "And finding sincere friendship? It's like trying to find a needle in a haystack, with the fear of betrayal lingering in the back of your mind. We become so skeptical that we end up trusting no one at all. Our circle of friends grows narrower, limited to those in the industry. But fame doesn't make someone a good person. More often than not, it brings out the worst in people. I yearn for the days when I could talk to a stranger about a book they were reading or a game they were playing. Life was simpler then."

He paused, remembering his closest companion from his school days, who just so happened to be a celebrity in his own right. "I'm lucky for my best friend. He's my anchor in this sea of uncertainty."

She nodded, her heart aching. No words would ease his suffering. All she could do was lend an ear.

"Every day, thousands of people say they love me, but it doesn't carry the same significance. It's like I'm immune to it. My admirers—would they love me if I wasn't on TV or in magazines?" He didn't expect her to answer. "I'm waiting for someone to tell me something different when I feel like I've heard it all. I gained the attention I craved, sure, but the limelight left me empty. It's like the more you have of something, the less you value it."

"What you have is an abundance of admiration, when what you seek is love," she answered. "It's no wonder you feel the way you do; admiration can be just as intense."

His shoulders slumped. "I've never heard something so hopeful while being so hopeless."

She reached for his hand. "Hanjun, do you remember the night the pap caught us in the rain, and I said I wasn't sure if I could go through with whatever this is?"

The image of her pressed against the jagged brick featured permanently in his nightly fantasies. "How could I forget?"

She gazed up at him, her eyes full of curiosity. "Part of my reasoning is because I want to know who *you* are. I love your music, but I don't know much about the real you. Who is Ryu Hanjun? You're the only one who can tell me."

Meeting her eyes, he dug deep. "I don't know myself. How can you know me?"

Recalling the small glimmers of his soul he had shown her over the previous weeks, she positioned a hand on his cheek. "Show me what's beyond the fake smile you wear. I want to see the grit and dirt—anxiety and passion. I'm dying to find out if you care for the happiness of others because it took so long to find your own."

He cupped a hand over hers. "What if I'm afraid?"

"What are you afraid of?"

Holding eye contact, he spoke with uncharacteristic honesty. "That I will be the only one to fall."

"I can't make promises. All I know is that right now, you're the brightest star in my sky."

Dipping into the depths of his soul, he drudged up the thing he feared most. "What if we fail?"

"You're right. Let's agree not to fall in love."

Stunned by her sudden change of heart, his throat sank into his stomach, leaving him breathless. "I thought you wanted—"

She rose from the deck, offering a hand. "Let's not waste time falling in love. Let's rise in love. Together."

He gave her a cynical glance, dropping his head to the side. "Rise... Where?"

Kicking off her pumps, she descended the stairs to the beach, motioning for him to follow. "Come on."

"You know it's cold, right?" Hesitating for a moment, he bounded after her. Walking along the rocks, they reached a small cliff where a mounded dune awaited. His toes cramped in the rough terrain, and he stumbled, folding under his bulk. "It's too uneven."

When she stopped to help, he grabbed her arm and pulled her down, ensuring she would be covered in just as much sand as he was. She chortled, playfully pushing him away and inadvertently setting off their balance. Rolling down the hill, they landed near the swells, where she straddled him. Ripples crashed onto the shore, sending small sprays of salty water into the air.

His smile exaggerated his dimples, his cheeks hiding his eyes, while the wet sand chilled him to the bone. "Why'd I let you talk me into coming down here? It's freezing!"

"But you can feel it, right? That's what makes you alive. Pain and worry are temporary." She tilted her head back, gazing into the star-studded sky. Returning her eyes to him, she sighed. "We're living right now."

Thrusting his hips, he flattened her onto her back. A gasp spilled from her as the coarse earth scraped her skin. He adored how her tresses spread like a golden halo and her eyes sparkled in the moonlight. Scooping up a handful of sand, he let the grains slip through his fingers like time in an hourglass. "This makes you feel alive?"

"You make me feel alive." She stroked his hair, reveling in the warmth of his body.

Resting his cheek on her chest, he held his breath, afraid she might notice his rapid heartbeat. "Did you ever dream you'd be on a beach in South Korea?"

"Never in a million years would I have thought it was possible."

"That's what's so strange, right? Think of all those things that needed to align for us to be here." His fingers dug into the sand, wishing to do the same to her. "It can't be a coincidence."

"The few times I thought about the future, I was disappointed." She sighed and ran a hand along his back. "The only thing I can control is me."

He couldn't argue with the unpredictable nature of fate. But with her, he dared to imagine a tomorrow. His fortifications were crumbling by the day; it wasn't a biological fascination but a uniting of two wounded hearts. Staring into her eyes, he considered kissing her until she unexpectedly giggled.

"I hate to end this moment, but I'm going to freeze to death if I don't find warmth soon."

⋆⁺₊⋆☾⋆⁺₊⋆

"There's our free birds." Swinging the back door open, Ha-Rin greeted Hanjun and Jen. The faint aroma of fig incense wafted through the air, calming their nerves, but their relaxation was short-lived with his next statement. "Jenilyn wasn't in our ranks when we rented this accommodation. Upper management wants Jun, Hanso, and Jen to share a room. And by *sharing a room*, I mean they want Jen and Hanso to occupy a bed. You know, because of the whole dating thing?"

"Why?" Hanso groaned.

"What he said," Jen agreed.

"Listen, as long as there's film of you two together, it should be enough to convince them." Shooing them from the room, he performed a vague Mizaru gesture.

Jen and Hanso exchanged glances. It wasn't how they envisioned the trip going, but they were determined to make the most of it. After all, nobody knew about the arrangement but them—and the photographers documenting their every move.

Grabbing the handle of his suitcase, Hanjun set off for their shared bedroom. "Let's get this over with."

Lugging their luggage down the narrow hallway, each step was a challenge. The bedrooms were barely wider than two cots. A three-legged nightstand left enough room for a lamp and phone chargers. Even with small beds, there wasn't enough room for their bags.

Hanjun maneuvered Jen's suitcase next to his, though she opposed the move. "My belongings go next to Hanso's."

He shot her a sharp glare. "It's just luggage."

She agreed but held her ground. "Anti analyze. Let's not give them more to talk about."

Caught in the middle of the tension, Hanso sank into his foam mattress. "I should have spoken up."

Hanjun tossed his backpack on the comforter and settled in with his back against the headboard. "I'm not mad at you. I'm mad at the situation."

Jen sat next to Hanso. "It's not your fault, Ho-Young. Hyun is punishing me. We only need to stick it out until he finds something new to play with."

While she comforted his bandmate, Hanjun reached for a notebook and sketched absentmindedly. Eyes glued to her, he struggled to comprehend how they ended up in such a mess. Despite knowing Jen's actions were fabricated, it stung to watch her put on a show for the ever-present cameras. Her artificial display of affection was a reminder that their lives were manipulated for consumption. Though a part of him admired her, and he questioned if she should pursue a career in acting.

During the farce, a cameraman came too close for comfort, provoking Hanjun to hide the sketchbook against his breast. The guarded drawings reflected his innermost views, and he refused to reveal them to judgmental lenses. The agency had taken enough from him. But the small act of resistance was futile, and he had an awful suspicion it would only get worse until it got better. Dae-Hyun would make sure of it.

As if hearing his thoughts, another camera shuttered, and he closed his eyes, wishing the operators would disappear.

★⁺₊★☾★⁺₊★

After enduring hours of intrusive cameras swarming their space, the companions were left in relative peace. Hanso was the first to doze off. Hanjun watched in amazement, unable to believe he fell asleep so easily. Jen, perched on Hanso's bed, took precautionary measures. She wedged a blanket between their bodies, and all attempts to drape an arm over her were thwarted. Scooting to the edge, she nearly toppled off.

Reaching for her hand, Hanjun resigned to a sleepless night. She responded by clutching his palm, proving she was just as upset as he was.

CHAPTER NINETEEN

The Water Listens

Hanjun untangled his hand from Jen's, propelling a sharp pain through his arm and shoulder. After the tingling sensation subsided, he wrote the former day's journal entry.

*The sea was cold but beautiful. Jen had to pretend to
date Hanso. Was this Dae-Hyun's plan?*

Finishing the blurb, he eased off the mildly uncomfortable bed and padded to the kitchen. Eyes drawn to the table, there were five boxes nestled in a row. He opened the one boasting his name and pulled out an outfit handpicked for him. The material was scratchy, promising a day of irritation before it began.

Disheartened, he started a pot of coffee and considered how J&I handled Blackmirror's wardrobe. The constant pressure to sport designer threads, often borrowed or rented from fashion houses, left them with little say in apparel. With no option to alter, they struggled with oversized clothing cinched together by pins. Shoes posed a greater problem; any pair could be one to three sizes too large or small. The dilemma became more dire when it was performance time; their heavy dance routines turned dangerous with ill-fitting footwear, leading to embarrassment or injury.

Waking shortly after Hanjun, Jen showered before the others dragged themselves out of bed. Exiting the bathroom in an oversized beach towel, she sat on Hanjun's bed. Smoothing lotion over her arms, she was grateful for the small moment of self-care amid their busy routine. She bypassed makeup, as it would be perfected on set, but she couldn't go without a dab of perfume.

Zipping the toiletry bag, her attention shifted to Hanso on the opposite bed. She smiled at his peaceful expression; he melted into the space she abandoned, and she wondered how frequently he was coerced into doing something he didn't want to do. Of course, anyone with a job had to complete unpleasant tasks; that was the name of the game when you weren't your own boss. Still, she thought the agency was over the top in its demands. Chalking it up to an insufficient understanding of a complicated industry, she left the room.

In the hall, three of her roommates were engaged in a heated argument over the bathroom. The door hung ajar, and Soogi could be heard singing while his bandmates vented.

Blocking the doorway, Jin rose over the crooning. "You've been in there forever!"

Discharging a vexatious laugh, Soogi clutched the flimsy curtain. "It's not my fault you woke up late!"

"I'll just rinse my hair in the sink." Deok-Sun turned on the tap, dispatching a cold message.

"Damn it!" Soogi shrieked, his spray suddenly turning icy. "Wait your turn."

Rolling her eyes, she stepped out onto the back porch. Sitting peacefully, Hanjun gestured for her to join him on an adjacent rocking chair. A carpet of morning fog spread over the sea. Calming and rejuvenating, it was a moment only described as soul-healing, far removed from the chaotic energy inside.

⋆⁺₊⋆☾⋆⁺₊⋆

Gusts whipped through the bank, though the team trudged on, prepping the shoreline for Blackmirror's campaign for their upcoming release, '*Miss You*.' Lighting equipment was established among the jagged rocks, along with tents offering respite from the cold. When the quintet arrived, their stylistically chosen outfits contrasted the sand: charcoal suits with pops of color. Despite their formal appearance, they went barefoot.

Slated to accompany Hanso, Jen was clothed in a button-up shirt with a faux leather panel over the bust, black snakeskin pants, and a sun hat that engulfed her shoulders when there wasn't a ray of sun to be felt. The stylists layered her in jewelry: chunky bracelets, dangling earrings, and a statement choker threatening to submerge her if she dared to step in the water.

Separated from the band, Hanso and Jen were instructed to mirror her moonlight encounter with Hanjun. From sitting with their legs intertwined on the landing to lying in the grit near the shore, it was clear they hadn't been alone the previous night.

Hanjun stood off-camera, questioning the similarities. "Does this seem familiar to you?"

"Overfamiliar." She struck a pose.

The photographer, acknowledging her rigidity, rattled off instructions to achieve the perfect image. "Suck on your tongue and hold your shoulders back."

Hanjun pondered aloud while Jen complied with orders. "Someone could have followed us."

"Place a hand on your knee, elbow away from the lens."

"Yeah, maybe." Jen shifted uncomfortably.

Frustrated with her lack of experience, Hanso grumbled. "The faster they get the shot, the sooner we're done."

Fighting the urge to squirm, she forced a smile. "I know I just... It's really weird."

Hanjun lowered his eyes. "Maybe Dae-Hyun has ulterior motives."

Locking her jaw, she snapped a reply. "Of course he does."

After what felt like an eternity, the photo session came to an end, and the performers were granted a brief break while the handlers prepared for the next promo. Seeking solace, the musicians flocked near the coast, though their usual playful banter was absent.

Joining them, Jen identified widespread agitation. Hanjun advertised a subdued frown, and Hanso's discontent was obvious. Jin complained about his get-up, tugging at the tags. Soogi whined about wearing a hue that clashed with his coloring, and Deok-Sun fed off the tension.

Clapping her hands, she tried to inject positivity into their spirits. "You can do this!"

The group mewled, barely acknowledging her. It wasn't like them not to snap back into hooting and horseplay. They were a comical lot who never stayed angry for too long, but even Jin, who was usually full of pep, radiated displeasure.

"Okay, let's try something. Up, up, up!" Motioning for them to stand, she performed a sprightly twirl and pointed to the ripples. "Yell at the water!"

Deok-Sun evoked an ocean of mirth. "Why would we?"

"The water cannot speak, but she listens. I'll start." Exemplifying, she flung her floppy hat into the water. "I *hate* these heels! And this stupid hat!"

Playing along, Hanso cupped his hands around his mouth. "I *hate* having to fake a relationship! Sorry, Jen."

She encouraged free speech. "Don't apologize."

Jin aired his peeves at the sloshing current. "I *hate* not being able to eat tteokbokki whenever I want!"

"I *hate* waking at five in the morning!" Soogi joined in. "And interviews! And dancing! And doing anything at all! All I ever wanted was to produce music."

"I *hate* having to pretend I don't feel the way I do!" Hanjun shouted against the freezing wind.

The breeze carried their troubles away. Events they couldn't change. People they missed from home. Things they wished they could do. Their desires mixed with the waves, forging a symphony of longing. Releasing their turmoil, they ended the affair by yelling random profanities in every language they knew, breaking into gut-busting giggles.

While waiting for the call to resume, Hanjun noticed Jen shivering, using her hands to cover her neck. Standing behind her, he wrapped his suit jacket around her body and held the buttons closed in the front.

Deok-Sun spotted the chivalry and couldn't resist interfering. Kneeling before them, he proposed to Jen. "Marry me?"

Refusing, she burst into laughter. "Why are you so obsessed with asking me that?"

"We get asked all the time. It's fun to ask someone else for once."

⋆⁺₊⋆☾⋆⁺₊⋆

Wrapping up after six additional hours of filming, the supporting staff arranged a party to celebrate. A bonfire was constructed on the rocks, its flickering blaze kissing the night sky. Though the cameras continued to roll, the artists and crew gathered around the fire, roasting meats and sweets. The eldest of the entourage lounged on logs while Deok-Sun bustled back and forth, cooking treats over the pyre.

After Jen was force-fed a third fire-roasted sausage, Hanjun apologized. "It may seem strange to you, but feeding each other is a sign of affection."

She swallowed a bite that was much too big for her mouth. "Now that I know I should expect food flying at my face, I'll be more aware."

Jin held a caramelized peach with chopsticks. "Try this."

"Mmm!" Biting into the warm fruit, Jen's eyes doubled in size at Deok-Sun.

Hunched over, prepared to take a flying leap, he had a not-so-bright idea. "Do you think I could jump over the fire?"

Pulling him away from the flames by his collar, Ha-Rin chuckled. "Not unless you want to walk home with a broken leg."

The night wore on, and the fire dwindled to a smoldering flame. Hanjun and Jen remained the last two on the beach. Huddled on a bumpy log with his arm draped around her, they swayed to the rhythm in their hearts.

Rhymes spilled from him in a melodic stream of longing and hope. "If falling in love is too much, let's make a pact between us two. You won't fall in love with me, and I won't with you. And if a time comes when keeping our word is too hard, let's promise to rise in love. We'll aim for the stars."

Swept away by his timbre, her body relaxed. She didn't know what they were to each other, but in stolen moments, she wished for more. Gazing at the sky, her heart skipped a beat when he voiced the thought running through her mind.

"It's too cloudy to spot a shooting star."

★⁺₊★☾★⁺₊★

After smothering the fire with heaps of dirt, Hanjun and Jen returned to the rental home. Jen frowned at Hanso sprawled out on his bed, leaving no room for her. "On the couch it is."

"I can sleep on the floor." Hanjun patted a pillow on his bed. "Or you can sleep next to me."

Her eyebrow shot up. "Isn't that too tempting?"

He held his hands in front of his torso as if he were surrendering. "It's not like that, okay? As much as you were surprised by your actions in that alley, I was too."

"Scoot over." Crawling into his bed, she mashed a ruffled blanket between their bodies. "Hands to yourself."

Shifting near the wall, he positioned his arms over his chest. "I won't move unless you tell me to."

She giggled. "Not even if I tickle you?"

Biting his lip, he hid a smirk. "No guarantees."

"If you flinch, you lose." Cuddling closer, she traced his knuckles, taking in the rough calluses and tiny cuts. Spinning the rhodium-plated rings on his fingers, she contemplated his hands and everything he did with them. In the music he made. The mixing he did. It would all be impossible without them.

His gaze never left her. "What are you thinking about?"

There were infinite subjects she wanted to discuss, but she was too tired to start talking. "You always wear rings on the same fingers."

"It's where they feel most comfortable."

She tapped his pointer. "Did you know the astrological association of this finger is Jupiter?"

"I didn't know that." He admired her admiring him. Removing the ring, he placed it on her, trying several placements before finding one he didn't think would fall off immediately—the middle finger of her left hand. "It looks better on you."

Squeezing his hand as a thank you, she rolled to her side. Awaiting the soft purrs of her slumber, he reached for a pen to immortalize the moment.

I'm no longer interested in dreams, illusions, or fantasies. Please, let her be real.

CHAPTER TWENTY

A Possible First

Sunlight filtered through the blinds, disturbing Hanjun's rest. Cracking one eye open, he found Jen cuddling next to his side. Patting her head, his eyelids lowered. "Snooze."

"Jun, get up." She shook him a second time.

"You're too adorable to say no to." Biting his lip, he reached for his phone, capturing a moment of lazy intimacy.

"Aren't I?" Propelling off the bed, she gathered her toiletries and disappeared into the hallway.

Watching her leave, gratitude flooded his heart. Had she not been so insistent, he wouldn't have had enough time to rise, caffeinate, and rouse his mates.

Shuffling through the home, he found the coffee pot primed with a reservoir of water and a filter of grounds. He flicked the switch and slumped into a chair at the table. Waiting for the java to brew, he scrolled through his phone, catching up on trending news.

HAMAS GUNMAN OPENS FIRE IN THE ALLEYWAYS OF JERUSALEM'S OLD CITY, KILLING ONE MAN AND WOUNDING THREE OTHERS BEFORE BEING SHOT BY ISRAELI FORCES.

FRANCE DEPLOYS GENDARMERIES FOLLOWING RIOTING AND LOOTING IN THE ARCHIPELAGO OVER PANDEMIC SAFETY MEASURES. AT LEAST THIRTY-ONE PEOPLE WERE ARRESTED.

MALAYSIA SURPASSES 30,000 DEATHS FROM COVID-19.

FIVE KILLED AND FORTY INJURED BY A HIT-AND-RUN DRIVER IN WAUKESHA, WISCONSIN. A PERSON OF INTEREST IS IN CUSTODY.

Discarding the device, he shook his head. "Why do I look when I know what I'll find?"

"Sorry I woke you." Jen appeared in the doorway with a towel situated on her head. "I was afraid you'd be late."

"I'm glad you did." Jumping to his feet, he poured a mug of coffee. "I need a few minutes to myself before I deal with the boys."

She sank into a chair. It was something she noticed about him—his strict adherence to efficiency. Most people disliked being tardy, but he took it to another level with his unwavering commitment to production. There was no room for idleness; every moment exercised purpose. He even advanced mundane tasks with passion. If he couldn't doze at the designated time, he tossed and turned. And if he couldn't concentrate on a book during instants of relaxation, frustration set in. Any disruptions to his carefully crafted routine were sure to put him in a sour mood. If waking him in the morning meant his day went a little smoother, she was happy to add human chronometer to her list of responsibilities.

Jin shambled to the fridge. "Do we have milk?"

"There's chocolate and strawberry on the lower shelf." She pondered how they coexisted. With five distinct individuals in one house, disagreements were inevitable, and she had stepped in more than once to prevent arguments from escalating into fistfights.

In Hanjun's ideal world, the entire condo would ascend with the sun, jumpstarting their day with a brisk jog around the complex. They would have checked off half of their chores by the time they made it to the office.

If Soogi had his way, they wouldn't stir until noon. A self-proclaimed night owl, he thrived under the moon's spell and struggled to leave his bed. To him, productivity was determined by creative output, not time.

Hanso's temperament was somewhere between the two extremes, influenced by his energy levels, priorities, and workload. Like a chameleon, he adapted to his surroundings without complaint.

Jin was a vibrant mix of spontaneity and free-spiritedness. He was notorious for staying up, but he also retired earlier than his peers. The witching hours plagued every member of Blackmirror, though Jin bore the brunt with reoccurring nightmares.

Partially due to his age, Deok-Sun's strength was nearly endless. He played video games all night and somehow woke with enough pep to tackle the schedule. When he wasn't socializing, his nights were occupied with alcohol and animations. He drank until the morn, getting as little as three hours of shuteye before rolling out of bed.

★⁺₊★☾★⁺₊★

The morning dawdled on, and the musicians convoked in the kitchen to have their faces transformed into idol-worthy perfection. Layers of concealer and powder were applied to hide imperfections, and once deemed flawless, they were fitted with colorful tracksuits and designer beachwear.

Jen's ensemble consisted of ripped skinny jeans seemingly designed to cause discomfort and a flimsy tank. Holding a smile when she wanted to scream, she changed in the bathroom and revisited the kitchen, tugging on the neckline of her blouse. "It's official. This is the most intolerable thing I've worn to date."

Jin reached under his sleeve. "Is this made of fiberglass?"

"Let's just go." Hanjun beckoned to the back door. "The sooner we get down there, the sooner we can get out of these clothes."

Barefooting sharp rocks on her way to the beach, Jen experienced a squirmy sensation in her belly. Fear or disgust—she wasn't sure which—her tummy troubles were overshadowed by Ha-Rin and Dae-Hyun waiting for them near the shore. Lowering her voice, she glanced at Hanjun. "Why is *he* here?"

"He wasn't supposed to be."

She was instructed to standby while Blackmirror prepped for photos—a series of pictures with the band romping on the shoreline and separate portraits of each member, staged and candid. It was all lighthearted fun until Dae-Hyun called her over to Hanso's photographer. She marched to them, trying to ignore the swarm of bees buzzing in her stomach. Standing awkwardly next to Hanso, her fists balled, and she was sure her face reflected the discomfort.

Hyun snapped two fingers, commanding a chain of poses. "Hanso, sit in the sand. Jenilyn, drape your legs over his and twist your body to face away."

She did as she was asked, adding a sultry curve. Holding her mass with her core, she alleviated Hanso's uneasiness by keeping her extremities close. "I'm sorry you're caught up in this."

"Clutch her thigh. Make it look good!" Hyun barked another order, and Hanso fixated on Jen, searching for compliance. She nodded, reassuring him.

Hovering behind the photographers, Hanjun had a grand panorama of the circus. Wincing at Hanso's hands on Jen's body, he refused to give Dae-Hyun the satisfaction of seeing his distress. Instead, he crossed his arms and drew deep huffs while Hyun shouted commands.

"Hanso, lay down. Jenilyn, get on top of him!"

Shifting his hands from his thighs to under his head and then at his sides, Hanso strived for comfort. Stiffened, vulnerable, and lost, Jen approached him, lifting her knee over his abdomen. Pausing midway, she wasn't sure how to assist without violating him further. "I don't know how to do this."

"Today!" Hyun squawked.

Hanso granted her permission to straddle him. "It's okay."

Positioning her body over his thighs, she sent an apologetic glance to Hanjun. Blinking to divert his tears, he averted his eyes. Her spirit ached at the sight, but she had no choice. She was required to fulfill Dae-Hyun's outrageous demands.

Taking cues from the lensman, Hanso tilted his head to face the camera. The angle had him staring down the lens. Had she not been intimidated into performing the pose, she would have thought it was an attractive perspective. Regardless of him looking petrified, he was tremendously handsome.

Squeezing his forearm, she encouraged him to power through. "You're doing great. Just a few more—"

"Grab her hips!" Hyun hawked.

Hanso draped his hands over her waistline, his fingertips barely touching her. "Jen, this doesn't feel right. It's not right."

"One last photo, and we're done." Yanking them by their arms, Hyun positioned them near the bonfire, leaning on the same log she and Hanjun shared the previous night.

Pushing past the violation, she focused on the lens. But when she spotted Hyun smiling at Hanjun's distress, she knew it wasn't a coincidence; he was purposely tormenting them.

"Place your hand on her thigh." Hyun issued a double snap.

Hanso hesitated to touch her, and she appreciated that even in their situation, he looked to her for consent. "It's okay."

"*Kiss!*"

"Alright, alright." Hanso smooched her on the cheek the same way he would his sister. Swift and painless.

Hyun vocalized his unhappiness. "On the *mouth!*"

Cringing, her gut knotted. Even the way he commanded the kiss was repulsive. He was a grown child, smashing his toys together. "Why are you doing this?"

Unable to watch his friend and his prospective lover forced together, Hanjun turned his back on the spectacle. Even if it was the reaction Dae-Hyun wanted, he couldn't look any further. "Just take the photo!"

Hanso sought approval once again, but she had reached her breaking point. Accepting the fact that she would be paying off her debts for the next decade, she stood tall. "No."

"*Kiss!*"

"No!" Rotating in defiance, she apologized to Hanso. "Anyone would be lucky to kiss you, but I can't."

Gasping between breaths, Hanjun doubled over, planting a hand over his chest. "I can't breathe."

Deok-Sun rubbed soothing circles on his back. "You know she doesn't want to do this."

Dae-Hyun smirked as if he wanted to see what wrongs she would endure. "Kiss him like you kiss Hanjun!"

"What are you talking about? I've *never* kissed Jun!" Her confession aroused silence from everyone on the beach.

Deok-Sun leaned into Hanjun. "Didn't the pap catch you?"

Hanjun's expression turned dark. Shooting daggers at Hyun, he divulged the truth. "I kissed her neck. That's it."

Suspicion leaped from Jin's larynx. "You haven't?"

Swinging his attention to Jen, Hanjun's volume softened. "Sorry to disappoint, but it's not like that."

Hyun's scrutiny pendulated between Hanjun and Jen; he was positive their relationship surpassed a first kiss. "You haven't..."

"No, we haven't, but that isn't up for discussion." Terminating the gossip, giggles gurgled out of her. It wasn't humorous, but contemptuous. Her heart teemed with spite at being put in such an onerous position, but she wouldn't let them make her the scapegoat in their quasi-tragedy. "I can't do this."

Unsure what else to do, she set off for an unoccupied part of the shore. Away from everyone and everything. Hanjun scoured Ha-Rin for help. Finding him just as powerless, he followed her. "Wait!"

"Your whole company is asinine!" Kicking at the sand, she gestured wildly while she walked. "What is even happening?"

Hanjun yanked her elbow. "Jen—"

"He's torturing us!" Pointing a finger, she addressed Dae-Hyun and his forced photography fetish. She knew it wasn't his fault, but she needed to unload on someone, and he happened to be there. "When I signed the contract, I didn't know I'd be giving the agency permission to use me as a puppet. And it's not just me; it's Hanso, Deok-Sun, Jin—"

Seizing her arm, he spun her to face him. His gaze darted between her eyes; all he could think about was how cute she was. "Jen..."

"The look on your face—you were being torn apart. As much as I want to stay—" Grounding her toes in the earth, she mustered up the courage to admit her limitations. "I can't watch you suffer."

He marveled at how quickly her lips moved. Her usual speech carried a heavy Midwest cadence, though her outraged enunciation took her back to her roots as a young girl living on the streets of Chicago. Grabbing her hand, he pulled her towards him. Dropping to their knees, he encased her in a protective hug. "Everything worth something is hard. I'm sorry you were dragged into our world, but I'm so happy to know you."

She felt the intensity in his delivery. A lifeline he was clinging to. "*I can't.*"

He strained to sway her decision, desperate to change her mind. "If you give up, you let him win."

She clung to his wrists, letting the words sink in. He was right. She wasn't the type to let someone manipulate her; why was she allowing Hyun? The answer was simple: she made the decision to stay. Backed into a corner, there wasn't a way for her to escape without making Hanjun resentful, Hanso uncomfortable, and her hate herself.

On the other end of the shore, the remaining bandmates huddled, displaying a myriad of reactions. The pair often spent time alone in the evenings, but nobody knew how friendly they were. Outside of playful gestures, they never exhibited outward signs of affection. Potential amorous involvement was purely speculation among the friends.

Jin placed a palm over his heart. "Hanu *likes her* likes her."

Deok-Sun chuckled. "Hasn't that always been obvious?"

Hanjun held onto Jen until her trembling ceased. Once her body relaxed, she slipped from his grip, though she remained eerily quiet. From his knees, he pleaded for discord. "Say something."

Crashing waves provided a peaceful backdrop for the turmoil she didn't voice. "I've said everything I can say. I can't stay. I can't. I'm just making things worse for you."

"He's trying to take this from us." Rising from the sand, his boiling hatred for Hyun suffocated his rationality. Hyun *wanted* him to lose control. He *wanted* Jen to see his worst qualities and smother their flame before it ignited. "Whatever this is, he wants to ruin it. How are you going to let him?"

"Take *what* from us?" She scoffed incredulously. "We don't even know what—"

"*This*—" His body bulldozed into hers, sending them toppling to the ground. He pulled her into an embrace as natural as breathing. She melted into his arms, enjoying the rough grains grinding into her skin. His hands caressed her neck, and their lips met in a long-expected explosion.

Gentle and possessive, he wiped away the matcha gloss he smeared on her. "I should have kissed you sooner."

Returning his enthusiasm, she tugged him close, savoring the fusion of their labored panting. "Yes, you should have."

The cinematic first kiss was witnessed by their friends, colleagues, and supporting staff, who cheered from a distance. Especially Jin, who was the couple's biggest supporter.

"Finally!" Hanso jumped up and down, creating a starfish with his body. "We can end the bet on whether they've kissed! You've made me a mildly richer man."

"Get it!" Deok-Sun pumped a supportive fist.

"*HanJen!*" Soogi started a chant, and soon, everyone on the beach joined in. "*HanJen! HanJen! HanJen!*"

Lying on the deserted strand, Hanjun gazed at Jen with admiration. Rubbing his lips together, he licked the spicy sweetness she transferred to him. "Cotton candy... And cinnamon?"

"My lip balm is flavored." Pulling an oversized tube from her shirt, she handed it to him. "The lady who makes them started the company from her kitchen. The brand is a little expensive, but it's important for me to support small business."

"It has a lot of slip." He swiped a coat over his lips and returned the product. "And the cinnamon?"

"I'm obsessed." Slipping the container into her bra, she rose to her feet. "Gum, sweets, tea—I can't get enough cinnamon."

Meeting her height, he thought she tasted like his all-time favorite snack: cinnamon sugar chips. If given the chance, he would devour her every hour of every day, but he settled for a kiss, anticipating the next opportunity to taste her.

Hiding her mortification, she motioned for him to follow her back to the crew, where she hung her head and offered an apology. "I'm sorry I left. I should have fought harder."

"Don't blame yourself." Deok-Sun trapped her in his arms.

"About time." Jin patted Hanjun's back.

Reeling from the romantic display, Soogi assembled the roommates, camera ready to capture a photo. "Group hug!"

Smashed between warm bodies, Jen skimmed the dunes for Dae-Hyun. "Where'd he go?"

⋆⁺₊⋆☾⋆⁺₊⋆

Jen intertwined with Hanjun on his bed, her body forming a cocoon around him. Hanging onto his midsection, she didn't care if they were official because she was officially falling for him, one slow day at a time. Eventually, she drifted off, her respiration steady against his back. In the quiet stillness of the night, he extracted his phone and drafted a journal entry.

> *What is a first kiss? It's that electrifying energy you only experience once. A rare elixir that can never be replicated. These are the moments I've dreamed of.*

CHAPTER TWENTY-ONE

Truth or Dare

Rising in an empty bedroom, Jen half expected a slew of messages from the agency's CEO about her run-in with Dae-Hyun. After a good night's rest and enough time to reflect on her actions, she decided she shouldn't have walked off set. Her conniption likely caused a deficit for the agency, and she needed to apologize, if not beg for forgiveness.

The only good thing that came from the situation was a glimmer of honesty from Hanjun. Closed off and perhaps a bit scared; he wasn't someone who professed his mysteries. Though she had suspicions of his affection for her in the aftermath of her date with Dae-Hyun, she couldn't be sure without admittance. His line of work included a long list of fan-pleasing gestures; she couldn't take a light amount of flirting as an absolute sign of fondness.

Departing the room, she entered the kitchen, finding Hanjun in an apron, barefaced with straggly hair. He greeted her with a cheeky smile. "Morning."

She studied the table to find half-prepared earthenware, as if he were assembling a feast. Trays of vegetables, platters of meats, and bowls of fruits lined the tabletop with orange, yellow, and brown leaves covering the spaces between. "What are you making?"

Looping an arm around her back, Hanjun directed her to a chair. "It's Thanksgiving in the States."

"We're whipping up something to remind you of home." Jin kangarooed in his seat.

Hanjun squeezed her shoulders. "*Loosely* remind you of home. We have limited knowledge of American cuisine."

Suffering from a loss of words, she surveyed the table a second time. For a group of men who didn't do a whole lot of cooking and had even less familiarity with the holiday, they did an exceptional job of replicating the coveted meal. The only thing missing was a wildly contested can of jellied cranberries. "You didn't have to do this."

Jin reached for her hand. "We're sorry you couldn't spend Thanksgiving with your family."

For a little over two months, it had been only them in her life. Moving to a foreign location was difficult, but they ensured her transition was light-years easier. "You're my family."

The hours passed, and the roommates cooked pork, ham, and duck. Observing how hard they were working, Jen didn't want to tell them turkey was traditional. She wasn't even sure the meat existed in South Korea, as she hadn't seen it the entire time she'd been there. At least not in the form of a whole bird.

"Food's ready!" Wearing thick potholders, Jin moved steaming pottery onto trivets while Deok-Sun staged the table with porcelain dinnerware.

"While I'm not religious, I'd like to mention a few things I'm thankful for." Taking a seat between Hanjun and Jin, Jen squeezed their hands, setting off a chain reaction of handholding. "I'm thankful we have food to eat and a safe home to stay, and our health affords us the ability to enjoy today. I'm thankful I had the opportunity to be here."

Suppressing a giggle, she made eye contact with each roommate. "Thankful that your bus broke down at my place of work."

Weaponizing a grin, Soogi challenged her from across the table. "Marry me?"

Scoffing, she shook her head. "No."

Hanjun ignored the raillery. "I'm thankful we're together. Thankful for Anti. Thankful for our company and crew."

He paused, holding a hand over his heart. "A very happy moment."

Jin's lips quivered. "Stop, you're going to make me cry!"

Heartfelt tears were shared over the hour, and the warm glow of a rustic chandelier reflected light from the silver serving spoons. Emptying pan after pan of delicious food, they reminisced over the previous months, commemorating stories of co-existing by calling attention to each other's worst habits.

Struggling to stay seated, snickers bubbled from Jin. "You'd have to go in with air freshener after Deok-Sun!"

Deok-Sun, choking on a roasted chicken leg, retaliated. "At least I have the decency to put toilet paper *in* the trash bin."

Hanjun returned his glass to the table. "Can we save this conversation for after we're finished eating?"

Shoveling food into his mouth, Soogi interjected. "They're not hurting anyone."

Hanjun's eyes flicked to Jen, prompting a retort from Soogi. "She doesn't seem to care as much as you do."

Caught in the middle of their disagreement, Jen spoke up. "It's natural. Talking about it is humanizing."

"See?" Soogi nibbled on a caramelized carrot. "You were worried for nothing. Let them poo in peace."

⋆⁺₊⋆☾⋆⁺₊⋆

Following a waistband-stretching dinner, Jen stepped out onto the back porch. A vicious wind jerked at her blouse; a storm was brewing on the horizon, and the temperature plunged by the second. Despite the cold, something about the waves crashing against jagged rock swathed her in tranquility. Having never lived near the beach, she was mesmerized by the liberty of the sea.

Wrapping his arms around her frame, Hanjun rested his chin on top of her hair. Slanting over her, he matched the ebb and flow of the dangerous waters, rocking her in his arms. "I'm thankful for the ocean and the sky. The clouds and the rain. The air that we're breathing and the chill of the day—"

"The cold of the winter and the leaves in the fall. I have only love in my heart—" He placed a wet smooch on her cheek. "To you, my soul calls."

"That's beautiful." Sighing, she caressed his wrists. "Thank you. It couldn't have been a more perfect Thanksgiving."

"Isn't that what boyfriends are for?" Spinning her to face him, the shock she displayed was exactly what he hoped for.

Blinking, she stammered. "B-boyfriend?"

"If you'll have me." He rubbed her nose with his.

"Of course!" Plummeting into his arms, her eyes welled, though she pulled back from him. "Wait. My contract says—"

He placed a finger over her lips. "We can't date publicly. I'm sorry it can't be like a normal relationship."

Tugging his waist, she parked her face on his chest. "I'd rather keep what we have for us."

"Me too." He hugged her the way he'd wanted to hug her for months. "We should get inside before we turn into ice."

"You read my mind." Opening the door, they found their roommates sitting in a circle, preparing to play a game.

Three glasses into a jumbo-sized bottle of wine, Jin beckoned them over. "Truth or dare! If you refuse, you take a shot."

"Dare." Collapsing to sit, Hanjun accepted the provocation.

Jin plucked a lone piece of shrimp from the living room table. "Eat this."

Taking a seat, Jen's face contorted into disgust. They feasted in the kitchen; she couldn't fathom how seafood had gotten in the lounge. "Where did that come from?"

Deok-Sun's chortle gave him away, and he admitted to dropping a plate of crustaceans. "I guess one escaped earlier."

"Easy." Hanjun popped the arthropod into his mouth. Swallowing the morsel whole, his stoic guise faded.

"Truth or dare?" Hanso posed the question to Jen.

She steeled herself for embarrassing queries. "Truth."

"Marry me?" He deadpanned.

Eyeing Hanjun, she declined. "Absolutely not."

The night stretched on, and the game of do or don't intensified. The once orderly room was strewn with empty bottles of soju, plates of leftovers, and throat candy wrappers. Speech slurred and movements unsteady, Deok-Sun hatched a loaded question for Jen. "Truth or dare?"

Tipsy but eager to participate, she gave a quick retort, aware he never shied away from the risqué. "Truth."

He fired off the request faster than she thought was possible, given his high blood alcohol level. "If you weren't into Hanjun-Hyung, who would be your second choice?"

"Why'd you have to ask that?" Pouting, she didn't want to answer. Unfortunately, she had already skipped too many questions and felt concerned for her liver. "Ho-Young. He looks innocent, then you hear him speak—"

"You *do* have a type! Maybe Dae-Hyun is on to something."

Jin sulked, inciting a compliment from her. "You're handsome, and your voice is beautiful."

"Okay! Okay! Okay!" Soogi devised the perfect plan to add a bit of spice to the game. "Hanu, truth or dare?"

Having experience with Soogi's awful dares, Hanjun hesitated. "*Truth.*"

The roommates anticipated a juicy reveal, but rather than digging up controversy, Soogi went simple. "Do you love Jen?"

Hanjun fidgeted with his sleeves while his friends sounded a chorus of oohs. "I have feelings; that is true. It's too soon for a commitment, but I hope we make it there."

Hoping to divert attention away from his crimsoning cheeks, Jen turned to Deok-Sun. "Truth or dare?"

"Truth."

"What was your first impression of me?" It was a question that had tickled the back of her brain since she met them—how they felt about her the night they crossed paths.

"You looked tired and smelled amazing." Stifling a laugh, he signaled to Jin, who mimed breasts in front of his chest.

She gasped and gave him a curt shove. "Jin! That's sexist."

Jin offered his analysis once she cracked into an eye-scrunching laugh. "I was intimidated. You're strong."

"That's just my face."

"I thought you were calm and serene, like a gentle stream." Soogi emitted an animated chuckle. "How wrong I was..."

"*Sexy!*" The room erupted into hysterics at Hanso. "What? I answered the question truthfully."

Falling into a hushed silence, all eyes swept to Hanjun, who concealed his face in his bicep. "The first thing I noticed was your voice and how your eyes were between blue and green. You were confident, but also aware and sympathetic. Then you walked around the counter, and I was like, 'Whoa! The whole package!'"

Looking at Jen, Soogi spilled the tea, prying Hanjun's hands from his blood-rushed face. "I *knew* Hanjun liked you."

Refusing to remove his defenses, Hanjun whined. "No—"

"At the concert, when I fell and you jumped right in, I knew he was interested," Deok-Sun added.

"Please no—" Hanjun's cheeks flushed, but he knew it was his fault. What he told his companions in private never stayed private.

Jin mimicked how Hanjun cuddled on her sofa as if he had dwelled there for years. "When we went to her apartment, he sat on the couch and burrowed under the covers like a stray cat."

Hanjun hid his face in a pillow. "Don't tell everyone!"

Jostling Hanjun's shoulder, Jin smiled at Jen. "What did you think of us?"

She addressed the team before breaking them down individually. "You were all so grounded, and you're more impressive than people know. U-Jin, you were dapper and kind, but your thoughtfulness and wisdom impressed me. Deok-Sun, you had a boyish naivete, full of wonder and pride. Ho-Young, you have an inquisitive mind. But behind your upbeat facade, I sensed a hint of sadness, yet you manage to wear a smile. Soogi, you were as I anticipated, yet different. You're easygoing and quiet, but your affectionate nature surprised me."

"Jun—" She whispered his name, and her expression softened. "Of course I thought you were attractive. I mean, I do have eyes. But it's not the superficial that captivated me. I admire how you carry yourself with confidence, even when you may not feel it."

Calming the expanding anxiety in her sternum, she grew more reflective. "To be honest, I'm not easily attracted to others. It takes more than physical appearance for me to engage. It's about *personality*. Like Hyun; at first, I thought he was good-looking, but then I got to know him, and it was just..."

She gagged over the thought of Hyun. "I thought you were a great guy, but that's only your outer layer. You show me a little more of the real you every day, and sometimes it's dirty and messy, but it's also fascinating and beautiful. You have a lot of little quirks, and I look forward to learning more."

Met with silence, she fussed with her phone, wishing to break the tension. "I now realize I've said too much."

Hanjun studied her. There were many things he wanted to say, but he couldn't manifest the words. From first sight, his heartbeat hastened when she looked at him. Within days, he yearned to learn everything about her. Regardless of his interest in her progressing quicker than it had for anyone else, he couldn't measure their connection in time. Only in intimacy. His love was all-consuming; mentally, spiritually, and physically, there was one milestone they had yet to reach.

Hanso interrupted his musing with a query. "Jen, truth or dare?"

A coy smile graced her lips. "*Dare.*"

Hanso pointed across the room. "Take Hanjun in the closet and hang out for *one whole song.*"

"What are we? Twelve?" Hanjun rolled his eyes at the childish suggestion. But before he could protest too much, Jen tickled his curiosity.

"Do I get to pick the song?" Receiving a nod from Hanso, Jen grabbed a dining chair and strolled to the cubbyhole. Hanjun followed, sensing all eyes on him. Closing the doors behind them, she produced a smile. "See you in 3 minutes and 59 seconds."

Light spilling from the lounge bowed to the darkness. Hanjun perched on the creaky, worn seat amid a jumble of musty coats and spare blankets. The rich spice of her perfume masked a cluster of mothballs nestled on a shelf above him. Hands trembling, he fiddled with the fabric of his jeans, anticipation and nervousness battling for supremacy in his mind. Scrolling through her playlist, the screen projected shadows over her silhouette. He held his breath, wondering which tune she would choose. Something sultry or erotic, he prayed. He wasn't sure how long it was—a minute, maybe two—when she settled on a provocative hip-hop beat and discarded the phone on the floor.

Moving her fingertips down his forearms and up his chest, she detected the exact moment his breathing hitched. "Is this okay?"

"Yes." He planted his arms at his sides, regulating his exhalation. Conquering his desire to take control, he wanted to see what she'd do if he didn't make the first move.

Lifting his shirt, she traced along his stomach, inching to his groin. He groaned, his head staggering back. Grabbing his shoulders, she climbed into his lap, depositing soft kisses below his ear. Encountering the bulge growing in his denim, she purred into his collar, leaving traces of her scented balm on his skin. "Tell me what you like."

"Everything."

"*Everything?*" Guiding his palms to the cups of her brassier, she urged him to squeeze.

Fingers interlaced, he pulled her close and claimed her neck with hot kisses. "Everything."

His mouth roamed over her body, extracting a gasp from her. "I love when you touch me."

Grasping a chunk of her hair, he tugged hard enough to let her know he was beyond serious in his appetite for her. "I could touch you forever."

Disrupting their motionless tango, she rose in a graceful motion, moving in sync with the rhythm. He clutched her hip possessively in one hand while the other slid under her blouse, fingers brushing the band of her bra. Pulling her down, his throbbing erection rammed against her thigh, provoking a short squeal.

Restrained by four flimsy layers of clothing, he bounced her on his thighs, caging the raw hunger surging through him. He longed to strip her naked and take her right on the hardwood, but he held back. His bandmates were lingering outside, and they didn't know they were official. Instead, he shut his eyes and imagined what it would be like to rail her. Would she moan or whisper? Did she have hidden kinks waiting to be revealed? How badly did she crave him? And how deeply was she willing to let him serve her?

Fantasizing about banging her wasn't enough; he wanted her body entangled with his. Elevating his glutes, he drilled against her. With each smooth thrust of his hips, her thighs fell further apart, and her chest expanded, inviting him to explore her magnificent body. He ventured down her abdomen, creeping to her waistband, though he ripped his hands away at the last second. "If we keep fucking around like this, we're gonna pass the point of no return."

"Do you want to stop?" Leaning against his torso, she threaded his arms around her waist.

Trailing a hand up to the base of her neck, he applied gentle pressure. "I *never* want to stop."

"Then don't." Hopeless in the moment, on the brink of surrender, the repetitive riffs ended, shattering the illusion of privacy. Gasping for air and trembling with thirst, they were brought back to a bitter reality, left mourning a painfully lost probability. "We went way further than I thought we would."

In post-orgasmic haze, he confessed an embarrassing truth. "I need to change."

"Oh, you—" Propelling out of his arms, she averted her eyes. "Must have been quite a ride."

"I swear it's not normally like—" He positioned a hand over his crotch, his mind teeming with every excuse for why his body betrayed him. She dry-humped him until he released, and he was sure it was how the Gods created rivers and streams.

She yanked him from the chair. Standing on her tiptoes, she left a peck near his ear. Simultaneously snaking a hand to his belt, she adjusted his shirt to cover the damp spot. "It's okay. We were messing around, and there was a lot of buildup."

Adjusting his clothes, he wasn't sure what to say. He wanted to thank her—both for the lap dance and ensuring he didn't embarrass himself in front of his friends—but acknowledging heat that had already cooled seemed too gauche.

She nabbed her phone from the floor and opened the door. Shocked and disoriented by the noises coming from the closet, Deok-Sun protected his ears. "I'm just a baby!"

Jin broke into a fit of giggles. "We should have played *seven minutes in heaven.*"

"Seven minutes would have been too long." Jen wielded a devilish smirk.

Nodding, Hanjun agreed. Three minutes later and he wouldn't have been able to restrain his urges. With her explicit consent, he would have ravaged her every curve with his hands, lips, and tongue. He was at her mercy, and whatever she demanded, she could have. In the dark space of that closet, he was hers. Emotionally and devotionally on his knees, he besieged her to reciprocate the same intensity. He wanted her to use him until his body was depleted and all that was left of him was stardust. And when he was reduced to nothing but a cosmic puddle of dreams, he would consume her. Absorbing and devouring her fears, he would replace every shred of guilt, insecurity, and unworthiness she carried and replenish her with love, trust, and the purest of naughtiest intentions. He would have rearranged the planets until she begged him to stop.

Fantasizing about her body nestled beneath his gave another rise to his trousers. He bolted to their room, where he spent a long time hiding, partly from embarrassment but also to recollect the moment. It wasn't his first rodeo, but it was by far the most memorable. "She's going to wreck me, and she doesn't even know."

⋆⁺₊⋆☾⋆⁺₊⋆

Jen snuggled next to Hanjun, emphasizing delicate kisses on his fingers. Blowing on the tips, she admired the contours of his profile. The grooves, hills, and dips made her want to worship a higher power. Only someone all-knowing could create something so beautiful.

"You can't be doing that." He displayed a certain look when aroused; his puffy eyelids became heavy, and he fixated on her lips, then moved his lazy gaze to her eyes.

She pouted. "No? Why not?"

"Hanso is sleeping." He gestured to the opposite bed.

"That's a shame." Her lips traveled to his collarbone. "So I shouldn't do *this*?"

"You know too well what I like." Her scent ignited a familiar flame, flooding him with memories of their closet romp. Humming along to each of her kisses, his fingers twisted in her hair. "You're so bad for me, but I love it."

Though she would never admit it, she adored the way his voice changed when he was amorous. His diplomatic words dissolved into a jumbled mess, projecting innocence and vulnerability. Releasing his hand, she coiled up to sleep. "Goodnight, Jun."

"Sweet dreams, Jen." Reaching for a pen, he relived the night until he fell asleep.

When she said she loved my hands on her body, I exploded. She consumes every thought, and while I'm happy to move at her pace, I can hardly wait to express our emotions on a much deeper plane.

CHAPTER TWENTY-TWO

Desperation and Bravery

Lifting a cup of single-origin coffee to his lips, Hanjun savored the full-bodied aroma, though his focus was won by Jen. Strutting through the kitchen, she exuded comfort on a cold day, dressed in an oversized Adidas hoodie and jeans.

"Did you sleep well?" Moving to the freezer, she plopped a palmful of ice cubes into her insulated cup.

"Very." He tipped the mug toward her.

"I was thinking..." She leaned on a cabinet, running her fingers along the straw. "We should stay low-key. I don't want anyone thinking you're receiving preferential treatment."

He nodded. "I wouldn't want that, either."

"Friends at work, then?" She held out a clenched fist.

"Friends at work." Reciprocating the gesture, he checked his watch. "Do you mind waking the boys?"

"I don't mind." She abandoned her cup on the counter and turned for the hallway. Singing along to an earworm, she zigzagged door to door. "Up! Up! Up! Makeup in thirty!"

Reaching Soogi's room, she knocked more softly. "Deok-Sun and Jin are taking their showers; then you can take yours."

Soogi's muffled response came from the other side. "Okay."

Reaching their shared room, she found Hanso awake. Dipping to acknowledge him, she closed the door and tramped back to the kitchen. "Everyone's up; they just need to get ready."

Scoffing, Hanjun rinsed the carafe in the sink. "For some reason, they wake easier for you."

"I don't think that's true." She picked up her cup and took a long drink. "I think they just like annoying you."

⋆⁺₊⋆☾⋆⁺₊⋆

The musicians sat in front of traveling vanity stations, having their makeup applied. Standing front and center, Ha-Rin hosted a small summit of requirements while the cosmetologists worked. "We're filming another episode of Parallels, where you'll compete in boat races built by hand. We'll ask trivia questions during the building process; answering correctly will earn you upgraded parts for your boats."

Motioning to the back door, he gestured to the beach, where the challenge awaited. "Don't forget, we need a few shots of Jenilyn near Hanso."

"I know." Groaning, Jen trotted to the shoreline, trailing behind a parade of staff. Though she was initially in a sour mood over Ha-Rin's announcement, she wasn't forced to engage as much as the previous days. She was asked to hold lighting equipment, disperse hot drinks, and occasionally hover next to Hanso.

Their first scheduled break came faster than expected, and Hanjun gravitated to the water, combing the bank for seashells. A lifelong passion, he started in childhood and continued as an adult. His bandmates assisted in the hunt, bringing him handfuls of baubles and sea glass.

During her down time, when she wasn't mingling with the crew, Jen splashed in the shallows. Finding unique pebbles—the vividest of greens and the inkiest of blacks—she placed them in her palm to appreciate.

"Which one do you like more?" Jogging to her side, Hanjun showed her his treasures. Noticing her frown, his enthusiasm diminished. "Is something wrong?"

"I don't want to ruin your fun." She averted her gaze from the shells.

He bent to her height. "Jen, tell me what's wrong."

Glancing at the pearlescent shells in his palm, her shoulders drooped. "There's an issue with critters not being able to find homes due to overharvesting. Even if everyone only takes one or two, imagine how many that is."

"Oh." Dropping to his knees, he placed the trinkets in the sand. She started to apologize when he pulled out his phone. "I'll just take a photo. I don't need to possess something to admire it, right?"

"Right." Her spirit perked up. "I've heard people are 3D printing replacement shells using biodegradable materials."

He straightened up with the cheeriest of smiles. "Wouldn't that be awesome to leave some instead of taking them?"

"There's a tourist spot I've always wanted to visit in Florida—Hermit Crab Island. Perhaps we can go there one day."

Performing a small hop, he grinned. "I'd love that."

⋆⁺₊⋆☾⋆⁺₊⋆

The sun dipped below the horizon, casting a golden glow over the living room. Returning an empty bottle of Casillero del Diablo to the coffee table, Jen took slow sips from her second glass. Comfortable heat spread through her body, and she sank into the cushion. Her phone rang from her lap, and she passed it to Hanjun. "Guess who."

Checking the caller ID, he offered a curt greeting. "What?"

An outraged voice crackled through the speaker. "Let me talk to her."

Wearing a smirk, he refused. "You talk to me, or you talk to nobody. What do you want?"

"Are you deaf? I already told you!"

Hanjun terminated the call. Abandoning an empty bottle of beer on the table, he stuffed the device into his pocket. "Meet me outside."

Watching him walk past, Jin cowered under a blanket. "Hanu looks mad."

"He should be." Hanso licked his finger and turned a page in his comic. "That guy just doesn't get the hint."

"Welcome to my world." Resting her glass next to Hanjun's, she grabbed two blankets from their bedroom. Rendezvousing on the back porch, she followed him to the beach. He didn't speak, but she sensed the tension in his shoulders and saw the way his jaw contorted. Approaching a secluded spot where the white caps met the rocks, she let the covers fall to her ankles.

Gesturing to the water, he handed her the phone. "Throw it in."

She studied him and then the screen in her palm. Though it was a few years old, a little banged up, and had a finicky charging port, it was perfectly usable. "Why would I—"

"You told us to let the water wash away our worries." He imitated her optimistic twirl, kicking up dust with his feet. "He's a worry for you. Throw it in."

Curling her fingers around the galaxy-colored case, she pondered the idea. Aside from her email, it was the last way her ex had to contact her. She barely existed on social media, and the single account she used was unable to be viewed by friends of friends. There were a few she contacted on a regular basis: her best friend, a handful of old colleagues, and her previous employer. "You're right."

Sailing through the air, the device created a satisfying splash. Collapsing her legs, she plopped on one blanket and wrapped the other around her body. In the same way the phone disappeared under the current, her former life was slipping away, forgotten among the billows of her new one.

He snuggled next to her, cinching the cover in front of their chests. "I know you don't like to talk about it, but whatever's in the past, let it stay there. It belongs behind you."

Mirroring the turbulent waters of the roaring sea, her failed marriage was just as unpredictable—a constant struggle with highs and lows that were impossible to predict. "Two years ago, I wondered what was wrong with me. No matter what I did, it wasn't good enough. I'm not going to pretend I was the best wife in the world, but I wanted to be. I don't think I knew enough about love. It's not like in the movies. Love in the real world is conditional, cemented by boundaries, expectations, and accountability."

She hunkered into the warmth, recalling the most uncomfortable part of her severance: having her integrity torn apart by nearly everyone she knew. Even those who had never been married or divorced claimed to know what went wrong and never hesitated to offer unsolicited advice. "Making a promise to be with someone forever is easy, but loving someone unconditionally is irrational because there is always a fault line. Guaranteed, there's something your spouse could do that would be your breaking point. If there weren't, we would be captives. Slaves, even. Romantic love can't exist without conditions. It would be insanity, not love."

He caressed her hand. "Unconditional love doesn't mean absolute tolerance."

"I tolerated more than anyone should."

"Perhaps, but you gained wisdom only someone in your situation could have. The one who succeeds fails far more than the one who never tried."

She looked up at him, searching his eyes for hesitation. "It doesn't bother you that I'm divorced?"

"Your willingness to do what's best for you is the only thing I need to know." He gave her arm a reassuring jostle. "I've never been strong enough to leave someone, even when they were bad for me. I wish I had an ounce of your bravery."

"It wasn't bravery; it was desperation. It was choosing myself. I was going to lose one of us, and it couldn't be me." Her admission was prideful but also tinged with sadness at what it had taken to make herself a priority.

"I don't believe that." He shook his head. "The difference between bravery and desperation is thought. Desperation is the instinct to survive unthinkable situations. It's without consciousness."

"Bravery—" He paused to make direct eye contact. "*Bravery* is knowing the consequences of your actions and carrying through anyway. It's taking a leap of faith and accepting that the circumstances might not end in the way you hoped. Bravery is a choice."

"*Brave*." A surge of strength drowned her anxieties—the unmistakable awareness of her power. During her divorce, she was given many labels—some empowering, others hurtful—but never once had she considered herself brave.

"Perhaps unconditional love can only exist for ourselves," he mused.

"Or our children."

He admired her under the moon's spell. "Or our children."

Sitting in contemplative placidity, she had second thoughts about her contribution to pollution. "I can't leave my phone in there. What if a creature tries to eat it?"

"Ha!" Throwing his head back, he cackled at his lack of foresight. "I should have thought about that."

Shedding the blanket, she tramped to the water's edge, dipping a toe into the icy ripples. "It's freezing."

"Jump in!" Purposely snuggling into the covers, he razzed her. "It'll be over before you know it."

She backed away. "No way. It's too cold."

Springing to his feet, he sprinted the distance. "You need to find it."

She stepped forward, only to shake her head and retreat. "You're the one who wanted me to throw it! You get it."

Trapping her waist in his hands, he guided her to the water. "You got this!"

"Hanjun..." She yelped as the waves rushed over her toes and threatened to engulf her legs.

Despite her protests, he didn't stop until they were knee-deep. While her arms shivered uncontrollably around her chest, he posed a loaded question. "Ready?"

"No, I am not!" She closed her eyes, unleashing a dam of swear words. "Don't you dare—"

"Dare what?" Weaponizing a laugh, he tipped their bodies over the plashing surface.

"No—no—" Plunging into the icy depths, she struggled to catch her breath, and the salty water rolled over her tongue.

"Shit, that's cold!" Bursting out of the water, he slicked his hair back. "It's not here..."

"I found it!" Dunking to retrieve the device, she paddled out just as fast as she fell in. Tingling with pins and needles, she stripped out of her clothing with lightning speed. Tossing her blouse on the beach, she recommended he remove his as well. "Take your pants off."

"What?" He observed the way the fabric flung from her body. "I'm not taking my—"

"Seriously, we need to dry off." Standing in her bra and undies, she shook the sand from her clothes. "That water is cold enough to freeze. I read about it in a survival guide."

He unbuckled his belt. "You're crazy, you know that?"

"Maybe, but you love it." Utilizing her best Hanjun impression, she pointed to his torso. "Shirt, too."

⋆⁺₊⋆☾⋆⁺₊⋆

Just shy of midnight, Jen and Hanjun returned to the rental home, sheathed in damp comforters. The only source of light came from the wood-burning stove, billowing a cloud of choking smoke. Creeping through the back door, the wooden floor moaned, coaxing their giggles.

Jen knelt before the log burner. "Can we stay here for a few minutes?"

"Sure." Dropping the bedcover, he settled near the flames.

She held her hands out to the fire, chasing away the cold. Serving him a side-eye, she caught on to his quiet admiration. "It's kind of weird, Jun."

He added a small piece of kindling to the firebox. "Every day, you teach me something new."

"Is that so?" She restored her attention to the pyre.

"Before I met you, I longed to be normal. To go on simple walks or ordinary dates." The blaze illuminated her features, making her even more beautiful, and his true sentiments slipped from his lips. "I don't miss normal anymore."

"Hanjun—" She turned to face him, shuddering from the chill of her wet undergarments. "I dream of meeting you. The person you were, the person you are, and the person you're going to be. I want to meet all of you."

"I want you to know every part of me, too." Pulling her close, he caressed her hair, wishing the moment never ended.

$$\star^+_+\star\mathbb{C}\star^+_+\star$$

At the end of the night, Jen reclined on her back, her skin cold from the water. Hanjun nestled beside her, propped up on his elbow to shield her from the accidental gawk of Hanso. Their dampened clothing hung over the footboard, leaving skimpy undergarments as a boundary.

His fingers lingered in the space between her breasts, identifying her hastened heartbeat. Beyond her surface-level apprehensiveness and aversion to vulnerability, she was anxious about starting a new relationship. She survived a toxic past and was afraid of history repeating itself—a fear he knew all too well. Leaning in, he left the softest kiss on her forehead.

She mumbled for him to stop his fawning and drifted off to sleep just as fast. Patting her hair, he reached for his journal.

Her worry washed away by the sea. I can only hope
she grows to love the heart within me.

CHAPTER TWENTY-THREE

Argus Panoptes

Following a grueling day of photo shoots, Hanjun greeted Jen, flourishing a platter of prepared noodles. "We'll watch the footage while we eat."

Holding out a bowl, Jen couldn't shake the guilt that had haunted her since the kerfuffle with Dae-Hyun. "What if there isn't enough?"

He served her a generous portion. "We should have more than plenty."

"But if we don't..." Picking up her chopsticks, she struggled to position the utensils in her hands. Once she was too frustrated to continue, she tossed them in the sink and grabbed a fork.

Hanjun smiled at her failed attempt. She was determined to master the skill and gave it a try every time she ate. "We would have to move the schedule and stay an extra day."

"It will be fine." Soogi trotted to the living room. Abandoning his bowl on the coffee table, he primed the television for viewing.

Slumping into his seat, Deok-Sun mocked the narration. "Watch Blackmirror exploit their liaison."

"Let's hope they didn't play into it too much." Jen snuggled between Jin and Hanso.

"Shh." Hanjun stood in the doorway, adjusting the volume to drown out Deok-Sun's commentary.

During the opening theme song, Hanjun disappeared into the kitchen. Emerging with an armful of chips and a frosty can of cola, he lingered behind Jen, shoveling handfuls of salty snacks into his mouth. Offering to share by holding the bag directly next to her face, his eyes were glued to the screen.

'Stay tuned for clips starring Blackmirror, taken directly from the secret filming location of their newest single, 'Miss You.''

The tube flashed with brief shots viewers would recognize from the episode: the mates huddled on the coast, chaotic boat racing montages, and behind-the-scenes footage of their colorful concept shoot. Weirded out by the humiliation they endured, Jen and Hanso avoided acknowledging themselves. The program went on to display angles not captured by their videographers, including distant outlines of Hanjun and Jen on the shore, along with bird's-eye views from their bedrooms.

"Who was that on the beach?" Deok-Sun scooted to the end of his seat. "The only time we filmed at night was during the bonfire."

Fixing her attention on the screen, Jen tapped Hanjun's wrist. "We never filmed that."

"The indoor footage we took was first-person. Jen and Hanso were shown aerially." Hanjun rewound the show. "It couldn't have been us."

Deok-Sun observed the clip a second time. "If we didn't, who did?"

"I don't know." Handing the crisps off to Jin, Hanjun eyeballed every nook and cranny of the room. Concentrating on an old clock hanging above the back door, he stretched to his limits, yanking the timepiece from the wall. Tearing a wad of electrical wires from the back, he zeroed in on a microlens camouflaged within the two of the twelve o'clock. "A camera?"

Covering her mouth, Jen gasped. "Who would do that?"

"Molka." Eyes moving to Jen, Jin's bottom lip quivered.

She shifted uncomfortably. "What's molka?"

The room fell into an uneasy silence until Soogi intervened. "Spy cams, Jen."

"Why would someone—"

Finding hidden cameras was an all-too-common occurrence—a nasty blemish elected officials liked to pretend didn't exist. The crime of molka referred to images taken with any kind of camera or voyeuristic videos that were later circulated without the consent of those on screen. Although criminal,

South Korea's digitized society made it easy to circulate and difficult to remove once spread.

"It's illegal, but—" Pausing, Soogi hoped someone else would answer. "They're used to record sexual deviance and later distributed for personal gain."

"Sometimes without," Deok-Sun added under his breath.

Her stomach squirmed. "Should I be concerned?"

Pulling his attention from the clock, Hanjun's features softened. "I don't think so."

Discharging a long sigh, her troubles were eased until she remembered the drunken game of truth or dare. The memory of getting frisky with Hanjun made her quiver, though a different kind of tremor burned her blood. "Jun, the closet."

Catching the crack in her voice, Hanjun investigated the cuddy, pushing aside brooms and boxes. Pulling back a rod of jackets, his sights landed on a bizarre collage. Hung precariously, a quintain of frames were arranged in a circular pattern: majestic white cattle adorned with jewels and pearls. Affixed in the middle was a lone painting of a stunning peafowl. "What the hell?"

Hanso sprang from the sofa. "Did you find something?"

"I guess you could say that..."

Jen joined him in the cramped space, followed by Soogi and Jin. She studied the unusual grouping, and her gut told her it wasn't a coincidence. "Five cows?"

"And a peacock," Jin whispered.

Piecing together an explanation, she blurted out the first thing that made any amount of sense. "Callithyia!"

Confused glances were exchanged between Soogi and Jin, prompting clarification. "Also known as Io. She was said to be the ancestor of many kings and heroes. Perseus, Heracles, Minos, and generations later—"

"Dionysus." Hanjun's gaze shifted from Jen to the portraits.

Jin recognized symbolism he had only seen in textbooks. His limbs went cold, knowing there was something sinister on the horizon. "Are we supposed to know what it means?"

Hanjun traced the intricate details. "Io... Jupiter's moon?"

Soogi pulled out his mobile, performing a quick search. "Lover of Zeus and first priestess to Hera—"

"Hera? C'mon, think." Hanjun rubbed his fingers along his hairline. Ripping the framed peacock from the wall, he made a sudden exclamation. *"Argus Panoptes!"*

"Argus Pano-*what*-es?" Jin peered over Hanjun's shoulder.

"Argus Panoptes. The Greek God of Surveillance." Understanding the gravity of their situation, Hanjun's expression darkened. It was bad. Very bad. "Someone wants us to know they're watching."

Soogi gripped his phone. "According to this, Zeus fell in love with Io. Hera, consumed by jealousy, transformed her into a white cow and sent Argus to guard her. Eventually, Zeus employed Hermes to distract and kill Argus. Hera turned Argus into a peacock who, over time, became celebrated as the God of Surveillance."

"What the—" Deok-Sun hyperventilated.

Jin shuddered. "What does it mean?"

"It means someone saw everything," Jen whispered.

"No, they *heard* something. It was pitch black—" Fixating on the image, Hanjun's voice faded. The frame stood out from the others, thicker and more ornate, with elaborate scrollwork. Studying the portrait, he spotted a small pinhole bordering the edge. Snapping the casing over his knee, shards propelled from the frame while the remaining chunks crashed to the floor.

"Jun—" Jen's confusion shifted to concern. "There's glass everywhere."

Kneeling to retrieve something from the floor—no bigger than a tiny fuse—he held the item up to the light. "It's another camera."

⋆⁺₊⋆☾⋆⁺₊⋆

While Jen tended to Hanjun's injuries in the kitchen, their roommates scoured the rental home for cameras. Much to their dismay, they uncovered security equipment in every room except the bathroom—inconspicuous recording devices disguised as daylight bulbs.

Hanjun extended his hand, wincing as she rinsed his arm. Eyebrows crinkling, she gauged the damage, dabbing at his palm with a wet towel. His lifeline was marked by a sizable wound, though the blood had begun to clot. "What were you thinking?"

He chuckled. "I wasn't."

"We need to clean this." Glowering at him, she popped open a bottle of peroxide. "It will burn."

Splashing enough pain-inducing liquid over the injury to make him flinch, she took another look. "You're incredibly lucky the cut wasn't deep."

She heard a suppressed gasp escape his lungs and glanced up to find him flaunting a vexatious grin. "What are you smiling for? You could have seriously gotten hurt, Jun."

"If someone has that recording, and they release it—" He waited for her to look at him. "We won't have to hide anymore. We could be together."

"That would cause a scandal." She replaced the lid with a huff. "The agency would never allow it."

"Think about it—" His infectious smile coaxed her lips to curve, despite her reservations. "A scandal would get people talking. That's what J&I cares about."

"Not in a good way." Expelling a rueful simper, she rolled her eyes. "We have no choice but to wait."

Turning to rinse the blood-covered rag in the sink, she contemplated their predicament. She knew any connection they had—whether they were friends, acquaintances, or lovers— wouldn't be normal. His career simply wouldn't permit it. Her apprehension about entering a relationship with him was in direct relation to the issues it would spur. If anyone were to uncover the romance, her life would become a perpetual battle of sustaining appearances. As his ambassador, she would need to put her best face forward, and many of the same burdens plaguing him would infect her. Fame was a grotesque and crippling disease she wanted to avoid at all costs.

⋆⁺₊⋆☾⋆⁺₊⋆

Complaining of a headache, Jen retired earlier than usual. Hanjun remained by her side, his anxiety climbing to uncontrollable levels. He couldn't tell her what would happen if their secret tryst was discovered; the consequences would be unpredictable and disastrous. His uneasiness hid behind a facade of pipe dreams, but his cool composure was starting to crumble under the weight of his culpability. If anyone got their hands on the lap dance evidence, their private moment would be revealed to the populace, subjecting them to endless scrutiny. And while the agency's publicists would navigate the fallout, he would be reprimanded for jeopardizing Blackmirror's reputation, along with J&I's credibility.

But what troubled him the most was the possibility of Jen becoming a target. As the object of his affection, she would bear the brunt of the backlash. Their fan base, while brimming with millions of wonderful adherents, hosted a slew of irrational crazies. Devotees who would do anything to protect them, or so they thought. Jen would undoubtedly fall victim to their rage, and he couldn't stand the thought of her facing such cruel treatment. It wasn't the first time he had disappointed the company—it was a regular occurrence—but this time, the repercussions could be dire for someone he cared for. She would be crucified on the cross of social media, and if that wasn't enough to make her flee from his life, die-hard supporters would issue threats until she did.

Of course, the agency would make moves to shield her from the onslaught, but they could only counteract hurtful articles and comments. They wouldn't be able to prevent harassment from happening, and she couldn't outrun the news reporters, paparazzi, and stalkers who would stop at nothing to get the information they wanted.

He didn't know how to tell her why none of Blackmirror admitted to having significant others. It wasn't that they didn't date; it was that they couldn't announce their affairs publicly without it being a threat to their partners and their partner's friends and family.

Chewing on the end of his pen, he logged a journal entry.

*Every minute of our lives is monitored, yet someone
invaded the little privacy we have. I should have
warned her to stay away from me.*

<u>CHAPTER TWENTY-FOUR</u>

The Unknown

Morning rays streamed through the windows, projecting a radiant glow over the kitchen. Jen strutted in to find Hanjun slumped over the table. A coffee cup sat near his hand, steaming and untouched. He looked up at her with teary eyes, wiping away the evidence.

She joined him, hugging him to her chest. "What's wrong?"

He closed his eyes for a long moment. "I should have looked for cameras. The crew usually checks before our stay, but I should have looked myself."

She swiped a tuft of hair from his eyes. "It's okay—"

"No, it's not." Running a palm along his swollen cheeks, he groaned. "If anyone gets hold of—"

"We'll deal with it then."

Blinking the remaining tears from his eyes, he forced a smile. It was impossible for him not to worry. Throughout his career, precautions were taken to avoid scandals, and threats were avoided with direct intent. As much as he didn't like to admit it, he cared about the public's opinion, he cared about charting in every country, and he cared about being a role model. If he didn't care about any of it, he would produce for the simple act of creation.

The idol system was predatory, but it was still one of the best ways to get noticed, even if it required living up to an impractical standard. It was a grand opportunity—one that shouldn't be squandered by careless actions. Without Jen knowing the conditions he was subjected to, and the amount of energy invested in building an empire, he feared she wouldn't grasp the severity. The prospect of ruining his life's work over a night of fun wasn't something easily grasped by an outsider.

He adored her. It might even have been more than that. He liked her so much that he could hardly wait to see her. He split his time between working on external projects and spending time with her. He wanted her to stay in his life more than anyone before her, but he couldn't jeopardize his existence for her, and he hoped she understood that as an artist, entertainer, and public figure, his work would always come first.

He wasn't selfish. His profession was more than his livelihood; it was his savior. Music kept him sane in a world full of crazy. Even at the age of twenty-nine, music was the only reason he could roll out of bed some mornings. Music wasn't just music. It was love, and it was hate. And like all things he did, he loved music wholeheartedly. From the melody to the lyrics, he appreciated the raw grittiness as well as the harmonic aspects. Musicians, much like artists and authors, shared a piece of themselves in every work they touched, and he welcomed the bruises, bumps, and all.

Pulling away, he drew a breath. "The boys will be up soon."

She pushed the full mug into his palm. "You don't have to pretend to be strong for them."

Pressing his hands together, he rested his lips against his fingers with his thumbs tucked under his chin. Being strong was a substantial part of his job, even if it meant falling apart alone. There was no other option. He had to be strong.

He straightened up when he heard his bandmates shuffling around in the hall. Before they entered the kitchen, he splashed cold water on his face, removing the puffiness from his eyes. When they finally emerged to eat breakfast, he interacted as if nothing were wrong. He acted with such ease, as if he had faked a smile millions of times before.

Jen couldn't stand to watch it anymore.

★⁺₊★☾★⁺₊★

Following a busy morning of packing, the roommates settled into a van for the long trek back to Seoul. Smooshed between Hanjun and Hanso, Jen gazed out the window. Whizzing past expansive fields and tall mountains, the sun shone through the trees, dappling shadows on her forehead.

Gaze fixed on something far beyond the scenery, Hanjun bobbed in time with the tunes streaming through his earbuds.

He drummed along to the beat, but he couldn't hide his unease. The jitteriness, the harsh movements—he was more than agitated. He was pissed.

Resting her head back, Jen mulled over the drama that had unfolded over the prior week. Dae-Hyun, fake-dating Hanso, secret tapings—she was running out of ways to regulate her festering anger. Her usual distractions couldn't be utilized when she was contracted to her source of rage. She wasn't even certain she wanted to calm down; after all, her resentment was warranted. Anger had a bad rep, but it was a neutral emotion. It highlighted discrepancies, repression, and brutality. Coming to terms with her anger would mean she had given up, and she sure as hell wasn't surrendering. No, she was going to beat Hyun at his own game by being one of the most prominent public relations stunt girlfriends of the decade. When she was done, he would wish he had never messed with her.

Jen woke just as their driver pulled into the parking garage. Dark and musty, eclipsed beneath the tower, the parkade was only accessible by electronic pass. She tugged on Hanjun's sleeve, gesturing to the expensive cars in the lot. "I didn't see anything on the schedule about going to the office."

Removing an earbud, he flung the door open. "I requested an emergency meeting."

"Is there something you need? I could have called Ha-Rin." Slinging her bag over her shoulder, she scurried behind, nearly tripping over a parking block.

Dragging his feet, Soogi complained about the unplanned requirement. "I needed to visit the studio."

Hanjun scanned his identification, gaining access to the basement elevator. "We need to find out why there were spy cams at the beach house."

'Welcome, Hanjun. You are expected on business floor thirty-six in thirteen minutes.'

"It's a breach of agreement." Jin agreed. "Our contract specifies forewarning."

★⁺₊✱☾★⁺₊★

Leaning back in his chair, Dae-Hyun was bemused by Hanjun bursting through the door, followed by his teammates. "Was there a reason this couldn't have waited until—"

Projecting his deepest timbre, Hanjun refused to be questioned. "Why weren't we told about the cameras?"

"We took the liberty of capturing candid content." Sitting at the far end, Ha-Rin hoped to appease the angered musician.

"Why weren't we informed?" Hanso scowled, unable to understand why the agency would go to such lengths for a few extra shots of film.

"It comes as no surprise; you act different off camera." Ha-Rin discharged a chuckle. "You were trained that way."

Face twisting in disgust, Soogi sniffed out a lie. "That doesn't mean you can record us without our consent."

"You were aware we were there to film."

"The footage from the closet." Hanjun tapped the table. "I want the master and all additional copies destroyed."

Ha-Rin raised an eyebrow. "Closet? We would never—"

"Spy cameras?" Jin interjected, only to be met with a sassy retort from Ha-Rin.

"The only cameras we put up were in the bedrooms."

Leaning close enough to whisper, Jen squeezed Hanjun's knee under the table. "I don't think he knows."

"Never mind." Lowering into his seat, he conceded. If they didn't know about the potential leak, he wasn't going to be the one to tell them.

"Since that's resolved..." Hyun redirected the conversation. "I have a few things I'd like to discuss."

★⁺₊✱☾★⁺₊★

Gathering in the hallway at the end of the night, they discovered a small package sitting on the floor outside their door. There was no name or address indicating who it was from.

Tearing into the kraft wrapping, Jin found a paper heart. "That's it?"

"Could be from a fan." Hanjun wheeled his luggage through the doorway. "Windsor Heights is home to a lot of powerful people; many have kids who are Anti."

"Yeah, you're probably right." Jen followed.

Heading straight to his room, Hanjun couldn't ignore how their private time had been recorded. Slumping on the mattress, he stared at the ceiling, fixating on the overhead fan. A moment later, he found himself balanced on a desk chair, ensuring the fixture wasn't bugged. He then went to each room in the home, searching for cams. Checking every light he could reach, he didn't find a single bug. When he was sure the condo was clean, he returned to his room to record the findings.

Management installed all the cameras except for the lounge and closet. Who puts a camera in a closet? How long has it been there? And what are they doing with the recordings?

Jen flopped on her comforter, unsure how to support Hanjun. After scouring the residence, he performed a forensic examination of her dressers, mirrors, and vanity, convinced they were under surveillance.

Flinging through her belongings, he almost ripped open one of her stuffed animals, certain there was a camera buried inside. He only stopped when she cried over the thought of her favorite stuffie being torn to shreds. Standing in the middle of her room, his swivel-eyed mania turned lucid. He placed the cow pillow on her bed and left, muttering an apology.

She had never been in such a predicament; when someone cared about her so much, they ignored their feelings. She couldn't tell him to stop caring; she simply wished for him to handle himself. She would be fine, as she always was. Even if the press caught wind of the naughty closet dare, not much could be done to her beyond ridiculing. She was socially non-existent. Practically a ghost. His reputation was in jeopardy, not hers. His years of hard work and dedication were in danger, not hers. She was worried for him, not her. "How can I ask him not to care when I can't do the same?"

CHAPTER TWENTY-FIVE

A Secret Date

Hanjun climbed on Jen's bed, sinking into the cozy blankets. With his arms snaking around her waist, his lips vibrated against her nape. "I'm a jetpack. Brr."

Eyes fluttering open, she rotated to face him. Brushing the bangs from his eyes, she studied his handsome features. "We have the day off. We should do something."

A mischievous glint flashed in his eyes. "Like what?"

"How about visiting the museum?" Her eyelashes batted.

Expelling a wistful sigh, his grip loosened. "I wish we could."

"I have an idea." Shushing him with a smooch, she rolled off the bed. "Be ready to leave in fifteen minutes."

Conceding to her desires, a dimple dotted his cheek. He wondered what she was up to—it wasn't like her to do anything without an expertly crafted strategy. She was someone who had backup plans for her backup plans. With three minutes left on the clock, he slithered out of the covers and pulled on a pair of well-worn jeans.

In the kitchen, he found her dressed in a trendy outfit: a cozy pink sweater with a textured heart pattern and black leather pants. Retrieving her favorite jacket from the entry closet, he draped the fabric over her shoulders. "That's a good look on you."

Outlining the plan, she slipped into combat boots at the door. "I'll arrive before you so we don't raise suspicion. Once we're there, we'll play it by ear."

★⁺₊☽⁺₊★

Stepping out of the taxi, Jen hoofed it to the entrance. The imposing building loomed over the skyline, beckoning patrons inside. A line formed at the door, and she integrated in, waiting for her temperature to be taken. Once declared healthy and Covid-free, she surveyed the visitors, gauging to see if there was anyone to be wary of. Hanjun could be recognized at any given moment, but the probability was higher when there were children involved.

Relieved by the older couples, groups of businessmen, and internationals frequenting the establishment, her eyes landed on a mother, father, and pre-teen daughter. Assessing their designer threads, she assumed they were opulent, or at the very least, wanted to be. But what piqued her curiosity was their behavior. All three whipped out their phones, recording every spec of artwork within a ten-foot radius.

The youngster brandished a selfie stick longer than her arm, and her parents indulged her requests, promising to fulfill her wishes if she did well in school. "I want one like this!"

"Of course, honey." The mother snapped a picture of her near a giant mural.

"Mom, look!" The child pointed a finger at the entrance doors. "That's Ryu Hanjun of Blackmirror! Can I meet him? Can I?"

She dashed towards Hanjun, nearly knocking him over. Five Multiverse keychains dangled from her Celine backpack, and Jen was sure her plan for a peaceful date was falling apart. The girl begged for an autograph, and Hanjun, ever the gracious celebrity, obliged. Flashing a smirk at Jen, he pulled a marker from his pocket and scribbled his name on the girl's museum map. He then asked if she would like a picture. The girl nodded, and Hanjun turned to the parents, who had made little effort to calm their daughter. Mumbling thanks, they handed over their phones, though Hanjun's gaze remained on Jen. "Would you mind?"

"Uh, yeah." Bridging the gap, she served him a questioning side-eye, taking the phones in her hands.

Holding his arms at his sides, he readied an adorable peace sign. "On the count of three, okay? Hana, dul..."

On cue, Jen captured the moment. Without so much as a smile, the mother ripped the devices from her, though the father stopped to apologize. "I'm sorry about her."

The family left the area with brag-worthy pictures for their social media accounts, clamoring about meeting the superstar in the wild. "What's the chance we'd be here the same day as Rem?"

Waiting for them to leave the vicinity, Hanjun reached for Jen's hand. "You're a trooper."

Pulling away, she rushed to the nearest exhibit. Holding the door open, she ushered him through and spoke in whispers. "I was a fool to think it would work. Just go. I'll hang behind."

Accessing a vast white room, the walls were lined with oversized portraits. Soft light filtered in through high windows, casting a serene glow over the installations. Treading carefully, she watched him move from one piece to the next. Select artists held a special place in his heart, and he lingered at their handiwork. Removing the knitted beanie he wore, he bowed at every exhibit label.

Like two celestial bodies orbiting a sun, they traversed the room, never close enough for others to make assumptions about them. But every now and then, as rare and fleeting as an eclipse, she idled near him. One painting caught his eye: a striking monochromatic effigy of a Korean woman, her disposition reflecting a painful annulment. He stood before it for a long time, studying the tiniest brushstroke with unwavering focus. "What do you think she wanted to convey?"

"This was painted when divorce was highly stigmatized. The muted colors and lack of light highlight her descent into madness. Her family and friends ostracized her for wanting more..." Trailing off, he clicked his tongue.

"Not much has changed." The woman's lifeless eyes portrayed the same hurt she once suffered: a tangled web of shame, exhaustion, and frustration. Venturing into the unknown may have been intimidating, but it was something that needed to be done for her growth. In tearing down her old life, she discovered a little more about what she truly wanted.

He bent forward, nearly ninety degrees. "She died alone."

"Perhaps things are different." While the idea of dying companionless crossed her mind more times than she cared to admit, she would have rather perished than wither away. "In a loveless marriage, she would have died alone regardless."

His gaze bore into her. "That's frightening, isn't it? Even if you do as the world expects, there aren't any guarantees."

Nodding, she bit her lip. "We love knowing others could betray us. That's what makes it thrilling."

"Less thrilling when they do." Noticing her eyeing the monument a little too long, he sidestepped to another portrait. He identified hidden elements, passionately discussing his interpretations. The emotions invoked in him. The mental condition the painter might have had at the time of creation. How the artist's view transformed in the series. Writing a book report with his words, he swiped a tear from his eye.

"Would you like me to take a photo of you?" One thing she learned about him during their short time together was that he documented everything. Something simply didn't happen without photographic evidence.

"Please." Handing off his phone, he posed, and she shuttered away at his request. Roaming the room, he submitted to his penchant for digital souvenirs. "I'd like a photo with this one. And maybe that one over there? I'm sorry if I'm being too much."

"Your happiness is my happiness." Each click of the camera captured his perfectly poised smile.

His cheeks were rosy, bashful at his own indulgence. Backtracking, he paused once again to marvel at the divorced woman's canvas. "Thank you."

"You're welcome." She returned the phone, and they separated. To avoid unwanted publicity, she left the institution first. Seated on the concrete steps, she debated whether to wait for him or head straight home. "Not a very thorough plan, Jen."

After making a generous donation with the caretaker, Hanjun took his leave. Finding her outside, he pulled his hat over his eyes and settled next to her. "I didn't think it would be possible to go on a date, but we managed."

"Don't celebrate just yet." She avoided making eye contact with pedestrians passing by. "I'm not sure we went unnoticed."

"Do you like the arts, or did you come to be with me?" Tracing the bandaged cut along his palm, he would have loved it if she shared his fascination with art. If she didn't, he would be happy she wanted to be with him.

"I love to visit galleries, but I couldn't name more than twenty artists. The truth is, I have interest in everything, and I can only have so many hobbies."

He knew the feeling all too well. There were only so many hours in a day to pursue one's passions. "You know music is the love of my life. What's yours?"

"Poetry, and to a lesser extent, lyrics. While I can appreciate a catchy beat, it's poesies that do it for me. Dead or alive, poets weave their lifeblood into their work—something artificial intelligence will never replicate."

He felt the same about art. His deep appreciation for the visual arts began after he joined Blackmirror. During tours, they were confined to hotel suites, and there weren't many things he could do to escape his comfortable prison. With too much time to think, he often reminisced about being young. His father was an avid aesthete, and he fondly recalled visiting museums with him as a child. Hand in hand, they strolled through long halls, admiring works created hundreds of years before his birth. Afterward, they would purchase fish-shaped pastries from roadside vendors and discuss the sometimes difficult topics accompanying the images.

Catching a serious case of homesickness one lonely morning, he toured local galleries to evoke childhood nostalgia. Unchaperoned and standing among the Sixteen Pillars of Tadao Ando, he realized why his father was an enthusiast; for a few moments, it was as if time stopped. He stood shoulder to shoulder with an artist from a different part of the world and heard their voices loud and clear. They screamed in silent rooms, and he resonated with every internal conflict, existential war, and heartache.

From that moment on, he crammed his existence with artifacts. It was beauty that would never fade, and he was envious of the longevity of an artist's career. Some didn't sell their first commission until they were in their sixties. Other works outlived their creators and were appreciated generations later. His life as an idol was temporary, and he spent countless hours trying to figure out what to do after. When the stage lights flickered out one last time, who would he be? He longed to make his mark on the world—to be known for something greater than being a mere boy bander—but he didn't have the slightest clue where to start. Leading was the only thing he knew how to do.

His strong need for legacy was his drive—the reason he never gave up on his dreams, despite rivals claiming he'd never amount to anything. He couldn't afford to give up—his aspirations were too enormous to leave unrealized. Instead of letting ambition crush him, he became strong, and with time, his goals didn't feel too grand to withstand.

Raising his phone to memorialize the moment, he pulled her into the frame. "Smile!"

⋆⁺₊⋆☾⋆⁺₊⋆

The crescent moon hung high by the time they arrived home. Exiting the elevator, Jen spotted another gift waiting near their door. "Is that..."

Swiping the delivery from the floor, Hanjun tapped in his code. Slinking through the doorway, he tore the wrapping to reveal a small box of chocolates. "This is getting out of hand."

From his spot on the sofa, Jin scolded them. "Where were you? We've been looking for you all day."

"We went to the gallery." Hanjun throttled his excitement.

Ankles propped up on the coffee table, Soogi raised concern. "How?"

Ignoring the question, Hanjun shook the candies. "Did you see who left this? We live in a secure community; it can't be random."

"No, but I'll take them." Jin strained for the package.

Deok-Sun intercepted. "No, give them to me."

"You're seriously going to eat candy from a stranger?" Jen grimaced, witnessing them tussle for the sweets. In the end, they agreed to pick one candy at a time. "At least they share well."

Planting a hand on her lower back, Hanjun bid her goodnight and retired to his room. Settling in bed, he reached for his journal, eager to capture the day.

*The museum was inspiring. She shares my love of
poetry. I'm looking forward to the future.*

CHAPTER TWENTY-SIX

Lawless Lawyers

Marching out of her room, Jen's sight fell on the chalkboard calendar. Though it was the end of November, the blocks had been changed, showcasing an onslaught of recordings, appearances, and brand commercials. As she studied the schedule, Hanjun emerged from his room with a black Bottega backpack slung over his shoulders.

He inspected the agenda. "It's our last day off before December. Are you sure you want to leave the condo?"

Swiveling to face him, she scanned his sharp jawline. "I promised Jin I'd visit Jenny House with him. He'll be upset if I postpone again."

"I don't know why he doesn't use the agency's salon. It's what it's there for." His shoulders deflated. "You'll be safe?"

"We'll be with his guards." She brushed debris from his shoulder. "Are you spending the day with the boys?"

"Nah, Hanso left hours ago, and Deok-Sun wants to play video games."

She glanced at the tied curtain door next to her room. "What about Soogi?"

"All he does is sleep and eat tteokbokki." He chuckled, searching his pockets for his identification. "I'm gonna hit the office and get a workout in."

"Working on your day off?" She flattened his misshapen collar. "Won't winter be busy enough?"

He bit his lip, melting into a playful smile. "My work doesn't get done unless I do it."

Arms falling to her sides, she nodded. "In that case, I'll see you when you get home."

"Can't wait." Leaving a peck on her forehead, Hanjun left.

⋆⁺₊⋆☾⋆⁺₊⋆

Standing outside the condominium, waiting for his escort, Hanjun absentmindedly scrolled through the pictures on his phone, pausing on the selfie he had snapped in front of the museum. Smirking, he set the photo as his lock screen. Though Jen hated having her picture taken, she tolerated it for him. Her aversion wasn't about her strong dislike of overt narcissism or ego; she simply thought snapping selfies in the middle of life's precious moments was a nuisance. 'Life couldn't be experienced behind a lens,' she'd say. "One day, I'll convince her to like photos."

Warring with boredom, he searched for new rumors surfacing about Blackmirror. A bit of a guilty pleasure, he liked to stay on top of happenings within the fandom; there wasn't a day that went by without theories popping up about one thing or another. It was better he knew before an interviewer blindsided him with questions about something he wasn't prepared to answer.

The newest installment of Parallels was released only hours earlier, though the fandom was hard at work, clamoring to dissect the show's addition. To neutralize Dae-Hyun's reckless decision to throw Jen to the wolves, Ha-Rin insisted on introducing her as an assistant. The one and only employee allowed on camera without needing to be censored.

Fingers gliding over the glass, he sifted through an endless stream of articles when a bold title tempted his eye.

HANJUN: THE HAPPINESS KILLER

He clicked on the article and devoured its contents.

HI BLOGGERS, IT'S ME, BLACKMIRRORIFY!
AS MANY OF YOU KNOW, IT SEEMS HANSO HAS A POTENTIAL LOVE INTEREST. AS MUCH AS THIS BOMBSHELL MAY BREAK YOUR HEART, WE AS ANTI NEED TO ACCEPT THIS AS A FACT: WHEN OUR BOYS DECIDE TO DATE, WE SHOULD BE HAPPY FOR THEM. BUT THAT'S NOT WHAT I CAME HERE TO TALK ABOUT. I WANT TO TALK ABOUT REM AND HIS OBSESSION WITH OUR NEW IT GIRL. IF YOU ASK ME, HE'S A LITTLE TOO INTERESTED IN HER, AND I'LL BE UPLOADING DOCUMENTATION TO SUPPORT THIS CLAIM.

EXHIBIT A: IN THE AFTER-SPECIAL, PARTICULARLY IN THE BEDROOM FOOTAGE, THERE WERE TIMES REM COULD BE SPOTTED STARING AT THEM. YOU DON'T FOCUS ON SOMEONE LIKE THAT UNLESS YOU'RE CRUSHING ON THEM.

EXHIBIT B: YOU CAN SEE HIM DRAWING IN A SKETCHBOOK, BUT WHEN THE CAMERAMAN GETS TOO CLOSE, HE HIDES THE SCRIBBLES. WHAT IS HE HIDING? I'M SURE IT HAS SOMETHING TO DO WITH HER.

EXHIBIT C: IN THE BONFIRE SEGMENTS, HE LOOKED AT HER WHILE HE SANG. HE WAS SINGING TO HER. THERE WASN'T A SINGLE FRAME WHERE HE DIDN'T GAWK AT HER DESPITE AN ENTIRE STRAND OF PEOPLE.

EXHIBIT D: DURING HANSO'S SOLO SHOOT, HANJUN AVOIDED LOOKING DIRECTLY AT THEM. HE WAS THE ONLY ONE TO DO THIS.

EXHIBIT E: AMID THE BOAT-BUILDING SCENES, YOU CAN FIND HANJUN HANGING AROUND HER, SHOWING OFF HIS VESSEL. HE CONSTANTLY FINDS A REASON TO HOVER AROUND HER.

EXHIBIT F: BACK TO THE FIRE; HANJUN COULD BE SEEN OFFERING HER HIS JACKET. HANSO WORE A SIMILAR BLAZER BUT DIDN'T OFFER IT TO HER.

I COULD BE ENTIRELY BY MYSELF, BUT I BELIEVE HANJUN IS CREEPING ON HER. LET ME KNOW WHAT YOU THINK, AND DON'T FORGET TO LIKE AND SUBSCRIBE FOR MORE K-POP CONTENT!

Navigating to the bottom, the comments varied in opinion, ranging from supportive to aggressive.

'HANJUN'S BEING NICE TO HER! HE IS THE LEADER!' —JUNBUG

'HANJUN IS DEFINITELY A CREEP.' —HELLOJIN

'WHY WOULD J&I ALLOW THEM TO HAVE GIRLFRIENDS? DON'T THEY CARE ABOUT THE FANS?' —DEOKSUNSDONUT

'NO WAY! I THINK SHE'S SEEING BOTH.' —ONETWOSTEP

'HE'S FALLEN FOR HANSO'S GIRL.' —GRIZZLEDHONEY

'LOOK AT THE EVIDENCE! THE FIRST DAY, THE GIRL DIDN'T WEAR ANY JEWELRY. ON THE SECOND, SHE FLAUNTED A RING HANJUN HAD WORN THE DAY PRIOR. HE GAVE IT TO HER.' —BLACKMIRROROBSESSED

'YOU GUYS ARE SLEEPING ON THE MOST OBVIOUS ANSWER. HANJUN IS IN LOVE WITH HANSO!' —HANSOXHANJUNSHIP

"Not fucking happening." His eyes rolled. The shipping of idols was nothing new; it emerged at the dawn of Korean pop. Regardless, he refused to welcome the fantasies as healthy fan-to-artist interactions. He found it to be an unsettling fetish for someone to have. To make matters worse, agencies sometimes played into the mania for publicity, and the discomfiture was known to wedge teammates apart, stimulating division among friends.

At the office, Hanjun dove into an intense workout, using physical exertion as an outlet for his pent-up frustration. Squats, pull-ups, jumping jacks, planks, mountain climbers, burpees, crunches, leg raises, and Superman exercises. His breath expulsed in short bursts, sweat drenching his athleisure. The burn in his muscles was a brief distraction, but it did little to calm his apprehension. He wasn't sure what he should be more concerned with—the deliveries left at their condo or how the public would react to a dating scandal. No member of Blackmirror had been linked to anyone prior to Jen being forced into the position of girlfriend, and he didn't know what to expect.

The fabricated love affair spread like wildfire, gaining national coverage within hours. Columnists scrambled to dig up information on the unknown girl, though they were faced with scarcity. But it was only a matter of time before they unearthed something; they never failed to find dirt, even if it was falsified. The paparazzi were masters of generating headlines and would manufacture a whole persona if necessary.

He was fearful of Jen getting dragged through the mud when the media discovered the romance was a sham. No matter what she did, she would be ridiculed. If she claimed responsibility, she would be derided by supporters and critics alike. If she told the truth about the coercion used on her, she would be portrayed as weak and impressionable. And that's after she was slammed with defamation suits. Bound by cruel contracts and lawless lawyers, there was no winning for her. J&I Entertainment was too influential to fight.

Finishing a rep of bicep curls, he came to an educated conjecture: the management pushed her into a corner on purpose. Contractually binding her to the agency meant she wouldn't be able to leave until her release. Not without paying a lifetime's worth of damages, anyway. Ruminating on the reasons behind

J&I's proposal to bring her on, a strangling revelation crept into his mind. There had to be a greater motive beyond holding the band together. Perhaps they saw her as their golden ticket—their salvation for the next four years. Just enough time for Blackmirror to squeeze out a few more albums and fulfill their military obligations. But they weren't satisfied with having her on the crew; they wanted her to bear the same fate.

He experienced simmering anger on Jen's behalf and sympathy for Hanso, who had no say in the matter, either. It was common for the directors to employ questionable tactics, but stripping the group of their autonomy was a new low. Nobody pressured them to become famous; it was their own free will that led to them becoming trainees, and all career-altering decisions were made as a team with majority rule. It wasn't a system without flaws, but it was democratic and fair. Never had they been thrust into prevarication for exposure.

The cameras. The shots of them on the shore. Dae-Hyun's demands. The strange cow frames in the closet. The eerie parcels on their doorstep. It was all unreal. He was convinced they were actors in some kind of cheap, never-ending psychological thriller. The only good news was that the lap dance recording hadn't made it into circulation. Yet.

⋆⁺₊⋆☾⋆⁺₊⋆

Hanjun arrived home, encountering another package leaning on the door. Ripping the paper to find a box of chocolate-covered strawberries, he left the gift on the kitchen counter for Jin, who had a nearly sexual obsession with the fruit. Heading straight to Jen's room, he knocked on the open door. "Can I come in?"

Sitting with her back propped against the headboard, she moved her laptop to the nightstand. "Sure."

Slipping through the doorway, he noticed a change in atmosphere. The smooth jazz she enjoyed in the evenings had been replaced with a more sinister version. "Are you alright?"

"Just a bout of the morbs." She pointed to a colorful word-of-the-day flip book on her vanity. "Victorian slang for temporary melancholia."

Plopping on the bed, he eyed her ultramarine-colored manicure. "Did you enjoy your day off?"

Wiggling her fingers, she grinned. "Yeah, we had a good time. Jin chose the color."

"Of course he did." He tapped the ring he gave her at the beach house. She had wrapped a piece of broken elastic around the band to ensure it wouldn't fall off. "I don't think I've ever seen you take this off."

"Should I?"

"I'd be happy if you never did. Jen..." Sighing, he cut to the point. "On the way to the gym, I stumbled upon a blog; Anti are suspecting a lot of things."

"I'm surprised you bother with those comments."

"They think I'm in love with you." Cheeks flushing, he backtracked. "They think I'm stalking you."

"You sometimes do." Her playfulness faded at the genuine concern in his tone. "Are you worried?"

He met her eyes. "Can I be honest?"

"Always."

He nodded. "I am."

"Do you want to talk about it?"

He shook his head, then decided to reveal his troubles. "Being with me comes with a price."

She placed a hand on his knee. "What do you mean?"

"I just—" The words caught in his throat. He didn't want to scare her away, but he also didn't want to sugarcoat their predicament. The fact was unforgiving; he didn't know if she could handle the approaching storm. "I'm afraid when you see what my life is like, you'll go running for the mountains. It's not all negative, but it's ugly when it's bad."

"Jun." She grasped his hand, rubbing his knuckles. "I'm not frightened by the darkest parts of you."

"What if I am?" A flicker of hope sparked in his heart, though it was quickly extinguished by doubt. "I've always pretended I'm fearless, but I'm not."

"Fearlessness is a rare virtue, but it's never acceptable to let fear stop us."

"Thank you." He kissed her forehead and returned to his room. Picking up a pen, he scribbled a journal entry.

Today was a day of rest. I'd like to find out who's leaving the packages. I have a few things to say.

CHAPTER TWENTY-SEVEN

Settling Roots

The first of December brought boatloads of Christmas cheer. Jin began playing jolly tunes at the stroke of midnight, and Deok-Sun hung decorations everywhere he could reach—mistletoe over doorways, wreaths on each cabinet, and scented garlands tucked under the television. Red and white pillows livened up the sofa, and tacky gingerbread baubles littered every surface.

Dressed and ready to tackle the day, Jen joined her roommates in the kitchen. Huddling around the table, the performers prepared to start their live broadcast. The task? Sharing Christmas wishes. Happiness for Anti, world peace, and the end of Covid were popular answers.

"I want all those things, too." Hanso stared into the lens. "I have all the stuff I want."

Aware of Hanso's weekly retail therapy, Jin chuckled. "Because you bought it yourself."

Soogi turned to his left. "What about you, Hanu?"

"I want to see our fans again." Hanjun's gaze swept the room, landing on Jen. She stood amid the videographers, camera in hand, and he instinctively smiled. "I have everything I need."

The production carried on, and the musicians shared heartwarming stories about being on tour. Of course, they made it seem flowery; frolicking in new cities, feasting on local eats, and forming bonds with roadies sounded like great fun until you experienced it.

What nobody says about the life of a touring artist is the soul-crushing boredom. And all those cool places you thought you'd enjoy? Consider them nonexistent. If you're not sleeping in the back of a bus, you're rehearsing for a show. And if you're not practicing for a gig, you're on stage. And if you're not doing any of those things, you're confined to your hotel, where you're reliving every failure until you fall asleep for a few short hours. You'll have a catering crew, and you'll eat well in the beginning, but the repetitive foods you consume for breakfast, lunch, and dinner will soon become tasteless. You'll gorge on chain restaurants to fill the void, but even that doesn't cure the depression. You'll miss your mom's kalguksu, how she refused to use canned kimchi, and the way she cut your meat into bite-sized pieces even when you were an adult.

On the road, you discovered everything you overlooked, took for granted, and couldn't live without. It's just you, your bandmates, and a ninety-person posse—most of which you love like family. Some you tolerate; others you loathe and wouldn't care if you never saw again.

In the evening, Jen relaxed in the lounge, cradling a steaming mug of tea, while her roommates discussed ideas for incorporating good deeds into their busy schedules. J&I was known for its contributions around the holidays; every personality from the agency was expected to perform at least one act of kindness. While most stars made a big show of visiting children's hospitals, donating truckloads of toys, or instigating pay-it-forward chains, Blackmirror filled in the gaps. Leveraging their fame, they explored ways to assist those living alone, surviving on the streets, or struggling with low incomes.

"What about caroling?" Jin bounced in his seat. "We've never done that before."

"I'd like to help needy animals," Hanso chimed in.

Feigning disinterest, Soogi shrugged, but there was a glimmer of belief in his eyes. "Something for the homeless."

"Or perhaps a secret fan giveaway?" Deok-Sun proposed.

Nodding along with each bid, Hanjun scribbled in a notebook. "I'll get your suggestions sent to Ha-Rin."

Following a knock, Hanso rushed to the door. The hallway was quiet, though there was a package leaning on the wall. He scooped up the parcel, admiring its red wrapping and oversized bow. Pulling at the tape, the inside housed a quarto-sized photo, dark and blurry, as if it were shot in a poorly lit room.

Returning to the condo, he waited for the automated lock to chime. "There was nobody there."

"Gifts don't deliver themselves." Jin reached for the picture and held it under the overhead light.

Deok-Sun tittered. "They do if you believe in Santa."

Snatching the print from Jin, Hanjun used his phone to backlight the pigment. "There's one, maybe two people."

"It's low-quality." Soogi eyed the still from across the room. "Or blown up too large."

⋆⁺₊⋆☾⋆⁺₊⋆

Hanjun stared at the ceiling, a blanket tangled around his ankles. Despite trying to enhance the oversaturated photo, the pixels remained distorted. "Do you think it's Dae-Hyun? I mean, he's the one who rented the condo for us. I'm sure he has access to—"

"Why would he need to harass us at home? He's doing a good enough job at work." Nose buried in a horror comic, Hanso turned a page. "Someone's just messing with us."

"Why now? If someone wanted to stalk us, why didn't they start years ago? You don't think it has something to do with—" Before Hanjun finished, there was a guest at the door.

Eyes rolling, Hanso had no doubt it was Jen, evident by her melodious rapping. "Good evening, Jenilyn."

"Hey, Ho-Young." She wore baggy pajamas; a blue two-piece printed in an adorable kangaroo motif. Drifting to Hanjun's side of the room, she perched on his bed.

"I love the kangaroos." He stroked the soft fabric.

She brandished a teasing smile. "I know you do."

"What's your Christmas wish?" He traced the delicate patterns along her neck.

Leaning her head on his shoulder briefly, she brushed his hand. "For this year or in general?"

Unamused by the affectionate display, Hanso scowled. "I'm going to spray you two if you don't stop acting cute."

"Sorry." She pushed his hand away and hiked her collar higher. "I live in a beautiful home, have a well-paying job, and have the *best* boyfriend—"

"Boyfriend!?" Hanso discharged a mimicking laugh. "I didn't know you made it official."

"We were trying to keep it private." Grumbling, Hanjun tossed an empty water bottle at his bandmate. Turning back to her, he fingered the spaces between the buttons on her top.

She swatted his hand. "I suppose Deok-Sun, Jin, and Soogi will know within the hour."

"Try a minute." Hanso reached for his phone, reporting the change in Hanjun's relationship status. "She needs a Bluetooth speaker so she stops using ours."

She chose to ignore Hanso. "I'd like to be a mother."

"Hard to have children as an idol." Hanso swapped the device for the manga.

"I'm talking years from now, not tomorrow." She imagined herself with children. Two, maybe three, with the possibility of adopting. Providing a safe home to one teen before they were kicked out of foster care would be enough. "Unfortunately, I have a condition that makes it difficult to conceive."

"Oh." Hanjun caressed circles on the sensitive plot between her breasts, his expression washed with sadness. "You can't have children?"

She leaned into his embrace. "I can, but it comes with risks. A high chance of miscarriage, among other painful complications."

"Don't worry too much." He dappled kisses on her forehead. "Ten percent of the population struggles with infertility, and we've come a long way with drugs, assisted reproductive technology, and surgery."

"I've heard the journey is physically and emotionally taxing." Slumping, she sighed. "I'm not sure when I'll be ready."

Patting her hair, he pressed a kiss on her cheek. "Either way, I can't wait to see you as a mom."

She nuzzled a hand into his. "I can't wait to see you as a dad."

"That's *it*—" Storming out of the room, Hanso returned moments later with a spray bottle of water and proceeded to hose them down.

"Why is the water so cold?" Shrieking, Jen hid her face in Hanjun's shoulder while he sprayed them like cats in heat.

Hanjun laughed uncontrollably, covering his face to avoid the watery assault. Pushing Hanso's arm away, he admitted defeat. "Okay, we get it!"

"I'm not joking." Hanso squirted him three more times for good measure. "*Knock. It. Off.*"

"I'm going to my room. *Alone.*" Hurling a smile at Hanso, Jen emphasized her plans to sleep solo. "Goodnight Junie."

Dabbing his face on his sleeve, he held her hand until she slipped from his grasp. "Goodnight Jen."

Muttering, Hanso returned to his covers. "You two make me sick."

Hanjun smirked, knowing that while Hanso liked Jen as a person, he wasn't fond of their romantic involvement. He had expressed his concerns about their courtship and the issues it could cause on numerous occasions. Ultimately, he knew he couldn't drive a wedge between two lovers without inadvertently pushing them together. "You're going to have to learn to deal with it."

"Just be careful." Hanso hinted at an incident that predated Jen. "After what happened with your ex—"

"I have it under control." Hanjun signaled an end to the conversation. He may have had no clue what he was doing, but he didn't want to admit it to Hanso.

Settling on his side, he retrieved his journal from under the pillow. Opening the cover, the pages were laced with spilled ink. From their first meeting, Jen became a prominent feature in his diary; her name memorialized alongside his own. Skipping to a blank section, another precious moment evolved into a sacred memory.

> *Hearing her talk about starting a family makes my heart beat faster. I find myself wondering what kind of future we could have. Where would we lay down our roots? Seoul is nice, but if I had a choice, I would live closer to my parents or grandparents. If we chose to settle in my home city of Goyang, our children would have an upbringing like mine. If we lived near my grandparents, they could be wild and explore the mountains and streams.*

CHAPTER TWENTY-EIGHT

Oven Lovin'

Waking to her alarm, Jen trudged to the bathroom, washing away traces of rest. Returning to her room, she dressed in a pale pink cropped sweater, light jeans, and ivory chenille socks. She found the cameramen hard at work in the kitchen, running logistics for a long day of shooting. Grabbing her task sheet, the script threw her for a loop.

Blackmirror were challenged with creating two cookies, one resembling a classic gingerbread man, and another modeled after a member of the band. The kitchen's surface was cluttered with an array of ingredients and color-coded utensils. Behind the table, the boy banders faced a line of cameras with red game-show-style buttons situated next to their hands.

Taking her by the shoulders, Ha-Rin ushered her to the middle of the commotion, where a man she was semi-familiar with evaluated the scene. "Jenilyn, this is the lead production manager for Parallels."

"Sehoon Sohn." The man held out his hand. His beard was neatly trimmed, though his hair was frazzled, perhaps from ripping it out on an hourly basis. He donned a mix of smart and casual—an oversized sport jacket and flat-footed sneakers—and the intensity behind his eyes suggested a focus on his work. "We're filming you today."

"On purpose?" She failed to cover her skepticism. "I thought the plan was to phase me out."

"Upper management wants to keep you on." Ha-Rin gestured to the buzzers. "All you need to do is stand by, and when they press their buttons, assist for two minutes."

"But—" Jin closed his eyes for a final round of face powder. "If we use it while you're helping someone else, you have to leave that person immediately."

She nodded, understanding her instructions. "You can sabotage each other. Got it."

"Keep your back to the lens at all times. We still need to be cautious." Sehoon pointed out hidden camcorders among the table decorations. Snapping two fingers, he solicited a fashion advisor by his side. "Let's get her prepped for film."

"Yes, Sir." A young woman hurried over, spraying frizz control over Jen's roots and taming her flyaways.

A second hairdresser joined, curling her bangs with a cordless heat tool. "This will give you more volume on camera."

Sehoon circled her like a hawk, inspecting every inch of her outfit from head to toe. Tugging and tucking her clothing to better fit her frame, he asked her to give him a spin. After a moment of consideration, he gave the green light to proceed. "Get a mic on her."

Another helper appeared at her side, securing a body pack to the small of her back. He wrapped a strap around her waist, muttering step-by-step instructions under his breath. "These allow us to record without visible wires."

Yanking on the back of her blouse, he threaded a thin wire down her spine and plugged the cable into the pack. "You'll need to keep an earpiece in for your cues."

He connected a tiny microphone and spun her to face him, handing off a fuzzy decoration. "Clip this on your collar."

Checking his watch, Sehoon moved behind the cameras. "Are we almost ready?"

"Just about..." Hastening his pace, he hid the extra wiring in her hair and clothing. "She's wired and ready to roll."

Jen faced the table of musicians while Ha-Rin commenced a countdown. "Recording in three, two..."

Slipping into character, the bandmates broke into smiles, initializing their introduction. "Making the impossible, possible! Blackmirror!"

Hanjun took charge. "And today we're doing something that's not so impossible: making gingerbread cookies!"

"But—" Hanso interrupted as if his lines were rehearsed. "There's a catch."

"We'll be working separately," Deok-Sun added.

"I hope we'll have help." Jin tagged a playful whine at the end of his proclamation. "This is my first time baking cookies."

"Thankfully, we have someone to lend us a hand." Hanso signaled to Jen. "But remember, you can only call for help once."

Cackling, Soogi pushed his buzzer multiple times. "And using the button during someone else's turn, sabotages them!"

"Our assistant is Jen," Hanjun inaugurated with flair.

Jenilyn, that's your cue! Keep your back to the camera and give a friendly wave. Sehoon blared in her concha. Employing her inner princess, she raised her hand vertically, adding a half twist from the wrist.

Replicating the greeting. Hanjun snapped his hands together. "Shall we begin?"

Jin slapped his button and held out the recipe card to Jen. "Read to me while I make the batter."

Stepping forward, she skimmed the directions, noticing the stove wasn't prepared for the occasion. "Preheat the oven to 177 degrees Celsius."

"What next?" Jin turned on the oven, giving her an adorable thumbs-up. The remaining members listened, following along with her advice. Annoyed by their intrusion, he pouted and covered Deok-Sun's ears. "It's *my* turn. Don't listen to her."

After Jin's two minutes were exhausted, Soogi called her. "Can you show me how to shape the dough?"

"Of course." She wasn't fooled by his pouty lip. Soogi was no stranger to gastronomy—he often taught her tricks in the kitchen, especially when it came to traditional cuisine. He just didn't want to knead the mound himself. Obliging regardless, she started shaping the dough, and the mates imitated her actions.

Hanjun deadpanned a serious delivery, though he cracked into a smile. "This has been cooking with Jen, brought to you by Blackmirror."

"Blackmirror!" Hanso parroted in his best announcer voice.

"I'm going to call her 'Mommy Jen.'" Laughing, Jin punched a hole into the unsuspecting dough.

Jen glared at him. "*No.*"

"Wouldn't that make Hanjun 'Daddy?'" Unable to resist cracking a joke, Hanso instantly regretted his decision. "That went too far."

Deok-Sun fixated on the lens, harnessing a vacant expression. "Oh God, yes."

"That needs to be edited out." Hanjun covered his face, mashing remnants of wet flour in his hair. Catching the blunder, a stylist rushed over to fix the mishap while the main camera veered toward Hanso.

Combining the dough to the right consistency and flash-cooling the clump in a laboratory cooler, Deok-Sun summoned Jen. "Cut the shapes for me?"

"I would suggest making more than necessary. I don't know about you, but I always end up breaking cookies." She dusted the metal shaper with flour and pressed it into the dough. Within minutes, the forms were prepared and sent into the oven for ten minutes.

During the baking process, the crew took a brief breather. A flurry of stylers descended upon Jen, fixing stray locks and smudged eyeliner. Hanjun materialized next to her, munching on a handful of banana puffs while an aide worked to remove crumbs clinging to his designer clothes. "How is your first time on Parallels?"

Stealing a puff from his palm, she shrugged. "Different from the video set. More relaxed."

He chuckled, flashing her a winning smile. "Music videos are all about precision and perfection. Parallels is all fun and spontaneity."

"I'm a little concerned about the jokes." She leaned into his shoulder. "Mommy? Daddy?"

He laughed, wagging his head. "Don't worry. It won't get past postproduction."

"Break's over!" Producing a sharp whistle, Sehoon commanded the floor. "In three, two, one..."

Jen darted back to her designated spot. Adjusting her footing to stand exactly where she stood before the break, she nodded at Hanjun, who addressed the camera. "Now that the cookies are cooled, it's time to make them pretty."

Keep in mind they've never made icing before, Jenilyn. Ears buzzing, she moved forward as if she wasn't prompted. "Icing can be a little finicky. You might need to add a bit more water or sugar."

The entertainers sifted powder into mixing bowls, and drops of food coloring were introduced to create a thick, dreamy glaze. First to complete a batch, Hanso requested Jen's services. "Help me with the frosting?"

The exact moment she stood in front of Hanso, Hanjun slammed his hand on the table, sending his button flying. "Nope."

The staff erupted into hysterics, and Soogi dropped to his knees, piecing together what was left of the plastic bits. "Medic! We need a medic!"

"You got cock blocked!" Deok-Sun taunted Hanso.

Jin performed a dramatic karate chop. "Fatality!"

Holding a hand over his heart in mock distress, Hanso pretended to fall out of his chair. "Death comes for me!"

"She's mine!" Hanjun stuck his tongue out at Hanso, as if acquiring her assistance was an accomplishment.

Maintaining patience and poise, Jen stood in front of Hanjun, shaking her head at their theatrics. Instead of taking command, she held his fist, guiding the icing bag over each loop and line. When they were finished, he booped her on the nose with a fingertip of frosting, melting her nervousness into a smile.

The shoot ended with the attending personnel holding a vote for the best-looking biscuit. To everyone's surprise, Hanso's creation won the prize for traditional design, while Jin took home the award with his artistic reimagining of the leader.

Hanjun examined the dessert with grayish-blue hair and a handsome smile. "What's that red thing on my cheek?"

Jin exhibited a smirk. "A kiss from Jen."

He grinned, confronting the camera one last time. "That needs removed, too."

★⁺₊★☾★⁺₊★

Once the house was clear of cinematographers, the roommates gathered in the living room. Action-packed anime served as background noise for the remainder of the evening. While her companions discussed ways to enrich future episodes, Jen felt self-conscious about her acting. "How do you think it went?"

Jin wiggled in his seat next to her. "You were great."

"You were stiff." Soogi received a disapproving scowl from Hanjun, though he held his ground. "Being honest isn't a crime. She won't improve without feedback."

Noticing Hanjun's lips beginning to separate, Hanso acted to defuse the tension. "It was her first time."

Deok-Sun remained glued to his phone. "Imagine what would happen if nobody gave *us* criticism."

Frustrated by their critiques, Hanjun challenged the room. "A little sympathy would have helped us, too."

Eyes dancing between speakers, Jen interjected. "I appreciate the honesty. I'd rather someone be truthful than blatantly lie."

"Sorry." Jin's happiness deflated. "I wasn't lying, though. I thought you did a great job."

"Jin, that's an opinion, not a lie." She patted his head.

Hanjun's lips pulled into a smile. Despite Jen's lone-wolf tendencies, she showed remarkable sensitivity towards the vulnerable. A perpetual people-pleaser, Jin was quick to apologize for any perceived wrong and often made self-deprecating quips. Bullied from a young age, he coped with his tormentors by utilizing extreme flattery. Unfortunately, complacency was something he never healed. Caving to demands was all he had ever known, and fame did little to help.

It was a curious thing, stardom. Celebrities lived in a different world. Equivalent to high school, oppressors were journalists, obsessive fans, and keyboard warriors who aborted their own dreams. Blackmirror ran in circles that ninety-nine percent of the population would never experience, yet it was somehow easy for others to judge their lives. The reality was that few would scratch the exterior. And sure, there was a certain amount of pandering to the press, but the public weren't their friends.

Lost in thought about how Jen was their friend, Hanjun was startled by a loud thump at the door. Hoping to apprehend the sender in the act, he found the hall empty and a package on the floor. Returning to the condo, he flapped the parcel in the air. "I've talked with security. They haven't found anyone lurking around."

Hanso peered out from behind a comic. "We used to prank J all the time. Maybe he's getting us back."

Deok-Sun cackled from the kitchen. "Remember when we replaced his backing vocals with rubber chickens?"

"After all these years?" Hanjun paced in front of the television, tearing at the gift wrap. "He's not even in the country."

Jen monitored his anxious steps, experiencing his unease creeping into her. "It's been a long day. I should get some sleep."

Ditching the picture on the counter, Hanjun followed her into her room, fixated on her figure. Slinking into bed, he peeled off his shirt and tossed it near a pile of garments she had tried on that morning. "Your room is relaxing."

"I'm a glutton for luxurious textiles." Fluffing a pillow, she admired his broad shoulders. "You usually don't undress until you're ready to sleep."

"I'm comfortable with you." His timbre was warm, and he wiggled close to her, leaving a few inches of space between their bodies.

Taking in his toned physique, she reached for his bare chest before pulling her hand away. "Can I touch you?"

He nodded. "You can always touch me."

She lowered her fingers to his shoulder. "After being manhandled all day, I didn't know how you'd feel about—"

"Jen..." He moved her hand to his heart, flattening her palm for maximum contact. "Part of my job is to accept the fanfare, even if I don't like it."

"You don't like being doted on?" Tracing the center of his impressive frame, she had never noticed how defined his pecks were. If he were Greek, he'd be the ruler of gym memberships and athleticism. "Seems like something you'd love."

"It's not that I don't—" His gaze traveled from her hand to her face, spotting the glimmer of fascination in her eyes. She was impressed, and he made a mental note to use her as encouragement whenever he wanted to skip a workout. "When your name carries significance, invasion of privacy becomes a price tag."

Her stomach squirmed, imagining how many times he had been exploited for pay. "Why do you trust me? Aren't you afraid I'll—"

"At first, I didn't." Tucking a strand of hair behind her ear, he took on a soft, wistful quality. "After being betrayed too many times, I've learned not to trust."

Her fingertips meandered over his collarbone. "What changed your mind?"

"In Chicago, when I said it didn't have to be goodbye—you turned me down. And the night we met, while I laid on your sofa—" He scoffed and shook his head. "You should know the first thing I do when I meet someone is look up their socials..."

"You *searched* for me?" Tilting her head back, a burst of humor fell from her throat. It was highly unlikely he had found much of anything. "How'd that go?"

"Not very well. It was refreshing to find someone with little online presence. While the rest of the world wastes their days inflating their lives for the approval of others, you exist as you are. You own your life, your flaws, and the chaotic flames fueling your actions, and you never try to document our relationship as if you're preparing an exposé." Reaching for her hand, he spilled the biggest reason he fell for her. "You remind me what being human is like. How caring and considerate people can be without money serving as motivation. Truth and wisdom can be unsettling, but they don't need to be inhumane."

"I'm glad you're learning to believe in people again." Nodding off, she accepted sleep's embrace.

Patting her head, he moved from her bed, retrieved his shirt, and returned to his room to archive the day.

> *We made gingerbread cookies. Not something I would eat again, but I enjoyed making them. Jen asked why I trusted her. I could only think of a few reasons, but the list is endless. There isn't one single thing. It's everything.*

CHAPTER TWENTY-NINE

A Daring Rendezvous

Sharing a home with five other bodies was a juggling act. Amid the chaos of morning routines, Jen was grateful the condo offered two bathrooms. Though she usually carted her toiletries around, she sometimes forgot to grab them when she left. After discovering Deok-Sun preferred the scent of her shampoo, she left the containers behind for him. He never admitted to using feminine products, but she detected the fragrance when he emerged.

Breathing in the aroma of sudsy bubbles, she tested the acoustics of the wet room. After the fatal drowning of her phone, Hanjun was kind enough to let her borrow his to create a playlist on his Spotify. Lost in her own little world, she sang along to her eclectic compilation, spanning over three decades of artistry, when Blackmirror's chart-topping hit, 'Valiant,' burst from the portable speaker.

In the living room, Jin sprawled on the sofa, his ears perking up at the hint of his voice. "Is that Jen?"

Hanso snapped his comic closed. "Sounds like it."

Deok-Sun muted the television. "She's listening to us?"

"Let's surprise her." Hanjun popped up from the floor.

Creeping toward the bathroom in a single file line, their footsteps barely made a sound. Piling in the hall, each pressed their ear against the door, straining to hear Jen croon at the top of her lungs.

'Rise up! Rise up!
Our determination, our drive!
Our voices, our lives!
We are the valiant!'

Jin executed an upbeat seaweed-style dance. "She likes us!"

"Is it weird that I'm excited?" Deok-Sun piped along, as the lines were his to belt.

Hanso smiled at their harmonizing. "Her voice goes well with Deok-Sunnie's."

"Take it, Sunnie!" Jen giggled at the rumble of their chants drifting through the door, though her amusement dissipated once she heard warbling inside the walls. Swiping water from her eyes, she found four of her five companions crowded around the vanity, crooning with gusto. Deok-Sun twirled a hairbrush as if it were a microphone, while Jin strummed an invisible guitar. "Wait, what? Get out!"

"The stall gives the best echo!" Hanjun yelled over the coordinated chorusing.

"Guess I'll have to get in the shower!" Jin squeezed into the opposite end, followed by Hanso and Deok-Sun.

"Are you serious right now?" Concealing her body with the shower curtain, she erupted in a mixture of shock and frustration. "I share my life with you; can I please cleanse in peace?!"

Met with a chorus of laughter, she pleaded with their ringleader. "Hanjun! Control your minions!"

He paused his serenading. "They *can't* be controlled!"

Protecting his already-perfected hair, Jin avoided scalding droplets bouncing off her head. "Why is your water so hot? You could roast a chicken in here."

"Because women are from hell, and it feels like home." Holding a straight face, she splintered into a hearty laugh. "If you don't get out, I'm going to flash each of you."

Giggling, Hanso challenged her. "You wouldn't."

"Try me." Lowering the curtain to expose the décolletage of her breasts, she held smoldering eye contact.

"She's not joking!" Fleeing the shower, Jin leveraged Deok-Sun's shoulders to escape. Scurrying behind him, the accomplices roared about the interruption and went to tell Soogi about it.

Grabbing a squeegee to clean up the watery mess they left behind, Hanjun hung around, jamming out to the next song on her playlist—a desperate rap-rock beat covering the artist's troubled past. Finishing up, he listened as Jen's vocals cut through the steam. Crisp and deliberate, she poured her heart out in the third verse. Her accent, typically camouflaged by flawless English, surfaced in flashes of intensity during her delivery.

Shackles of want, our shadows dim
Greed takes hold swift and grim
Millions of childhoods marked by need
A tapestry woven with broken thread

Food scarce, a luxury denied
Empty bellies cry without pride
A constant battle against hunger's sway
Our morale wilted day by day

Holes in our boots, battling perpetual shame
A symbol of poverty's unending claim
We yearned for warmth amidst the cold
But dignity was often too hard to hold

Education came at a price too steep
Books and pencils but a distant dream
Knowledge became an elusive chase
Our futures uncertain; our names disgraced

Society judges with scornful eyes
Labeling us as failures, second prize
Yet in our hearts, a flame still burns
Longing for the fate we earned

But again, our hopes were crushed by circumstance
Crumbling beneath desire's relentless dance
Opportunities vanished like morning dew
Leaving us fractured, our spirits subdued

Amidst the darkness, hope still gleamed
A flicker of light refusing to be tamed
We found strength in unity
A lifeline setting our souls free

From the ashes of want, our resilience grew
A fire fueling our dreams anew
We vowed to break the cycle's hold
And build a future of gold

Through hardship and struggle, we'll prevail
Growing from the dirt, we could never fail

We have our ancestors unwavering will
We'll forge a path and be better still

The ending notes faded, and she turned off the water. Pushing back the curtain, she realized he hadn't left with the others. "Jun, why are you still here?"

Sitting on the floor with his back against the door, he rotated just enough to see her. "Your voice—that song meant something to you."

"Oh, you heard that." Tying a bathrobe over her waist, she kneeled beside him. "At one point, music was my only ally."

"You never talk about your childhood. Was it that bad?"

Biting her lip, she nodded. "Yeah, it was."

"Why didn't you tell me?" Lips quivering, he sniffled.

"Jun, I am who I am *because* of what I've been through." She cupped his cheeks in her hands. "When I look in the mirror, I see someone I would have admired as a child. I try to be the person little me needed, and sometimes I think I fail miserably, but I also think defeat is just as important as success. Little me needed to know adults can fail, too."

He dabbed a tear from his eye. "Little you would be proud."

"Little me would have thought I was ancient by now." She jostled his shoulder. "C'mon, you need to get ready."

Springing to his full height, he started peeling off his clothes. "I'll be a moment. Will you let the boys know?"

"Of course." She returned to her room and dressed in comfortable clothing. Heading to the lounge, she overheard the chatter of her roommates and Ha-Rin's aggravated tone. A handful of production editors were also in attendance, discussing their plans for the day. "Hanjun's showering."

"Again?" Hanso groaned from the floor. "He showered at four this morning—his terrible singing woke me up."

"He did?" She plopped next to Jin.

Deok-Sun's eyes remained on his phone. "Hanu sometimes showers multiple times a day."

"Why? We haven't done anything to get dirty."

"It's not about being clean." Jin nudged her shoulder. "It's about maintaining a schedule."

Entering the room, Hanjun clutched a towel, rubbing his hair. "What'd I miss?"

Ha-Rin checked his watch. "A few minutes later, and you would have missed the entire episode."

"Sorry." Issuing an apology, he sat next to Deok-Sun.

"Now that we're all here—" Ha-Rin ejected an annoyed huff, gesturing towards the television. "Let's get started."

Sehoon stood by the screen, eager to demonstrate the work. "Throughout the editing process, we took great care to only include shots of Jenilyn from behind. In accordance with your request, we also probed for surfaces reflecting her image."

He skipped through certain parts, occasionally pausing to make a statement. "We scrubbed the risqué jokes and spliced scenes of Jenilyn and Hanjun to avoid romantic speculation."

"Is that me?" Jen caught her voice emanating from the speakers. "I sound cute."

"Jen looks like a teacher with her students." Soogi chuckled at a particularly heartwarming moment.

"Look at our dumb faces." Jin pointed out their silly grins.

Watching Hanjun break cookie after cookie, Hanso broke into a chuckle. "He looks like he's ready to resign."

Sehoon turned to Hanjun. "As you can see, we removed footage related to the kissy cookie."

"Thank you, Sir." His tense jaw relaxed at the news.

⋆⁺₊⋆☾⋆⁺₊⋆

A creature of habit, Jen enjoyed a cool stroll in the evenings to explore more of what Korea had to offer. Or at least imagine she could. Though she couldn't exactly walk into any establishment, she admired the stores, niteries, and bars. With over nine million cramped in the metropolitan area, there was never a lack of interesting people on the prowl.

"I'll be back in a bit." She retrieved a puffy overcoat from the closet. The frock, constructed of biobased insulation and a nylon exterior, was space cadet blue—reminiscent of a darkened midnight sky—and stuck out against the solid black coats of Seoul's denizens.

"Don't forget gloves!" Jin called back from the kitchen.

Springing from his spot on the couch, Hanjun joined her. Throwing on a thin jacket, he pulled the oversized faux fur-lined hood over her face. "You look like the Stay Puft man."

She tilted her head back, her blonde locks cascading down her back. "Perhaps, but I'm a toasty little marshmallow."

Venturing into the bitter night, their breath materialized, and their footfalls echoed off the cobblestone, accompanied by the satisfying crunch of fallen leaves. The pathways were quiet, save for the occasional chirping of nightjars flying out for the evening. Dragging her along, Hanjun convinced her to join him for a trip downtown. Despite spending countless nights wandering the streets surrounding their castle, with its opulent shops, lush gardens, and fine-dining restaurants, they had never wandered too far. She was unsure if it was something they should do, but with the way he held onto her hand and how he spoke with such enthusiasm, she almost couldn't say no. After some gentle persuasion, she finally agreed to hop in a taxi with him.

The cab screeched to a halt, temporarily illuminating busy streets. They jumped out at a cross-section, surrounded by a spritely crowd. Vibrant storefronts lined the paths, their colorful neon signs competing for attention. Strains of chords drifted from various establishments, tempting them into the herd. Bumping into pedestrians, they moved with the flow of the flock. Every thirtieth stride, a roadside vendor tempted them with an expansive array of Korean delicacies. From sticky, syrupy aromas to the sweet smell of fresh squid, there was magic in the air.

She absorbed the ambience. "The city's beautiful at night."

"Be glad it's almost winter." While waiting on a street corner, Hanjun's breath matted in his throat. The self-filtering mask he wore did little to protect him from choking smoke.

She covered her masked mouth with a palm. "What's wrong with the rest of the seasons?"

He gestured to the pavement, where pockets of garbage littered the drains. Unwanted flyers, torn and tattered, fluttered like confetti at a sad party, and an overabundance of spittle violated the soles of visitors' shoes. "In spring, the fine dust peaks and clings to everything. In summer, the sewers emit a putrid odor. Fall brings relief, but it's still dry and dusty."

"Yikes. There must be *something* you enjoy."

Cracking into an eye-crunching smile, he offered an improved description. "The villages and palaces have always been my favorites. And Seoul boasts some of the biggest attractions, like the world's largest underground shopping mall."

"At night, the city transforms into an explosion of color. Some say Seoul has one of the most active nightscapes in all of Asia." Painting a portrait with his words, he waved a hand over the horizon. "I wish I could show you more."

Underwhelmed by the idea, she shrugged. "I've never been a nightlife kind of person."

"I was heavily interested in the lifestyle for a while. The clubs, the outfits, the fame—" Keeping his eyes on the side-walk, he expelled a sigh. "I don't know who that person is anymore. It's all too much. Fast fashion and even faster people."

"The dying pieces of you made room for the present you."

"I've never been so thankful something died." Eyes crinkling as they approached the Mojeon Bridge, he was thrilled to show her the waterfall feature. But his happiness was shortened when his name cut through the lively district.

Is that Ryu Hanjun?

"We need to go." The second he picked up the shrill voice, he knew they were ambushed. Glancing over his shoulder, he spotted two figures in hot pursuit and began formulating a plan to lose them. Grasping Jen's hand, he pulled her along, hoping the imposing structure would provide some cover. Weaving in and out groups of people, he formed obstacles between them and their chasers. Reaching the aqueduct, he loosened his grip and leapt over the concrete wall.

She stumbled after him, but as she reached the edge, her body froze. Peering at the hard cement below, she couldn't make the jump. "I'm scared of heights."

Ducking under the overpass, he motioned for her to come down. "Hurry!"

"It's too high! I can't do it." Refusing, she fell back.

He held out his arms, promising to catch her. "You got this."

"Okay..." Hearing the pursuers drawing near, she lifted her legs over the ledge. Sliding down the jagged facade, the coarse surface scraped her outerwear, leaving a trail of scratches on the fabric.

Just as her toes were about to hit the ground, he caught her with lightning speed, tugging her into a dark alcove. "Now we just have to wait for them to pass."

She dusted off her knees. "Is this something you do often?"

"First time." Scooping her up in his arms, he yanked her close. "But it was exhilarating, wasn't it?"

She withdrew from his embrace. "The last time you manhandled me like this, someone put it in the tabloids."

"I'm done worrying about what people think." Spinning her to face him, he squeezed her waist through the bulk of her coat. Kissing her just as forcefully as he grabbed her, he pressed her against the wall like he had in the dark alleyway.

"What if the press gets ahold of—"

"Fuck them." With one harsh tug, he jerked down the zipper of her outerwear and tongued her jugular.

Her eyes fluttered. "What about Hanso? I'm publicly—"

Sinking his teeth into her soft flesh, his fingers tangled in her hair. "Who are you *privately* dating?"

"*You.*" She clawed at his wrists; he applied just the right amount of pressure to make her moan.

"That's right." His lips, hot and insistent, seared her neck, delivering a column of fire to her artery.

She tried to oppose, but his touch was like a flame. Arching in pleasure and pain, she caved into a blissful daze. "Junie, we have a meeting tomorrow. I can't have marks on me."

He pulled away. His hand lingered around her throat, his thumb tracing the deep hollows he left behind. "It's a little late for that."

★⁺₊★☾★⁺₊★

Hanjun spotted a mysterious package waiting outside their door. He tore open the box to find another picture, identical to the others. Tossing the delivery on the kitchen counter, the novelty was wearing off. Jen was the only thing on his mind.

He followed her into her sanctuary, where she lit a pillar candle on her nightstand. While she fluffed a pillow and prepared for bed, his eyes were drawn to the deep impressions on her neck, still red from their rendezvous. Petting her hair, his heart swelled with regret. "You have to tell me if I'm too rough."

She traced along the irritation. "Is it that bad?"

"Maybe..." Aiming his phone's camera at her, he brushed a few strands of hair behind her shoulder. Harnessing pride and concern, he snapped a photo and showed it to her.

"Junie, you're a vampire!" Inspecting the prominent indentions, she pouted before melting into a wicked grin. "I liked it, though."

He nuzzled her nape, his honeyed cologne mingling with her perfume. "Good."

"I'm worried someone may have seen us." Her voice was marked with distress.

Shushing her with a kiss, he didn't want to hear why they shouldn't be together. "If they did, it doesn't matter."

"It could impact—"

"That's not for you to worry your pretty little face over." He stared at her lips, fighting the urge to kiss her again. The softness of her skin made his heart palpate, and his restraint slipped. Certain he wouldn't be able to resist temptation, he pulled away. "Sleep well."

"Goodnight Hanjunie." She blew out the candle.

Shambling to his room, his mind was clouded with conflicting desires. Part of him wanted to return to her bed and solidify their emotions, but another part wanted to make sure everything was perfect before taking that leap. Sinking into bed, he pulled out his journal.

We went to the Cheonggyecheon stream, and I
kissed her under the bridge. I thought the first kiss
was the best, but it keeps getting better.

Hanso sliced through the silence like a sharp blade. "Where'd you go after dinner?"

"Cheonggy." He tucked the diary away.

"There's a video of you fleeing from a journalist circulating online. If Dae-Hyun catches wind of—"

"If the agency has a problem with it, they can talk to me." Turning away from his roommate, his focus shifted to the city. For as long as he had lived in Seoul, the stars twinkled off the water, beckoning him like a friend. But then, looking over the river from his concrete castle, the ripples were more like false promises, threatening to destroy everything he cared about.

CHAPTER THIRTY

#HanJen

Jen tiptoed to the kitchen in the early morning hours to find the normally quiet home overflowing with impishness. Her roommates gathered around the island, giggling as if they were up to no good.

Holding a finger over his lips, Deok-Sun stood off center, camera ready to capture their antics. "Shh."

She lowered her voice, nearly to non-existence. "What are you up to?"

Holding a sizable squirt gun, Jin struggled to contain his mirth. "We have a surprise for Hanso's birthday."

Her eyes dilated. "Oh no."

"Take this." Handing her a colorful box from a local bakery, Hanjun pointed to the hall.

Padding down the corridor, she pretended they were characters in a spy movie. Imagining a jazzy Henry Mancini tune in her mind, they approached Hanso's room, armed with cake and water guns. Pushing the door open, Soogi led the way, with Deok-Sun trailing behind, unsuccessfully suppressing their giggles.

Creeping to the bed where Hanso lay, Jin prepared to spray him with the pistol. Shoulders shaking in laughter, he smacked the toy on his palm. "This thing isn't working."

Hanjun, eager to take up the challenge, nabbed the plaything from his hands. Aiming at Hanso's forehead, he pulled the flimsy trigger, sending the plastic flying in a random direction. "Aish! Cheap piece of—"

"Ha!" Jin doubled over in hysterics.

Soogi pretended to clap. "Nice, Hanu! You almost took an eye out!"

"I know how to fix this—" Hanjun pulled the plug, dumping the contents directly on Hanso's face.

Startled awake by a sudden splash of cold water, Hanso recoiled and swatted at him. "What the hell—"

Before he could finish his sentence, the companions interrupted with joyful singing, though Jin belted the loudest. "Happy birthday, our Hyung!"

Amid the chaos, Jen presented him with the cake. "Happy birthday, Ho-Young."

Thanking her, he eyed the poorly written message. His friends decorated the dessert themselves, with varying degrees of success, but what caught his attention was the incorrect age alongside the cheery sentiment. "You know I'm thirty, right? We need to get used to using our international ages."

Jin nodded, his bangs swaying with the motion. "Do you feel any different than you did yesterday?"

Hanso shook his head. "No—"

"Then you're *still* twenty-nine." Deok-Sun expelled a hearty laugh. "For the second year in a row."

"You're only as young as you feel." Hanjun dipped a finger into the outer edge of the frosting. "Hate to do this on your birthday, but Ha-Rin wants us at the office."

"When?" Hanso deflated like an old helium balloon.

Hanjun checked his watch. "About fifteen minutes ago."

Muttering a few choice words under his breath, Hanso flung the covers from his legs. "I'll be right down."

⋆⁺₊⋆☾⋆⁺₊⋆

Hanjun settled in the back seat of a black Hyundai Palisade, itching to dive into the world of social networking. Clutching his phone, he opened a search tab for the latest episode of Parallels. In a matter of days, the web exploded in a frenzy of theory videos and heated disagreements, all centered around a single topic: his mooning for Jen. He sifted through countless celebrity gossip columns, experiencing a tinge of pride. Some fans were praising Jen's curled hair, her trendy outfit, and the barely visible tattoos on her upper back. However, a twinge of guilt tugged at his chest; once their relationship was discovered, the compliments would turn sour. But until he couldn't, he relished seeing her gain the appreciation she deserved.

Between the praise and speculation, one statement caught his eye. The commenter spoke of Hanjun's behavior towards Blackmirror's newest addition but also noted how in a recent live stream—when the musicians discussed their Christmas wishes—Hanso didn't seem to enjoy her company, while Hanjun confessed his affection to the cameras. The replies were flooded with fervent debates, and full supporters hypothesized that the theoretical couple should be referred to as #HanJen.

Spotting Jen approaching the vehicle, he closed the browser and greeted her with a smile. "Ha-Rin says he has good news."

Swinging the door shut, she sank into the seat next to him, mirroring his friendliness. "Oh? What kind of good news?"

Jin hung over his seatback. "Yes, what *kind* of good news?"

Hanjun responded coyly. "You'll see."

"Ugh." Pouting, he slunk into his chair.

"It's a few minutes. You'll be fine." He chuckled and gave Jin a friendly pat on the head.

Catching the tail end of Jin's sulking, Hanso chucked his bag on the floorboard. "Can we have one day without someone whining?"

Jin brooded. "Only because it's your birthday."

★⁺₊★☾★⁺₊★

Holding a warm smile, Ha-Rin sat alone in the conference room, stacks of binders on his left, and a state-of-the-art smart board displaying color-coded graphs on his right. "Good morning."

Taking a seat next to Ha-Rin, Jen expelled a contented sigh, grateful for the absence of Dae-Hyun. She eyeballed his empty chair at the end of the table, her breath rattling at the very thought of him.

Ha-Rin pulled papers from the folders. "Our quarterly poll results are in. Since the addition of Assistant Jenilyn, views are up twenty percent, and interaction is exceptional."

He tapped a diagram, bragging about a sharp increase in positive sentiments after Jen's appearance. Displayed in vibrant colors of organized input, the data highlighted her impact. "Anti may be open to having a girl around."

He gestured to an analysis on Hanjun's favorable public reception on the big screen, pivoting to address the couple. "The chemistry between you two cannot be ignored. We should play on that."

"What about me dating Hanso?" She gulped, knowing J&I was attempting to use her for some kind of publicity stunt, although she couldn't grasp why. Blackmirror was beyond popular. Nobody knew or cared who she was—or at least they didn't until she was caught in close quarters with them.

"You still are." Ha-Rin folded his hands over his stomach as if he held the power to pull an infinite number of strings. "We'll have you stage a breakup before the new year."

"It would be best if I broke up with her," Hanso suggested.

Ha-Rin nodded, scrawling notes in a leather-bound notebook. "The research department will devise an exit strategy. Providing everything goes according to plan, you should walk away with the least amount of pushback."

Hanso looked at Jen apologetically. She gave him a sympathetic smile and twisted to face Ha-Rin. "Thank you, Sir."

Rising to leave, Ha-Rin tugged on his jacket, his mood shifting from business to dismissive. "That's all I have for today."

⋆⁺₊⋆☾⋆⁺₊⋆

The chauffeur maneuvered through traffic, protecting precious cargo hidden behind tinted windows. Ignoring blaring horns and screeching tires, Hanjun was engrossed in his mobile. Looking away during a non-skippable ad, he glanced at Jen. She was the only passenger not sucked into cyberspace. "Why haven't you replaced your phone?"

"I have one from the agency." Digging in her pocket, she produced a company-mandated mobile. Rose gold—one of two colors available—the unsmartphone was specifically created for use at the J&I tower. Given to all low-ranking associates, the device served as a direct line to the company heads and was modified to prohibit content leaks. Different from smart phones in almost every way, the handheld operated as a basic phone or walkie-talkie when activated.

"You can't be serious." He spouted raucous sarcasm. "It's a brick with slightly more functionality. The only thing it can do is make and receive calls."

"That's all I need."

He brandished a convincing smile. "I would feel better if you had something more reliable."

Jin inserted his opinion. "She doesn't need to be glued to a screen like you, Hanjun."

"Jin—" Hanjun emitted a low growl. "Mind your business."

"Not everyone wants a phone," Soogi emphasized from the front seat.

Hands whipping through the cabin, Hanso erupted into a mind-scrambling rant. "That thing's so old; it's a Sam-*Hyung*, not a Samsung. We live in an internet-based reality. Not having a phone doesn't make sense. How do you expect to do anything? You can't even buy tickets to a show!"

Paying no mind to his incessant rambling, she slid out of the vehicle as soon as it came to a stop. Sprinting through the parking lot, she was the first to enter their complex; a calculated maneuver to bait any lurking paparazzi that may have tailed them. Once the coast was clear, the bandmates followed her to the elevator.

"Another one?" Stepping out on their floor, Hanjun snatched the anticipated gift from the carpet and tore it open, revealing another photograph. Tapping his code into the keypad, he tossed the parcel on the kitchen counter and headed straight to his room, grumbling about the lack of security. "You'd think it wouldn't be hard to catch someone leaving unaddressed packages."

Deok-Sun slipped past Jen in the kitchen. "He tends to get angry when he's worried."

Her gaze swept the hallway. "I should give him space."

Opening the door to his room, Hanjun heard Jen asking about him, but he was too furious to vocalize his unrest. He collapsed in bed, hoping to alleviate the anxiety plaguing him day after day. Restless, he reached for his cell, shopping for security cameras. It may have been a small precaution, but he wasn't sure what else to do. Placing an order with expedited delivery, he discarded the device and opened his journal.

> *Happy 30th birthday, Hanso. Fans deemed us Han-*
> *Jen. I'm looking forward to their breakup.*

CHAPTER THIRTY-ONE

Any Kink for You

Stirring from sleep, Jen found a note taped to her door. The edges of the paper were curled, as if the missive had been there for some time. She peeled the memo from the surface, uncovering Hanjun's hasty handwriting.

Went to the office. —Jun.

Affixing the keepsake to her vanity mirror, she ensured it would catch her eye every morning. She never told him, but she loved it when he left her notes. In a world dominated by instant messaging, she found his old-fashioned gestures charming. He was a person of tradition in most aspects of life. His prose and musings were written in a tangible notebook with ink and paper, while his younger colleagues utilized tablets.

Though it was a Sunday—reserved for repose—the condo was eerily still. Disappearing into the bathroom, the rush of water overpowered the silence. She assumed the rest of Blackmirror were also at the office, working on upcoming projects or catching up on unfinished tasks.

Dressing in a chic ensemble of black ripped jeans and a crisp white button-down blouse, she grabbed a leather jacket from the closet. Clearing the condominium gates, she hustled to the J&I headquarters. Normally bustling, there was not a soul to be found. The sidewalks surrounding the tower were devoid—no fans hoping for a glimpse or reporters clamoring for an interview. Even the lobby was empty of crew, artists, and trainees. Wondering what could cause the anomaly, she slid into the elevator.

'Please scan key card.'

She scanned her identification, waiting for the blue light to signal approval. The system chimed a soothing melody, and she tapped her foot in time with the rhythm.

'Welcome, Jenilyn. Members of Blackmirror Hanjun, Deok-Sun, Hanso, and Jin are located on recording studio floor twelve. Soogi of Blackmirror's whereabouts are unknown.'

She shook her head. Soogi was known to dodge security by hopping in the lift with unsuspecting workers and having the hijackee flash their card. She only knew because he did it to her on a handful of occasions to visit the unoccupied floors. From there, he sat in empty lounges and composed lyrics in extreme silence.

Stepping onto the private floor, she discovered Deok-Sun in a luxurious massage chair. Lifting one arm, he directed her toward Hanjun's workroom. Following his directions down a narrow corridor, she was struck by artwork adorning the stretch. Hung three feet apart, the works created a mini museum. Traveling along, she examined the beautiful flowerwork and colorized koi featured in many of the collections. Inching to the door at the end, the designs became progressively darker, as if they were purchased based on mood until the purchaser entered a madness of his own.

Appreciating a painting hanging above the door, she recognized it as Karak Sam Kuk Yusa—the legend of six princes emerging from golden eggs. Its hieroglyphic style intrigued her, and she noted the twin fish in the background—something Soogi often referenced in his works.

Tearing her vision from the canvas, she raised a fist to knock, discovering his studio name matched the one plastered on his social media: Hanu. What most of the world didn't know was that he also had accounts under a pseudonym, which he used to talk with family and friends.

"Hanjun?" Placing her ear against the door, she heard a loud crash.

He quickly recovered from the blunder. "Yeobosayo?"

"Jen. Can I come in?"

He swung the door open with an exaggerated grin. "Hey."

"Hey." She peered inside; the lights were dimmed depressingly low, with a stack of empty coffee cups abandoned next to his computer mouse. The mother-of-pearl trinket box sat under his monitor, proudly on display. "Your collection is impressive."

He scratched the back of his neck. "Mr. Yun's advice was to purchase a piece for each award we win."

She inspected the hall. There weren't enough to represent every Blackmirror trophy. "Aren't you missing a few?"

He flashed a charming smile, widening the door. "The rest are in here."

Proceeding inside, she was greeted by an overwhelming display of mementos, figurines, and treasures he had collected during his travels. Each item was arranged aesthetically—a surprising contrast to his usual clutter. "I didn't know you collected so many things."

"I like everything." He monitored her reaction closely. "I get bored after a while, but I can't get rid of them."

She bent down to admire a set of Sailor Moon collectibles on an acrylic shelf. "These are adorable."

Reliving his previous girlfriend's disapproval, apprehension plagued him. "I've heard it's immature to collect toys."

"Who told you that?" Shaking her head, she straightened up. "We all have an inner child. I'm glad you spend time with yours."

Relieved, he shut the door. "You didn't have to come all this way for me."

"Your studio is iconic." She noticed a production program open on his desktop and the microphone on his desk. "I wanted to see it for myself."

Wrapping an arm around her waist, he guided her to the computer. Collapsing into his seat, he played the unprocessed version of a song he was working on. "I've been considering this one, but I think it might be a better fit for Deok-Sun. I don't have the vocals for something like this."

She listened, eyeballing the cluttered shelves and disorganized corners. Despite the organization, there were piles waiting to be dealt with. Without a window, the plot was dreary, as if there were a thunderstorm brewing inside the walls. "Have you gotten any sun today?"

"I like the darkness." Tugging on her waistband, he snuggled against her side. "Besides, you're my sun, and I'm the snow that melts beneath you."

"Mi Sol," she insisted. "It means 'My sun' in Spanish."

"Then you're *Mi Sol*." He replicated her smile.

Blushing, she admired him in his happiest place. His workspace was his home, and music was his comfort. Sitting in an empty chair next to him, she observed how engrossed he was, wavering between clenching his jaw and bouncing his knee. Dissecting his recordings note by note, he shook his head. She contemplated that he could have been nervous, but she knew brooding was his process.

Standing, she massaged his shoulders. "Take a break."

He caressed her wrist. "Gwenchanayo."

"You are not fine, Ryu Hanjun." She wagged a finger. "Don't try to hide it from me; you have a tell when you're frustrated."

He snickered at her use of his full name. "Do I?"

"You drop your head and rub your fingers along your hairline." She positioned a hand on her hip. "And you've done it four times since I walked in."

"You think?" Holding eye contact, he rubbed a forefinger along his lower lip.

"Come on." Dragging him from the chair, she led him to a sofa tucked in the corner, urging him onto the cushions. "Sit."

Settling in, he licked his lips. "This is new."

"Close your eyes," she whispered, her voice velvety. He relaxed his hands at his sides, and she shifted in his lap, relishing the solid warmth of his body. Holding his chin in her palm, her thumb swept down his lips, taking in their fullness and the clear coat of balm he applied religiously. Tracing the curve of his bottom lip, she noticed a slight gap between his teeth—a small imperfection adding to his attractiveness. "You can open your eyes."

Without breaking eye contact, he clamped down on her finger, applying soft pressure. "This is my idea of a break."

"Junie," she murmured, experiencing universal heat developing between their bodies. "I think you have a biting kink."

Raising an eyebrow, he leaned his head back. "I could have any kink for you."

She tugged on his hair, rousing an animalistic groan from him. "Is that so?"

"Everything you wanna do." He held his breath, a surge of fixation afflicting his exhale. Mind wandering, he was disturbed by the sinful acts he wanted to commit with her. "And I do mean *everything*."

His voice was impossibly chasmic when he was aroused, making her pelvis quake at his trembling. She trailed kisses down his torso, pulling the collar of his sweater down to reveal bare skin. Moving her tongue to his neck, she grazed her teeth along his collarbone. "*Everything?*"

"You're trying to get it." He squeezed her hips, provoking a squeal from her.

"Am I?" Harnessing a wicked smirk, her fingers worked at the buttons of her blouse, revealing a patch of delicate lace.

"That's not fair." Unable to remove his eyes from the dangerous curves of her breasts, he scolded her.

"*No?*" She flirtatiously whined. "Why not?"

"You're torturing me." Holding his arms behind her back, he yanked her closer.

With a seductive lick of her lips, she locked eyes with him. "It's only torture if you can't have what you want."

"It's like that?" And there it was. *Consent*. Staring at her, he weighed his options. He wanted their first time to be memorable, but he wasn't sure if he wanted it to happen in his bottega. If a relationship didn't work out between them, the memory would haunt him during every studio session.

Without further hesitation, he rolled her onto her side, his body eclipsing hers in a possessive shadow. His lips tracked down her neck and shoulder, igniting sparks along her skin. Revisiting her mouth for a heated kiss, he tore her shirt open with primal ferocity, unveiling the lacy bra underneath.

"Hey, that was expensive!" She broke away from her pleasure but was quickly reeled back in.

"Don't worry your pretty little face. I'll buy you ten more." Snaking up her figure, his hands traveled behind her back. Just as he reached the third clasp, his phone started to vibrate.

Incapable of ignoring the persistent ringing, she rapped his back. "Junie, your phone—"

"It doesn't matter." Grunting, he refused to be interrupted.

"It could be important."

His body sank into hers, his fingers clawing the sofa's fabric. "Is a little privacy too much to ask?"

Amused by his exasperation, she chuckled. "I'm sorry."

Tramping through the room, he answered in a disgruntled mutter. "Yeah?"

"Oh shi—" He nodded in response, terminating the call.

Lunging forward, she held her torn shirt together with the scraps. "What's wrong?"

Smoothing the wrinkles in his clothes, he blushed. "I'm supposed to be on live."

She giggled while he strove to look like he wasn't making out with his girlfriend. "Your hair is a mess."

"Bansa." He brandished a shy smile. "It's slang for 'back at you.' Something school kids would say."

Repeating the word, she panicked when he turned to face the desk. "Wait! Let me get out of here. I can't leave like this."

"Stay. It won't take long." Plopping into his chair, he adjusted the webcam. "I'll move the lens so you're not in the frame."

Tossing her a hoodie hanging from a floor lamp, he simultaneously greeted his audience. "Sorry, I lost track of time."

Pausing, he stole a glance at her; she fixed her partially undone bra and slipped into his hoodie. Forcing his eyes back to the screen, he wanted to postpone the stream and finish her while the moment was lukewarm. Once the flame died out, he would need to wait until the next opportunity. And he was getting tired of waiting.

Retreating to the sofa after putting on his sweatshirt, she watched from the best seat in the house. He seemed anxious, jerking his legs and fidgeting with items on his desk. It was endearing to see him have butterflies over something he had done countless times.

"My hair is messy?" He choked on his viewer's observations. "Um, yeah, I recently woke up."

"My voice sounds deeper?" Another commenter caught his eye. "My throat hurts a little."

A new query popped up, and his mouth twitched, though he shook his head in vague denial. "Is Hanso dating Blackmirror's assistant? Not for me to say."

"Is she pretty? *Beautiful.* You're gonna love her." Reading another comment, his phone vibrated against the desk. He checked the caller and answered on speaker. "Say hi to Anti!"

"Hey, Anti!" Deok-Sun's distinct vibration imbued the room. "Hanu, have you seen Jen?"

"Uh, yeah." Hanjun focused on the camera, biting his lip. "She's in the studio."

"I didn't need anything; I was just wondering where she was!" Deok-Sun released a howl and abruptly ended the call.

Curious about the sudden guffawing emitting from the hall, Jen kept her back to the computer and went to investigate. Opening the door, she caught her roommates laughing at Deok-Sun's impromptu interruption. "You got jokes, huh?"

Taking advantage of the situation for comedic effect, Soogi encased his arms around his chest and pretended to canoodle his reflection. Deok-Sun and Jin feigned devouring each other with their lips and hands. Hanso shook his rump, grinding on the door frame.

Jen maneuvered past the exuberance. "I'm getting him another coffee. Behave while I'm gone."

Hanjun gawped at the camera, shaking his head at his bandmates twerking beyond the threshold. Holding a straight face, he finally burst into cachinnation at the stupidity. "This is what I deal with. Every. Damn. Day. Be the leader, they said. It'll be fun, they said."

He revolved to face his friends, who were captured in fits of giggles. But when he spotted Jen returning with a cup of fresh brew, he strutted through the room, blocking her from view. Returning to the sofa, she sat down, and he couldn't help but stare; her hair was disheveled, and the hoodie hugged her form, layering her in his scent.

Pointing to the desk, she passed off the coffee. "You should finish that."

Remembering he was in the middle of streaming, he closed the door in his friends' faces and returned to his chair. "I'll answer one more question before I go."

Leaning in, he found the inquisitiveness he knew the viewers would have. "Why was Jen in my studio?"

"She brought me coffee." Taking a sarcastic slurp, he waved goodbye. "Thanks for watching."

Making a heart by crossing his thumb and pointer, he severed the stream and turned to Jen. "That was awful."

"Deok-Sun thought he was funny. I hope he didn't get you in trouble."

"The company is lenient. Without proof, there's not much that can be done." He grinned at the sight of her wild, tousled hair from their earlier activities. Her legs were crossed, giving him a glimpse of her meaty thighs. Purging the dirty thoughts from his mind, he realized he needed to release some energy before he pounced on her like a rabid animal. "I'm gonna hit the gym. You can stay here if you'd like."

Accompanying him, she didn't feel comfortable staying in his territory without him. "I'll hitch a ride with Jin."

⋆⁺₊⋆☾⋆⁺₊⋆

Jin reached the door first, fetching the wrapped gift abandoned in the hall. "This is getting scary, don't you think?"

Unfazed, Soogi tapped in his code. "At least the packages are *outside*. Imagine if they were being left *inside*."

"I don't want to think about that." Jin bulldozed through the home, dumping the mysterious parcel on the counter.

Shimmying out of her outerwear, Jen shuddered. "Me either."

Hanso disappeared into the kitchen. "If they do, I'm moving out."

Tramping to the lounge, Deok-Sun sprawled on the sofa. "We only have a year on the lease. I'd stick it out."

"A year?" Jen settled next to him. "Ha-Rin never mentioned that."

Jin nodded with his whole body. "After that, we can live separately."

"I suppose I should start looking for a new place." She made a reminder to scout for serviced apartments, knowing how difficult it was for an expat to find housing in central Seoul.

Soogi collapsed on a chair, kicking his feet up on the coffee table. "Don't worry too much. J&I has connections in everything. They'll help you."

Jin wriggled an arm around her shoulder. "We could be roomies!"

"We'll see about that, Jinnie."

Thirty minutes later, Hanjun arrived home just in time for dinner, his skin glistening with sweat and his muscles taut from harsh exercise. "Has Deok-Sun taken his evening shower? I'd like to clean up after dinner."

"I believe so." Preparing the table, Hanso handed him the first plate. "You didn't shower at the office?"

"I did." Hanjun ravenously shoveled noodles into his mouth. "But then I rented a bike. I guess I cycled harder than I meant to."

Hanso suppressed a frown. "Is everything okay? You usually turn to biking when you're sad or stressed."

"Just work piling up." Hanjun wore a calm facade, but his angst was visible.

Serving him another helping, Hanso squeezed his shoulder. "It's okay to rest, you know."

"There was another package." Summoned to the table by clinking cutlery, Jin slipped into his seat. "I haven't opened it yet."

"I'll take care of it." Hanjun finished the last bite of his meal before anyone else had a chance to touch theirs. Discarding his bowl in the sink, he snatched the delivery and retreated to his room. Hearing Jen ask if everything was alright with him, he closed the door. He was fine and, in many ways, not fine.

Locking the knob, he pulled out a trunk from under his bed, brimming with photos sent to their residence. Taping pictures to the wall, aligned like pieces of a puzzle, he rearranged the images until they formed a semi-recognizable scene. "Two silhouettes, a cramped, blacked-out room, coats, blankets—are these from the beach house?"

Just as he started to unravel the mystery, his phone pinged with a notification. Scrolling through the group chat, he smiled as his bandmates teased him about his facial expressions during the broadcast.

He cast the device aside and reached for his journal. It was a day of laughter and flushing cheeks, but it was also the day he found the courage to express his desires for Jen. Convinced their first sexual encounter was on the horizon, anticipation mounded in his belly. He needed it to be soon.

Today was just short of an amazing day.

<u>CHAPTER THIRTY-TWO</u>

Yoo Junyeong

Jen was glad the day's schedule would be relatively easy. Though her job wasn't laborious, the psychological stress was unmanageable. Or perhaps it wasn't the mental strain she was under, but the lack of ways to manage her anxiety.

In her previous life, before she made the move to Seoul, her preferred way to decompress was by observing. Mug in hand, she read compositions from all over the world. From travel blogs to scientific studies to dissertations, she enjoyed uncovering the unwritten within the written. There was a hidden meaning behind the thinly worn public veils of those who wished to be heard. And much like those who watched true crime and tried their hand at cracking unsolved murders, she wanted to discover what went unsaid.

Diving into the motivations of strangers was her favorite pastime, and since the evolution of telecommunications, she didn't have to frequent coffee shops or people watch at the Home Depot to get an inside scoop into someone's life. Though it did wonders to regulate her cortisol levels, she attributed many of her best traits to the not-so-guilty pleasure. Imagining the lives of others, from their triumphs to their struggles, kept her thoughts fluid and her heart compassionate because life was never all roses or unicorns—there was a lot of hell in every heaven.

The world was categorized into digestible labels of cultural indifference, but she saw something else: people were mosaics of everything and everyone they touched, loved, or hated. It was a powerful and distressing reminder that even the smallest thing could have a grand impact on those she encountered.

Since being forced to fake date Hanso, she couldn't do what she once treasured. Like some kind of karmic intervention, opening a browser would inevitably lead her to hearsay about herself. Or Blackmirror. Or her and Blackmirror, collectively. Sure, she could have deluded herself into believing she wouldn't click into the crudely chronicled pieces. And maybe she wouldn't, but reading the headers was enough to know she didn't need to see what was lurking inside, even if she found the tabloids mildly amusing.

Seoulvia, one of South Korea's trending celeb lifestyle columns, was the first to dispatch about Jen after the initial commotion.

'THE SEARCH FOR SEOUL'S CINDERELLA IS AFOOT.'

Koreana, a young adult print boasting fashions and disasters, was the second to cover the story, running bulletins on the suede Jimmy Choo's she ditched during her narrow escape with Hanjun.

'HANJUN OF BLACKMIRROR JIMMY CHOO'SES MYSTERY WOMAN.'

Izentity, a dating and scandal startup, launched a full-blown investigation in cahoots with celebrity stalker Haeseong. Luckily, the steam dissipated with the discovery of another budding couple within the band.

'BLACKMIRROR, BLACKMIRROR ON THE WALL, WHO IS THE GIRL FOR WHOM HANSO DID FALL?'

Seoulcialite, Korea's leading gossip column on the one percent, focused on her humble way of life.

'BLACKMIRROR'S GAN HO-YOUNG 'VALIANTLY' FALLS FOR COMMONER.'

Even Seoul Star, an up-and-coming mag dedicated to fair, unsensationalized news, boasted Jen's likeness.

'ONYX SHEEP IN WOLF'S CLOTHING; THE SOCIAL MEDIA HUNT FOR A GIRL NAMED JEN.'

Not only were the bloggers and press conspiring to bring awareness to the calumny, but there were also employees at J&I having their own laugh. She ignored the side-eyes of antipathy and snide quips about her residing with Blackmirror, but she wouldn't turn a blind eye to the freshly Xeroxed memes appearing in the restrooms. Derogatory in nature, one prankster made it their life's mission to keep a particular idea afloat by photoshopping Jen and the five members of Blackmirror into a casting couch scenario.

The agency did its best to weed out the aggressor, and he did an excellent job of hiding his identity until he made an ignorant mistake. Manager-in-training for an up-and-coming idol group, he went to fetch pastries from a local shop and returned with boxes closely resembling the meme: one white-frosted donut surrounded by five yellow donuts. He found it hilarious, though the apprentices he was working with found it appalling and turned him in to the CEO. Ousted from the company, he was slammed with defamation lawsuits for each member of Blackmirror. With the trainees as witnesses, along with a handful of staff who saw him with stacks of circulars, he was required to compensate for the damage.

Jen didn't find out about the incident until a company-wide email was sent out just before the legal proceedings. Though the correspondence didn't specify the what or who of the situation, she knew it was about her based on the mention of bathroom propaganda. Within days, the harassment ceased, though there were still a few whispers floating around the cafeteria.

Weeks later, she ran into the young men who halted the aggravation. The quartet, which was in the late stages of development, had little more than a name at the time. Aged twenty to twenty-five, the soon-to-be stars had an elegant, mature theme with vogue vocals, juicy jazz harmonies, and masculine appeal. Their trademark—F.U.T.U.R.E.—was an acronym for 'Friends Until The Universe Reaches the End,' and their pre-debut fan base were known as the Eternals. The moniker tied directly to their concept: polished, refined billionaire heirs on the rise to take over their family businesses. Fabricated clones of provocative studs from women's erotic novels, the dark, sensual vision landed somewhere between the realms of Kwon Si-Hyeon from Tempted and Christian Grey from Fifty Shades.

Underneath the rented designer suits and modern quiff haircuts were four young men who envisioned success, much like the characters they portrayed. They admired Blackmirror and believed it was their responsibility to call out injustice. As the youngest quoted, 'Watching someone drown is just as bad as holding their head underwater.'

Jen shook her head, bringing her mind back to what she was supposed to be doing: accompanying Hanjun to a slew of markets in Namdaemun. Fulfilling the schedule Ha-Rin carefully laid out, the musicians were split into groups, tasked with procuring Christmas presents with their camera crews in tow.

"Do you know Yoo Junyeong?" She felt textured pillows while Hanjun meandered through aisles of kitschy gadgets.

"Of Future?" Reaching for an expensive Spam gift set, he nodded. "He's the leader, right?"

"Right. He's half Korean and half Native—"

"Ah. I remember. I heard him practicing Korean on the trainee floor." Situating the box in its display, he pretended to be the young novice. "He was shouting through the door like this: ㅐ! ㅖ! ㅐ! ㅖ! ㅘ!"

Giggling at his impression, she unloaded what was on her mind. "Being the youngest and moving to South Korea, he's having a hard time staying firm."

Surprised, he turned to her. "Why didn't he come to me? I could have helped."

"Because you're his role model. I know you don't think of yourself as prestigious, but he only knows you as his senior."

"I'll talk to him." He fingered through a rack of girlish tops, pulling a frilly blouse from the bunch. "Do you like any of these?"

She checked the tag, calculating a rough won-to-dollar exchange. The price was much too high for a simple white blouse. "I'm not worried about it."

His head fell to the side. "I destroyed your shirt. I need to get you *something*."

"If you must, get something you'd like to see me in."

A snicker gushed from him. "I'd like to see nothing on you."

As if summoned by happiness, Hanso interrupted their shameless flirting by draping an arm around her shoulder. Plastering on a phony smile, she mouthed an apology to Hanjun while she was whisked away by another man.

Hanjun knew it wasn't real, yet his perception didn't stop him from hating every minute of the fake romance. Not just because he disliked seeing her with Hanso, but because he despised knowing she invoked unchecked jealousy in him. He thought he had grown past the emotion. Or perhaps he never felt anything worth being jealous of.

⋆⁺₊⋆☾⋆⁺₊⋆

Smooshed between shopping bags in the backseat of his escort, Hanjun browsed the comments of his most recent livestream.

'HANSO DOESN'T SEEM CONCERNED. MAYBE SHE'S WOOING ALL OF THEM.'
—XSANDOHNOES

'ONLY JUNIE COULD COME ON LIVE OUT OF BREATH, WITH SEX HAIR, AND STILL MAKE US LOVE HIM.' —WOWJUN

'AW, HE GAVE HER HIS HOODIE! BOYFRIEND MATERIAL.' —ONYXMIRROR

'THE WAY HE LOOKS AT HER! IT'S LOVE.' —SUNDAYWORST

'HIS DEEP VOICE! THEY WERE DOING SOMETHING.' —UNFINISHEDSENTENC

'GET YOURSELF A MAN WHO LOOKS AT YOU THE WAY HANJUN LOOKS AT ASSISTANT JEN.' —NOTSOBAD

Grinning at the critiques, he tucked the phone into his pocket. Exhibitionism wasn't on his list of kinks, but there was something thrilling about the world knowing he was pursued by her. He was living every man's fantasy by catching the attention of his ideal woman. She wanted him—not just the best parts of him—and was willing to make her stance known.

But his attachment was about so much more than sexual gratification. She held him when he was having a hard day and told him she was proud to be with him. Reminded him of how strong he'd been and that she couldn't ask for a better person. If she went a day without seeing him, she was as happy as a dog to talk to him for a few minutes at the end of the night. And even though she had a certain aura that aroused the male gaze, he had little worry about betrayal. He wasn't stupid enough to believe she was incapable of cheating, but he believed she would need to be pushed past her breaking point to consider the idea.

He wanted the world to know he had found the thing everyone longed for: genuine love. Something he didn't think existed after the fallout with his ex-girlfriend. After spending too much time and too many funds on a woman who had few intentions other than to cross him, he vowed to proceed with caution. While his mind urged him to shower her with lavish gifts, he honored his father's advice.

'Test her affection with fruit. If she complains, she isn't the one.'

A Casanova of his time, Mr. Ryu was not new to the world of courting. Though Hanjun had fame and fortune on his side, his father had physiognomy and charisma, and somehow he married his mother, who was fiery-tempered and obscenely outspoken. She was the exact opposite of his father: jagged around the edges and highly demanding. Despite their goals sometimes misaligning, they navigated every hardship together.

That's what he wanted: love like his parents. Maybe the relationship would be choppy, and maybe the boat would rock, but they would never capsize because they cooperated to remove the water threatening to drown their vessel. He believed Jen would be the perfect shipmate; she wasn't afraid to get her hands dirty and didn't spout instructions on how to fix a problem without putting in the work herself. She was a lot like his mother, who never let her husband sail a worrisome storm alone.

But Jen wasn't his mother. His father won her heart by ensuring she would live a comfortable life. The family wasn't rich, but they certainly weren't poor, and he never had to worry about many of the things Jen did. On the contrary, Jen had hustled since she was a child, establishing multiple routes of security to guarantee she would never be homeless again. Standard courtship practices would go unheard; he couldn't impress her by buying a home or requesting her hand in marriage, and he had no idea what she wanted beyond experiences.

So he did the only thing he could do: buy her a crate of produce and observe her reaction. While Jin carried the massive coffer to the table, she was amazed by sweet persimmons, yuja, green plums, hallabong mandarins, and oriental melons. Picking up a ripened peach, she stared at Hanjun in disbelief, and he thought the plan might have gone awry when she finally spoke.

"This is more fruit than we could possibly eat."

Over the next three days, after finishing her work shift, she prepared the fruits to feed her allies, along with dishes she gave to coworkers. With a little help from Soogi and Hanso, every fruit went to use, right down to the rinds, which made a delicious citron tea. They were eating persimmon salsa every day for a week, and she even returned the container to the market on his behalf.

He went to his father with the results. Devouring persimmon kimchi fresh from the dish, he shared a slice of wisdom he learned from his dad. "Women are not equal to men. They are far superior. Whatever you give her, she will multiply. If you give her a house, she will give you a home. If you give her groceries, she will give you a meal. And if you give her love, she will love you in a way you didn't know was possible. But if you give her nothing but grief, do not expect less in return. That's all you need to know about women like your mother. And Jenilyn."

Trudging to their condo, the roommates were greeted by another package waiting on the doorstep. Soogi wasted no time in placing it on the kitchen counter, where he began prepping dinner. Jen offered to help, and together they scuttled about, chopping vegetables and seasoning meat. The remaining mates joined in, each taking on a task. Deeply engrossed in a mysterious project, Hanjun scurried away.

Nosiness getting the best of him, Deok-Sun probed Jen for answers. "What *were* you doing in Hanjun's studio?"

Stifling a smile, she refused to divulge information. "That's confidential."

Jin rested his chin on his palms, swinging his legs daydreamingly. "I love the Jun-Jen saga. It's like our very own drama."

"Sorry to burst your bubble, but nothing happened." Knifing a bundle of scallions, she shook her head. "You made damn sure of that."

Deok-Sun covered his ears. "My innocence!"

Hanjun entered the kitchen, silencing the oral examination. Although the companions were curious about the romance, they knew better than to pry. When they tried in the past, he dodged their questions with meticulous accuracy and made it known he wanted the intricacies of their relationship to remain unseen.

$$\star^{+}_{+}\star\mathbb{C}\star^{+}_{+}\star$$

Swathed in a cocoon of warmth, Jen's rhythmic breathing lulled her into a dream state. Just as her eyes began to close, she was jolted awake by a sharp knock. "Come in."

"Hey." The door creaked open to reveal Hanjun.

Her eyes remained closed. "Hmm?"

He crawled to her side, but there was an underlying tension in his plea. "Can you tell me Hanso-Hyung means nothing to you?"

Pivoting to face him, she ran a hand along his cheek. "I care about all of you, you know that."

Pulling her close, he savored her soft body pressed against his. "I need to hear you say you don't want to be with him."

"I don't want to be with him."

He threaded his little finger around hers. "Promise me; when all of this is over, you'll choose me."

"I promise." She planted a kiss between his eyebrows. "Since you came into my life, it has only been you."

"Thank you." Wrapping his biceps around her in an embrace Hanso could never replicate, he dreamed of breaking free from their constraints.

Holding her until she drifted off, he reluctantly peeled away and returned to his room. Slinking under the covers, he pulled his journal from the nightstand.

I have mixed feelings of love and jealousy. I await the day I can walk with her in the sunlight. Mi Sol.

CHAPTER THIRTY-THREE

Spin the Bottle

Bulldozing through a sea of bodies, Jen maneuvered through the kitchen. Animated conversations and raucous amusement buzzed a chaotic symphony in her ears. Against the walls, a dozen of the agency's top makeup artists, hair stylists, filmers, and production managers stood like statues with cameras trained toward the center of the room.

Blackmirror were gathered around the dining table, surrounded by an array of textiles. Chenille stems in every color, fuzzy pompoms, sparkling glitter, wispy feathers, and hot glue guns littered the surface. The project? Crafting ugly sweaters from thrifted apparel.

"Did everyone get a name that isn't theirs?" Waving a red Christmas stocking, Hanjun rose above the commotion.

Jin focused on the leader. "I'm making a sweater for Rem."

"You could paste a picture of Jen on it." Soogi snickered.

The statement rang loud and clear on Hanjun's face. Melting into a lighthearted chuckle, he focused on the lens. "We need to edit that out."

Acquiring her task sheet for the day, Jen stood between two cameramen. She always wondered if Blackmirror were as close as J&I portrayed them to be. Working with them allowed her to see the truth. It wasn't that they were buddies and spent every waking moment together; they were associates who learned to coexist. They didn't always get along, and they didn't always like each other, but they persevered. They were a band of brothers, not best friends.

Hours passed like minutes, and the group devoted themselves to decorating. They jollied and jeered, sipping hot tea and singing holiday tunes. By the wrap, Deok-Sun's creation won over the staff; applying a variety of ribbons and rhinestones, he fashioned a darling sloth on the front, knowing it was Soogi's favorite animal. So much so that his Multiverse character was a dashing folivora.

While the cinematographers packed up the recording equipment, Hanjun checked the door for any sign of a package. As expected, another puzzling gift was left despite the gathering at the residence. Defeated, he flopped on the couch and reviewed the tracking number for the door camera he ordered days earlier. "Delivery never takes this long."

Placing a comforting hand on his shoulder, Deok-Sun joined him. "Windsor Heights has CCTV in every corner."

"I watched the footage; they're avoiding the cameras as if they know where they are."

Jen approached from behind. Tossing her arms around Hanjun, she passed him an open can of beer. "Let's not worry until there's something to worry about."

Sitting cross-legged on the sofa, Jin poured an entire bottle of wine into an exceptionally large glass and placed the empty container on the coffee table. "Let's play spin the bottle. If you refuse to kiss, you complete a dare!"

Hanjun scoffed, gesturing to Jen. "There's one girl here."

"Then I guess we'll have plenty of dares to go around." Jin gulped a sarcastic swig of vino.

Sliding to the floor, Hanjun rolled his eyes. "Fine, U-Jin."

"Me first." Jin spun and fluttered his eyelashes at Hanso, who begrudgingly braced for a smooch.

Hanjun lurched forward. Giving the bottle a whirl, the vessel slowed and almost struck Soogi before pointing at Jen. Cheered on by his mates, he prowled to her like a tiger stalking its prey. Leaning in, he grasped her cheeks and kissed her sweetly.

Deok-Sun landed on Soogi. Much to everyone's surprise, he shook his head in refusal. "Nah."

"Do the chicken dance!" Hanjun shouted the command, and Deok-Sun began to jiggle. Seconds later, Hanso harmonized, and soon all six roommates hummed to the tune.

Emboldened by three bottles of soju—seventy-five percent of his tolerance—Soogi performed a children's dance. "Baby Shark, doo-doo, doo-doo, doo-doo!"

Clapping along, Jen spun, parking on Hanso. She examined him, then Hanjun, and decided she wouldn't. "Dare."

Deok-Sun supplied his extra-expensive jug of bokbunjaju. "Drink the rest of this."

She seized the weighted canister, sampling the rich raspberry aroma. "This is an awful lot."

"Chug! Chug!" The friends chanted, pumping their fists in the air.

Holding a hand under her jaw, she guzzled until she choked. Pausing to catch her breath, she analyzed the label. The spirits were far too potent to be mere wine. "Deok-Sun, what is this?"

Hanso snatched the decanter, taking a sip by pouring from high above his mouth. "Did you mix it with soju?"

"Oops." Deok-Sun pounded a fist on the floor. "I forgot I combined them the last time I drank."

"Seriously?" Swiping the bottle from Hanso, she finished the elixir in one gulp, thankful the berry flavor masked the burn.

Deok-Sun spun next, landing on Jen. He kissed her weakly on the forehead, retreating to his seat just as fast. "This game likes girls!"

On Hanso's turn, the bottle ticked around the circle like a slow-moving clock until it pivoted toward Jen. Without looking at her or Hanjun, he declared his premeditated choice. "Dare."

Deok-Sun's eyes doubled in size, almost as if he were awaiting an opportunity to disrupt the peace. Before anyone uttered a word, he challenged Hanso with the most daring ultimatum he could think of. *"Kiss her on the lips!"*

A deafening hush settled over the room, and all eyes turned to Hanso. He studied Hanjun; he showed concern, but not enough to dissuade him. Crawling to Jen, he kneeled at her side and stole a glance at Hanjun one last time. Finding reassurance in his friend's nod, Hanso leaned in for the kiss. One smack later, he retired to his seat, evading eye contact with the room. There was an underlying discomfort in the atmosphere, and despite his nonchalance, Hanjun hopped to his feet and vacated the area.

"Uh oh." Jin observed his painfully clenched mandible.

Hanso turned to Deok-Sun, granting him a hard tap on the leg. "You issued the dare; you go check on him."

Taking the eldest's advice, Deok-Sun scurried after Hanjun. Discovering him resting on his bed, he hovered in the doorway. "Hanu, I didn't think it was a big deal."

"It's not your fault." Running a hand through his hair, Hanjun patted the spot next to him. "The whole fake dating Hanso thing has me on edge. It *haunts* me."

Deok-Sun padded across the floor. "They hardly talk because of how weird things are."

Hanjun clasped his hands together. "I know I shouldn't be jealous, and I try not to be, but I am. I'm a jealous person."

"She loves you, you know? The way she looks at you—that's what I imagine love is like. She takes an interest in everything you like, and she stands up for you when we're teasing you too much. You're the first person she sees when she walks into a room—she sees through everyone to get to you." He wished he could shake some sense into him. "Don't let your jealousy ruin—"

Jen knocked on the open door. "Junie?"

"That's my cue to leave." Deok-Sun nudged Hanjun's shoulder. "Remember what I said."

Timidly entering the room, she slumped against the wall. "Thanks, Deok-Sunnie."

"No problem." Wielding a grand smile, he closed the door behind him.

Patting his knees, Hanjun puffed his cheeks. "Do you think they're still playing out there?"

"I'm not sure." Swaying from her buzz, she mumbled. "I shouldn't have let—"

"It's just a stupid game." Biting the inside of his cheek, restraint suffocated him in a thick fog. His anger wasn't about childhood games; it was about shackling his possessive nature and concealing his worst traits. Greed, envy, arrogance—they were his toughest habits to combat, and he wasn't sure he wanted to resist; after all, what musician would succeed without drive, desire, and defiance? But he didn't know if she would accept his shadowy side or consider him a monster, just as everyone else had.

"I should've backed away." Her thoughts were lucid, but her sentences were slurred. "I shouldn't have put you in—"

Running a forefinger along his bottom lip, he admired how her joggers accentuated her frame—fitted at the waist and baggy in the legs. Scanning her body, his mind wandered to what was underneath. As if pulled by an unseen force, he floated through the room, craning her chin to graze her lips. Her hands tangled in his hair, and without thinking, she wrapped her arms around his shoulders. Lifting her from the floor, he pinned her against the wall, his palms roaming her contours.

"I only want to be with you." A soft, breathy moan released from her parted lips as he slid his hands under her shirt, trailing up her sides like wildfire. Discarding her blouse, he paused to appreciate her undergarments: red lace with black trim. Before he could fully take in the view, she grabbed his face and assaulted him with hungry kisses.

Tongues flicking in feverish sync, his palms migrated to her backside. Carrying her to the bed, he pushed her flat on her back, never breaking impact on her lips. Introducing scorching kisses along her neck and breasts, he trailed from her hips to her calves, slowly unsheathing her legs. Peppering her bare flesh with his tongue, he ascended from her ankles to her tummy and chest. "God, you're amazing."

"Aren't I?" Melodic giggling bubbled from her lungs; his soft petting clashed with the rough, calloused texture of his palms, launching shudders into her core. Censoring her moans, she bit her lip, captivated under his weight.

Returning for a second taste, he inspected her eyes; riveted in unadulterated surrender, her body arched, and her hands tugged at his hair. She was unlike herself—wholly consumed. "Jen?"

Pouting, she nibbled on the tip of her finger. "Don't stop."

He tried to decipher if she was serious. "Are you drunk?"

Eyes rolling, she snorted. "Maybe a little, but it's fine."

Jerking away, he sat upright. "No, it's not."

Startled by his sudden recoiling, she propped up on her elbows. Deflating under his gaze, she used an arm to shield her exposed chest. "Is it something I did?"

"No, you're perfect." Fingers trembling, he traced the curve of her nearly naked body. Warmth radiating from her exterior fueled his growing arousal, and he retreated a second time.

Confused by his mixed signals, she slumped. "It's okay if you don't want to—"

"You have no idea how bad I want you." Plunging forward, he pressed her against the headboard, conveying his deepest desires: to intimately experience every inch of her with his hands and mouth. But then he withdrew, pausing to cover her with the blanket. "But not like this."

Her eyes expanded. "Why?"

"I want our first time to be—" Exhaling, he held her hand with both of his. "Euphoric."

"*Euphoric?*" She wasn't sure what his expectations were—intercourse wasn't something they discussed, as they rarely found time to be alone. Even when they managed to escape, they were either in public or at the agency. The only private time they had were the fleeting moments they stole.

He squeezed her hand. "Our first time needs to be something we *both* remember."

"You're right." She clicked her tongue, fluffed the pillow, and snuggled with his Joey stuffie. "Goodnight Junie."

He ran a hand through her silken strands. Hearing her breathing morph into light purring, he reached for his journal. Pulling a pen from the spiral ring, he battled conflicting poignancies. A jumbled mess of anticipation, fear, and longing, he knew they would reach the point of full intimacy, though he couldn't pinpoint when.

The thought of being with her in an intimate way was exhilarating, but with the excitement came a tinge of sadness; once they crossed that threshold, the tension between them would dissipate. No longer would they have to fantasize—fantasy would become a reality. And seldom did actuality compare with imagination. What if he didn't live up to her expectations? What if she hyped the moment to be something extraordinary and he fell short?

Even worse, what if he built her up in his dreams and became disinterested after the initial thrill waned? It was something he hadn't told her; he was notorious for engaging in shallow relationships and moving on just as fast. But his withdrawal was never about the explicit; it was about having his mind fucked at the same time as his body. He craved a lover who aroused his brain as much as his emotions, and he had yet to find a suitable partner. But God, how he wanted it to be her.

Today was almost the day. I need to better control my possessiveness when it comes to her.

<u>CHAPTER THIRTY-FOUR</u>

The Seven Sisters

Hanjun's focus drifted to the silhouette at his side. Jen relaxed in a comfortable slumber, her hair falling over her face. The blanket tangled around her legs, exhibiting the velvety curves of her hips. Sliding out of bed, he draped the covers over her form, trusting Hanso hadn't caught sight of her during the night. It would be even better if he hadn't realized she was in their room to begin with.

The game of truth or dare continued long after they left, with the remaining participants consuming alcohol with reckless abandon. Hanso stumbled into their shared space sometime after dawn, footsteps unsteady and words slurred. Hanjun, immersed in atypical songwriting, watched with amusement and anxiety. Propping his knees, he shrouded Jen, allowing her a peaceful snooze.

Prowling through the room to retrieve his shirt, he marveled at the possibility of waking up with her for the rest of his life. He yearned for a lifetime of her, anchoring him to his dreams.

★⁺₊★☾★⁺₊★

Jen awoke in Hanjun's bed, daydreaming about the previous night. The memory of his pure intentions lingered, but she wished he would have resumed. Despite her intoxication, she was aware of her desires and knew what she wanted—for him to bend her into every position and fulfill months of erotic teasing. But as she sprawled alone, she could only imagine what could have been.

She sought to test their compatibility, and her only goal was to please him. Impatience coursed through her veins; each encounter became more heated, and she wasn't the only one subjected to the magnetic pull. Hands roving her thighs and eyes threatening to consume her, he knew how willing she was to be devoured by him. He may have even enjoyed delaying her gratification.

Deciding to be a productive human—one who didn't fantasize about missed steamy encounters—she padded around the quiet room in search of her discarded clothing. The morning sun cast a faint glow, illuminating the arc of her pillowcase-concealed body. Spotting her shirt near the door and her pants next to the bed, she vaguely recalled the fabric being stripped from her. All she remembered was the intoxicating swelter of Hanjun's breath on her bare thighs, the scratchiness of his palms against her breasts, and the burning in her belly.

Rushing through a quick shower, she dressed just as fast and met Hanjun in the kitchen. He sported an eye-catching sweater embellished with a quirky mosaic. "Is that a seashell?"

"Jin made it. I have to wear it at least once." He pulled at the fabric to reveal a spiral shell crafted from rhinestones, pompoms, and curled chenille stems. Spying the kitschy reindeer-shaped bag pulled over her chest, he fondled the glitter motif. "So cute."

"It's gaudy, but I love it." She haphazardly swung the purse from side to side. "The schedule says you're filming today."

Sipping from a mug of coffee, he nodded. "It's the first portion of a two-part special. We'll be out in the city all day."

★⁺₊★☾★⁺₊★

Chaperoned to a lively district, Blackmirror were separated into pairs, tasked with finding holiday trimmings to reflect their distinctive styles. Amidst a team of guards and a horde of cameramen, they maneuvered among congested aisles. Jen trailed behind Hanjun, progressing through walls of firs in every color, from classic green to striking black and rainbow hued.

He inspected each conifer, pausing to speak to the cameras about his decision-making process. After much deliberation, he selected a seven-foot pine in frosty white. "I like this one because it's a blank slate."

With the assistance of a friendly crew member, he lifted the oversized box into the shopping cart. Meanwhile, Jen browsed racks of ornaments. Running a hand over delicate glass baubles, she turned to him, pointing out various plant-themed adornments. Amid them was a sakura, no bigger than her palm. "Jun, look at these."

He chucked the ornament and a handful of others into the basket. "Those are adorable."

Over the hours, Hanjun skimmed every cranny of the store. By the end of the production, his buggy overflowed with embellishments, tinsel, and garlands fit for a grand tree. Inching toward the checkouts, his eyes were drawn to the pink blossom ornament in the cart. "Have you ever visited the cherry blossoms?"

"I always wanted to." She could have drummed up a dozen reasons why she never had, but claiming she didn't have enough time or didn't know where to go would be an excuse. She had just as much time and just as many resources as everyone else. "I was just too lazy."

"I visit them every year." He dangled the pendant in front of her eyes. "And I've been growing one for a while. It's at my family home."

"I've killed every plant I've ever touched." She laughed at her misfortune.

"It takes a lot of care. But everything worth something does."

⋆⁺₊⋆☾⋆⁺₊⋆

Drained from a long day of shooting, the roommates found another package left at their doorstep, along with the delivery Hanjun anticipated. Retrieving the package from the floor, he tapped in his pass code and barreled through the door. "Took long enough."

Tossing her coat in the closet, Jen made a beeline for the kitchen. Knowing Deok-Sun had been craving pizza all week, she started prepping dinner. Since three out of five Blackmirror members were on strict diets, she needed to get creative. Hunting for suitable ingredients, she devised a plan to make a healthy pie without sacrificing taste.

Shoving his hands in his pockets, Hanso stood nearby, his eyes shifting to the vegetables on the island. "Can I help?"

She pointed to the produce. "The kabocha needs to be quartered, garnished with salt and olive oil, and roasted until tender. We'll caramelize half to make the toppings and purée the rest for the sauce."

Jin watched Hanso prep the pumpkin, marveling at his knife skills. "What about me?"

Passing him a variety of greens, she smiled at his eagerness. "Wash the spinach and Swiss chard. Dice the delicata, scallions, and Brussels sprouts."

He carried the bundle to the sink. "I can do that."

While they worked like a well-oiled machine, Deok-Sun roamed the kitchen, ensuring all necessary ingredients were present—mainly the must-have side of sweet pickles. "Cinnamon? Nutmeg? Honey? Gochujang? Are you sure you're making pizza?"

"Yes." Jen pressed the dough on floured pans. "A seasonal veggie pizza with a bit of warmth and sweetness."

His eyes landed on a triangle of Gruyere, a chunk of Parmigiano-Reggiano, and pearls of mozzarella. "As long as there's cheese involved."

"There will be plenty. Don't you worry."

Fleeing the kitchen before he was roped into helping, Deok-Sun barged into the living room, giggling at Hanjun's struggle with the door cam. The open container sat on the floor, contents strewn about as Hanjun fiddled with the gadget. He spent more time fumbling with the manual than discerning the diagrams. "I'm doing more harm than good with this."

Jin poked his head out from the kitchen. "It's even more painful to witness."

"Play nice, Jinnie." Jen chided Jin after noticing Hanjun's irritation. A sizable vein bulged in his neck, and she knew he was two mishaps away from scrapping the idea.

Unable to watch Hanjun struggle, Soogi motioned for him to stand back. He inspected the partially assembled mass as if he were disarming a bomb. "You were trying to install it backward."

Connecting each piece, his tongue protruded from the corner of his mouth. Snapping the final components into place, he read off key features from the manual. "Motion detection and voice recording—I'll send you a link to download the app."

Within minutes, the camera was installed and ready for use. Jin and Deok-Sun rushed to test the alarm, their giggles echoing in the hallway. With boundless energy, they jumped in front of the lens, causing everyone's phones to chime with notifications.

Hanso mocked their enthusiasm. "At least we know it works."

⋆⁺₊⋆☾⋆⁺₊⋆

At the end of the night, Jen lay in exhaustion, seeking solace in the comfort of her sheets. Just as sleep whisked her away, a thump jerked her awake.

"Can I come in?" Hanjun called from behind the door.

She offered a weak reply. "Sure."

Slinking through the room, the floorboards creaked under his weight. Climbing under the covers, he wrapped his arms around her waist. "Who were your celebrity crushes?"

She snorted. "I had a fondness for Blackmirror."

"You're hilarious. Who was your *first* crush?"

"As a young girl, I didn't grasp celebrity worship. While my peers fawned over male vocalists and sports models, I didn't understand how someone could favor somebody they didn't know. It wasn't until I went to my first The Base Gene show that I experienced the relationship between artist and fan. I heard about them early on. They played local gigs and were openers for larger artists at the time."

"Oh?" Mesmerized by the tale, he tracked gentle shapes down her arm. "You've been an enthusiast from the beginning?"

"Yeah, and I've attended all their Chicago concerts since the moment I fell in love with them."

He smirked at her unapologetic fangirling, wondering if he sounded similarly enthusiastic about Eminem, Nas, or André 3000. "Were they your only celebrity crush?"

Her eyes dilated. "Kyle Richmond has been my biggest crush since I was fifteen. He had a blog during The Base Gene's hiatus, discussing his struggles as a performer and as an individual. People didn't like the musical direction the band went in, and the stress bothered him. He went on to say the universe wanted him to disappear—and he did for a long time."

Each word pained her, as if she were reliving the band's dark past herself. "It's awful that someone who brought so much joy to his fans could feel so joyless."

As an entertainer, he battled the emptiness accompanying achievement. Regardless of his desire to dabble in diverse genres, he feared backlash from his supporters. While he hoped his backers would support him through artistic change, he knew they would desert him one day. There was only so much room at the top; with an endless pool of talented musicians all vying for recognition, few would be commemorated beyond their active years, and less would be celebrated for generations. It was the Michael Jackson's, Paul McCartney's, and Taylor Swift's of the world whose legacy would outlive them. His work would die with him and his listeners.

"I know Blackmirror's going through something similar. Your sound is evolving, and your audience is upset." Her inflection was laden with frustration. "I don't understand that. If you truly love music, you can find beauty in every song. If your favorite idol creates something different, you might not love every single, but how can you not like *any* of it? I can listen to any band or singer and find something to appreciate."

Tucking a strand of hair behind her ear, he forced a smile. "That's beautiful, Mi Sol. Unfortunately, J&I uses the Western business model; success is measured by sales."

"Profits shouldn't be held over your head, and appreciation should be given on both ends without expectations." Huffing, she rolled on her stomach. "It's not my fault, but I apologize for those who believe they own you."

She had nothing to do with the horrific things imposed on him, yet she grasped his pain. In an industry where he was deliberately misunderstood, she was a precious gem—the only person who came remotely close to understanding him. Suppressing the overwhelming emotions welling in his chest, he outlined a geometric solar system resting between her shoulder blades. The dark pigment peeked out from the edge of her tank, with detailed lines and dot patterns connecting the work. "You've never told me about your tattoos. What does this one mean?"

"It means, at some point, I had an extra two thousand dollars." Her giggle tapered off. "I love to admire the sky; I can drown in thoughts about the universe and how vast everything is. We're so small—not even a speck within existence—and we'll be dead longer than we're alive. Sometimes I wonder if anything matters."

In the depths of the night, when loneliness crept in and his mind pivoted to existential crisis, his gaze would drift to the heavens. He wondered if she searched for meaning among the twinkling constellations at the same time he did. Perhaps their paths crossed in those fleeting moments.

His wandering fingers trailed a matching minimalistic tattoo of the Pleiades on her shoulder. "What about this one?"

"It's the—"

"Seven Sisters. In Korea, we call it myo-seong." Having read countless legends, he traced along the design. "Every culture has a story about the cluster; most tales carry the same elements. There are always seven sisters, and there is a reason to explain why there are only six we can see."

"It could be the world's oldest myth."

"It's kind of sad," he whispered without moving his gaze from the thin lines. "In the stories, the seventh sister is lost."

"Lost is a temporary state. When we're lost, we're on the way to where we're needed."

Grabbing a lock of her hair, he tickled her back with the ends, imagining vivid watercolors flooding the ink. "If you inked your body, it must mean something to you."

Shuddering, she explained the significance. "When I was a teen, I was part of a girl group. We performed songs from popular boy bands. It was something we did for fun, but we took it seriously. We even had dance rehearsals."

He revealed a pair of charming dimples. "*A girl group?*"

"At the time of the group's split, I was writing a paper on John Michell. He pioneered insights into a wide range of scientific fields: astronomy, geology, optics, and magnetism." Fondly remembering the short-lived venture, she chuckled. "He calculated the likelihood of so many bright stars aligning to be one in five hundred thousand, making the pattern a rare occurrence. Knowing that fact, we agreed to get matching tats with each star representing a teammate."

"You're serious?" Cackling, his deep voice rumbled like distant thunder. "*You?* In a girl group?"

"What's that supposed to mean?" Her laughter heightened, filling the air with melodic vibrations.

Soogi pounded on the wall. "Will you two shut up?!"

Hanjun suppressed his bemusement. "You're enigmatic and guarded, shy away from the spotlight, and revel in mystery. You're so elusive even the most skilled journalists haven't been able to dig up shit on you, and you're telling me you *willingly* joined a girl group?"

"I swear!" Throwing her head back, she howled. "We went all out! Typical girl ensemble with nicknames and synchronized outfits. I created some of the choreography, though I found myself hurt a lot."

Quelling his embarrassment, he buried his face in her shoulder. "We might be soulmates."

"One time, we were working on this move where we'd jump on a folding chair, tip it back, and walk off as it folded beneath us. I fell on my ass like thirty times trying to perfect it. One of the girls still contacts me to this day whenever she thinks about it. It will never not be funny."

Tapping the asterism, he counted the number of stars. Six. Connected by fine dots, he assumed the troupe was a sextet. He probed for more information, but she succumbed to sleep. His first instinct was to shake her awake; after all, he hadn't told her about his first crush—someone few knew he admired. Instead, he tucked the comforter around her and retreated to his room. Hiding a giddy smile from Hanso, he reached for his journal.

> *She shares the perspectives I do. She's done many of the things I've done. I don't know how to calculate the probability of our hearts uniting, and I've never been one to believe in fate, but I do believe in luck.*

He shut the notebook only to open it again, jotting down a lyric under the entry.

> *She is the sun that lights my path. I am the crescent moon searching for my other half.*

CHAPTER THIRTY-FIVE

Kimchi

Mid-afternoon light filtered through the curtains, tossing eerie shadows on the wooden floorboards. Rising from bed, Jen glanced at the calendar; everyone had the day off—except for Jin and Hanso, who were required at the office for a high-profile advertisement shoot. Crossing the hall, she reached Hanjun's room and slipped inside without knocking. Crawling under the covers, she cuddled against his chest, placing gentle kisses along his neck. "We slept in."

"I needed the rest." He coiled an arm around her frame, sighing at her pecks. "You know what that does to me."

Nearly purring, she laced her fingers through his. "The house is quiet. I thought we could go for a walk before the boys notice us missing."

His eyebrows shot up. "You do realize it's freezing, right?"

She returned a flirty grin, leaning in to challenge him. "There's this neat invention; you may have heard of it. You wear it around your body, and it keeps you warm."

Flinging the blanket from his legs, he interrupted her witticism. "Ha! You're so funny."

"Get ready to leave." She leaped off the bed and vanished into the hall. "It'll be fun, I promise!"

He sauntered to the bathroom and stared in the mirror while brushing his teeth. Not to ogle himself, but to sort out his mindset for the day. It was easier for him to reflect when he could hold his thoughts accountable. Spitting in the sink, he inspected his image. His eyes were red from too much sleep, and his face was puffier than it had been in weeks, but he didn't think Jen's plan would involve crowds. She was alarmingly proficient at evasion.

Dabbing his face with a towel, he couldn't overcome his all-consuming penance. He enjoyed spending time with her, and his affection grew by the day, but her suffering weighed on his conscience. She wasn't one to seek fame, and the constant apprehension of an eventual invasion of privacy generated sleepless nights. Despite the careful concealment of their courtship, she couldn't escape the expectations. On any given day, their relationship could be broadcast for all to judge. Embodying the ideal partner, she battled unrealistic standards set by his stardom. Subjected to the same extreme pressures he faced, her appearance would be under the microscope. A floret on display for all to admire; if she wilted under exposure, she risked being deemed unworthy by millions.

He didn't care if the media captured her with frizzy hair or clothing from seasons ago. His only concern was her happiness, but he knew finding relief was difficult when living in fear of criticism. Though she concealed her anxiety for his sake, he felt immensely guilty. If he were an ordinary person—without devoted supporters and an equal number of detractors—she wouldn't have to bear such difficulty.

In a cruel irony, grandeur rendered love—the thing he yearned for—inaccessible. Music was his professional vision, but Jen was his amorous dream. The one who made his heart thump and his soul bloom. The notes he sang to audiences paled in comparison to the melodies he composed for her.

⋆⁺₊⋆☾⋆⁺₊⋆

Exiting the condominium, Windsor Heights shrank behind them. Cars zoomed along the roads, spewing gray sludge on the sidewalks. Kick-scooters weaved in and out of traffic, delivering freshly prepared food to customers. There was even an older woman steering a motorized vendor, selling cold yogurts to those on foot.

Reaching a cross-section, Jen's grasp on Hanjun's sleeve loosened, and she looked back at him. "Don't follow me."

"Where are you going?" Dumbfounded, he watched her strut away. Cocking his head, he wondered what she was up to. She was a planner, always devising ways to avoid publicity. Most of the time, she took it more seriously than he did.

Evading the question, she hastened her pace, creating a basketball court's length of distance between them. Her movements were intentional, dodging fellow pedestrians along the way. Nearing an isolated stretch of path, she dropped a vending machine capsule into the snow. He paused at a nearby tree, scanning their surroundings for anyone who may have noticed the drop-off. Once she disappeared from sight, he retrieved the bauble, popping the lid to reveal a tiny note tucked inside.

Meet me at the playground in ten minutes.

Seated on a weathered bench, he tapped his foot, waiting for time to pass. Phone in hand, he scrolled through the comments of Blackmirror's most recent stream, feeling comforted by the relatively positive remarks. At his persistent request, the agency agreed to test the waters by introducing their partners. The management was apprehensive, and for good reason; rather than coming out in the open and facing potential backlash, they introduced her as the group's permanent assistant—a calculated move to gauge global reaction. If, at any point, suspicious activity was detected, they would pull the plug on the project. Jen was hesitant about the idea; he told her everything would be fine, though he had no concrete way of knowing. As with much of his career, he was navigating uncharted territory.

He trudged to the nearest playground. The ground was shrouded in powdery snow, unbothered except for her footprints leading up a metal stairway. With each step, the cold saturated his boots, numbing his toes. His breath came in puffs, creating a foggy trail behind him. Reaching the landing, he discovered her huddled inside a colored tube slide, surrounded by an assortment of takeout.

"This is an odd place to be." Maneuvering to sit on the molded surface, he flashed an affectionate smile. Shifting his long legs, he contorted into a position that didn't make him feel like a ship trapped in a bottle.

"We can't go on a date, but we can have a little meal right here." Like a magician pulling a trick from their sleeve, she produced a small candle. With the flick of her wrist, she lit the wick and stationed the jar between their thighs. "Voilà! This should keep us warm."

It had been weeks since he expressed his longing for a normal, college-style date. Going to the movies or dining at a restaurant was an impossible feat with the country reporting his every move. But somehow, she made his desire an actuality.

He took in the distinctive bags—vibrant red and yellow lettering from a local Korean hangout where the staff didn't speak English. "How'd you order that?"

"I pointed at pictures and handed them money. I didn't know they only accepted cash..." Her voice tapered into a sheepish giggle. "Luckily, Soogi saved the day."

"I bowed before I ordered. I hope it was polite." Turning pensive, her eyes lowered. "Deok-Sun always told me how sweet the couple who owns the shop is. The woman kept grabbing my cheeks and saying, 'Mochi hada!'"

"She found your face to be velvety and matte." Stuck on the idea of Soogi borrowing her funds, his mouth hung open. It wasn't something he was known for without asking twenty intrusive questions. "Soogi lent you money?"

"I'm glad I thanked her, then." She reached for a bag and tore at the paper. "Yeah, he did. I've tried talking to Ha-Rin about my card, but he's been preoccupied."

It was hard for him to remember that South Korea wasn't her home. When she made the move, their dissimilarities were painfully obvious. But as the weeks passed, their differences overlapped, blurring the lines between their worlds. He no longer viewed her as an American woman. She was someone who relocated to a foreign country and just so happened to be employed at the same company as him.

"I remembered you liked kimchi soup and bulgogi." Holding a confident smile, she held up two foam containers. "I couldn't remember the names of anything else."

"This is lovely." He reached for the offering, grinning as she struggled with her chopsticks. Once she situated the utensils properly, he commended her efforts. "You've improved."

"I've been practicing." And she had. While Blackmirror was engaged with filming or pictorials, she snuck away to the cafeteria, honing her skills with small candies and crisps. "I'll be a pro before you know it."

Shoveling marinated beef into his mouth, he relished the savory flavor. "I received an email this morning; based on the interrogations from Mr. Yun, Ha-Rin believes we could tour as soon as next year. They're looking into regional sales and working on a schedule."

"Congratulations! You've been dying to perform!" Hugging him with one arm, she ditched her chopsticks.

"I haven't told the boys yet. They were devastated when our last tour was postponed."

"They'll be ecstatic."

"I'm sure. Unfortunately, opportunity comes with obligation. Rehearsals, fan signs, promotions..." His expression turned somber, purposely avoiding her gaze.

"You don't need to worry; I know you're going to be busy." She planted a hand on his knee. "Your career comes first."

The weight of responsibility sat on his shoulders, but he found solace in knowing she would be by his side. For the first time, he would have someone waiting for him at the end of every long night. His heart fluttered at the thought of having her support him in the aftermath. Or the after*mess*. The intervals on stage were fleeting, but the time after—when he took off his costume and melted into a puddle of insecurities—he was a mix of two people. A blended time of confusion and disillusion, he realized Rem wasn't real; he was simply the character he played. His reality fractured, and he endured the harsh truth: his fans admired him as a celebrity, not Ryu Hanjun. They liked him because they didn't know him.

But Jen did. She saw him, or at least the pieces he felt comfortable sharing. No matter how rude, whiny, insensitive, or catty he was, she validated him. She listened more than she talked, and she saw through his egotistical charm. She studied his nuances and knew when he wasn't doing well, even if he said he was. She allowed him to make mistakes and never chastised him when he did, all while providing gentle encouragement. Most of all, she made him feel content with the idea of imperfection because she didn't think in terms of winning or losing. She acknowledged the gray area between and believed humans should find what they're good at and what they love, and that the two weren't mutually exclusive.

Most people viewed success as perpetual, and anything less than eternity was failure. An author who ceased writing after a few books was a washed-up scribe. A rock band that created three albums before their disbandment were failed musicians. If you weren't triumphant, you were defeated.

But not Jen. She recognized the necessity of ill-fated ventures. Life was an assembly of moments, and moments were all anyone had. The future was uncertain, the past could be warped and forgotten, but the present was ever evolving. She thought people depended on the vanity concept of everlasting—a hypothetical eternal state of glory—too much. Breakups didn't erase emotions felt during a fling. Divorce couldn't take away the happy times in a marriage. And the death of an artist wouldn't remove the mark they left on the world.

She found a way to weaponize apathy. To her, nothing mattered; anything that went wrong could be altered into something greater. She believed in a galaxy of opportunities, almost as if she sensed realities beyond her own, and it was everything to him. The belief that he couldn't fail when there were so many possibilities was enough for him to want to take risks—in love, in art, and in his life.

Finishing the meal, he sighed. "We should go before the primary students let out."

Once the wax solidified, she slid the candle into her coat pocket and stuffed the leftover containers into her backpack. Sliding down the chute with him right behind her, she rushed to a snow-covered merry-go-round. "Spin me?"

"You have a half hour until we're overrun with kids." Checking his watch, he grabbed the cold bars and spun, joining her at the last second. Hanging onto each other, they wobbled and leaned as the world revolved, swirling the colorful play equipment into indistinct streaks. The child's ride came to a slow stop, leaving them dizzy.

Holding his stomach, his jowls puffed. "I'm gonna vomit..."

Supporting his arm, she helped him sit on the bumpy flooring. "Maybe not such a good idea right after eating."

Waiting for the dizziness to subside, he knocked his shoes together. "It's been a while."

She kicked at the rocks. "I haven't been on one since I was a child."

"A long time since I felt like this." Resting his temple on the frosty bar, cold imbued his skin. "Happy."

She suppressed a frown. "I wish I met you sooner."

He couldn't imagine wanting to be anywhere else. "I think we met at the perfect time."

★⁺₊★☾⁺₊★

Stepping off the lift, Hanjun spotted another wrapped gift—not directly in front of the door, but close enough to bait his irritation. "The person doing this knows there's a camera."

Jen hurried after him, a hand resting on his arm. Entering her passcode, she nudged him inside. "As long as they're outside, let's not worry."

"How can I not?" Snapping a reply, he tore open the package. Deserting remnants of paper on the floor, he retreated to his room, taping the photo to the wall with the others.

"That's weird—you keeping all those photographs." Hanso tossed a comic on the nightstand, questioning his obsession with the deliveries. "Where were you earlier?"

"Jen took me on a date." Remembering the makeshift picnic made his lips curl into a smirk; despite the damp tunnel, the retreat was one of the most romantic dates he could ask for.

Hanso crossed his arms. "Haeseong is hunting her. What will happen if he catches her with you while the agency claims she's dating me?"

"I know." Thumbing through the group chat, he wondered how long they could continue their forbidden love before someone discovered them.

> **Jinja**: Where is Hanu?
> **Soogins**: He's out with Jen.
> **Sunnie**: How is that possible?
> **Honsa**: I hope Hanjun uses that big brain of his.
> **Soogins**: It's Hanjun. He's smart. Let him enjoy what he has.

Grabbing a pen, he turned to his journal, though he couldn't bring himself to divulge the truth. He felt truly happy at the park for the first time in years. But with happiness came regret; his momentary bliss meant eventual misery.

The snow at the park was beautiful.

CHAPTER THIRTY-SIX

Whirlissimo

Blackmirror were divided into groups, each taking up residence in separate rooms of the home. Scented with pine and cinnamon, Jen's pristine bedroom provided a cozy atmosphere for Hanso, Hanjun, and Jen. Forming a triangle on the rug, the room was modified into a festive utopia; mountains of themed paper, boxes of varying sizes, and colorful ribbons covered the floor.

"Today, we're wrapping gifts." Gesturing to Jen, Hanjun beamed at the cameramen. "Our lovely assistant will guide us."

"Hey." Jen greeted the cameras without looking at the lens.

Hanjun swiveled toward Hanso. "How confident are you about your wrapping abilities?"

Biting his lips, Hanso shook his head. "I'm not."

Chuckling, Hanjun selected an item from the pile. "Let's start with this retro camera. Soogi's a photography enthusiast, so he'll love this. Jen, how do you think we should wrap it?"

She couldn't help but tease him. "It's in a box, so it just needs to be wrapped."

"I got it." Snatching the box from Hanjun, Hanso began tucking and folding.

Hanjun moved on to another present, humming a holiday tune under his breath. "Next up, we have a snack basket for Deok-Sun. He has a bottomless appetite; this will be perfect."

Jen examined the oddly shaped gift. "That will be a challenge. I'm good at wrapping, but not *that* good."

"Let's circle back." Hanjun placed the bundle aside. "We also have a variety of comics for Jin."

Portraying the role of aid, Jen stole glances at her roommates; Hanjun reminded her of a child helping his mother, while Hanso took on a gentler approach, as if preparing presents for his offspring. It was rare to witness them so engrossed in capering. Usually, they took it or left it, but they were entirely immersed in the festivities. She contemplated the idea of pushing their boundaries as a unit, perhaps even asking Ha-Rin to incorporate their ideas into future episodes.

"I'm hoping for sunglasses or books." Hanjun shrugged, recalling his wish list. "But I wouldn't mind artwork."

Hanso grappled with a present. "Movies."

Hanjun analyzed his bandmate. "Really? Movies?"

"Romantic movies." Hanso rocked on his knees, holding a hand over his chest. "Crying's good for the heart."

Hanjun reeled toward Jen. "Any Christmas wishes?"

Caught off guard by the question, she searched the staff for assistance. Sehoon nodded, and she proceeded to answer. "I haven't thought of anything."

He cocked his head. "I hope someone gets you a phone."

Her eyes rolled. "What is your obsession with me having a phone? You're always going on about it."

"I worry about you." Encountering the genial expressions of the camera crew, he backtracked. "I worry about all of you."

Suffering a bout of anxiety, she fixed her fascination on Hanso, who struggled with the same gift he'd been wrapping since the beginning of the recording. "Would you like help, Ho-Young?"

Brandishing a charming smile, he slid the semi-wrapped gift to her. "Could you hold the paper?"

She obliged, resting a hand on his. "Glad to."

Taping the edges, he pretended to blush. "Thanks."

Third wheeling, Hanjun refused to look at them as they played happy Hanso home. Their chemistry was undeniable, though the forced smiles and practiced movements were insincere. Annoyed, he sought respite in the kitchen, where he retrieved a glass of water and took deep breaths. He returned just in time for them to finish.

Jen affixed a curly bow to the untidy package. "And we're done."

Humbled by their messiness, Hanjun chuckled. The floor was cluttered with half-used rolls of paper, crumpled bits of stickers, and balls of cording. "Well, there's a clear winner in wrapping. Thanks for joining us. We love you!"

Hanso waved goodbye. "Thanks for watching!"

The moment the cameras ceased rolling, Hanjun jumped to his feet. His muscles screamed from hours of sitting, but he paid no mind and sprinted to the door, expecting another package. His suspicions were confirmed by an ominous box. Inside was a dark photograph secured in white tissue. "Of course, more photos."

Hiking a camera bag up on his shoulder, Sehoon whistled. "You've received a few of those, haven't you?"

Hanjun studied the image. Obscured by shadows, it was difficult to discern details. "I've spoken with security; they won't take any action until there's proof of something malicious."

"Have you told Ha-Rin? He would want to know."

"No." Hanjun wagged his head. "He would use it as an excuse to keep our relationship hidden."

Firming up his grip on the recording case, Sehoon nodded. "Hopefully it's an overzealous supporter."

Returning to the condo, Hanjun placed the mysterious package on the kitchen table and hurried to Jen's room. Balancing a garbage can at her side, she plucked leftover tape from the carpet. He scooped up her arm and dragged her to the terrace. "I have something to show you."

"Hanjun, my room is a disaster." Jen shadowed him like a balloon floating in the breeze. Protesting about the mess, she tittered at his overt enthusiasm.

"And it will be there when you get back." Transmitting an infectious laugh, he urged her to gaze beyond Windsor Heights. "Look."

Hit by a frigid gust sapping the heat from her body, Jen's breath stifled in her throat. Piercing air prickled her exposed skin, sending shivers up her arms. The balcony, normally a sanctuary for sun rays and chirping birds, was transformed into a frosted wonderland. A thin layer of snow blanketed the seating, and her sights fell past their gated community: the cityscape glistened, and the river was cloaked in freshly fallen powder, melting at an impressive speed. Establishments across the city installed twinkling Christmas lights in every color.

Admiring snowflakes pirouetting from the sky, a surge of unbridled bliss overtook her. In spontaneous childlike wonder, she spun in circles, kicking up a cloud of white dust at her feet.

Head tilted back and arms outstretched, she welcomed the droplets on her face. "This reminds me so much of home."

Watching her rotate until she felt dizzy, Hanjun faked a shudder. "What's so great about the snow? It's freezing."

"Without winter, the flowers would bloom all the time. We wouldn't be able to appreciate them—we wouldn't even notice them. They would become nothing more than background noise." Ceasing her twirls, she clutched the guardrail, stretching to catch a single flake. "Spring exists *because* of winter."

The vexatious glimmer in his eyes transformed into a genuine smile, and he joined her in catching puffs of snow. Braving the cold without coats or scarves, they competed to nab the crystals. Hanjun spotted a jumbo-sized snowflake, mystical in size. Extending a hand, he emitted a triumphant shout as it descended on his palm. "Look at this one."

She was amazed at its beauty. "It must have combined with another on the way down."

Summoned by melodic giggles, their roommates gathered near the door. Through the frosty windowpane, they viewed them frolicking like a pair of school-aged children. Eager to join, Deok-Sun stepped forward, but Soogi latched onto his collar, yanking him back. "Let them have their moment."

Jin leaned into Hanso, his eyes glittering. "They're so cute."

Hanso monitored the couple; the flurry seemed to dance around them like fairy dust. He kept his distance from Jen, thinking her involvement was contractual. Watching them rejoice in their joy, he couldn't deny the probability of the romance becoming permanent. There was no mistaking a man in love. And Hanjun was inexplicably in love with her.

It was saddening as much as it was heartwarming. Witnessing their leader fall in love signified transformation. True love was Hanjun's end-game goal, and his devotion could be the demise of their careers if he chose to apply his ambition to family. With commitment came a slew of press coverage when their courtship went public, and it meant a change in the direction of their sound. Though Jen went out of her way to remain oblivious to their unreleased work, she had a massive impact on Hanjun—and Blackmirror by proxy. The muse of an artist lived well beyond the years of the art, and she would be glorified for as long as people remembered him.

Turning his back on the lovers, Hanso trudged to the kitchen. It wasn't his night to cook, but he needed a distraction. He began removing ingredients from the fridge and aggressively chopping vegetables into pieces, each slice serving as liberation. Filling a pot with water, his stomach churned at the possibility of losing the team. The only chance for continuance was if Jen cared for the act as much as she claimed; if she did, she would push Hanjun to create music, thus keeping the spirit of their beloved band alive. After all, the only thing Hanjun loved more than love was music.

Jen strode into the kitchen, shaking off the remnants of snow clinging to her sweater. She grabbed a worn apron from the auxiliary and tied the strings around her waist. Scanning the counter, her gaze landed on a rice cooker, surrounded by fresh veggie peelings. "What can I do to help?"

"You scared the Jesus out of me!" Startled, Hanso cursed and turned to face her, placing a hand over his heart. Tying off a bag of scraps, he pointed to the appliance. "I haven't had a chance to make rice."

"On it." Pulling storage containers from an upper cabinet, she measured out grains—short, brown, black, and barley—and poured them into the pan.

Hanso rinsed his hands in the sink. "Where's Hanu? I figured he'd be right behind you."

Dumping water into the device, she used her finger to measure the depth—the way Soogi taught her, and his mother taught him. "He wanted to make a heart with our initials in the middle. I guess he saw it in a movie once."

Hanso worked noiselessly, wiping the countertops with a wet rag. "I've never seen him like that."

Closing the lid, she set the timer for twenty minutes. "I'm not sure what you mean."

"Hanjunie. Even when he does something he loves, he's always quiet. He's afraid of having the things he loves taken from him. The happiest I've seen him is when he searches for shells at the beach—he's like that with you all the time."

"I didn't know he was different around me." Her voice was soft, barely above a whisper.

Without giving her time to object, Hanso hugged her, spewing a torrent of apologies. "I'm sorry for how I've treated you."

She stood frozen, reaching to pat his back. "You didn't do anything wrong."

"I've thought awful things about you. I was jealous of your relationship with Hanjun, and I feared you would hurt him." He pulled away, reaching for her shoulders. "Forgive me."

She took his hands, giving him a jostle. "Hanso, you've never treated me poorly. You're a good friend to Hanjun—it's only natural to want to protect him."

"Thank you for coming into our lives." Hanso pulled her against his chest a second time. "Not just Hanjun's life, but all of our lives."

Hanjun stood near the doorway, straining to hear the conversation. A wave of relief washed over him; one of his closest friends validated their relationship. Suspiring, his angst shifted to the next daunting task: gaining acceptance from the entire Blackmirror fan base. It would be no easy feat, but with his bandmate's approval, he was ready to take on the challenge. Unfortunately, their journey couldn't begin until the agency released her from Hanso.

★⁺₊★☾★⁺₊★

The night brought a sense of finality, and Jen moved the wrapped presents to the corner of her room. Collapsing in bed, she let her consciousness drift to what she wanted for Christmas. She preferred practicality to consumerism, but she still strove to find an answer.

Uncertainty swirled through her mind, a maze of possibilities, and she considered a trajectory beyond her contract. The world was full of options, making it impossible for her to plan ahead. The only thing she knew for certain was that fate held countless variables.

Disrupted by unfamiliar rapping, she was taken aback by Jin lingering in the doorway. "Is everything alright?"

"No." Bearing a pouty bottom lip, he crossed the floor with dejected steps, settling next to her in bed. Tugging the comforter from her, he hid his swollen cheeks.

She swiped unruly strands from his eyes. "What's wrong?"

"I was reading the feedback from our last live." Concealing his face, he muttered from underneath the covers. "Do I look like a girl? Is that why they keep saying those things?"

"Were the comments in English?" She ran a finger along his temple, and he nodded, watery-eyed. "Jinnie, you're youthful, which can be intimidating to those who adhere to narrow standards of masculinity. You don't need to meet the expectations of those who aren't even satisfied with themselves."

"You don't understand what it's like." His voice wavered, and tears threatened to spill from his waterline.

"You're right, I don't." She pulled him close, tangling their limbs together. "But I *do* know what it's like to have others judge me based on assumptions."

He nuzzled against her shoulder. "Like when?"

Assembling her wits, she released an extended exhale. "Do you remember the company-wide email about Future's ex-manager?"

He recalled the correspondence provoking a massive stir within their workplace. "Yes."

"Well." She brushed a lock of hair from his tear-stained jowls. "The lawsuit was about me."

"Really?" He looked up at her in disbelief. "I heard it was a sexual assault suit, but I didn't know it was about you."

Nodding, she squeezed his hand. "The harassment was confined to the trainee floors, and though the manager was fired, I still hear the whispers. I'm called a lot of nasty things daily."

"You've done nothing wrong."

"As a woman who lives with five men, there are many speculations about our living arrangements. I receive the bulk of the hate, while the men I live with receive praise."

"But we're friends." He shook his head, unable to comprehend the double standard. "You're like my sister."

She forced a rueful smile. "You may feel that way now, but do you remember how you felt when I first moved in?"

"Awkward, I guess." He thought back to a time when the kinship was new. "But I stopped seeing you as a woman. You're just Jen."

"Regardless of how you feel, there will always be someone who will only see what they want." She caressed his puffy cheek. "Don't worry about people who only want to hate."

Emerging from a cocoon of self-doubt, his hand reached for hers with newfound determination. "Mr. Yun says we should work hard enough to make our critics believers."

"Jinnie." She tucked the blanket under his chin. "Regardless of what Mr. Yun says, you will *never* please everyone. Our lives are fleeting, and at the end of yours, you won't regret not caring about what others think. You will regret not taking every opportunity and every gamble. Not seeing everything beautiful and tasting everything delicious. You will regret not doing all those wonderful things, but you will never regret not caring about the opinions of others. You will regret not living for you."

Hanjun prepared to knock on Jen's door, but before he could, the muffled vibration of Jin's troubles reached his ears. He peered through the crack, finding him snuggled with Jen, their bodies radiating warmth even from a distance. Though he wished to visit her, he understood Jin needed her more.

Expelling a resigned sigh, he retreated to his room to check the group chat.

> **Sunnie**: Anyone seen Jin?
> **Soogins**: Is he not in your room?
> **Sunnie**: Haven't seen him since dinner.
>
> *He's with Jen.*
>
> **Honsa**: What happened?
>
> *Rude comments again.*

Setting his phone aside, he reached for his journal to capture the day. Intense jealousy, the flutter of snowflakes on his palms, and sudden breakthroughs of acceptance—the moment was worth remembering.

> *I'm glad Jin has someone he can confide in. He will talk to us, but with her it's different. I often wonder what she'd be like as a parent. Her kindness and patience are ideal.*

CHAPTER THIRTY-SEVEN

Larger Than Life

Jen woke to the heat of Jin's body outstretched next to hers. She tucked the covers around him and slid out of bed, discerning the muffled prattling of cameramen preparing for the day.

Treading to the kitchen, she discovered Hanjun wide awake, stirring his second cup of coffee. "I saw the schedule, but there's a chunk of time blocked off."

"We're attending an awards show." Revolving with an affable smile, he gripped the hot mug. "And performing."

"So that's why you've been rehearsing five nights a week." She flattened his collar, smitten by his puffy complexion. "What you really mean to say is that you'll be cleaning up the awards and proving why on stage?"

He glanced down bashfully. "You'll be watching, right?"

Scoffing, she raised an eyebrow. "What kind of girlfriend do you take me for?"

"The best." Grinning, he flourished a cherry blossom ornament between their eyes. "But before we leave, we're decorating Christmas trees."

A tinkling, melodic laugh accompanied her to the freezer, where she grabbed a handful of ice for her cup. "Of course you are."

"Jin still sleeping?" Savoring a sip of caffeine, his eyes peered over the rim.

"He was when I left. Should I wake him?" She turned on her heel to rouse him.

"Let him sleep." Trapping her in his arms, he swayed in a slow-motion dance, nuzzling into her neck.

As they twirled around the island, Soogi walked by. Shooting them an unamused glare, he mumbled a groggy greeting and shook out his unruly hair. "Morning, Jen."

Dipping low to the floor, Jen giggled. "Morning."

Hanjun brooded at the second eldest, guiding Jen to her feet. "Doesn't anyone say good morning to me anymore?"

Guzzling milk straight from the carton, Soogi returned a blank stare. Wiping his mouth on his wrist, he snapped a cold reply. "No."

Deok-Sun entered, acknowledging her warmly. "Good morning, Jen."

Hanjun's neck jerked at an abnormal angle. "Are you kidding me?!"

Pulling out of his grasp, she jostled his arm. "They're messing with you."

"I'm here." The last to rise, Jin smoothed out his attire. Studying his reflection in his phone's camera, he tampered with his locks until he was satisfied. Behind him, photographers bustled about, erecting cameras in every corner of the home.

Checking his watch, Sehoon separated the mates for the filming. Hanso's mission was to raise a tree in their shared bedroom, while Hanjun's was to assemble his in a corner of Jen's room. Jin was in the kitchen, Soogi in the parlor, and Deok-Sun in the entryway.

Cameramen in tow, Hanjun meandered down the hall into forbidden territory. Beckoning to the girlish space, he clarified his reasoning for recording in the feminine domain, though he didn't explicitly state whose room it was. "Hanso's in our room, but this room is much more visually pleasing."

A pleasant splendor of fairy lights danced off the mirrored surfaces, and the spicy aroma of cinnamon and vanilla swelled, inviting guests into a cozy winter wonderland. Lace curtains filtered sunlight, gleaming against chic golden decorations. "Beautiful, right?"

"Today I'll be trimming this tree." He proceeded to the windows, where a friendly handler awaited with the unopened spruce. Battling the well-taped box, his confidence wavered, and his fingers floundered. "Starting with opening it."

Howling erupted from behind the cameras, and Ha-Rin shook his head, hurling orders at Jen. "Assist him."

Stepping in, she held out a pair of shears. "These should help."

He stretched for the scissors and stabbed at the packaging. "I chose this one because it was pre-lit and white."

Freeing segments from the cardboard, he discarded the box to the side. He snapped the metal legs into place, recovering from his initial embarrassment. "Now that the bottom is on, we need to add the middle section."

"And finally—" Sliding the upper wedge into the base, he reached for an accessory from a paper sack stuffed with baubles. "It's time for the fun part—decorating."

"It's a lighted tree, Hanjun. Plug it in." Ha-Rin's prompt evoked laughter among the staff.

"Plug it in." Repeating the command, he searched for the nearest socket, his face lighting up with each illuminated tier. But his expression faded when only the lower bulbs flickered on. "Huh?"

"For God's sake..." Leaning into Jen, Ha-Rin gestured to the musician. "Go help him. Keep your back to the camera."

Inching forward, she pointed to the trunk, where the connectors dangled freely. "Jun, you need to join the plugs."

He plunged his arms deep into the sprigs, and the twinkling globes came to life. "Now it's time for the ornaments."

"I love little things." Plucking trinkets from the bag, he fixed them on the twigs, hovering over the delicate cherry blossom. "This one suggests spring."

"And this tiny bonsai reminds me of the Spirited Garden on Jeju." Reaching for another charm, he spotted a small giftbox containing twin adornments. "Here are a couple of cacti."

Tiptoeing around the tree, he poised Blackmirror's Multiverse characters at eye level. A dapper sloth with languid arms. An owl with sunglasses and sharp, observant eyes. A suave axolotl with a cute and curious face. A turtle ready to compete in any race. And of course, Joey, the somber kangaroo. "These remind me of our group."

With his fingers forming a pistol shape against his chin, he withdrew to admire his work. Reminiscent of a Charlie Brown tree, droopy branches cried for help. The decrepit appearance summoned giggles among the crew, and he wasn't sure where he went wrong.

"Hanjun..." Ha-Rin stationed a palm over his face. "You never cease to amaze us."

Standing off-camera, Jen voiced her opinion. "It just needs to be fluffed."

Hanjun studied her. "Huh?"

"The needles need to be spread like a peacock's tail." Circling the sparse limbs, she arranged the tips, and the tree transformed into a fuller, more vibrant variant.

Staring down the lens, Hanjun flashed a disobedient grin. "Meet Jen, Blackmirror's fluffer."

Pausing her branch-spreading, she served him a shrewd scowl. "Ryu Hanjun, what is wrong with you?"

Chuckling, his eyes landed on Ha-Rin. "Let's edit that out."

Jen unfurled the withes until the model was a beautiful vision, and Hanjun stepped back to laud once again. The monument was no ordinary tree—it was a representation of Blackmirror's cherished memories. "It's perfect."

"Oh, I almost forgot." Reaching into her pocket, Jen retrieved a pearlescent crystal shell. "I thought you might like this."

"This belongs at the top." He received the gift, admiring its intricate design and smooth surface. True to his word, he positioned the talisman in a place of prestige. "And there you have it; my Christmas tree. I wish it could have been better. Thanks for watching. Love you, Anti!"

⋆⁺₊⋆☾⋆⁺₊⋆

Black cars encircled Windsor Heights, and suited guards lined up, ready to escort Blackmirror to the ceremony. Hanjun's defense ran late, but he welcomed the delay, grateful to spend a moment alone with Jen. Limelight suffused the complex's parameters, filtering through the closed drapes. The outside of their home was crawling with reporters, but they focused on each other until it was time for him to leave.

In the peacefulness of the kitchen, their bodies intertwined, creating a private sanctuary amid the whirlwind of his stardom. "I need to go."

Sensing anxiousness in his labored breathing, she burrowed her face into his neck. "Have a safe performance."

Fingers knotted in her hair, he pressed his lips to her forehead. "I'll do my best."

"Your best is enough." Letting him slip from her grasp, she tarried until the door alarm chimed. Meandering to the bathroom, she shed pieces of clothing along the way. Sitting on the edge of the tub, she reached for a bottle of bubbles, squirting a glob under the rushing water.

Sinking into the fragrant foam, she pondered Blackmirror's ascendancy, wondering if their one hundredth award felt like the first. Perhaps she didn't understand the full extent of an artist's longing for recognition, but she was no stranger to chipping at goals—it was something she couldn't survive without. At all times, she carried out a specific set of objectives—short and long-term—along with end-of-life missions.

As a child, the first thing she sought was a Tamagotchi, and she almost had enough saved at the time her mother abandoned her. Even though they were under twenty dollars at the time, a Jackson note in 1997 could afford a week's worth of food if she ate mostly ramen. From that point on, she gave up on obtaining the plaything, as surviving proved more costly than expected.

A few birthdays later, her friends worked their butts off to purchase her a secondhand digital pal. She remembered holding the thing she desperately wanted in her hand; the toy was a symbol of her dreams, and it was the moment she began to believe anything was possible.

She aged through adolescence and acquired another cyberpet, bought with her first paper paycheck. Yet, the accomplishment didn't surpass the first. Although warm and fuzzy, she didn't get the elated sensation she once did. Nothing felt like the first.

On display at the J&I tower were nearly one hundred glittering awards. A powerhouse in the industry, Blackmirror knew the thrill of winning, and she had doubts that attaining more would be comparable to the first. The only accolade able to invoke that excitation was a Whammy, the Music Institute's most prestigious honor. The elusive trophy was their wettest dream, as Soogi would say.

Slipping into her clothes, the comforting scent of eucalyptus lingered on her skin. Reconvening to the lounge, she sank into the cushions, clutching a near-empty bag of chips. Live preshow action featured on the television, and she watched as celebs stopped for interviews along the blue carpet. Spotting a few performers she had subbed for at the agency, she cheered for the recently debuted groups, happy to see their music drawing an audience.

Loosely watching the program, she was acquainted with only a handful of acts. While she appreciated the dedication propelling Korean pop, she found the furor overwhelming. She couldn't invest the time needed to go beyond casual listening and couldn't compete with the extensive knowledge of die-hard netizens. "Everything takes a small piece of your life."

When it came to trends in Korea, she was only semi-familiar with what her roomies favored. Second-generation groups and soloists filled their playlists, with additional entertainers thrown in the mix. The rap line favored royalties such as Epik High and Big Bang, though Hanso stuck to early 00s bops. Deok-Sun had a soft spot for Western artists and exclusively listened to billboard hits. But it was Jin who stood out with his eclectic taste; he enjoyed rhythm and blues from any era and had a particular affinity for Jodeci.

Each time Blackmirror won a plume, they took the mic, expressing heartfelt gratitude to their fans. J&I cultivated an audience with undying love for them, and it was as beautiful as it was scary. Good or bad, Anti were ready to defend them to the death.

Though she didn't agree with how their fans rallied behind their every decision, she grasped why; the devotees saw a curated version of their lives. They didn't know the hardships integrated with celebrity or the pressures a devout fan base could hold over them. And she didn't know, either. She only knew what the managers wanted her to know, but even then, it wasn't always glamorous. "Paragons can only exist if you disregard faults."

During their late-night talks, Hanjun voiced the difficulty of gauging their success. He believed their fame had reached a point where releasing mediocre music would render hits. Their larger-than-life following was consuming just to consume, and the pleonexia made him question his vision. Carving such an expansive listenership was an achievement in itself, but he fretted about losing his ability to create art. Even worse, he feared falling in hate with his career, trapped in a cycle of slogging to appease universal demographics.

In the past, when unease about their compatibility troubled her, she mustered up the courage to ask him why he was drawn to her—after all, she was a listener at the time of their meeting. Though she didn't own any of their albums or merchandise, she kept up with the group's activities whenever life allowed, and she worried previous admiration could complicate the relationship.

While the idea of crushing her perception was unnerving, Hanjun explained it rather simply: to the majority, Blackmirror were infallible, yet she understood they were just as human as anyone else, if not more vulnerable. Even with being held to a high standard, they would always make errors, and she recognized their responsibility to own up to those mistakes without allowing their coalition to bully others into thinking they were indefectible.

"Is that why he likes me?" She tossed the controller aside. "You don't need me for that, Hanjun."

★⁺₊★☾★⁺₊★

Shortly after nine, chatter floated into Jen's consciousness, stirring her from sleep. Blinking repeatedly, she focused on the overhead light, and the lively voices grew more distinct when Sehoon burst into the room, his arms loaded with expensive recording equipment. "We're back!"

Rummaging through the kitchen cabinets, Deok-Sun called for Jen in a sing-song voice. "Where's Jen?"

Lying in a disheveled mess, she rubbed her eyes. "In here."

Jin strode in wearing a tailored suit, juggling two bottles of champagne. "Did you miss us?"

"Honestly..." She paused to brush crumbs from her shirt. "I wasn't expecting you home so soon."

Hanjun dropped a pile of takeout on the coffee table, placing the mysterious package he found in the hall next to the bags. "Instead of partying, we stream as a thank you to Anti."

Favoring his elbow, Soogi erected tripods around the living room. Passing around clip-on microphones, he offered a subtle reminder about the broadcast. "Let's not get too tipsy this time, yeah?"

Jen, still bleary-eyed, slunk to the floor, remaining hidden from the camera's view while they poured drinks and rehearsed procedures under Sehoon's guidance.

⋆⁺₊⋆☾⋆⁺₊⋆

In the hushed stillness of her room, with only the hum of the humidifier keeping her company, Jen settled into bed with her laptop. Notification pings interrupted the silence while she navigated her one and only social media feed. Friends she hadn't spoken to in weeks inquired about her whereabouts; she mentioned South Korea as her destination, and though they specifically asked if she was with Blackmirror, she never confirmed her association with the quintet. Nor did she plan to.

With a hopeful heart, she opened the messenger, pleading for her best friend to be online despite the massive time difference. The pixels blurred as she waited for the little green dot next to Kristen's name to appear, signaling her availability.

> *I'm sorry we haven't talked in a while.*
> Girl! I miss you! How is Korea?
> *It's beautiful, but I miss home.*
> Home misses you. Can you visit soon?
> *I'll let you know.*
> You never told me what you're doing there.
> There are some interesting things in the news.
> *Please don't tell anyone.*
> You know I won't!
> Listen, I'm at work. I'll message you later.
> I miss you so much! I love you!
> *I love you, too!*

Closing the lid, she hated to admit she was homesick. Despite her efforts to fuse with the populace, the country would never be home. The sidewalks were dappled with stunning architecture and markets, and the people were mostly kind and welcoming, yet she couldn't shake the annoyance of being a foreigner. Even with wistful representations of domestic surroundings, Seoul reminded her that imitations could only shadow authenticity.

Gazing out her window at the busy streets below, she knew no matter how long she stayed—whether it was four months or four years—she would never fit in. Every time she left Windsor Heights, she sensed the eyes of strangers, labeling her with whatever stereotypes they held. Positive or negative, there was a brand seared into her back.

She was a lone tree, uprooted and planted in unfamiliar soil. An anomaly among native vegetation. Perhaps a bitter pill to swallow, the realization also brought a strange sense of liberation. Without a sliver of a chance to integrate, she was granted full permission to be herself. Any attempt to adapt would be futile, as her distinctiveness couldn't be hidden. Her only choice was to lean into her uniqueness, finding strength in her differences—not so easy in a nation built on conformity.

Despite the slow-acting poison of exhaustion seeping into his bones, Hanjun scribbled a few lines in his journal. His mind was abuzz, but his hand felt too heavy to capture his thoughts.

> *She gave me a seashell ornament. I will treasure it forever. The broadcast went well, but there's always room for improvement. I'll try harder.*

His gaze drifted to the half-open door, revealing blue light pooling from the threshold of Jen's. He had barely spoken with her since arriving home and longed for the energy to do so. The exertion from the telecast drained every ounce of his vitality, leaving him feeling like an empty vessel in the bowels of fatigue. Depleting the last bit of strength left in his muscles, he messaged her goodnight and apologized for his absence throughout the day.

CHAPTER THIRTY-EIGHT

Lipstick Kisses

Eyes popping open, Jen sprang into motion, hopping into the shower to wash away the remnants of dormancy. Rushing back to her room with a towel cloaking her build, she prayed Deok-Sun would be gone. But he wasn't, and she tiptoed to her closet, selected an outfit, and backtracked to the bathroom.

It became routine for one of her roommates to search her out in the middle of the night ever since Jin started sleeping in her bed. Sometimes it was to ask a question; other times, it was to seek comfort. But Deok-Sun's visits were different—he suffered from night terrors and couldn't relax without someone massaging his forehead.

Hanjun stood in the kitchen when she entered, brewing a pot of coffee. Sneaking up on him, she bound her arms around his waist and breathed in his honeyed scent. "Can I get you to order me a room divider? I'd purchase one myself, but navigating the online markets is frustrating."

Swaying from side to side, he aligned his hands over hers. "Sure, but why?"

She nuzzled into his back. "A few times a week, one of the boys sleeps in my bed. I'd like to have somewhere to dress without leaving the room."

He swiveled to face her. "I've noticed, and I have to say I'm a little jealous."

"Don't be. I'm just doing what I can for them." Standing on her tiptoes, she placed a tender kiss on his cheek. "You're the only one I want between my sheets."

The moment of intimacy was broken by Jin passing through for a drink of water. "Mom and Dad are kissing again!"

"You used to think it was cute." She slipped out of Hanjun's grasp to prepare a cup of liquid caffeine.

Hanjun's curiosity peaked. "I didn't take you for a coffee drinker."

"I don't love it as much as you do, but I like it iced every now and then." She added a handful of ice from the freezer, dumped in a pouch of concentrated cold brew from the fridge, and tried a tentative sip. Pulling milk from the shelf, she stared at the carton, remembering how Soogi drank straight from the spout. Opening the opposite end, she poured in a healthy dose of dairy.

He lifted his ceramic cup in a toast. "Good to know."

Revolving to meet his eyes, her fingertips slinked up his shirt. "You know, since it's my job, is there anything I can do for you?"

Eyebrows bouncing, he grinned. "I have some ideas of things you can do for me."

Jin returned the glass to the sink. "Mom and Dad are making sexual innuendos again!"

"I'm going to wake Sunnie." Eyes rolling, Jen situated her tumbler on the island and set off to rouse the youngest. "Deok-Sun, you need to get ready. You have a recording today."

Turning his back on her, he refused to budge. "Ten more minutes."

Chuckling, Hanjun stood at the threshold. "He's never going to get up like that."

"Deok-Sun!" She tugged on the covers. "Get up!"

Stepping into the hall, Hanjun called for the eldest. "Ho-Young! Come wake Deok-Sun!"

Strutting in, Hanso focused on the half-naked form sprawled on Jen's bed. "What did you try?"

Shrugging, her inflection held a tinge of annoyance. "I tried shaking him."

"When he stays up too late, shaking won't work." He ripped the blanket from Deok-Sun and delivered a firm wallop to his bare chest. "*This* is how you have to wake him."

Surprised by the brute force he used, she stumbled back. "I am *not* doing that."

Deok-Sun jolted upright, kneading the sore spot on his breast. "It would have been nicer if you did."

"You should have gotten up for her if you didn't want me to wake you." Cackling, Hanso high-fived Hanjun on the way out the door.

"Yeah, yeah." Deok-Sun crawled out of bed and staggered to the washroom. Running a comb through his strands, he tamed wild curls sticking up in every which way. Wearing a fresh set of clothing, he joined his bandmates in the kitchen.

The moment his rear hit the seat, Sehoon began a countdown. "In three, two…"

"Hello, we're—" Hanjun paused, allowing the mates to hail their band.

"Blackmirror!"

"And today, we're making personalized Christmas cards for Anti! At the end of the film, our lovely assistant, Jen, will pick five lucky winners. Be sure to drop a comment for a chance to win."

The dining table was transformed into a colorful workspace. Tubes of acrylics sat in neat rows, jars of speckles sparkled under the chandelier, and reams of cardstock awaited, ready to be folded. Jin reached for a container of gold specks and a glue stick. "I'm going to put glitter *all* over my card."

"And we'll be cleaning it until the day we move." Hanjun transferred his attention to Hanso. "What are you putting on yours?"

"Kisses!" Smiling from ear to ear, Hanso's excitement deflated when snickers erupted from behind the cameras.

Ha-Rin didn't hesitate to crush his crafty dreams. "We don't have any lipstick."

Jen stepped up. "I have some; want me to get them?"

Receiving a nod from Sehoon, she retreated to her room. Rummaging through her vanity, she gathered a handful of unused samples. Returning to the cameras, she offered what she found. "It's not much. I don't usually wear colored products."

"Go ahead and assist him." Ha-Rin gestured towards Hanso, issuing a gruff reminder. "Keep your back to the cameras."

Crossing the kitchen, she perched on the tabletop next to him. Twisting the tube of tint, her mouth curled into a shy smile. "This is my first time applying makeup to someone else. I apologize if it's bad."

"It will be perfect." Hanso held his lips pursed.

Finishing the application, she replaced the lid with a click. "I brought a few shades just in case you'd like more than one."

He kissed the inside of the cards until the hue faded and requested another color. Holding his chin steady, she applied a second coat over his perfectly shaped lips. Eyes roaming his features, she identified the symmetrical beauty of his contours and the subtle hint of injections in his forehead and cheeks. "This one is so sparkly."

"I love it." Hanso made use of the vivid rosy shine.

Replacing the lid, Jen felt Hanjun's scrutinizing gape from the other end of the table. In a futile attempt to ease his suffering, she flashed a smile in his direction.

"Thanks, Jen." Following an in-ear command from Ha-Rin, Hanso tipped forward, leaving a peck on her cheek. The bold pigment transferred to her skin, leaving a blemish that taunted Hanjun.

"It's time for Jen to pick the winners." Interrupting the cutesy spectacle, Hanjun grazed Jen's arm, handing over an expensive tablet.

She reached for the device. The touchscreen illuminated a chat box of rolling praise from Blackmirror's supporters. "Let's see what we have here..."

He watched her scour the comments for something particular. Something *different*. She had a knack for discovering novelty, and comments were no exception.

"Blackmirrorforlyfe, sweetlikehoney34, onyxbronx, jinsbabie, and hexielexie." She used a moment to clarify why she deemed their narrative worthy. "Words of support, jokes, or memes were what caught my attention."

Hovering at the end of the table, Hanjun stood parallel to Jen, his shoulder bumping into hers. Fixated on the display, he was immersed in whatever was playing out in his mind, unaware of his surroundings until she poked his shoulder. "Earth to Hanjun."

He returned to reality and reached for the device. "If you were chosen, our staff will contact you."

The moment the live stream ended, Jen scurried to the bathroom. Scrubbing at the lip print, she wished to erase the evidence. "Damn it, Ho-Young."

Standing in the doorway, Hanjun's stare darkened. "Your cheek is ridiculously red."

"This obviously wasn't meant for skin." Leaning into the mirror, she inspected the stain; the pink patch contrasted her pigmentation, growing more crimson by the second.

"Let me try." He nabbed the cloth from her hand and began rubbing at the splotch, nearly scouring her raw.

"Jun, I have an epidermis for a reason."

"We'll try cleanser." He opened the cabinet door and grabbed a bottle of soap, squeezing a dollop onto his finger. Raising his hand, he draped a palm over her neck, using his thumb to massage the substance into her skin. "I don't know why Ha-Rin would have given Hanso that order."

"I don't know, either." She felt overwhelmed by his intense gaze. Suddenly, tears streamed down his cheeks in an uncontrollable surge. "Hanjun, is everything okay?"

"You're just so beautiful." Blushing, she turned away, but he pulled her into a tight embrace. "Every day when we're taping, I find myself looking at you. I don't know what I'd do without you."

Hearing his heart thump against her temple, she snorted. "You'd do whatever you did before I came here."

He cradled her, cherishing the weight of her body rocking against his. "There was nothing before you. I went through the motions, pretending to be happy, but I didn't truly live."

He swiped at the mark; the cloth revealed her flawless complexion, and a serene stillness settled over his mind. "It worked."

"Thanks." Shocked by his vulnerable confession, she pulled the washcloth from his hand.

Detecting her discomfort, he twisted away. "I should check for today's delivery."

★⁺₊★☾★⁺₊★

"Why do they insist on taunting us with these pictures?" Slipping into a pair of house slippers at the door, Hanjun sighted a package propped on the wall, swaddled in festive paper. Trudging back to the kitchen, he gave up trying to decipher the photo and abandoned the parcel on the counter.

Retreating to Jen's room, he found her cocooned under the comforter like a caterpillar. He flopped on the bed, sinking into the mattress as if he owned it. "If we go on a world tour, is there anywhere you'd like to visit?"

"I never left the States before I came here." Twirling a piece of hair around her finger, she pondered aloud. "Umbrella Sky.

And I've heard Narita International Airport gives out origami. And there's Bunny Island—"

Eyes narrowing, his brow twitched. "Just Japan?"

She wiggled into her pillows. "There are too many to name. Life is too short to do everything, but that doesn't mean I can't try, right?"

He nodded, brushing wild bangs from her temples. "We can."

She trailed her fingers down his arm. "What about you? What's left on your list?"

A warm flourish engulfed his body, his eyes airing a trace of longing. "The Uffizi Gallery in Florence. I want to see The Birth of Venus with my own eyes before I die."

Sitting up, her eyes widened. "Let's go. We might have to find more creative ways to blend in, but we'll figure it out."

The conversation meandered lazily, drifting through destinations and adventures, though he posed an interesting question. "When you travel, do you prefer to plan or go with the flow?"

Her laughter bubbled like a clear spring. "I think I know your answer, but let's say it together."

"On three." He initiated a count. "Hana, dul, set!"

Their voices vibrated in a blended torrent. "Both!"

Breaking into a belly laugh, he wrapped a hand around hers. "I don't like strict plans, but I create a general outline of where I want to go. If I don't, I'll miss out on everything I want to do."

"I need a bit of structure, but I also enjoy spontaneity. It's important for me to savor the moment."

Discussing possible vacation arrangements into the early morning hours, he remained by her side until she gave in to exhaustion. Navigating to his room, he slipped under the covers, ordered her a partition from a local artist, and reflected on the day.

I'm counting the days until they break up.

CHAPTER THIRTY-NINE

A New Tradition

Eyes fluttering to find Jin slumbering at her side, Jen slid out of the covers and went for a shower. Returning to her room, she decided on an ugly sweater adorned with a comically large Tyrannosaurus. The garish pullover clashed with blue jeans, but she couldn't resist its festive charm.

Stepping into the kitchen, her eyes fell upon Hanjun. Perched on a bench, he was surrounded by a team of makeup artists. Five empty mugs were situated on the table. "Let me guess, you're making hot cocoa."

"How'd you know?" Scrunching his nose, Hanjun received a final swipe of powder over his forehead.

"It could be the mugs. Or perhaps the cocoa." Her colleagues erupted into giggles.

"Morning." Lumbering to the table, Jin wrapped an arm around Jen's and dragged her to the chair.

She ruffled his unwashed hair. "Did you not sleep well?"

Shoulders slumping, he eyeballed Hanjun. "I heard you guys talking about the photos the other night, and I was afraid you'd leave."

She squeezed his hand. "The deliveries have me concerned, but I'm not going anywhere without a good reason."

Within twenty minutes, every member of Blackmirror had found their way to the kitchen, where they were primped and preened by their stylists. After an hour of impeccable grooming, Ha-Rin tapped a finger on his watch. "Let's get this show on the road."

"On it." Jen floated through the space, cleaning up the set. In one hand, she gathered stray makeup brushes, while the other stashed away scattered hair clips. Satisfied with her work, she took her place behind the cameras.

Sehoon's hand shot up like a flag, signaling the beginning of the broadcast. "We're going live in three, two..."

On cue, Hanjun greeted the lens with a wave, urging a red stocking towards Jin. "Today, we're making hot cocoa. Draw to find out which flavor you're making."

Jin reached into the sock, his knuckles brushing slips of paper. "White chocolate."

He passed the stocking onto Deok-Sun, who took his time drawing. "Mint chocolate."

"Mint choco?" Face scrunched, Hanjun mewled. "Why'd it have to be mint choco? I'm glad I didn't get that one."

"Let people like things." Soogi scolded him, handing the stocking off to Hanso. "Chocolate raspberry."

Hanso fetched his scrap and returned the stocking to Hanjun. "Pumpkin spice. Isn't it too sweet?"

Hanjun rummaged for the singular bit of paper left. "That leaves me with—espresso hot chocolate."

Scrambling for ingredients, they followed detailed recipe cards supplied by the crew. Soon, the indulgent aromas reached every corner of the kitchen, blending with the heat radiating from electric kettles.

"We've prepared a topping bar." Amid the clanging of utensils, Ha-Rin rang out from behind the cameras. He passed the treats off to Jen, who advanced to the table, revealing an array of toppings. Pillowy marshmallows, peppermint coins, cinnamon sticks, crunchy sprinkles, and enough whipped topping to satisfy the most playful of inner children.

Snatching a can of cream, a burst of sugary foam landed on Deok-Sun's tongue. "This is the nectar of the gods."

Choking on his beverage, Hanjun released a feline wail. "Geukyeom!"

"I love mini marshmallows!" Hanso dropped a handful into his cup, sending some of the fluffy confections tumbling to the floor.

Deok-Sun dove under the table, unwilling to let the sweets go to waste. From his hands and knees, he stuffed the morsels into his mouth, referencing an age-old myth. "Three-second rule!"

"Sprinkles!" Jin released a fistful of rainbow speckles. Bouncing off the rim, the candies sprayed in every direction.

Shielding his mug from the blast radius, Soogi went about making his hot drink. "Jin made a bomb."

For the ending shots, the mates assembled around the table, holding their handcrafted cocoas. They then swapped mugs, sampling each other's concoctions, and talked about what they learned during the process.

Once the cameras ceased filming and the home fell to a hushed lull, Hanjun slipped outside to retrieve the anticipated package. He placed the wrapped box on the kitchen counter, among the clutter of unopened mail. Without uttering a word to anyone, he cradled his steaming cup of cocoa and disappeared to the terrace.

Noticing his silent retreat, Jen retrieved a blanket from her room. Draping the fabric around her shivering frame, she followed him into the cold. "It's still snowing."

"I love to marvel at the snow when it's undisturbed by people." Handing her the cup of cocoa, he patted the concrete next to him. "Did your family have holiday traditions? I mean, when your family was a family."

Collapsing to sit, she tapped her fingers on the ceramic mug. "Each part of my family celebrated differently."

His left eyebrow arced. "How did your German grandparents celebrate?"

"On Christmas Eve, we gathered for a feast and opened one present before bed. Stockings were also a German thing. And we had something called stollen—it's like a sugar-dusted fruitcake." Taking a sip, she recalled the most amusing element of a German solstice. "And there's Krampus."

His features twisted. "What's a Krampus?"

"If you're good, Santa brings you gifts..." She passed the tepid cup back to him. "When you're bad, you receive a visit from Krampus; he beats naughty kids with branches."

He nearly spit out his drink. "Sounds kind of like the Dokkaebi."

She splintered into an animated giggle. "What on earth is a Dokkaebi?"

Obstructing chocolate from dribbling down his chin, he wiped his lips with the back of his hand. "Dokkaebi are mythical creatures said to have supernatural powers, allowing them to interact with humans. They can be helpful or hurtful, but they are known for being tricksters."

"That's fascinating. I've always been drawn to folklore." She accepted the mug with both hands, reveling in its warmth. "The Hungarian side of my family was like the German side, with Christmas Eve being celebrated. Christmas Day was reserved for dinner, and the day before was a festive time spent admiring light displays. It's why I enjoy looking at the lights so much."

He couldn't imagine the logistics of trying to please everyone. "Let me get this straight: you had four sets of great-grandparents, who all immigrated to the country—except for your Native American grandmother, of course. Did you have multiple get-togethers?"

"No—" Her eyes reflected the exhaustion of acting as a bridge between generations of vastly different cultures. "What's worse is that I had three great-grandmothers who wanted me to cook like them. And they smacked me with a different object when I messed up. Grandmother Borbala would chuck wooden spoons, Grandmother Ingrid would hurl cabbages, and Grandmother Achukma would chase me with whatever was within reach—moccasins, umbrellas, and on one occasion, a ceremonial drum."

Cackling, he imagined her being chased by the matriarchs. "I'd ask about the fourth, but you said you didn't know them."

She jostled his shoulder. "Don't laugh! The drum made a rhythmic thumping every time she hit me."

"I've always wondered how you can cook without measuring; you just drop ingredients in the pan and go to town." He lowered the quilt from his shoulders, reenacting how she sautéed with one hand and added spices with the other. "And I must say, your exceptional use of garlic surprised me."

"Garlic is measured with your heart." She planted a hand on her chest. "I don't think I've ever eaten something too garlicky. Too salty and too sugary, but never too garlicky."

"I feel the same." His stare lingered on her profile in the pallid moonlight. She tilted toward the railing, eyeing the hectic city below. The river was coated in a layer of snow, its surface reflecting neon signs surrounding the water. On the sidewalk, two shadows collided. One fell to the ground, and the other reached to help them up.

In a graceful motion, she lifted her arms as if she were holding an old-fashioned camera. Imitating a shutter, she preserved the image for as long as she lived. "My great-grandparents were from another time. It was unheard of for a woman to not be able to cook, but honestly, I feel like everyone needs to know how to feed themselves."

His gaze followed hers to the city dwellers, their laughter ringing like chimes in a seaside breeze as they brushed off snow from the sidewalk blunder. Pulling out their phones, they exchanged contacts under the glow of streetlamps. Conquered by jealousy, he wished someone had done something comparable for them. If a bystander photographed the fated meeting, he could have held onto the memory as a reminder of when his life changed. "Maybe you can teach me?"

Pulling her attention from the falling snowflakes, she glared at him. "What makes you think I can?"

"You don't make me feel like a failure." He ran a clammy palm along his arm, fiddling with his sleeve. "There's a proverb that says, 'By doing nothing, you remain neutral.' If you try and succeed, you make it to the top. If you try and fail, you land at the bottom. But if you do nothing, you exist in a state of mediocrity without experiencing triumph or defeat."

"Failure is the fertilizer for success."

"I wish someone would have told me that when I was young." One sentence was all it took for her to comfort him, but it wasn't the words—it was her belief. "You have a flair for inspiring, did you know that?"

"You only think that because you like me. Anyone who seems as if they have it all figured out, doesn't. Sometimes my sanity is held together by superglue and wishes." Tsking, she slurped the cooling cocoa. "Our parents taught us the way they were taught, but the truth is, our parents were kids. The body withers under the strain of accomplishment, but we're all children of the earth. If you think they reared you wrong, they just didn't know any better."

He met her eyes, taking note of the way her lips pursed and the movement of her tongue catching her lower lip. "You really think that?"

Head bobbing, she relinquished the chilled vessel. "Go to a place from your development years and tell me it doesn't take you right back to those days. Hand your grandmother something from her youth and watch her turn into a young girl again. Adulthood is exhausted in one of two ways; we're either making childhood dreams realities or reclaiming the innocence we lost."

"I suppose I'm doing both." His mind drifted to the complexities of her family. "Was it difficult to host four distinct nationalities?"

Her forehead creased. "Each side preferred different dishes, but they overlapped somewhere in the middle. The Hungarian side liked carp fish soup, fried fish, and beigli, which is a rolled poppy seed pastry. The German side enjoyed duck, goose, sausage, and mulled wine. The Chickasaw side ate something called Three Sisters. They drank corn tea and ate mountains of vegetables and jerkies—"

"Corn tea? Like the kind we drink?"

"Yep. They also dried corn to make bread and porridge. As for my dad—I don't know. He demanded Asian dishes, but I don't remember what they were. All I know is that there was a bowl of rice at every meal." She released a wistful sigh. "When I have a family, I want to do that. Traditions. Even if I'm on the road with you, I still want to have traditions."

"What's something you'd want to do?"

Hesitating, her gaze bore into the distance. She liked to believe she could plan for the unknown, but life was full of surprises. While some strove for an organized existence, she believed a life without unexpected twists would make a boring story. "When my family was a family, we'd have this elaborate Christmas dinner, and everyone was required to attend. Maybe one of the reasons I like the season so much is because, even though my family was irreparably broken, they pretended to be happy."

He reached for her hand, stroking the back. "You want a giant celebration?"

"Forced gatherings cannot repair bloodline rifts, and I have no desire to argue with my estranged family over simmering resentment, alleged favoritism, misaligning politics, or social values." Perhaps it was her previous occupation that amplified her cynicism, but she knew all too well that festivals, holidays, and religious events were just as damaging as they were restorative, especially for those burdened with the pressure of making everything perfect.

Touted as the most wonderful time of year, Christmas hid a dark side. In a frenzy of consumerism, shoppers mutated into maniacs willing to injure for discounts, and guardians labored tirelessly for overpriced gadgets that would be forgotten within a matter of months. The days between Halloween and the New Year were supposed to be the jolliest time of year, when everyone was expected to carry a smile. But most turned a blind eye to the world's greatest atrocities to maintain the illusion of joy.

The season brought the burden of expectation. Parents poured their hearts into creating the perfect atmosphere for their children, determined to give them everything they never had. Trees sagged under the weight of the best presents, carefully chosen and decorated with love. Goodies scented the air, a result of someone slaving over a hot oven.

Christmas was a mirage, created by the toil of its participants. Santa didn't wrap gifts, nor did he prepare lavish dinners or clean up the mess afterward. It wasn't Mrs. Claus who exhausted hours baking treats or filling stockings. And elves weren't hanging lights in major cities; they also weren't assembling toys for children around the world. The holiday was born from the compassion, empathy, and enjoyment of humans. It was selfless acts that made the season magical—not a fictional man in a red suit.

"I'd rather have something small and intimate with all of us here in the condo. On Christmas Eve, I could make cheese fondue, and we could get drunk on cheap wine. We'd watch movies in matching pajamas until we couldn't hold our eyes open. And in the morning, I'll help Hanso make the unhealthiest breakfast. We'd exchange presents and listen to Deok-Sun and Jin serenade us."

Comfort seized his lungs at the thought. "What's stopping us?"

⋆⁺₊⋆☾⁺₊⋆

The kitchen clock chimed two in the morning when they finally returned to the home. Jen stumbled down the hallway, clutching the cold blanket to her chest. Each time her eyelids fell, she bumped into the wall, mumbling an apology for relying on Hanjun to steer the way.

He dashed ahead and opened the door to her room, nudging her inside. Tugging the bedspread from her arms, he retrieved an extra throw from the hall closet. Though the faux mink fabric clashed with her bedding, she pulled the cover over her shoulders and rolled onto her side, succumbing to sleep's embrace. Patting her hair, he placed her phone on the charger and tossed the wet blanket in the hamper. Shuffling across the hall, he checked on Hanso. Finding him snoozing comfortably, he crept across the floor and settled into bed.

Laying in the darkness, he raised the collar of his shirt, inhaling her perfume. Neither fruity nor floral, the scent lingered on fabrics for weeks. Though he would never admit it to a living soul, he sometimes sprayed his clothing with her perfume. The spicy feminine fragrance served as a reminder of her; the subtle hints of cashmere and gardenia, mixed with something exotic, stirred his olfactory senses and made him want to kiss her. But not just any old kiss; he wanted to leave her standing frozen, breathless, savoring the way his hands gripped her waist. His pecks would follow the scent to her neck, brushing her throat and stopping at the collar of her shirt. Tugging on her nape, he'd draw a gasp, leaving her lips in a permanent pout.

Shaking his head to rid himself of carnal thoughts, he deliberated a journal entry, wondering how he could surprise her for Christmas.

I've never thought about what my future family would be like, but she makes me want to think about it. Christmas days with our friends. Matching pajamas and films. I think I want the same things she wants, and I'm sure I want them with her.

CHAPTER FORTY

Dirty Little Fantasy

Yawning, Jen rose from bed. She selected an outfit—a fuzzy ivory sweater adorned with pearls along the neckline and dark wash denim. To complete the ensemble, she picked a gray-taupe jacket, imagining she'd nab matching suede booties from the entry closet. Shuffling to the kitchen, she spotted a note on the island.

> *I made you a coffee. It's in the fridge. I'll be at the office. —Jun.*

Giving the cup a shake, she lifted the rim to her lips. "Not bad for him watching me make it once."

With her day bag slung over her shoulder, she slipped her shoes on at the door. Exiting the ornate wrought-iron gates of Windsor Heights, she hopped into the backseat of the first taxi that stopped. "J&I Entertainment."

"J&I?" The cabbie turned to address her, his gruff appearance softened by a small chuckle. He appeared weathered and tired, likely from years of working in a people-pleasing profession. "Isn't that where all those pop stars hang out?"

Unsure how to respond, she was relieved when he returned his eyes to the road, though he had an additional query. "What's that group's name? The ones who are always appearing on the news? Blacksomething…"

Refusing to entertain his questioning, she couldn't shake the jitters wriggling up her spine. "I'm not sure."

The way he stared at her in the rearview mirror made her skin crawl, and she couldn't tell if his creepiness was intentional. "You aren't one of their girlfriends, are you?"

Her white-knuckled grasp on the door handle tensed as the car maneuvered into traffic. "Actually, I'll walk from here."

"Are you sure?" The driver flicked the meter. "We're five minutes from the headquarters, and it's below freezing."

"I'm sure." Ignoring his annoyance, she stepped out onto the wet sidewalk. Trudging to the building, she situated her coat's hood over her face. Holding her vision to the puddles, she aimed to dodge the fans lurking outside the establishment. To her surprise, large trucks were parked near the path, blocking views of the building with protests. Looking up long enough to catch the English version of a complaint plastered on a scrolling LED sign, it seemed an actor contracted to the agency went public with plans to wed his pregnant girlfriend. It was safe to say that his supporters were not happy.

Finishing an icy tour of the snow-covered sidewalks, she entered the lobby, catching a glint of recognition from the guards. Scampering to the elevator, a rosy flush adorned her face. The doors opened, and she stepped inside, rubbing her nose with ungloved hands. Unable to feel her fingers, she cursed herself for forgetting her gloves again.

'Please scan key card.'

"Welcome, Jenilyn—" She performed a little dance in hopes of thawing her frigid bones.

*'Welcome, Jenilyn. Members of Blackmirror Hanjun
and Soogi are located on recording studio floor
twelve. Deok-Sun, Hanso, and Jin of Blackmirror's
whereabouts are unknown.'*

Choosing the studio floor, she went back to warming her cheeks. When the lift slid open, she found Soogi in the lounge, legs outstretched. Spotting her, he leaped to his feet and snatched her hand, towing her to an elongated hallway. Breathless from her wintery stroll, she failed to keep up with his long strides. "I've never seen you so excited."

Reaching the door to his workroom, he clasped her hands, rubbing them between his palms. "Did you walk here? You're frozen."

"I caught a taxi, but the driver must have recognized me." She tugged at her sleeves, warming her wrists and forearms.

Swiping his thumbprint on the biometric scanner, he tapped in a four-digit code and opened the door. "Seven. Eight. Four. Two. I call it the 'Spark of Brilliance.'"

"Fitting." Upon first inspection, she was struck by the modern aesthetic. On one end of the room, illuminated by soft lighting, a skinny bookshelf stood with photographs of musicians he had collaborated with. Musical equipment lined the floor—an electronic keyboard, guitars on stands, and a drum set tucked into the corner. "You play a lot of instruments."

"I mess with everything." He turned to face her after registering her statement. "We need to be more careful about letting you go out alone."

"I'll be okay." Stepping inside, the space was how she imagined it—heavily inspired by his love for music and incorporating the colors black, red, and white. His computer featured an attractive blonde alongside posters of nearly naked models on the walls. Trinkets and basketball memorabilia were scattered throughout, rivaling the most impressive man cave.

He encouraged her not to ignore the incident. "I'm sure you will be, but it's still a good idea to let Ha-Rin know, yeah?"

Distracted by the sheer volume of audio equipment on his desk, she nodded. It would have been excessive if he wasn't a musician. "That's a lot of speakers."

"I spend a lot of time in here." What he didn't say was that when he worked, he rarely left at all. His studio was his home, while their condo was his vacation spot.

Her eyes fell to a trio of candles on his desk. A surprising detail, as she had never known him to be one for scented items. Or much of anything, really. He wore expensive brands, but she assumed he rolled with his moods and didn't care about impressing anyone.

His eyes followed hers. "Can I show you something?"

"Sure."

Pulling up a seat for her, he settled into an oversized chair and wheeled to his computer. His appreciation for composition was evident from the number of cords snaking across the floor. "I've been working on this one for a few weeks and was hoping it would make it on the new album."

Jiggling the mouse, his voice spilled from the speakers, accompanied by a lively beat. Soogi had always been drawn to adrenaline-inducing music—a stark contrast to Hanjun's preference for melancholic melodies. "I've been messing around with double time, but it's visually confusing to look at."

Each syllable neared desperation, and through the delivery, she experienced his desire to break free from the grips of pride. But there was also a hint of regret for opportunities lost due to his unyielding self-importance. "Hanjun says you create the track before the lyrics, right?"

"There are times we come up with lyrics and build the melody around them." He opened a folder on his organized desktop and began playing an earlier, slower version. "The more you mess with a recording, the more alien it sounds. I'm afraid this one is overproduced. The chorus doesn't suit the vocals anymore. I suppose I could add new lyrics and scrap the double time."

Fidgeting, he restarted the tune and belted out the first verse as if he were standing on a mountain, proclaiming his truth to the world. "Pride is a luxury I can afford, but if I ever find something I love more, I'll bend a knee to prove my support."

Singing along, he tapped the desk, reaching for an elusive rhythm. Failing to summon a spontaneous chorus, his mind went blank. Falling silent, he paused the work and shook his head. "Verses are the easiest. Choruses are hard."

Music had always been a source of inspiration for her, and each score held a story. When she was young—and too poor to buy music—she listened to instrumentals, brainstorming lyrics to fit the tune. It was a cheap way to pass the time and hone her skills. "Would you mind if I gave it a try?"

He nipped his lip. "Not at all."

She closed her eyes, and the melody swelled, quilting the small area with magic. And like a burst of fireworks illuminating the sky, she rendered a chorus from her soul, weaving a tale of love and loss.

'All the lies I've told
Have bruised my pride
But I pick up the pieces
And continue to hide
Despite the fact
I'm dying inside
I continue to tell myself
You're gonna be fine

Finishing the addition, she opened her eyes to find him scribbling the refrain before it waned. Tucking a strand of hair behind her ear, she blushed. "That's what came to mind when I heard the beat."

"I'm shocked." Tossing the notebook on the desk, he stared at her with newfound admiration.

Blowing her breath, she revealed an unknown fact. "I've been writing since I was a child. That was from a poem called 'Next Time.' You can use it or change it. It doesn't matter to me."

"I didn't know you wrote poetry. Would you mind if I picked your brain? I'd like to see what concepts you can come up with."

"Sure, but why? You have an entire band with ideas."

"The team hasn't—" Silencing his tongue before he spilled a secret the size of an atomic bomb, he halted to craft an answer that wouldn't get him into a heap of trouble with J&I.

Whispers floated around the company, but the truth was a guarded secret: after Blackmirror's triumphant return from the states, they were to begin a series of emotional farewell shows and announce their official disbandment. Creating new content had come to an end, and the bittersweet moments they shared were fading memories. The video for the song they filmed at the beach was meant to be a goodbye to their beloved fandom, fittingly titled 'Miss You.'

The composition—crafted by Soogi—served as the final masterpiece Blackmirror would promote. While supporters swooned over the romantic lyrics, there was a deeper meaning only they knew; the song was a heart-wrenching ode to the struggles and sacrifices of change.

'Holding you like I miss you
Even before I let you go
It's how I know I'll never forget
You are part of my soul'

The conversations between the band after the initial Covid outbreak were emotionally draining. Each harbored reasons for wanting to quit, producing an onslaught of tears that could have filled an Olympic-sized pool. The weight of their collective sadness hung heavy—a looming storm of regret and loss for what could have been if they were stronger.

Envisaged as a sex symbol from a tender age, Deok-Sun ached to separate from his childish image and embrace the man he was. The saccharine world of pop music, with its glossy surface and manufactured perfection, had lost its allure, and he itched to explore the complex and sometimes taboo aspects of his sexuality.

Jin's struggles were rooted in his public visage. Within the quintet, he portrayed the reserved, introverted teammate, but in reality, he was an attention-grabbing stimulation seeker. He was so deeply immersed in his alter ego that he second-guessed every word and action.

Hanso craved time. Time to indulge in his passions, and time to immerse in new experiences. Despite dating two women during his contract, he never had the opportunity to connect on a deeper level. In fact, he hadn't even met one of his lovers in the flesh before the relationship fizzled. He dreamed of love, and while the agency provided ways to satisfy their physical desires—along with enough non-disclosure agreements to protect their privacy—their emotional needs were ignored. In the next chapter of his life, he expected to find his person and experience the fairy tale romance waiting for him.

Hanjun wanted everything without having an idea of what he wanted. He desired to remain the leader of Blackmirror, yet he also yearned to pursue his own musical journey. He craved a life where he could work hard and have time to enjoy simple pleasures. Fighting a constant battle for love and freedom, he was drowning in his dreams. Most of all, he wished for clearance to figure out what he wanted. Music would always be a part of his life, but he intended to find the rest of his missing pieces.

Soogi never aired his worries. He did everything he needed to do as one-fifth of the act and believed his qualities were best utilized in the background. His job was a supportive role, and he didn't pull focus from his teammates by acting as the protagonist. Though his leisure time was spent creating chords without the group's interference, he wanted to keep the unit together for as long as possible. They were his brothers—the people closest to him—and witnessing them shed tears over their hardships was enough for him to agree to the disbandment. From that point on, he viewed the band as a novel of combined struggles and looked forward to each member's stories in the series.

And then—by divine intervention—two days before their scheduled departure from Chicago, fate brought them Jen. She didn't know the day they walked into her life was the day everything changed. The group chat they had stopped using became a hub of chatter. The next morning, the companions conversed more than they had in months, and they somehow found themselves bonding over her. With a handful forming childish crushes and the others liking her general vibe, she was a hot topic of conversation. During soundcheck, they discussed her as if she were a movie star, quoting her cutest and most awkward moments. At the time, she was their only common thread beyond traumatic experiences.

Despite Ha-Rin's initial reluctance, Hanjun convinced him to invite her to the concert. He was almost too excited to call her, and the friends couldn't have been happier; the leader hadn't smiled in over a year. Following a heart-crushing breakup with his ex-girlfriend, he spiraled into a torrent of self-destruction. Fueled by alcohol and seedy sex clubs, the musician became a shadow of his former self. He was so immersed in the underbelly of Seoul that the company heads dreaded waking each morning, fearing they would find the front-page news of his untimely death.

But something miraculous happened the night Jen moved in—a switch flipped inside Hanjun. He started incorporating exercise into his daily routine and opted to eat healthier. His short fuse lengthened, and he no longer exploded at every little thing. He called his mom, who was worried sick, and met up with his best friend for the first time in months.

Hanso was the first to point out the positive changes. Hanjun began writing in his journal—something he brushed off during bouts of depression—and found inspiration after a period of artist's block. Witnessing him recover his vitality was like watching a flower bloom from dormancy. After surviving an endless winter, Jen was Hanjun's spring.

She had a way of breathing life into his world. It was too much to say she turned him around, but it wasn't enough to say her presence had a profound impact on him. He started caring for his body, mind, and career with the same passion he had as an aspiring artist. Whatever damage his ex-girlfriend did, Jen repaired.

She was an integrated part of the Blackmirror family. Unremovable, as each of them were. Her significance would remain a mystery to her, but to them, she was an essential piece of their dynamic. They had chosen her, knowing such a burden would weigh on anyone's shoulders. She was doing what the agency thought was impossible, and that was why she was respected in their eyes. She embodied the roles of mother, sister, roommate, friend, and colleague from the moment she joined them, and they vowed to protect her at all costs.

Suspiring, he finally answered the question. "It's not easy to get the group together."

She studied his features, wondering why he drifted off mid-conversation. "Have you tried asking Hanjun for help?"

He flicked his wrist dismissively. "I wanted him to chill out for a while."

She pointed to the open door. "Speaking of, I should check on him."

"He has a live stream today." Taking off his baseball cap, he plopped it on her hair. "Take this."

"Thanks, Shoog." Looking up at him from under the brim, the nickname slipped from her lips.

"Shoog? That's a new one."

"Soogi plus honey." Turning to leave, she paused at the door. "Make good music so I have something to listen to."

He scoffed, glancing at the scribbled reprise. "*Shoog.*"

⋆⁺₊⋆☾⋆⁺₊⋆

Departing Soogi's workroom with the hat pulled over her eyes, Jen moseyed to Hanjun's studio, approaching the open door with caution. "Jun-a?"

The room was blanketed in shadows, and a small lamp illuminated his face. He spun to greet her, motioning for her to keep her head down. While she wormed through the doorway, he positioned his body to block her from the frame. "I'll be back in four minutes."

Panning the webcam away from her, he strode across the room, leaving the vacant chair spinning in place. Settling on the sofa, he wasted no time in pulling her into his arms. "Come here."

She squealed. "Hanjun, what are you doing?"

"Enjoying the next four minutes." He bucked his hips and his hands swept under her blouse, pressing into the small of her back. "I swear you grow prettier by the day."

His touch launched a tremble up her spine, and she buried her face in his neck. "Hopefully longer than four minutes."

Smirking, he growled next to her temple. "Mi Sol, *it will be*."

Ignoring the electric pulse of desire boiling in her veins, she slipped from his lap. "I don't think it's a good idea for us to—"

Jumping to his feet, he wrapped a palm around the back of her neck, flattening his tongue below her ear. "You can tell me if you want me to stop."

Raw heat radiated from his body, making her knees weak. "Junie, you know better than to—"

"Better than to what?" Her pleas morphed into hoarse moans, and his mouth eased to the swell of her chest. His hands crept from below her bra line to cupping her breasts, eliciting a sharp wince from her. He kneaded the delicate fabric, erecting her nipples. "You don't want me to stop, do you?"

Lost in the moment, her eyelashes fluttered. "No."

"I didn't think so." Leaving a wet kiss on her forehead, he pulled back. "I have to start before people get antsy."

Releasing his hold on her, he returned to his chair, addressing his audience as if he had never left. "I waited four whole minutes."

She stood in the center of his studio, exactly where he left her, her head tilted toward the recessed lighting. Managing her elevating temperature, she fanned her face, desperate to cool off. He had consciously teased her, leaving her to grapple with a fiery fever, and she was eager to pay him back.

Shooting her a seductive glance, he leaned toward the monitor, his smoldering stare penetrating the lens. "Five hundred thousand viewers..."

The passion behind her eyes subsided, though she was captivated by his invisible nuances—the way he talked with his hands and how he absentmindedly fiddled with objects on his desk. But it was when he was lost in thought that made her heart flutter; in those moments, she understood the worries passing through him—and the truths he was too afraid to admit.

Meaningless dialogue tumbled from his tongue, and he pulled at his pants. His eyes were glued to her—a mixture of accusation and longing. Tempting his resolve, she held out a hand. Inching nearer, he shifted just enough to remain in the frame while locking fingers with her. Their gazes merged in a game of seduction, each daring the other to make the first move. She brought his hand to her lips, tracing the lines of his pointer finger with her tongue.

"Hold on, I'm trying to—" A ragged puff loosened from his lungs as she enveloped his entire finger. "Do something..."

"I need a moment." He disappeared from the screen and seized her wrists. His grasp was firm, almost bruising. Every kiss was a declaration of ownership, each more insistent than the last. "If you keep fucking around, you're gonna start something."

Her fingertips danced over the seam of his jeans, roused by the subtle ridges and dips. "You already started it."

"That's wrong..." The words plummeted into a bated groan, and his faculties fought to gain control. But the desire was too strong; he hungered for her acceptance and craved every inch of her hands all over his body. "You're playing dirty."

"I have an idea." Tugging on his belt, she inhaled his honeyed scent. "Do you trust me?"

Overwhelmed by the warmth of her fingers dipping into his waistband, he searched her eyes for deception—there wasn't any. The question was earnest, and he needed to know what she would do if he confessed his faith in her. "Always."

Releasing the denim, she nudged the office chair away from the desk. Crawling underneath the tabletop, she gave him a sultry glance and patted the leather seat. He stood agog, unable to move at the image of her waiting on her knees for him. "Seriously?"

For as long as he could remember, it had been a filthy fantasy of his—to have a ravishing bombshell of a woman tend to his needs. And what would make the encounter more perfect? If it happened while he was working. The thought of being pulled away from his ever-frustrating job for a stress-relieving sex sesh made his pants tighten, and he was ready to blow before she laid a finger on him.

Holding his breath, he approached the chair, trying not to act too enthusiastic. Wheeling to the desk, he panned the camera upwards, ensuring nothing could be captured on film. Before he managed to utter a word, she began massaging his thighs through his clothes.

"Sorry, I have a few things going on." Surrendering to her gentle kneading, he bit his lip, apologizing to the audience in a wispy gasp. Her palms climbed higher, and his lids fell in submission. Focusing on the screen, his voice rattled deep. "I'm good. I promise."

Discreetly unfastening his belt, she tugged the zipper, revealing more of his chiseled abdomen. He kept his elbows planted on the desk, concealing his face as she snaked her fingertips along his back. Breathing calmly, she seized the waistband of his jeans, exposing his lower body to her.

"I wanted to come—" Gulping, he was shaking even before she made it to his underwear, and he knew what was about to happen was going to be intense. "And answer questions."

Using open palms, she explored his body with fragile caresses. Moving down from his sculpted belly, she traced along his stiffened length, grazing the meat of his inner thighs.

"If you have any questions, drop them—" Gratified pants escaped him as her palm encased him in a hug unlike any he had experienced—gentle yet purposeful. Her vise on his shaft was secure but not too snug, the strength of her wrist balancing perfectly with his weight. And like a skilled sculptor, she worked with finesse, but it was her attention to detail that entranced him—each pump facilitated new sensations. He had dreamt of the moment since the day he met her, but never in his wildest dreams did he imagine it would happen in front of five hundred thousand viewers.

"In the comments." Eyes coiling, waves of arousal vibrated through his body, and he considered ending the livestream and railing her right on the fourteen-thousand-dollar koi rug.

His gaze flickered downward, meeting hers in a spirited match of eroticism. Lust burned in his gaze, but she knew she held the advantage. Adopting a sly smile, he raised his eyes to the lens, daring her to make a move. She tightened her grip, and his eyes widened, but he recovered and placed a hand over his face. "How was the hot cocoa?"

His eyebrows knit together as she licked up her palm, leaving a trail of moisture on the tip. "So good..."

"Did I get Jen a Christmas present?" He glanced down at her. With her eyes narrowing and her teeth sinking into her lower lip, she encouraged him to keep talking. "I did. She's gonna love it."

"Did she get anything for me?" Head falling back, he grasped the armrests. "Yeah, I'm pretty sure she did. She said she'd give it to me *real soon.*"

Peering up at him from below the desk, she caught the vein bulging in his neck. Straining to maintain composure but gradually losing supremacy, he was unraveling, melting in her hands. She loved to watch his phlegmatic facade crumble, and if it had been physically possible to masturbate at the same time, she would have.

"What do I think about Hanso and Jen?" Gripping the back of the chair, he stretched to give her a better hold. "I feel like we're closer."

For a moment, his mind went blank, and he released a guttural moan, diffused by soundproofed walls. "We spend a lot of time together, and honestly, she's such a *good girl.*"

Gazing up at him with doe eyes, she knew he had said it just for her. Heeding his raspy groans, a smirk graced her lips. She enjoyed the manipulation to the fullest degree. Faster, slower—she probed for clues on what served him. He loved her enthusiasm and how she glorified his dick as if his ex were watching. Stroking liberally, she knew from first sight that it would only be a matter of time before she had her hands on him, and something about his pensive, melancholic disposition made her want to submit. The only way to cure someone who felt overlooked was to make them feel worshipped.

He fumbled for her fingers, desperate for connection. "Yeah, she did help me get it up."

"Put the tree up, I mean." Legs bouncing, he edged to orgasm. Right before she thought she'd need to pull away to avert a broken hand, he exploded into a puddle of satisfaction in her palm. "Oh fuck—"

His brow was slick with a thin sheen of sweat, the salty droplets trickling down his temples. Shaking uncontrollably, his body betrayed him, and he tried to cover for his sudden groaning. "I pulled a muscle in my back. It hurts bad."

Her hand glistened—a radiant pearl nestled on porcelain canvas. Moving discreetly, he passed her a tissue, and she wiped away the evidence. Her fondling forced fiery trembles through his groin, making him pray for a moment of placidity; his genitals were overwhelmed, and the thought of engaging in another round so soon was unbearable.

"I-I need to go." He stumbled over a flimsy excuse and ended the broadcast. Relaxing his elbows, a burst of expletives fell from his lips. He rested his chin on his thumbs and pressed his nose against his fingers, staring her down under the desk. "That was so fucking hot, but there's no way nobody noticed."

She basked in erotic victory. "Are you a little less stressed?"

He reclined in his executive chair, stretching his arms above his head. "You have no idea how relaxed I feel."

Climbing out from between his legs, she pressed her lips against his, reaching to button his pants. "Good."

He found it erotic that she took care of him after taking such good care of him. "Thank you."

Pulling a mini hand sanitizer from her pocket, she broke into a giggle. "I need to wash my hands."

Checking his watch, he blushed. "It's about time to leave anyway. I'll walk you to the restroom."

Using a moment to smooth out the wrinkles in their clothes, they inspected each other's appearance to ensure they didn't give off the impression of being up to something suspicious.

He ran his hands through her hair, taming her waves. "Is it okay if I say you've made my week?"

She flattened his collar. "I'm off the hook for a week?"

Pulling her against his chest, he served a devious chuckle. "I'm not that easy to please, Mi Sol. There's no time off when it comes to what I want to do to you."

"Junie." She pretended to pout. "You're going to work me so hard. What did I ever do to deserve such treatment?"

His hands glided down her sides, the scorch from his palms radiating through her shirt. "*This* is what you did. I don't know how you expect me to work when all I can think about is you."

She expelled a squeal when he squeezed her backside. "You'll have to wait until we find time to be alone."

"We're never alone."

"Then I guess we'll have to create opportunities." She grabbed his hand, drawing him towards the door.

Reaching the lounge, they were met with the unexpected sight of his bandmates. Deok-Sun clenched his phone, giving off an accusatory glare. "What were you two *doing* in there?"

Hanjun's nonchalant shrug revealed a hint of tension. "Nothing, why?"

Jen's cheeks flushed cherry red. She didn't have regrets about *what* transpired; she felt guilty about *where* it transpired. "You guys were watching?"

"That was..." Hanso's voice dwindled. "Hot."

Jin's eyes widened. "I learned so much about Mommy Jen!"

Cringing, she wished she could erase the term from his vocabulary. "Can we use Noona instead?"

Soogi muttered a sly remark under his breath. "Since everyone's happy, can we go home?"

★⁺₊★☾★⁺₊★

The roommates were met with another package waiting outside their door, though the novelty was wearing off. Hanjun lugged the wrapped gift inside and abandoned it on the counter with previous deliveries.

Scurrying to his room, he opened the group chat, expecting a slew of playful jabs.

> **Honsa**: I've watched some adult films that started that way.
> **Jinja**: That is my mom, please don't talk about her like that!
> **Sunnie**: How do you think you were born, U-Jin? ㅋㅋㅋㅋ
> **Soogins**: Watch it. Hanjun reads the chat log.

He read through every line, familiar disappointment cutting through his enjoyment. Shoving the device aside, his interest turned to his tattered journal. With creases telling the story of his life, the pages never judged him like the world did.

She lingers in my thoughts. Her soul pierces into mine. In her eyes, I see a future. Every moment with her feels like a lifetime. I never want this feeling to end, and it scares me because nothing lasts forever.

CHAPTER FORTY-ONE

Jealousy is Punishment

Taking advantage of an ultra-rare occurrence—complete silence in the usually lively condo—Jen indulged in an extra-long shower. Hot water cascaded down her back, soothing her muscles and rejuvenating her senses. Afterward, she draped a towel around her body and returned to her room.

To her surprise, Hanjun sat on the floor, a massive box situated between his legs. "Your divider arrived."

She crossed the room, her feet sinking into the ivory rug protecting the hardwood. Opening both doors, she admired her entire closet at once. "I'm glad to hear that."

"I ordered one I thought would match your aesthetic." Struggling to open the cardboard, his stare drifted her way.

"I'm sure it will be perfect." Pulling clothing from the racks, she contemplated options in the full-length mirror. She caught him staring at an instruction booklet as if its pages held the secrets of the universe, purposely avoiding her gaze.

His resolve crumbled when the towel hit the floor. Thanking his lucky stars for the partially assembled screen, he risked another peek. Forcing his eyes down, he fired a frustrated growl. "You dropped your towel."

Unfazed by his early morning grumbling, she slipped into a skimpy pair of scarlet panties. Adjusting the lace over her hips, she maintained intense eye contact in the reflection. "It's hard to get dressed wearing one."

His face flushed—every curve on her body was hand-painted by a master of their craft. While she pulled on a matching red bra and adjusted the straps, he countered her sultry stare. "I just needed to stand this up, and you could have dressed behind it."

Harnessing a naughty smirk, she wiggled into a pair of slim-fitted jeans. Checking her contours in the mirror, she gave herself a hard slap on the rear. "Why are you blushing? You've seen me next to naked a handful of times."

He stood back to appreciate her beauty before remembering his objective: setting up the room divider. Aligning the legs, he moved the contraption to the corner, leaving room for her to dress behind. Tall enough to tower over him and vast enough to conceal every member of Blackmirror at once, the masterpiece boasted a white iron frame with watercolor panes. "It was the closest thing I could find to a galaxy."

Crossing the room, she held a shirt in her hand while inspecting the sparkling glass. "I'll wire you the money later."

Glimpsing downward, he realized she wore a bustier fashioned from the same fishnet material as her lower undergarments. "Consider it a gift."

She pulled the blouse over her chest and tied a knot in the back. "Jun, it looks expensive. Please let me pay you for it."

He planted a wet smooch on her forehead. "It *was* expensive. There's only one in the world; I had it made for you."

Her tone grew stern. "I don't feel comfortable accepting—"

He shushed her with a finger over her lips. "If you want to pay me back, take me on another date."

She felt oddly threatened by the challenge. "I'm going to have to come up with something grand, aren't I?"

Before he could respond, Jin walked past her door, feigning disgust. "Ugh! They're kissing again!"

"At least you don't have to endure their constant giggling all night." Soogi's sarcastic huff came from the adjacent room.

Slinking away from Hanjun, Jen snagged a thick book from her vanity. Moving to the kitchen, they sat at the dining table, waiting for the rest of their roommates to emerge.

"*A History of Korea: From Antiquity to the Present.*" Stretching for the novel, Hanjun fingered the glossy jacket. "Beginning from the Neolithic period? That's impressive."

"Ha-Rin recommended it." She tucked a loose strand of hair behind her ear. "I wasn't expecting it to be so pricey. The hardcover was $100."

He lowered the print. "American?"

"Yes." She duplicated his timbre. "I had to start taking notes because it's a lot to digest."

He placed the book on the table. "We have four years until our contracts end. What are your plans for after?"

She reached for his hand. "I'd like to buy a cozy cottage outside Chicago. Maybe something overlooking the water."

"You plan on going back to the States?" The words snared in his throat.

"I suppose." She released an undecided sigh. "As much as I love it here, Seoul isn't my home."

Uneasy tension settled over the discussion. Despite their mutual affection, there were clashes they needed to address. Massive, relationship-ending differences. "Tell me about your family. You've mentioned your mom's side and your Native heritage, but you've never revealed the last quarter."

Soogi and Hanso joined them, listening in on her answer.

"From my mom; German and Hungarian. From my father, a mix of Native American and Asian. My great-grandparents believed my father was half-Malaysian, but I'm not so sure. I never knew that part of my family, and my father refused to talk about them."

"I knew it." Soogi clapped upon hearing the possible Malaysian revelation. "I *told* you she had Asian features, but you guys kept insisting it was her Native roots."

Hanjun covered his face with his hands. "The night we met, they were speculating about your ancestry—"

Soogi scoffed. "That twenty-five percent has strong genes."

"You'd think the German gene would be dominant." Hanso apologized for his offensive quip. "Sorry, that's just awful."

"I didn't look like anyone in my family. At one point, my parents traced our lineage to multiple kings and a princess. I don't remember much about it—I was too young to care." A hint of bitterness seeped into her tone. "When my father left my mother, he took everything—wedding photos, pictures, even the silverware. I didn't have anything from my childhood. Sometimes it felt like I didn't exist."

⋆⁺₊⋆☾⋆⁺₊⋆

Snowflakes came down in a relentless storm, swirling and dancing in the wind. At the J&I tower, Ha-Rin loaded the staff onto a bus, ensuring everyone had a thermos of hot cocoa and a bundle of blankets. Jen sat in the back row next to Hanjun, where they huddled under a cover. Offering her an earbud, he allowed her influence over the music. Thirty seconds into a lively pop-goes-emo song of her choice, his phone dinged.

"It's my mom." Spatting off an apology, he snatched the device from her grasp. He sent a reply with a boyish smile and opened the front-facing camera.

Finding her face on the screen, she tried to duck out of the photo, but he yanked her into the frame. "Did you just—"

"Send that picture to my mom?" He returned the phone to her. "She doesn't know we're dating—she knows you live and work with us. Seeing me with a beautiful girl will make her smile."

Reminded that their connection was a guarded secret, a jagged ache crept into her stomach. Due to the demands of their respective jobs, it often felt like they weren't together, forced to pretend they weren't infatuated with each other. She knew the risks and understood the necessity, yet it pained her to not share their truth with the world.

He petted her hair. "I'd like you to meet her."

She gawked out the window, afraid that if she looked at him, he would notice the sorrow plaguing her heart. "I don't ever want you to be dishonest with your mother."

"Dropping the news on her so suddenly would cause unnecessary drama." What he didn't say was that he wanted to ensure their compatibility before introducing her to his family, knowing his mother's reaction would be overwhelming. Whenever he visited, she was on him about when he would bless her with grandchildren. Bringing a woman of childbearing age home would do little to curb her delusions.

★⁺₊★☾★⁺₊★

Following a winding ride up the mountains, the bus stopped at a wintry clearing. Descending the steps, Hanjun was struck by awe-inspiring tranquility—the rolling hills covered in patches of snow and crisp air were a refreshing change from Seoul's pollution. "Beautiful."

Standing near the door, Ha-Rin waited for the crew to exit. "We have something special planned, but you'll need to put in the work first."

Strutting to a stretch of snowfield, he motioned for them to follow. "You'll be divided into two groups: rap line versus vocal line. Jenilyn will join the vocalists to even out the teams. Your objective is to build a wall—or multiple walls, if you can manage—within two hours. After which, you'll compete in a game of Capture the Flag."

Jen and Hanjun stood beside each other, exchanging playful gestures behind their backs. Ha-Rin shook his head, addressing them specifically. "Keep in mind the editors are not magicians."

"We understand," they replied in unison, their faces crimsoning with embarrassment.

Ha-Rin gestured for Sehoon to take control of the rowdy adult-aged children. "Alright, let's get moving. We only have three hours to film."

Jin gathered the vocal line, huddling to discuss a strategy. "Let's make multiple forts so we have places to hide."

Jen nodded. "We can split into groups; you two work on one, and I'll form another."

"Sounds like a plan." Deok-Sun placed a hand in the circle.

With their hands stacked, they shouted into the sky. "Vocal line, go!"

Getting straight to business, Jen sprinted to the far end of the grounds and started creating a fort. Deok-Sun and Jin worked on one closer to enemy lines. While her roommates mounded snow into piles, she nabbed a stick to map the size and depth of the wall she planned to construct.

Across the battlefield, Hanjun stood with his eyes fixed on her. Spearing the stick in the snow, she darted back to the bus, returning a few minutes later with an empty milk carton. Falling to her knees, she tore off one side and began packing the cardboard. Shaping each glob into a block, she established the bricks in a half circle and applied extra snow as mortar to safeguard the hold.

"Check out Jen's wall." Soogi pointed to her. "She's building a whole castle over there."

"How the f—" Glancing at their defense, Hanjun frowned. Sparse and poorly constructed, the structure wouldn't protect a pennant, let alone entire bodies. "How is she almost done?"

"I overheard her talking. She wants to go home?"

Nodding, Hanjun gathered a blob of snow with his bare hands. "I never thought about what would happen after our contracts end. We were just having fun, you know?"

He ogled wistfully in her direction, his breath turning into smoke. "We're still having fun, but it's different now."

Soogi listened, unsure of how to support his bandmate. Love was something he brushed aside. He couldn't burden someone with the challenges of dating a musician—the scrutiny, lack of privacy, and inevitable hate. Though he sometimes yearned for a partner in crime, he decided it was better to worry about romance in another chapter of his life. "That's a tough situation."

Hanjun tore his admiration from Jen. "I always liked her, but I ended up liking her more than I thought I would."

Soogi nodded, his hands busy shaping snow into bulwarks. "There's always long distance. She doesn't seem like the jealous type."

Hanjun bit his tongue. "Let's hope she changes her mind."

On the other side of the field, Jen assembled with her teammates. "I'm all done; we should have no problem protecting our flag. Do you need help?"

Jin admired the fortress-sized wall she built on her own. "You've done enough."

"In that case, do you mind if I make a snowman?" Eyeballing the untouched grounds, her inner child ached to frolic. "That snow is full of dopamine. I just know it."

Jin chuckled. "Make sure it's on our side."

Light on her feet, she gathered handfuls of snow, compacting the mass into a firm ball. With a gentle push, she rolled the first snowball, carefully avoiding barriers, until it grew to the height of her thighs. She then repeated the process twice more, creating the body and head. Digging a hand in her pocket, she retrieved two cinnamon candies and plopped them on the smallest sphere. Clawing at the snow, she searched for pebbles, using them as the mouth and nose.

She stepped back to admire her work; the snowman had an almost sinister expression. "A little demonic..."

Rearranging the features, she ate one of the candies, moved some rocks to the eye sockets, and tossed the extras back into the snow. She positioned the remaining candy off to the side, creating a kissy face. "Much better."

While warming her wet hands in her pockets, a sudden impact hit her back. Revolving to nab the offender, she discovered Deok-Sun fleeing the scene. "Did you really? You really did that?"

Walking backward, he shook his head. "Me? Why would—"

"You asked for it, Deok-Sunnie." She scooped up a fistful of snow. Deok-Sun saw her coming and tried to escape, but she was too fast. Hurling the snowball, she struck him square in the breast.

"Ow!" He rubbed his torso and grabbed a chunk of snow, barely missing her.

"You suck." Discharging a victorious snicker, she picked up a gigantic globe of snow. Deok-Sun fled in a desperate attempt to avoid the glacial assault. Wiping out in a patch of ice, he fell and held his knee, emitting an echoing wail.

Ditching the snowball, she ran to his side. "Are you hurt?"

Expelling a simper of triumph, he grabbed her arm and mashed a wad of snow into her scalp. They tumbled in the powder for some time, but he eventually pinned her to the ground. "It's cute how you thought you could beat me. I admire your tenacity."

Pleased with himself, he restrained her hands at her sides. Witnessing her with red cheeks made him gawp in awe, and he hadn't noticed how green her eyes could be. She smelled of the cinnamon candy hidden in her cheek and an intoxicatingly decadent perfume. Resisting the sudden urge to lay his lips on her, he rolled over and helped her up. "Sorry."

Brushing powder from her coat, she tried to pinpoint when the situation became awkward. The childish game turned into a moment of vulnerability for Deok-Sun, and she didn't know how to diffuse the tension without drawing more attention. "Let's not let that happen again."

Standing behind Hanjun, Soogi chimed in with a sharp observation. "Deok-Sun still likes her."

Hanjun folded his arms, disapproving of Deok-Sun's romantic interest in his girlfriend. "He isn't right for her."

"That's not up to us to decide."

"Deok-Sun is—" Giving him a critical side-eye, Hanjun's response was cut short.

"Time's up! I see the vocalists created dual defenses." Holding two white flags, Ha-Rin beckoned them over, scanning the area for structures. "And a snowman? The rappers made one and a half walls."

"Snow*woman*." Jen pointed to the creation. "The top portion is anatomically correct."

Hanso cooked up a hasty joke. "Frost-she!"

Purging an exasperated breath, Soogi muttered a flat remark. "Why are you wasting your potential as a musician? You could be a successful comedian."

"Snowoman," Ha-Rin repeated. "The rules are simple: to win, your team must capture the enemy's flag and bring it back to your fort. Getting struck by the opposing team will eliminate you. You may return to your fort and rejoin the competition if a teammate tags you in. Everyone understand?"

Six nods of understanding were exchanged between the players before they took their positions on opposite sides of the clearing. A pair of friendly assistants stationed white flags at each command center, signaling the start of battle.

As soon as Ha-Rin blew the whistle, Jen's teammates charged forward while she remained behind to defend. Jin was eliminated by Hanso, but she tagged him in when he fell back. Soogi rushed to the stronghold, and she nailed him in the face with a snowball, sending him back to his starting position with swears spilling from his tongue.

Hanjun opted to cover their shelter. Afraid of being pummeled by a hard-packed snowball, he dove behind the crude walls whenever someone looked his way. Deok-Sun used the opportunity to infiltrate the zone. Crouching near the enemy bunker, he clutched a handful of snow, molding it into a perfect orb. The exact moment Hanjun popped up, he launched the projectile at his face and swiped the pendant.

Hanso and Soogi chased after Deok-Sun, who sprinted away and screamed at the top of his lungs. Jin met him halfway, running back to their garrison with ease. At their base, Deok-Sun claimed the standard and sang a victorious melody. "We are the champions!"

"Excellent work." Ha-Rin initiated a round of applause. "Let's close the set so we can get warmed up."

While the employees packed away camera equipment, the bandmates gathered for photos with the snowperson. Jen, tasked with manning a camera, noticed undeniable tension between Hanjun and Deok-Sun.

Returning to the bus, Jen sat next to Hanjun, who stared out the window toward the icy trees. She noticed the phone in his hand and tapped his sleeve. He handed it over without looking at her. After typing her take on the awkward situation, she passed it back to him.

Please don't be mad at Deok-Sun. It's not an excuse, but I'm around you guys all the time. It's easy to have a crush on someone you're around 24-7.

Tapping on the keyboard, he drew a deep breath. Following a few moments of silence, he turned the device toward her.

I need a moment alone.

"Okay."

Dropping the phone in his pocket, he didn't understand why he was so angry. The youngest's fascination with her was no secret, but his attraction was elementary. He admired her in the way young boys favored their older sibling's love interests. But even if he rationalized Deok-Sun's actions, he still struggled with his own envy. He'd been plagued with jealousy when a former girlfriend clung to too many male friends, but he was envious over Jen in a different way. He didn't feel jealous when she talked to other men; he was angry that they were taking away the limited time he had with her. Maybe it was selfish, but he wanted the small amount of time they shared to be exclusively his.

Ejecting a frustrated breath, he pulled out his mobile once again, typing his conflicted emotions.

Jealousy is the punishment for believing in love.

★⁺₊★☾★⁺₊★

Upon arriving home, Jen spotted a package in the hallway. Kicking the gift through the doorway, she barreled through the kitchen, ignoring curious questions from her roommates. Her tolerance had worn thin, and she needed to ruminate in her room before she unraveled on someone who didn't deserve her wrath.

Hanjun recognized her agitation and decided not to follow. Withdrawing to his room, he scrolled through the group chat.

> **Soogins**: You guys built an awesome fort.
> **Sunnie**: Mostly Jen.
> **Jinja**: Jen and Deok-Sun?
> **Sunnie**: It was harmless.
> **Honsa**: You need to make it right with Hanu.
> **Sunnie**: I know.
> **Soogins**: Not later. Now.

Not a moment later, Deok-Sun's shadow appeared in the doorway. "Hanu?"

Shooting him a glare, Hanjun removed his earphones. "Do you need something?"

Shuffling through the room, he fidgeted with the zipper on his sweater. "I had an impulsive thought, but I didn't act on it. I don't know what's wrong with me—seeing you together makes me wonder what being in a relationship is like."

Hanso tossed his horror manga aside. "Sunnie, you don't *like* her. You like the *idea* of her. Stop idolizing their relationship because you think it's ideal. You're doing the same thing the media does to you."

Deok-Sun nodded. "I'm sorry, Hyung."

Hanjun patted his knee. "If she felt like she was coming between us, I don't think she'd stay. She'd be on the next flight out of Incheon. I'm trying to keep her here. Do better."

"I will." Bowing, Deok-Sun scurried from the room.

Hanjun leaned against the headboard, producing his journal to document the day when Hanso made a telling declaration. "You love her."

"Love could not accurately describe how I feel." Hanjun inserted his earphones and picked up a pen.

We lost two games of Capture the Flag. Deok-Sun
wanted to kiss Jen, and I overreacted. Possessiveness
is an emotion I thought I had left in the past.

'It is not love that is blind, but jealousy.'

CHAPTER FORTY-TWO

Spreading Holiday Cheer

The weight of guilt suffocated Jen as soon as her eyes opened. What started as an innocent wintry duel between housemates snowballed into an agitation for Hanjun. Exhaling a prolonged breath, she added a final swipe of balm to her lips and headed to the kitchen, hoping to find Hanjun in an improved mood.

His austere expression turned jovial, though he kept the conversation to a minimum. "I made you a coffee."

"Thanks." She reached for the beverage. Leaning on the cabinet, she deliberated how to resolve the conflict.

Shuffling through, Soogi greeted her and moved to the pastries on the counter. "Good morning."

"Morning." She drummed on her cup. Hanjun remained mute, browsing through his phone. Desperate to escape the tension, she pivoted to the door and retrieved a coat from the closet. "I'll wait outside."

Hanjun darted after her, catching the elevator right before the doors closed. "Are you not speaking to me today?"

She snorted, fumbling to adjust the toggle buttons of her outerwear. "I thought *you* weren't speaking to *me*."

He flourished a guilty grin and adjusted his jacket. "I'm sorry for how I acted last night."

Exiting the lift in the lobby, she hushed him, eyeing fellow condominium residents resting on decorative chairs. All it took was one nosy neighbor or media-savvy teenager with a few thousand Instagram followers to spark a slew of news reports. With Hanjun and every member of the band, she needed to assume the role of assistant.

While waiting for their escort, the rising sun cast a glow in their eyes. Enveloping one arm around her back, Hanjun pulled her close. "My jealousies get the best of me, and I revert back to having a lizard brain. All that matters to me is being with you."

"Not here." Longing for a heartfelt moment of reconciliation, she pushed him away.

Sulking, his hands fell to his sides. "Fame is a curse."

"You don't mean that."

"I do if it means I can't hug you. I knew what I signed up for, but I never imagined meeting you."

She chuckled at his flair for the melodramatic. "You met me *because* you were famous."

"You don't know." His face remained expressionless—a skill mastered from years of coping with the paparazzi. "We could have met at another time. I might have visited Chicago, or you may have visited Korea."

She jostled his shoulder. "This is the only reality that matters. There's no time for what-ifs."

Whining, he returned the bump. "Maybe not, but they sure are fun to think about."

★⁺₊★❬★⁺₊★

A black van rolled to a stop at an establishment just outside Seoul, and the musicians emerged from the vehicle, catching faint barking emanating from the doors. They ventured inside with their cinematographers and waited for Ha-Rin to go over the day's objectives.

"Welcome to Blackmirror's 'Spreading Holiday Cheer' campaign. Today, you'll be devoting time to our less fortunate companions." Ha-Rin signaled to an elongated corridor, eyeballing Hanjun and Jen. "Remember to monitor what you say on camera. Go on. Pick a pal."

Jen tailed Hanjun through the building, her heart aching at the sight of each confined animal. She released a cage as Hanjun called for a pooch, and a small ball of fluff hobbled to her—an underweight Maltese mix with snow-colored fur. Aside from a reddish-brown spot over his left eye, he looked to have been no more than two years old.

She scooped up the dog and twisted to show Soogi. "I found my guy."

"What a cutie." Soogi cooed, envious of the fuzzy friend.

Stroking the pooch's wispy chin hair, Hanso nudged Soogi out of the way. "Who's a good boy?"

Collapsing to sit on the floor, she formed a play yard with her legs. Hanjun joined her, accompanied by his furry side-kick—a goofy brown Corgidor. "He's a fluffy little guy."

She snuggled the dog's soft coat. "He reminds me of my first pet, Ofi. He was a stunning wolf mix."

"What happened to him?" He caressed the chocolate mutt's velvety muzzle.

"He went to the eternal petting zoo." She paused to fix his ears. "That's what I like to believe, anyway."

"It's heartbreaking, isn't it?" He petted the half-lab's chin, thinking of his companion. He welcomed the hairy friend in his twenties but relied on his parents to look after him. "We forget how fast they age. We must be like gods to them."

His timbre possessed a deep ache, but as the cameras approached, he slipped into his stage persona. "We're at our local sanctuary, spreading joy to our furry friends. Consider volunteering your time to enhance the life of an animal in need."

As a part of their affiliation with the organization, the shelter's staff members introduced each canine and shared their heartbreaking stories. Hanjun translated for Jen, who held the little dog next to her breast. "His owner didn't want him due to the brown spot over his eye. He's considered different. He's without a name, and the workers call him Splotch."

The caretakers carelessly dubbed him 'ugly,' but he couldn't bear to convert the term.

"That's so sad." She protected his ears. "Don't listen to them. You're perfect."

His heart palpitated as she cradled the animal. "You could adopt him, you know."

"When would I have the time?" She planted a smooch between the dog's eyes. "I hope you find your forever family soon."

⋆⁺₊⋆☾⋆⁺₊⋆

Ready to unwind after an extended day of taping, the housemates trudged home. They encountered another package in the hallway but were too exhausted to open it. Jin added it to a pile of unopened parcels on the kitchen counter, which the maid would later discard. With collective disinterest, they focused on their much-needed rest.

Drained, Hanjun climbed into bed, depleting his last fragment of energy by scrolling through the group chat. Despite the bizarre deliveries and mysterious sender, the conversation was overflowing with light-hearted repartee and festive cheer, providing normalcy in an otherwise peculiar situation.

> **Soogins**: Jen fell in love with her dog.
> **Honsa**: Mine was a cutie!
> **Sunnie**: He was a cute ball of fur.
> *Would you guys be against getting a dorm dog?*
> **Honsa**: Sure. I miss mine.
> **Jinja**: I wouldn't mind.
> **Soogins**: We'd have to work on a schedule for walking a pet.

Moving the mobile aside, Hanjun accessed his diary.

> *Arguing over Deok-Sun having a small crush on her*
> *will do nothing but cause a rift between us.*

CHAPTER FORTY-THREE

Breakup & Admittance

The weightlessness of waking up enveloped Jen. Feeling a familiar presence in her bed, she smiled as Hanjun crawled towards her under the covers. Bringing her lips to his neck, she relished their closeness.

Hands sweeping to her hair, he cautioned against teasing him. "Don't start anything you aren't prepared to finish."

A smile played at the edges of her lips. "It's like that?"

Too tired to engage in banter, he gazed at her with heavy-lidded eyes. "Yeah, it's like that."

"If you say so." She maneuvered onto her knees and pulled the blanket over her head. Through the shadows, he fumbled for her waist, drawing her closer, and his fingers traced up her spine, tugging on her shirt. She raised her arms, allowing him to remove the fabric.

Maintaining eye contact, he moved his hands to cup her breasts, flicking his thumbs over her hardened nipples. "Did you dream of me? You seem very happy to see me."

"I'm always happy to see you." Stifling a giggle, she pulled back from him. "Be quiet. Soogi hears everything."

Straddling his thighs, she felt a solid bulge rising to meet the occasion. Tracing her finger along his jawline, she trailed kisses over his sculpted chest. His body tensed at the sensation of her cool lips descending over his hot skin. Positioned between his knees, she ran a palm over his sweatpants and planted feathery kisses around the waistband of his boxers.

"Mi Sol..." Eyes screwed shut, he gasped as her wet kisses inched closer to his prized possession.

Tugging his pants down, she wrapped her hand around the base of his penis and began a tender stroke, forcing a mellow moan from him. Issuing a delicate reminder about remaining silent, she lowered her lips to him, holding a seductive gaze. Extending her tongue, she licked around the head of his erection before putting him wholly in her mouth, using both hands to rub in a gentle, twisting motion.

Haphazardly grasping a fistful of her hair, the muscles in his legs stiffened. "Fuck—"

She liberated him from her throat and flicked her tongue underneath his head. Expelling a lengthy groan, his body convulsed, sending waves of ecstasy from his groin to every extension. The sensation of her touch spread to his toes, leaving him wondering how she knew his body better than he did.

"Do you like that?" Continuing a rhythmic stroke, she stared up at him with innocent eyes. Accumulating a mouthful of saliva, a trail of spit left her tongue, lubricating her swiveling wrists.

Restricting his volume, he muttered the only word his brain would form in a moment of euphoria. "Yes—yes."

Biting his lip, he urged her to proceed. She held a sensual glare and descended without his guidance, filling her throat entirely. With each hastened pass she made over his length, he knew he wouldn't be able to hold out.

"I'mgonnacome—" Legs trembling, a groan slipped out of his mouth before he could stop it. His words scrambled, resembling a bizarre forum username. He had intended to give her more notice of his pending ejaculation, but he feared even taking a breath would result in him pleading for her hand in marriage instead of finishing down her throat.

She held him until the pulsations ebbed, and he uncaged a satisfied sigh. Slowly, his stiffened muscles relaxed, and he loosened his grip on her hair. Allowing the comforter to slip from her shoulders, she wiped the corners of her mouth and sat up. "I think *you* may have dreamt of *me*."

Reclining, every inch of his body pulsed with spent pleasure. He reached for a bottle of water on the nightstand, thankful for the refreshing coolness on his parched tongue. Leaning forward, he incited an adoring kiss on her lips. "You are in every dream and every dream I will ever have."

Gulping a few sips of water, she slipped off the bed and grabbed her blouse from the tangled sheets. Cracking the door, she peeked out to make sure their roommates were asleep. Satisfied with the silence, she scampered across the hall.

Turning on the shower, she shivered and stripped. Hearing him moan made her hot, and she thought it was sexy how he begged for her to continue. He wanted her to finish him so badly that he would have done anything to make it happen, and it was a power she enjoyed having.

Scrubbing her skin, she considered pleasuring herself, but Soogi lingered in the back of her mind. He complained of hearing their late-night conversations and easily recalled what they were talking about. "I hope he didn't hear anything."

Returning to her room cloaked in a towel, she found Hanjun lying on his side, the bedspread covering his waist. "Deok-Sun replaced the container of sugar scrub he used."

"He sure does love that stuff." He watched as she approached the closet, choosing a comfortable outfit: a white baggy sweatshirt and black jeans with an oversized red rose applique on one leg. "Going somewhere?"

"To the agency with Hanso." Yanking the bottoms over her hips, she buttoned the fly. "We're breaking up, remember?"

He sported the most ridiculous smile. "Fucking finally."

"I'm sure it will come with its own set of problems." She stuffed a tube of lip balm, her agency-provided phone, and a tin can of cinnamon mints in her pockets.

A public separation wouldn't make their headaches disappear. If anything, the publicity would heighten them. The agency warned her she could become a target for crazed fans who believed Hanso was mistreated. After weeks of research, the analysts at J&I predicted the media would refer to her as the *American Siren*. Of course, they promised to do everything in their power to keep the name from sticking.

"I'll call you when it's done." She edged toward the bed, plopping a kiss on his forehead.

Taking her hand, he left a peck on the back. Her skin bore the familiar scents of her favorite perfume and chai spice shampoo. "I'll meet you there. I need to get a workout in."

"Why don't you use the gym here at the complex? I've gone a few times. They have everything you could want."

He stretched out, adjusting a pillow beneath his head. "I don't have to worry about someone snapping photos at the office."

"Right. I sometimes forget you're famous." She turned for the door. Venturing down the hallway, she met Hanso in the kitchen, wondering how long he had been waiting. "Sorry, I—"

"Don't worry about it." He gestured to the door. "Are you ready to break up?"

"Beyond ready."

⋆⁺₊⋆☾⋆⁺₊⋆

Bypassing security at the J&I tower, Hanso escorted Jen to the twelfth floor. While Hanjun's studio was located on the east wing and Soogi's on the south, Hanso's was situated at the northern end.

"What's on the west wing?" Traveling the long corridor to his studio, she noticed how the walls were lined with candy-colored pop culture memorabilia.

"We share a floor with J." He flashed a charming smile, but there was a hint of envy in his tone. "He's a legend in Korea. And the golden boy of the agency."

Scoffing, she failed to understand how an artist could be promoted under a singular letter. It sounded like a copyright nightmare. "Is that his whole name?"

"His name is Hyun-Woo. He never officially released why he chose the stage name." Jiggling the handle to his workroom, he flung the door open. "I call it the 'Galaxy of Hanso!'"

She had no idea what to expect from his studio, but it wasn't what she imagined. The walls were burnt orange—a color she had never witnessed him wear—and the room was messy, boasting more elements of comfort than his bandmates.

In the corner, there was a cluster of plush toys, with plenty of room in the center for dancing. On one side of the desk sat a miniature fridge, fully stocked with flavored vitamin water. Although he had a collection of trinkets—mainly Star Wars collectibles—she was taken aback by how disorganized the shelving was. He was particular about maintaining order, both at home and at work, and was quick to point out any lapses in contribution, yet his space was lawless.

Kicking off her shoes at the door, she crossed the room and moved a Murakami stuffed toy from the sofa. Sinking into the seat, she kept her hands close to her body. "It's *orange*."

"It's *energizing*." Joining her on the other end of the seating, he relaxed his slippered feet on the computer chair. "The agency wants us to go live in fifteen minutes."

She nodded, feeling edgy in his workspace. Out of the roommates, she was the least acquainted with him, and she was positive that being coerced into dating created a rift between them. While the charade neared its end and freedom was within sight, she was appreciative of the experience. If given a choice, she would pick him again as her fake partner. His snarky and mischievous nature didn't hide his compassionate heart. He never manipulated their forced proximity, and their combined suffering only strengthened her discrepancy with arranged partnerships.

She refused when her great-grandmother suggested she marry Tisho as a young woman, though she sometimes doubted her rejection was the right decision. Marrying a full-blooded tribesman would have ensured their children were sixty percent blood, thus preserving culture through ancestry.

Back then, she entertained the idea for her family's sake. Tisho was praised among the tribe; despite the world's accusations about his appearance, he lived his life in such a way that nothing could stick to him. He had a pure heart, and at his core, he was devoted to being with one woman. For him, a committed bond was a priority, and he saw it as his duty to create a family. Unfortunately, life has a way of disrupting plans, as evidenced by the disaster of his first union. Though he lost half of his possessions, wealth, and self-respect during the merger, he took accountability for his actions and carried the guilt of infidelity.

Aside from a momentary lapse of judgment, he was respectable. Just as her elders educated her about ceremonial phytotherapy, he learned to treat others with honor: older men were like fathers, younger men like brothers, older women like mothers, and younger women like sisters. The teachings extended to all beings. Every cloud, every raindrop, and every speck of dirt on the earth were treated with reverence.

He was hardworking and exuded the qualities of impeccable superiority—confident eye contact, clear communication, and intelligent conversation. When he took on a new project, he followed through without making flimsy excuses. He was flawed, but when he made mistakes, he devised a plan to fulfill his commitments.

He exemplified the qualities of a cultural foreman. By day, he managed his own company, Raven's Nest Homes, which specialized in building timber lodging along the Great Lakes. In his free time, he volunteered at local libraries, reading to children and holding seminars to promote Chickasaw culture. He also convinced Jen to write tribal-based children's stories, which he illustrated himself.

She could spend her whole life listing all the reasons she should have favored Tisho. He was incredibly patient, genuine, and sincere. He retained discipline, integrity, and an impregnable moral compass. He wasn't easy to anger, violent, or argumentative. He was clothed in humility, and Jen suspected he was one of the holiest men who had ever walked the earth.

She couldn't even blame her dismissal on his appearance because the man was as close to a god as any human could be. His chiseled body, strong features, and smooth voice were the personification of tall, dark, and handsome—everything every book claimed she should swoon over. And it wasn't only Jen who noticed his attractiveness, either. His charms worked on every woman in his vicinity, including her great-grandmother, though she had a sneaking suspicion the matriarch held a fondness for him simply because he was the great-grandson of her first love.

A tragic tale known throughout the clans: many moons before Jen was an embryo, her great-grandmother roamed the land. Her father toiled to reclaim sizeable portions of their ancestral Homeland and moved their family soon after her birth.

Achukma was a gifted child who enjoyed escaping into the forests to gather wild grapes and nuts. During her excursions, she also collected medicinal plants like yaupon holly, willow, cedar, feverwort, and snakeroot for the elders in her community. Her grandmother—an experienced tribal alikchi—recognized her affinity for harvesting and purported she would one day prove a healer. One couldn't choose to be an alikchi—they were divinely elected and inherently possessed a vast store of knowledge about the fated gifts.

Committed to preserving the Homeland, she spent her childhood studying a blend of standardized education and tribal teachings. Entering adolescence, she recognized the necessity of learning sacred psychological, physiological, and spiritual healing techniques and embraced the teachings as a benison.

Sadly, the medicinal arts were negatively impacted by the suppression of Native culture in the twentieth century, and its practitioners were reluctant to share knowledge with outsiders. The practices dwindled until only a few retained comprehensive knowledge, and Achukma was one of the last tribesmen to safeguard a full catalog of remedies.

As a young girl, she didn't think much about her successors beyond the fact that she would have them. Both because she desired to start a family and because it was expected of her. In the Chickasaw tribe, as well as the closely affiliated Choctaw and Natchez tribes, kinship was matrilineal. Women held prominence, with heredity traced through the mother's bloodline. Children inherited their family name from their mother, and matrons were responsible for managing resources and dwellings. If a couple separated, it was the man who would move out of the woman's home.

By the time she came of age, the lineage numbers were decreasing, and despite relaxing traditions, her family encouraged her to carry out the sacred practices in hopes of preserving the nation. Her bloodborne clan, the Shawi', held high positions of dominion, with leaders and healers elected exclusively from the line. To promote unity, women from the clan were required to marry outside their class. Alliances were formed through bloodlines, resulting in a roulette wheel of commitment, and the remaining ten clans expected members from their ranks to be anointed by the ruling class. To facilitate the process, young girls were placed around boys from the intended family, ensuring eventual weddings.

But Achukma resided in her tribe's territory, not alongside the Chickasaw nation. Fellow tribespeople were scarce, and she didn't stop to think about the potential consequences before falling in love with a young man from the Nashoba' Clan. Known as warriors, they were esteemed for producing combat chiefs. His name, Hopaya, meant 'war prophet,' though she never saw him as the warmongering type. He was a sweet boy who accompanied her on herb gathering trips and won her affection by creating contraptions to make her foraging easier. They united over their family histories; his ancestor, Tishominko, was a noble counselor to her relative, Piominko, in the seventeenth century.

Through the years, they bonded through shared experiences, like any other young couple. However, when the time came for conjugality, she was faced with cosmic irony. The Nani', offspring of exceptional hunters, were pressuring her kin to provide a wife for one of their men. The issue had never been significant as there was a surplus or negative at any given time, which would be rectified with the next coupling. However, the Fish Clan were twenty promised marriages behind. The other nine clans were relatively caught up in terms of partnerships, leading the Nani' to believe they were intentionally unfavored.

Achukma was commanded to marry a man from the Nani' Clan, while Hopaya was tasked with finding a suitable bride from the Foshi' clan. Their love story became a legend among the tribe, but they fulfilled their duties as members of their communities and asserted it was for the greater good.

The matriarch revered Jen as her greatest accomplishment—not her own offspring or curative abilities. She was a source of joy and pain—the reason for the tragic circumstances—but also a symbol of hope for redemption. The same fiery spirit burning inside her blazed within Jen, and Achukma trusted she was destined to become the next healer. The matron made it a point to pass on the rituals, traditional restorative practices, and sacred fire preparation to her great-granddaughter. She organized gatherings with the ascendants, ensuring the child was well integrated. And on special occasions, she took Jen back to their Homeland to gather herbs.

It was during one of her foraging trips that Jen met Tisho. She was five years old, picking berries from a tree, when Tisho, a few years her senior, joined her. He teased her about being so selective and boasted about knowing the woods like the back of his hand. Jen didn't argue and pretended she had no idea what she was doing. Little did he know, she trained in herbalism from the moment she was born and could identify native plants by mere sight.

He plucked a basket of fruits, and she warned him that not all bushes were what they seemed. But he was too smart to listen to a five-year-old and continued picking. On the way back to their homes, he ate grapes by the palmfuls, his hands and mouth stained deep plum. By the time they reached their backyard, he was deathly nauseous. Before parting ways, Jen handed him a bundle of feverwort, insisting he eat the roots. Aware that her relative was a village healer, he ingested the radicles and vomited purple sludge. Only after did she tell him the grapes he ate were pokeberries—poisonous to humans.

Tisho learned a humbling lesson, and he never again exaggerated his skills. The awkward first encounter blossomed into friendship, and they visited each other every year. Some visits took place in Mississippi, while others were in Chicago. And as the children played outdoors, the grandparents relived the good times, sharing hope that their lineage would merge through the next generation.

Tisho was blindsided by something akin to a slow-acting poison. He didn't realize his love for Jen until he was nearly an adult. He had dated a few girls during middle and high school, but nobody compared to her. Much like Hopaya and Achukma, Tisho suspected everything in their family's history led to their conjunction. Jen's grandmother experienced justice after enduring decades of trauma, but there was more heartache on the horizon. She didn't share the same romantic attraction.

On paper, he was the perfect man. The type of hunk women would sell their souls to spend one night with. Everyone swooned over Tisho, but none of it mattered. She didn't feel the way he did, and not only did she crush his heart, but she also shattered her great-grandmother's hopes and his great-grandfather's pipe dream. In one confession, she dismantled their plan to break a generational curse.

Jen couldn't blame anyone except her own heart, and Tisho didn't deserve her rejection. She couldn't even offer a concrete reason. Love was a foreign concept to her, yet their families demanded a list of reasons for refusing the proposal. But how could she know what love was when she couldn't define it? And if she couldn't define love, how could she be sure of her feelings for someone else?

Achukma didn't take kindly to her lack of reasoning and pressured her into accepting the proposition using less-than-ideal methods. If love wouldn't work, perhaps guilt would. After all, she married Jen's great-grandfather to unite the clans. Why couldn't Jen do the same?

The constant pressure became too much, and Jen reached a point where she didn't want to be associated with the tribe. She burst into tears during a stomp dance and retracted her membership sometime after the new millennium.

The outburst from her disobedient grandchild incited embarrassment for Achukma, but Hopaya urged her to listen to Jen's plea. Standing before the eleven tribes, she apologized to Tisho for her refusal and explained how trapped she felt. Her tears streamed, and she found the courage to express her innermost thoughts about the ongoing marital war.

Her words were directed first to her grandmother. "Grandmother Achukma, I've watched you suffer from your father's choice. Maybe your marriage had some good times, but from the outside, all I see is misery."

She then addressed Tisho's grandfather. "Grandfather Hopaya, Tisho told me about how you used to pick roots. For years, you secretly left them on my grandmother's doorstep."

Revolving to address her kin, her voice trembled. "Two lovers were torn apart, left to mourn the ashes of a smoldering flame, and for what? It didn't bring our tribe back from the brink of nonexistence, nor did it teach our language to a new generation. It was nothing more than meaningless slaughter, breeding suffering and codependency of the mind, leaving only illness in the hearts of those affected."

Her accusations were harsh and unjust, but she was young and reckless. She didn't care to filter her words. "You've twisted a naturally occurring element into an unending cycle of destruction. You thrust yourselves into parenthood when you were too young and filled the gaping hole in your hearts with distractions. You depend on each other's pain—stuck in a perpetual loop of justification—because that's all you know. You cling to animosity with unyielding stubbornness, deferring a legacy of sorrow spanning generations."

And then it happened. She said the worst thing she could have possibly said. "What you call obligation, I call disease."

"You are a stupid girl." For the first time, Achukma violated her own rule and raised a hand to her grandchild. "If you weren't so busy tramping around with that Chicago beggar boy, you would be able to see what's best for you."

Squaring her chest, Jen's teeth ground together. "He has nothing to do with my decision."

Scoffing, Achukma cackled. "The boy you love will amount to nothing, and even if he does, he'll go back to his country. You know that, right? First loves never end the way you want."

Discomforted but not discouraged, Jen held a palm to her stinging cheek, quoting her grandmother's motto on corporal punishment. "Why is it when an adult hits another adult, it's called assault, but when an adult hits a child, it's discipline?"

Tisho stepped forward to offer his perspective. "She's right. Obligation has poisoned our way of life. Are we not matrilineal? Don't we value the women who bear our future? I'm tired of hearing what others think love should be. We're required to play these games of commitment, but not a single one of you has asked if we understand what it means to be in love."

He turned to Jen and spoke with the first bit of sincerity she had heard in months. "I'm asking you, not only as your friend but as someone who cares—how do you define love?"

"Imperfection." Her one-word statement caused a handful of chuckles, but she stood by her truth. "You're expecting me to give some kind of cliché metaphor to describe something infinite, but it's so much larger than words. It's more comprehensive than all of us. Love is simultaneous fondness and contempt. Effortless and arduous unease. Everyone talks about the pleasant parts, but why is no one talking about the bad times? The moments when you're fighting with your spouse and you're disgusted. Or when you feel so drained that getting out of bed is impossible? How can we anticipate successful relationships without knowing *both* sides? You can't understand something if you only know half of it."

Tisho nodded in forgiving observation. "We've been fed a fairy tale while tolerating nightmares."

Uniting with Achukma's obstinate gaze, Jen made use of the mother tongue, underscoring her decision. "I will never have a definition for love, but I know it's much more complex than everyone makes it out to be. I don't want anything to do with it until I can treat it with the consideration it deserves."

Achukma's hands balled into fists, though her anger simmered down when Hopaya placed a palm on her shoulder. "She's doing what we never had the courage to do."

Approaching Jen wearing cultural attire, Achukma reached for her shoulders. It struck her like a lightning bolt—the juvenile had surpassed the teachings of her elders. She was consumed with regret for pushing her grandchild to conform, just as her own father had done to her. "I can no longer force my dreams on you. You must forge your own path. Only you can know what's right for you."

For seven nights, the Holy Fire blazed, symbolizing the beginning of a new era—one defined by personal choices rather than inherited debts. Jen was freed from obligations that had plagued her since birth, and while she continued to embrace her origins, she also explored other aspects of her identity.

Tisho respected Jen's choices without resentment. In time, they married other people, though their bond was unbreakable. In many ways, Tisho gave her the freedom she longed for; without him, she would have had no choice but to bow to her family's demands or withdraw from the tribe. Only when he spoke on her behalf was her voice heard.

Years passed, and both Jen and Tisho went through divorces. Jen started to believe her family was right; perhaps true love didn't exist. Or maybe her life was a bad rom-com and her ideal partner was an overlooked friend the whole time. One year after her divorce—enough time to heal—she called Tisho for a possible reconciliation. But something felt wrong; choosing Tisho because of his blood was not her idea of love. And surely, it couldn't have been his ideal vision of love, either.

On the night of their first planned date—which coincidentally happened to be the same night she encountered Blackmirror—a series of unexpected events delayed their meeting. It was almost as if fate offered her one last chance before she threw in the towel.

Hanjun was a significant influence on her, but even if they hadn't started dating seriously, after her encounter with Hanso, she would never take love for granted again. She was grateful for the freedom to choose her partners, and she honored Achukma by following her heart, even if it led her into trouble.

Hanso rubbed a thumb along his shaved chin. "While I have you alone, I wanted to talk to you about Hanjun. What are your plans with him?"

Shrugging, she didn't have an answer. "I'm not sure."

He bobbed along, giving a long-winded response. "I've always looked up to Hanjunie. Seeing him with you brings my heart such happiness, but he is temperamental. He might push you away if he thinks he's losing himself. We've all made excuses for the things he's done, saying we're kids and make stupid decisions—we aren't kids anymore, and we can't make excuses for each other. He is a man in mind but an adolescent at heart. He thinks he's not worthy of love; time and time again, his lack of self-love causes him strife."

She slumped. From what she witnessed, Hanjun boomeranged between thinking he was the best thing on earth and feeling unworthy of anything. There was never a point where he wavered between the extremes. "I wish I could tell you we'll be together forever and give you bunches of nieces and nephews, but the realist side of me knows better. I love what we have, but I don't expect it to last. Being an artist is hard, and I sometimes feel like a burden."

"He has blossomed into a happier person before our eyes, and you are solely to thank for that." He wanted to tell her more about the old Hanjun. He battled demons, some of them disgraceful, but it wasn't his place to tell her who he used to be. He wondered if it mattered. The Hanjun she knew was nothing like his former self.

She compelled her lips to part. "I love him. I don't know if I could ever tell him that."

Leaning in, he wrapped his arms around her. "I know you do."

His hug was more comforting than hot cocoa on a wintry day, yet thinking about an indistinct future made her heart lurch. Caught between wasting her time and enjoying the moment, she was willing to navigate the eventual heartbreak. To her, he was worth an irreparably broken heart.

Pulling back from their embrace, he walked her to his desk, where he pulled up a chair. Retrieving a bucket hat from a table lamp, he concealed her face. He motioned for her to keep her eyes down and started a stream, greeting his fans with an affable opening. "It's me, Hanso! And this is my friend, Jen. We went live to clear the air. Jen, do you want to explain?"

"I-umm... Okay, so first, hi Anti!" Buffering, she tried to remember the carefully devised script given to her by the public relations department. "Hanso and I have been friends for a while, and we tried the whole dating thing—it's not for us."

"Jen, I like you in a sisterly kind of way." Brandishing a smile, he held out a fist. "We can still be friends?"

"I'd love that." She joined his fist with hers.

Moving his eyes to the camera, he gave her a soft tap on the back. "Jen's going to relax while I answer questions."

Returning to the couch, she tilted her head back. Though the relationship came to an end, she harbored apprehension. The fake media play was too publicized for it to fade into non-existence. She contemplated if she would ever escape the cruel headlines or if she would be attached to Hanso in the way Cher was connected to Sonny or Tina was joined to Ike.

Her thoughts ran wild with scenarios of not being able to shed Hanso's name when Hanjun walked in carrying a paper cup of coffee. Giving her a wink, he strutted to Hanso's desk and greeted the camera. "I hear there was news!"

"Hanjun is here, everybody." Hanso saluted him with a supportive introduction.

After a short greeting, Hanjun sat next to her. Pulling out his phone, he discreetly turned the screen toward her.

This morning was amazing.

Taking the device from his hand, she tapped in a reply.

I hope Soogi didn't hear anything. You were LOUD.

Retrieving the phone, he blushed and typed a message.

I couldn't help it. You sucked the soul out of me.

Reading the statement, she choked on a laugh.

I'm glad you loved it.

He sheepishly hid his face.

I loved it so much, I'd do it again.

She snorted and covered her mouth.

You're unholy.

"I can't wait to do it again," he whispered in his deepest, sexiest voice. "Except next time, I want to taste *you*."

She slapped his knee. "Junie!"

On the ride home from the office, Hanjun listened to music and combed through the comments of his recent live: the sensual broadcast with the impromptu handy job. Many fans were in favor of the racy stream, despite community forums dragging him for displaying hypersexuality.

'LOL @ THE COMMENTS ASKING WHAT THEY WERE DOING. GIRL, IF YOU KNOW, YOU KNOW.' —ANALBUMCOVER

'YAS GIRL, GET IT!' —IEXISTWITHOUTCONSENT

'HE CAME BACK AND ADJUSTED HIS PANTS FOUR TIMES. FOUR TIMES. WE MUST KEEP ASSISTANT JEN. SHE BRINGS US THAT REAL CONTENT!' — ONCEBITTENTWICEWRY

'WE CAN ONLY LIVE VICARIOUSLY THROUGH HER.' — YOUNEVERFORGETYOURFIRST

'THIS VIDEO SHOULD BE LABELED AS NSFW.' —BILLNYETHERUSSIANSPY

The video had the most views of any webcast he'd done in his career, generating a slew of articles, both positive and negative. Without hard evidence and no actual pornographic material shown during the visual, nothing could be proved beyond speculation. There was only one person on earth who knew what went on in his studio, and he knew she'd never tell a soul.

She held no shame for indulging in their needs in the same way any new couple would—in a constant state of lust and magnetized attraction with desperation to act on the desire.

Tucking the phone away, he was surprised he hadn't received a strongly worded email from Ha-Rin about the incident. Or even worse, Mr. Yun.

The roommates arrived home to find another package outside the door. Damaged and torn, the parcel wasn't protected with gift wrap and looked to have been battered.

"Did it fall down a flight of stairs?" Jen opened the box to find a photo of her and Hanso from the live stream. Her name was written above the photograph in red splotches, and the ink stained her fingers. "It couldn't have been here long. It's not even dry yet."

"Someone must be mad about you breaking up." Deok-Sun speculated from over her shoulder.

Her eyes shadowed in concern. "Should I be worried?"

Jin begrudged a smile. "We've received threats in the past. Most are from anti-Anti."

Nudging her through the threshold, Hanjun hugged her from behind. "It's a cause for concern. I'll discuss it with Ha-Rin and see what he thinks."

A knot formed in the pit of her stomach; it was the first time she felt scared since her move. "I knew ending the relationship would be too easy."

Dropping the photograph on the kitchen table, she retreated to her room. "I'm gonna lay down. Make sure you eat something other than noodles for dinner."

Unsure how to comfort her, Hanjun went to his room, pausing to check the group chat.

> **Honsa**: Jen's being targeted because of me.
> **Soogins**: Maybe not.
> **Sunnie**: Yeah, Hanu's livestream made national coverage.
> **Jinja**: Must be a stalker.
> **Sunnie**: What if it's Haeseong?
> **Honsa**: How would he know where we live?
> **Sunnie**: Who knows anymore.

Reaching for a pen, he tried to capture the uneasiness tearing through his heart, but the words were lost amid desire.

She's done with Hanso. It couldn't have come at a more perfect time. I have some concerns over the photo we received. God, I want to be near her all the time. I'm obsessed, infatuated, and drowning in her.

CHAPTER FORTY-FOUR

Are You Sure?

Jen trotted to Hanjun's room, peering in to find the pair of roommates awake. Hanso sprawled in bed, watching videos on his phone, while Hanjun scribbled in a notebook, pausing to greet her. "Good morning, Mi Sol."

Crossing the room, she poked his belly, knowing it would make him smile. With his smile came his dimples. "Morning."

He dropped the pen to address her. "We need to visit the office. I know you want to stay home, but I hope you'll reconsider."

"I'd rather not." She slumped against the headboard. "I could use some me time, plus, I have something I want to do after you leave."

Nodding, his knuckles brushed hers. "In that case, I'm gonna get my hair done before I leave the agency. We have a few appearances coming up. I need to look my best."

Accustomed to seeing blueish-haired Hanjun, she frowned. "What color are you going with this time?"

He held a mischievous grin. "Which did you like the most?"

She laughed, covering her early-morning swollen cheeks. "Anything but your pre-debut braids."

Hanso choked on his water. "That was an awful look."

"Yeah, I'm not doing that again." The box braids were something he wished he could erase from his past; during Blackmirror's conception and for a year after, his curated bounce rapper persona was infused with catchy call-and-return songs, woven strands, and saggy clothing. Only after the agency came under fire for appropriation did they permit a change.

Shaking his head to remove the embarrassing memory, he prodded again. "You didn't answer the question."

"If I had to pick my favorite, it would be Hanjun circa 2017." She threaded her fingers through his. "Blonde-haired Hanjun. I didn't know who you were back then, but if I did, I would have been a *big* fan."

"Is that so?" He remembered the cut—the first style he had following the braids. Though he would have been happy with any trending 'do, he chose a fringe with messy bangs.

"Also, natural-haired Hanjun from the *'Galactica'* tour. And your blue hair from the *'Distraction'* era." She stopped herself from gushing over his previous looks before she unraveled.

He gave her a shy smile, squinting at her subtle fangirling while she added another statement. "But you in platinum, dressed in black and white, does things to me."

Shuddering, she couldn't imagine seeing him with the coloring. "Gives me some kind of feelings."

He winked, eliciting a smile. "Oh, so you like a bad boy?"

Standing to leave, Hanso threw an empty water bottle, hitting the wall next to Hanjun's bed. "Cool it!"

Dragging Hanjun to the kitchen, she produced a seductive smirk. "Yes, Sir."

Hanjun stood behind Jen, placing a hand on her shoulder. "Jen's gonna stay home."

Looking over the room, he acknowledged the disapproving groans from his mates. "We can't make her go on a Sunday."

She held a confident smile. "I know you're worried about the packages we've received, but I'll be okay. I'm going to catch up on Netflix and have myself a little spa day."

Collective grumbles filled the room, and each roommate vocalized their unease while they pulled on their shoes.

"I wish you'd come with us," Deok-Sun pleaded.

"Please be safe," Jin mumbled.

Hanso crossed his arms. "You're stubborn, you know that?"

Though Soogi didn't say a word, he slammed the door.

"Geesh," she whispered after they left.

Nuzzling into her shoulder, Hanjun inhaled enough of her perfume to last him the day. "If someone knocks, don't answer. We'll be home this evening."

"I won't. I hope you hear good news about the tour."

"Yeah." Flicking his neck, he harnessed a sad smile. "I should go before they cause trouble."

Left alone, she let a few moments pass. Once she was sure he wasn't backpedaling, she went to her room and reached for a package hidden in her closet. Moving to the living room, she rearranged the furniture, grunting as she pushed the oversized pieces into place. Positioning the sofa to face a bare wall, she opened the box, pulling out bubble-wrapped components of a home theater system. Propping the machine on a stack of Hanjun's to-be-read books, she pointed the lens toward the far end of the room. Several moments of adjusting later, she turned the projector off with a satisfied sigh.

Hurrying to the kitchen, she set up a concession stand on the counter with sweets, snacks, and munchies. Opening the fridge, she added cans of cola and bottles of sparkling water to the shelves, double-checking to ensure Jin had a chilled bottle of wine waiting for him.

Finishing the buffet, she stopped by her room and slipped into comfortable clothes: a strappy bra, black joggers, and a fitted white ribbed tank. Draping an oversized waffle-weaved robe over her shoulders, she was sure the fabric was roomy enough to conceal her body when her roommates returned.

Reconvening to the lounge, she settled on the sofa with the remote in her palm, hoping they would like the surprise. Deok-Sun and Jin were anxious to visit a cinema but couldn't due to their fame. Though the theaters in Seoul were open twenty-four hours, the city never slept, and neither did the paparazzi. Of course, they could have braved the crowds with security, but most of the time, they didn't bother. 'Too much work for too little payoff,' as Soogi would say.

★⁺₊⋆☾⁺₊⋆

Walking into the office, the bandmates took their seats around the conference table. Greeting them warmly, Ha-Rin noticed Jen's empty chair. "No Jenilyn?"

"She stayed home." Hanjun handed him the photo from the night before. "Someone's threatening her."

Ha-Rin inspected the photograph. "There isn't a lot here."

"We've received a package every day over the past few weeks." He rubbed the back of his neck. "It started as candies, but then it was photos. And now that."

Ha-Rin inspected the red ink splotched over Jen's face. "You've been getting these for weeks?"

"It seemed strange but not threatening."

"This is harassment. I'll speak with Mr. Yun and arrange to have security situated outside your residence."

"Isn't that a bit much?" Hanso asked from his seat.

Ha-Rin dropped the picture on the table, letting it fall like a dead leaf. "We don't know what someone is thinking when they do things like this, but the agency has an obligation to protect you."

Pulling out his chair, he read over the group's agenda. "It seems we will be touring in 2022. We're still working on finalizing the dates. As you know, tours come with expectations, and your schedules will be strict leading to the departure."

"Hanso, as the eldest, you're required to serve your military term following the performances. Soogi and Hanjun shortly after. We've failed to reach a decision on how to handle your requirements in the past. You have the option of enlisting as you approach thirty." He paused, emitting a low growl. "Without exemptions, the Maknaes will be left alone. Likewise, Blackmirror would lack vocals when they depart. You could enlist together, forgoing promotion for almost two years. I fear the move would be suicide for your careers."

"I have an idea." Soogi raised his hand. "What if we stagger the enlistments over a four-year period?"

Motioning for Ha-Rin to hand him a pen, he reached for the photo of Jen and drew a rough timescale on the back. "First Hanso and I would serve. We would be away for roughly eighteen months, leaving Deok-Sun, Jin, and Hanjun. Around the nine-month mark, another member would enter—let's say Hanu. This would leave Jin and Deok-Sun. Halfway through their enlistment, Hanso and I would return, allowing them to enroll. Military service completed in four years. It's the fastest way without a complete hiatus."

"How do you suppose you'll stay relevant?"

"We'll produce music until the point of induction, releasing it in intervals after our departure. It would leave at least two of us to attend interviews, concerts, appearances, and feed the fan base." Soogi reclined in his chair. "Plus, we could pursue solo ventures and pre-film Parallels."

"We would be relying on luck and Anti," Jin whispered.

"You can't generate income," Ha-Rin rebutted.

"*No*," Soogi acknowledged. "We can't *work* during admission. If we record enough *before* the enlistments—"

"That's a heavy load to bear." Ha-Rin groaned. "Producing music hasn't been easy for any of you, and if you remember, we began outsourcing hits. Hell, with your decision to disband last year, we thought your promotional days were over."

Soogi chewed on the end of his pen. "Jen's helping me with a set of lyrics. She has a lot to learn, but she could be an asset."

He wiggled in his seat after noticing Hanjun's accusatory glare. "I showed her a track, and she wrote part of the chorus out of nowhere. You read the words, and the flow is there."

"Noona can write?" Jin clapped his palms together.

"I guess so. The melody needs fleshing out, and I'm polishing the arrangement, but it wasn't half bad. There's something different about her. Maybe it's because she's not neck deep in the industry, but she has a fresh quality. She's brought me a few ideas, and she's innovative—"

Hanjun countered. "She doesn't have experience—"

"None of us did," Soogi snarked. "The best way to achieve a new sound is to find an outsider who isn't persuaded by big industry. It would be wise to see what she's capable of."

"Couldn't we try for non-active duty?" Deok-Sun interjected, breaking the tension between the musicians.

Slumping, Jin kicked his feet. "Why does service have to be two years? The war has been over for—"

"It's an honor to serve your country," Hanso announced before anyone could answer. "It would be unjust to expect our rights without serving as our elders have."

"Should we take a vote? All in favor of staggering the enlistments over four years..." Ha-Rin closed the schedule book. Each member raised their hands, with Jin and Deok-Sun reluctant to do so. "So it shall be."

Making a note on his phone, Hanjun looked at Ha-Rin. "Are we talking a world tour?"

"It's likely. And we're working toward a larger North American leg. This will be a long trip, boys. Make sure you're well rested." Ha-Rin aligned a stack of papers on the table. "One last thing: we haven't had a chance to finalize a stage theme. Since you produced '*Time Machines and Dreams*' during the pandemic, we could base our concept on the album or finish where we left off with the '*Distraction*' tour. Email me with your suggestions; we'll get the ball rolling with the production company."

⋆⁺₊⋆☾⋆⁺₊⋆

On the seventh floor of the J&I tower, an elderly stylist walked Hanjun to a hydraulic chair. "What are we wanting today?"

Hanjun pulled out his phone to show a picture of himself from years earlier. Sporting black leather pants and bleached blonde hair, the photograph flooded him with memories of a time when he was unsure of his life choices. "I'd like this cut and for the color to..."

He swiped to find a photo of Jen with red streaks peeking out from underneath her curls. "Match her."

She glanced at the screen. "*Girlfriend?* She's gorgeous."

"They might as well be married," Hanso snarked.

Blushing, Hanjun nodded. "Yes. Girlfriend."

"Serious?" The woman brushed out his fluffy strands. "It's been a while since you dated, hasn't it?"

"I feel it is." He stared at his mobile, wishing he could text Jen the good news. She couldn't fully understand how amazing the announcement was, considering Blackmirror went from a possible disbandment to planning a world tour, but she would share his joy.

Holding the device, he decided he would purchase her a phone for Christmas. One capable of receiving texts and photos. If required, he would sell the idea as a present for him. The gift of peace of mind.

Thinking about the hairdresser asking if his relationship was serious, he realized he didn't hesitate to admit it was. It was more serious than he had previously considered. Mustering up a bucket of courage while the stylist placed dye on his hair one strip at a time, he called his mother on speaker. "Hi, Mom!"

"Hi, son!"

"We're touring in the new year!"

"Han-juna! You've come so far! You'll visit before you go."

"I will." He bit his lip hard enough to hurt. "Mom?"

"Yes, son?"

"I—" He tugged at the collar of his shirt. "I met someone."

"The American girl?"

"H-how did you know?"

Chuckling, she responded in a mother-always-knows tone. "Halmoni isn't the only one who reads the tabloids."

Glancing at Hanso for encouragement, he reassured himself. "We've been dating for a few weeks. I was afraid to tell you."

Squinting as if her response might physically hurt him, he relaxed when she said, "Han-juna, you should be with someone who makes you happy. Does she make you happy?"

"The happiest."

"When can I meet her?"

"I—" He panicked, unsure what to say without speaking with Jen.

"If you like this girl, I would like to meet her."

Caving to her demands, he agreed. "I'll make it happen."

"I'm expecting you. Dress warm so you don't catch a cold."

Tucking the phone away, he held a smile he was unable to hide. "That went better than expected."

Soogi shook the half-cut hair from his eyes. "Guess you're official official."

"Yeah." As one weight lifted off his shoulders, another settled on his chest. The meeting of parents was a mere formality in the States. He didn't know how to explain the significance to Jen without making her nervous.

★⁺₊★☾★⁺₊★

Arriving home with fresh haircuts, the bandmates found a wrapped package in the hallway. Hanjun opened it to find another photo of Hanso and Jen. He snapped a picture and sent it to Ha-Rin. Tapping his code on the keypad, he tried entering and battled an unknown opponent. "It feels like the door's stuck."

On the opposite side, Jen tittered. "I have a surprise for you. Close your eyes!"

"A surprise!?" Jin spun around.

Opening the door and waving a hand in front of their faces, she led them to the parlor in pairs. Last to enter, Hanjun covered his eyes with both hands. Noticing the red tips on his blonde locks, she pressed on his shoulders until he sat and leaned in close enough to whisper. "Your hair is fierce."

"Today, Jen." Hanso veiled his eyes with one hand, searching for the side table with the other. "Where's my manga?"

Appreciating the rays from the setting sun, Deok-Sun broke into a laugh. "Why is the sofa facing west?"

Tip-toeing around the couch, she flipped a switch on the projector. The machine whirred, launching a beam of white light on the far wall. "You can't go to the movies, so I brought the movies to you. There are concessions on the counter. Drinks in the fridge."

"I *knew* I was facing the window." Deok-Sun rushed to close the curtains overlooking the river.

Admiring their new entertainment equipment, they agreed to watch Home Alone. Soogi distributed snacks to each roommate while Hanso passed around glasses.

Jin poured a generous glass of alcohol and broke the good news before anyone else could. "We're going on tour!"

Popping up from her seat, she squealed and reached for a hug. "Congratulations!"

Bending to meet her, he smashed the stemware between their bodies. Red liquid spilled down her tank, soaking her white top and bra. Apologizing, he tried to dry the mess with his sleeve. "Sorry, Noona."

Hanjun pushed him away from her. "Jin, what the hell?"

"You're fine, Jinnie. It's just a shirt." Getting up to change, she held the soiled fabric away from her body. "Go ahead and start the movie. I've seen it a million times."

Hanjun's eyes followed as she walked past. Deciding to join, he entered her room just as she peeled off her stained blouse. Perched at the edge of the bed, he ran his hands through his newly styled hair. "I'm enlisting after the tour."

She turned to face him, pulling a clean blouse over her chest. For the first time, she saw undeniable fear in his eyes. "How does that make you feel?"

"I've heard awful things about people exploiting celebrities—the abuse during basic training." Before she had time to react, his arms were wrapped around her. His embrace was a wholly different kind of hug—the caliber of clutch when you're afraid to release the only thing you know. "I'm worried I won't be the same."

Locked in his biceps, she squeezed her eyes shut, only able to imagine that the mandatory service would be strict and his small personal freedoms would vanish. The singular silver lining was that it would be a great reset—a time to live as an average countryman.

"I'm afraid you won't like the new me." He stood tall, taking her chin in his palm. "Tell me you'll be there when it's over."

"I promise." Nodding, tears formed in her eyes.

Searching for closeness when all he could think about was being ripped apart, his hands migrated to the back of her thighs, lifting her to his hips. Her arms encapsulated his shoulders, and he carried her to the vanity, placing her on the surface. In one motion, he swiped the cosmetics onto the floor and kicked the bedroom door closed. Pausing long enough to twist the lock, he removed his shirt.

Following suit, she shed hers and dropped it on the desk. Running her hands down his chest, he felt smooth and athletic under her fingertips. The dips of his collarbones were pronounced, and his neck was well-defined.

Interrupting her admiration, he pushed her against the mirror and devoured her mouth, reaching to unclasp the bra she had put on moments earlier. Replacing the strap with rough kisses, he migrated to her breasts, lapping up remnants of sticky wine. He wasn't sure which was sweeter—the candy flavor of Jin's favorite drink or the taste of her supple skin.

Trailing her hands down his body without breaking eye contact, she unbuttoned his jeans. As she tugged the zipper down, he let the fabric fall to the floor and stepped out, reaching to remove hers. Unobstructed, her thighs slid apart to reveal wet fabric, and the hour of reckoning was at hand. D-day had arrived, and after months of teasing and close encounters, they would erode each other's boundaries.

Emerging from his boxers, he stroked himself, imagining how she would feel. He had passing thoughts about her since the moment they met, and nothing could be wrong. Every single molecule in her body was created to fit with his, and he wanted to discover what kind of explosives they would create grinding together.

He bit his lip, watching as she licked her fingers and trailed down her torso. Holding a sensual glare, her lips parted, a moan escaping her lungs as she massaged her guarded secret. With her knees spread and her fingertips digging into her swollen, pink flesh, the look in her eyes suggested he wasn't the only one who thought about a sexual encounter multiple times a week. He was her fantasy as much as she was his.

Knowing he would explode if he had to wait any longer, he kissed her neck. "Are you sure?"

She nodded between moans, and he placed a kiss on her pouty lips. "I need to hear it. Do you want me to fuck you?"

"Yes." She drew him in with her calves, and he savored the moment, staring into her eyes as she pleasured herself. Holding her panties to the side, she permitted him to invade her.

"Junie—" Penetrated for the first time, she dragged her nails down his back. Only able to fit the first inch of his erection, he pulled out and pushed again, causing a shuddering moan to escape her. Her eyebrows wiggled together, her nose scrunched, and her mouth hung open, unable to catch a wispy breath.

Even if it took an entire military operation to occupy her fortress, he would carry out the mission. "Does it hurt?"

"No—" She shook her head. "It's a little uncomfortable. It's been almost two years since—"

"Two years?" Dismounting, he licked two fingers and positioned his hand between their bodies. Up and down, he mirrored the way she had pleasured herself. Running his free hand over her shoulders, he searched for erogenous zones. With slow, erotic touches over her thighs, wrists, neck, and shoulders, he heeded the subtle lip bites of pleasure and quivers of gratitude, relishing in her silent cries.

His traveling fingers moved to her calves, where her legs instinctively curled, and her trust awakened to him. She gripped the edge of the vanity and stared at him in disbelief, and he knew she was his. Even as she held back her pants, her soul spoke to him in a language only they knew.

Reaching orgasm, her body elevated to meet his, and she pulled him close enough to consume. "There. Don't stop."

Unwilling to remove his eyes from hers, he wondered if she knew the deep desire he held for her. He asked her if she wanted him to fuck her, but what he really thirsted for was to make love to her. To make love *with* her. The moment was theirs, and he was grateful to experience a period of universal growth. If everything went according to plan, their first sexual encounter would open the door to many more, and she would come back to him every time she craved a good fucking.

He dipped a finger inside her entrance, and she grasped his wrist, whining while he wound up her favorite toy. He began stroking her roof, and her breathing hastened, adjusting to the pressure. Panting, her neck fell back, and he thrust deeper, applying friction to her g-spot and a-spot. Body vibrating, she clawed at his arms when he sent her shooting into a cluster orgasm. "Jesus Christ, you're not playing."

"I told you I couldn't wait to please you." With her trembling and dripping wet, he positioned himself in her aisle, barely inserting the tip. "Are you ready to try again?"

Her eyeliner ran to her clavicles, but she refused to tap out. In her disheveled state, she was as far away from beautiful as she could be, and he needed to solicit her inner succubus. Only once he saw her—all of her—could she decide if he was worth her time. If his energy meshed with hers and if they were compatible on all planes of existence. She needed to see what he was capable of, not the romanticized version she toyed with in her fantasies. "Yes."

Kissing her cheek, he quivered at how soaked she was. "You know what I need you to say."

Staring into his eyes, she refused to utter the words he wanted to hear. "Hanjun, I want to fuck *you*."

"That's my girl." Harnessing a satisfied smirk, he draped a palm on the side of her neck and began a steady stroke. For every slow plunge, her eyes widened, and moans surged from her lungs. Concerned about the paper-thin walls, he wiggled his thumb over her tongue, muffling her pleasured cries. Caressing his wrist, she wrapped her lips around him. With his other arm, he pulled her to the edge, allowing for deeper penetration. "Fuck, you're incredible."

Masking his unexpected groans while her sweet whimpers passed over his finger, his eyes moved to her breasts, cherishing the sight of her body's gentle flow beneath his. Rolling and curling, they were two rushing currents, crashing to form a single violent confluence of pleasure. It was instinctive for him to stare into her eyes, and he swore he saw a moment when the coloring flicked from blue to green.

Dragging his lips along her neck, he squinted, remembering how she asked what he wanted from her every time they found a moment to fool around. "Tell me what you like."

Loosening the suction on his finger, she gulped, issuing a command during the downstroke. "Harder."

Attending to her desires, he slammed into her, bouncing the desk off the wall. Refusing to orgasm despite the burning rising through his belly, he bit his lip. "Fuck—"

"Just like that—" Wrapping an arm over his shoulder, she tugged at his hair, stifling her whimpers against his neck. Ridden to her peak, she arched her back and came in an explosion of ecstasy; her tongue hung on her lips, her body stiffened, and her legs fell from his waist.

A pleasured squeal escaped her before he covered her mouth. Hammering into her, he savored every second inside her warm Vallie Fountaine. Feeling her orgasm vice around him, he thought the pressure of her contractions might force him out when the pulsating subsided. Shuddering, he released with one extended groan and buried his face in her shoulder, sinking his teeth into his lip.

An instant sensation of euphoria clouded his mind. His hips rubbed into hers, his breathing labored on her skin, and he could feel her thumping heartbeat through her flesh. Remaining rigid, he didn't want to back away because, when he did, the rapture would fade. "Holy fucking hell."

Unable to hold her eyes open after experiencing a series of back-breaking orgasms, her eyebrow piqued. "Huh?"

"You're intoxicating." Coming down from his sensual high, he couldn't believe they shared such an intimate moment. If she hadn't been in his arms, he wouldn't have accepted the union as a reality. On the outside, she was the kind of girl you took home to mom. Inside, she was willing to take what she wanted, when she wanted. Whether it was five weeks into a relationship or two years of celibacy, she pursued her needs. There were no games or assumptions, and it was incredibly attractive to him.

It was the sex he'd been longing to have. Beyond a cognitive encounter, the experience was psychologically binding. He was aroused on all levels—spiritual, emotional, and intellectual—and felt the full acceptance she offered. In turn, he was confident in his ability to take her, and thus him, to new sexual heights. His mind wasn't haunted by every bad experience of his past, and he was charmed by her never-ending support.

And all he could think about was doing it again and again until he was an expert at blowing her brain and body.

While she leaned against the mirror breathless, he fixated on her moistened mouth to find a small amount of blood. Opening her tired eyes, she rubbed the matching ichor from his. "Junie, you're bleeding."

In the afterglow, she displayed innocence, and he considered he could have been dreaming—a girl who exuded such natural purity wouldn't engage in a sinful act with him. Fate had to be playing a cruel joke on him. She was unreal. A mirage. Pushing the self-loathing aside, he retrieved her shirt. "You're amazing."

"You aren't so bad yourself. I'm gonna wash up." Heading for the door, she pulled the article over her nearly nude body. Slipping into the hall, she ensured their interaction went unnoticed. Amid her pleasure, she wasn't thinking about their roommates or how her vanity knocked on the wall; she only thought of Hanjun's intensity and how he stared into her soul.

Discerning repetitive holiday jingles, she was confident the high volume was enough to cover any commotion they caused. Scurrying to the bathroom, she jumped in the shower. Running a soapy loofah over her breasts, the water was barely hotter than her skin. The emprise was mind-altering, though unexpected; she thought their first time would be planned based on his desire for a poetic beginning. She wasn't surprised, though—they came close to ripping off each other's clothes multiple times.

In Jen's room, Hanjun retrieved compacts that had fallen during the rollick. A few shattered on impact, leaving broken remnants of eye shadow as evidence of the tryst. Checking behind the desk, there were definite scuff marks, and he bit his lip, remembering how she begged him to stroke harder. He worried he might hurt her, though his worries dissipated with her pleasurable pants. An exquisite vision burned into his mind—he couldn't wait to taste her again.

Following a quick shower, Jen exited the bathroom. From the corner of her eye, she caught Soogi sitting in his room. Wearing a pair of oversized headphones, he scribbled in a notebook. She hoped to sneak through the hall unnoticed, though he raised his chin and locked eyes with her.

Soogi retreated to his room after Jen left to change. Drowning out the festive film he was outvoted on, he put on a headset, concentrating on the lyrics he was working on.

After witnessing Hanjun act as Jen's protector at the agency, he created a song about favoring his best friend's girlfriend. Throughout the writing process, he realized he wasn't the best suitor for her but made a vow to support her through any means necessary. His feelings couldn't be removed because she didn't reciprocate, and he wouldn't treat her differently because he couldn't gain something from her.

To him, a one-sided attraction was still valid even when it was unknown. Loving her was safe; he couldn't get hurt if she never knew his true feelings, and for as long as she dated Hanjun, there would be no fear of rejection. He could admire her from afar without the risk of misery.

Closing the notebook, he glanced up to find Jen tiptoeing into the hallway. With wet curls cascading down her shoulders, she clung to a towel, giving off a short wave when she spotted him. Averting his gaze from his secret love interest, he retrieved the pad a second time.

My psyche has always been shadowy. As a child, as a teen, and as an adult, dark thoughts have always filtered in. Perpetual night.

My mind changed the day I met her. With her hidden smile and aloof mannerisms, she lit up a corner of my brain, and ever since, everything has been brighter. Every burden lighter.

I don't understand it, and the not understanding poisons me. How dare she add clarity to my darkness, giving me a taste of something I will never achieve?

She doesn't love me, but that doesn't stop me from wishing she did. My heart aches at the thought of her being so close yet unreachable. I see her shining from my inescapable night, and I think, 'How pointless it is for those in hell to yearn for heaven.'

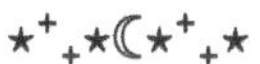

Smelling of decadent shampoo, Jen slipped into bed next to Hanjun. Smiling, he tucked a wet strand of hair behind her ear. "That was everything."

She pulled the towel over her bare breasts. "Everything?"

"*Fantastic. Beautiful. Amazing. Euphoric.*" An entire galaxy of adjectives couldn't capture how wondrous the sex was.

"I can't say you're wrong." She cuddled under the covers. "You fucked me good."

He snaked an arm around her waist, pressing a kiss on her shoulder. "You're so sexy when you come."

"I can't control what happens when I'm lost in it." Her smile faded as she weaved her fingers in and out of his.

He sensed her reeling thoughts. "Wanna talk about it?"

Wagging her head, she was apprehensive about sharing the truth. She didn't give herself to people without restraint, and her sexual attraction was explicitly linked to her intimacy status. If she didn't feel cared for and if she didn't experience emotional attachment, she wasn't able to enjoy sex. And oh boy did she enjoy it.

The chemistry was undeniable, and she favored the encounter more than previous sessions. Her overwhelming pleasure meant she was exceedingly attracted to him, and the moment she knew how comfortable she was with him was the same instant she realized he could hurt her. He could wreck her world, and she was too far gone to stop it. "It's just sex, right?"

He knew she was fibbing but didn't want to pressure her. "I think we both know it was more than sex."

They cuddled and talked over the following hours, and he stayed until she fell asleep. Once settled in his own bed, he checked the group chat before cataloging the day.

Honsa: The theater setup is cool!
Sunnie: We should use it more often.

I've looked forward to this moment since I met her.
If the book of life consists of meaningful memories
and happy coincidences, she's the greatest so far.
She's everything.

CHAPTER FORTY-FIVE

Dream a Beautiful Dream

Lying in bed, Hanjun contemplated the most unusual dream. Evocative, the imagery went well beyond an involuntary brain response.

In the vision, he traversed through a verdant grove until he reached a clearing of pink azaleas. Stooping to pick a bloom, he relished the lush fragrance. Hearing the faint snapping of twigs, he straightened to find a coffee-colored doe tethered to an enormous oak by a thick scarlet rope. On the ground was a piece of bread—fried golden and dusted in sugar. Tugging the constraints, the being struggled to reach the delicacy.

Retrieving the loaf, he offered sustenance to the doe. Telepathically, the creature cautioned him to nourish himself. He split the bread into two, taking a bite of one half and giving the other. The beast ate from his palm, and he spotted a polished ring dangling around its neck. Moving slowly, he pulled the tie to loosen the restraint, sending the hoop to the soil. The animal thanked him and galloped away. Left alone, he recovered the loop lost within a flowerbed. The metal gleamed in the rays filtering through the canopies, and in the center, an otherworldly-faceted gem cast a spectrum of reflections. Fumbling, the ring tumbled from his fingers and morphed into a hunk of lead during its descent, striking him on the chest.

He arose, perspiring and wheezing, suffering physical pain from a penetrated heart. The taste of cornmeal persisted on his tongue. Sweet and fresh-out-of-the-oven warm, the flavor reminded him of hotteok—his favorite Korean street snack. Besides the bizarre hallucinations, he felt rejuvenated. Almost like a new man.

Hopping off the mattress, he visited the bathroom to polish his teeth. In the reflection, he caught prominent scratches down his back from the previous night's entanglement, and he grinned, knowing Jen was well satisfied.

When he returned to his room, Hanso pelted him with questions. "What happened to your back?"

"I went crazy with the back scratcher." Pulling a shirt over his chest, he searched the closet for a pair of leather pants.

Unimpressed with his answer, Hanso wasn't discouraged. "Why were you up so early?"

"I had a weird dream." Sitting on the bed, he pulled on his socks.

"Huh…" Hanso fevered during the night, hallucinating a lucid illusion in a dark forest. Lost among the foliage, he assumed a state of hopelessness until the sun illuminated his path. "That's uncommon for you. What kind of dream?"

"Just a dream." Pulling a notebook from the nightstand, he handed the pad to Hanso. "I wrote it down."

Hanso studied the scribbled passages, detecting significant imagery. "There's a lot of symbolism here."

Disregarding the comment, Hanjun slipped across the hall. Venturing into Jen's room, he kneeled next to her bed. Mellow jazz infused the air, calming his fatigued spirit. He wasn't a saxophone enthusiast until she relocated; following her arrival, the sound began to signify the nighttime hours—when she selected a soothing melody. For as long as the audio was broadcast, she was without worry.

Tucking the blanket around her body, he was divided between allowing her to rest and shaking her awake. She was adorable when she slept, and as her chest moved with every beat of her breath, she remained at her most comfortable. Caressing her cheek, he perused what ideas she carried in her beautiful mind. Which distant lands she flew through and what adventures she participated in.

He wondered if he featured in her dreams the way she starred in his. Years before he had the pleasure of standing next to her, he dreamt her into existence by wishing upon thousands of stars. Countless nights were spent staring at satellites, praying one would quench his thirst for connection. He wasn't interested in garden-variety associations; he lusted for an anomaly equal parts ally and paramour. He didn't know her name, and he didn't know her face, but he knew her heart.

Stirring, she mumbled. "It's getting weird, Jun."

Retracting his hand from her cheek, he went pink. "I didn't realize you were awake."

"It takes very little to wake me." Her blurry vision focused, finding him wearing a fitted white tee and black pants. "Sir, it's way too early for you to be this sexy."

Too energetic for the morning hours, he lifted his shirt, revealing a prominent set of pleasure marks carved down his back. "Look what you did to me."

"I'm sorry." She hopped off the bed, giving his back a delicate stroke on the way to the bathroom. He reached to slap her rump, making full contact with his palm. "Ow, Junie!"

Embracing a coquettish smirk, he passed over his phone. "I can kiss it and make it better."

Rotating her eyes at his shameless flirting, her head fell back. "I'm taking a shower."

Entering the bathroom, she listened to his Spotify daylist—dance pop—while she scrubbed. While crooning her heart out to a java house jam, the door creaked open. Spying around the curtain, she discovered Hanjun sneaking in, suppressing a cunning snicker. Making grand strides, he jumped in the shower with her despite being clothed. While he sheltered behind the curtain, she twisted the tap and revolved to kiss him. He lowered the barrier, pulling her nude body against his.

"You better be careful, or I'll make you moist." She giggled, aware that he hated the word.

"I guess I'll have to return the favor."

"You've grown quite indecent these days, Ryu Hanjun." Slipping from his arms, she reached for a towel.

"It's your fault." Stepping out of the stall, he removed his wet socks.

Eyes rolling, she enveloped the cloth around her body and returned to her room. He trailed behind, resting on her bed while she picked out a frilly white button-up and black faux leather pants. "My mom wants to meet you."

Staring at him, she froze. "Your mother?"

"I told her about us yesterday. I mean about dating; I didn't tell her about the—" His head bobbed, eyebrows raised, and lips pursed to create a whistle.

"W-what—" Tripping over her words, she was concerned about meeting the matron. "Did she say?"

"She raised me to be myself." He snatched a lip balm from her nightstand and coated his lips. "And to visit before we leave."

"How much do I need to learn?" Tugging on the pair of pants, she worried she wouldn't make the cut on such a brief warning. "I'm wildly unprepared."

"She knows I won't give up on something I want." He flushed and positioned his head down, knowing she was someone his mother would approve of. "You're pretty, polite, well-spoken, dress well, and speak multiple languages. Trust me, you check all the boxes."

She also had the ideal complexion. He couldn't bring himself to vocalize how her appearance was a good quality, knowing she would object. The solitary time he praised her coloring, she reprimanded him for putting too much emphasis on her complexion. He wouldn't be doing that again, and he hoped his mother wouldn't, either.

"Still—" She dabbed a touch of perfume on her clavicles. "I'd like to make a good impression."

"I'll teach you what you need to know." He extended his arms, anticipating a hug.

Plunging into his embrace, she placed a peck on his forehead. "Should I shop for a more appropriate outfit?"

He held her hands, thumbing her knuckles. "Wearing something traditional wouldn't hurt."

A pound on the door disrupted their chat. Pulling out his phone, he studied the camera, finding Ha-Rin's stern expression on the screen. "What's he doing here? We're supposed to meet him at the filming location."

Migrating through the home, they met with Ha-Rin, who waited in the hall with another male. The lofty man showcased an unyielding disposition, evidence of comprehensive sentry training. Sporting a shaved head and sturdy shoulders, he appeared active military. "This is Suk-Chin. He's one of three door guards the agency has hired for you."

Suk-Chin extended an arm, and Hanjun reached to meet the gesture. Supporting his right forearm with his left hand, he glanced at Jen. "Lesson one: when shaking hands, support your forearm. It's a sign of respect. If they bow, bow in return. Women don't usually handshake—you will most often bow."

She analyzed the action. "I'll remember."

Spotting Ha-Rin's confusion, Hanjun clarified. "My mother has requested to meet Jen."

"Good luck to you." Ha-Rin assented, understanding the severity of the situation. Steering his attention to the guard, he directed an order on behalf of J&I. "Suk-Chin, this is Jenilyn. She's under contract with the boys as well as Hanjun's girlfriend. Keep a close eye on her."

Suk-Chin bowed and turned to stand guard.

★⁺₊★☾★⁺₊★

Jen exited the escort van at a busy cross section. A series of black cars surrounded their vehicle, pouring an unusually large amount of security from the doors. "Wow, the agency assembled an entire team."

Jin grasped her shoulders, directing her to a narrow walkway congested with reporters. "We wouldn't make it through here alive if they didn't."

Diverting from the crowd, she captured a glimpse of the guards. The company dispatched an intimidating crew to shepherd them through the packed pathways. Formulating a strategy, the sentinels encircled them from all angles, using their bulky bodies to obstruct camera flashes. Yanking her arm, Jin dragged her into the eye of the storm, assuring she wasn't lost among the fanfare.

Heading the entourage, Ha-Rin led them through the main access point of a frenzied mall. "As you know, we're filming another episode. You'll be split into teams, singing carols and urging patrons to donate. The team that receives the most donations wins."

Understanding their objectives, the musicians played a game of rock-paper-scissors. Jin, Hanso, and Soogi tied and became a unit, while Deok-Sun and Hanjun were left as partners. Ha-Rin then explained the details. "Choose a spot at least one hundred meters away from the opposing team. You will carol in intervals of twenty minutes, with twenty-minute breaks in between. Jenilyn, you may go with Hanjun to balance the teams."

Hanjun clutched Jen's sleeve and led her to the food court, with Deok-Sun and the camera crew chasing behind. Positioned next to the youngest, he addressed the camera. "We're at the Myeongdong Underground Shopping Center, singing for donations."

"That's right," Deok-Sun tweeted along. "All offerings will be given to a local girl's orphanage."

"And we'll be matching every donation to the won."

Plunging into the challenge, they sang Christmas songs and performed viral dances, accumulating a wealth of donations. Jen gathered the offerings in a Santa hat, thanking supporters with smiles. After their first set, she passed the donations to Ha-Rin for tallying.

Sticking close to Hanjun during their break, she followed him to a snack stand, where he purchased a banana hazelnut crepe. He offered to order one for her, but she declined. "I'm still digesting purple rice from breakfast."

"You at least have to try it." Taking a pause from stuffing his face, he held the treat in front of hers.

Sinking her teeth into the chocolatey confection, she hummed. "Mmm! That is good."

"I have to enjoy this because after today, it's back to dieting, rehearsals, and working out like it's my job." He savored another bite, staring longingly at the delicious food he wouldn't be able to enjoy in a matter of hours. "Because it is my job."

Stepping away from the camera crew, they meandered through narrow walkways, evading stores selling collectibles. Hanjun avoided eye contact with hopeful stall attendants, while Jen hid behind oversized sunglasses. Passing a compact disc shop, she spotted a rack near the path showcasing yearly calendars with Deok-Sun and Jin printed on the covers. "That must be weird for them."

He lowered his voice for her ears only. "When you're an artist, you don't notice the impact you make. You create music and hope it reaches the people who will benefit from it. Seeing someone buy the merchandise is proof of our success."

"Impressive proof." Jen halted at a shop displaying artfully crafted hanboks. Presenting beautiful fabrics, the antique forms and iron skirt cages evoked elegance in an otherwise contemporary boutique. Feeling the textures, she was captivated by a stylish black gown with gauzy sleeves. "This is gorgeous."

"Those are trendy, but my mom would love you in that." He garbled a mouthful of crepe, gesturing to the attire.

She chuckled, happy to see him eating well. "Do you mind if I go inside?"

"Not at all." He wagged his head, sucking chocolate from his fingertips.

She entered the store, relieved to find the woman behind the desk speaking English. Although she had picked up a few phrases from the agency, she wasn't anywhere near fluent.

"Can I help you?" A few inches shorter than Jen, the shopkeeper was around the same age with a wide nose and chubby cheeks.

"I'm looking for something to wear when I meet my boyfriend's family." She blushed; it was the first time she uttered the term to a stranger.

"Traditional or modern?"

"Modern, please."

Bending her wrist, the woman guided her to a sewing room brimming with artisanal frocks. "We have hundreds of samples, or we can create something for you."

Spellbound by the collection of styles, she couldn't decide where to begin. Drifting from rack to rack, she shuffled through countless designs when one caught her eye: a black pleated skirt affixed to a vintage-inspired top in a delicate floral pattern. Sheer sleeves added sophistication, and a wide belt finished the look. "Can I try this one?"

The seamstress gleamed, affirming her choice. Prompting Jen to stand on a round pedestal, she helped her into the dress. "Elegant and timeless. Young women don't choose fashion like this anymore."

"We add zippers for ease." She fastened the side and pinned the garment to her form. "It may need to be taken in for a proper fit."

"Would it be okay if we didn't?" She smoothed her palms over her hips. "I'm hoping to hide some of my figure."

The woman nodded, turning Jen towards a row of mirrors. "You chose well."

"Would you do me a favor?" She swished the skirt over her legs. The material was luxurious, though Hanjun's opinion could sway her decision. "Can you get my boyfriend? He's the tall one in the black jacket just outside the store."

★⁺₊★☾★⁺₊★

Hanjun examined people as they passed by. Minding the idiosyncrasies exposed by individuals who were unaware they were being watched helped him feel less alone in masking normality. Everyone had a secret to hide.

Eyeing his jacket and the crepe in his hand, the store owner approached him. "Excuse me—"

The unexpected vocalization startled him, sending the chocolate treat to the floor. Releasing a suppressed whimper, he saluted her while crouching to clean up the mess. "Hello..."

The seamstress motioned to the doors. "Miss Jenilyn would like your opinion on a dress she's considering."

"Yeah, sure." He clutched the soiled snack and followed her into the store. In the backroom, Jen stood on a platform beneath a glimmering chandelier.

She twirled in the dress, billowing the skirt. "Is this too modern? I love the details, and the fabric is quality."

He sat speechless. Someone designed the dress specifically for her, and nothing would change his mind. "My mom will love it."

The dressmaker nodded. "It's true. You've elevated my work."

Peering in the mirror, she wanted to wear the gown forever. "This is the one."

The couturier helped her disrobe while Hanjun lingered near the registers, appreciating the menswear. Stumbling into the formal section, he envisioned their marriage announcement and pondered Jen's preferences for a wedding. Date? Colors? Season? Planning out their entire future in a matter of minutes, his daydreaming was shattered by the beeping cash register.

"That'll be 686,000 won."

Jen fumbled with the payment, but Hanjun tapped his card on the contactless reader from behind her.

"Jun, I—" Cutting her rebuke short, she detected the shopkeeper's inquisitiveness.

He grasped her forearms, lowering to meet her eyes. "It's for my family. I should be the one to pay."

Uncomfortable with the gesture, her head jiggled. They hadn't negotiated how to handle purchases. "You don't need to—"

The shopkeeper handed him a receipt. "I'll need to make a few alterations. Your purchase will be ready tomorrow."

Tucking the receipt away, he gave thanks and turned to Jen. "You can return the favor by wearing it more than once."

Sighing, she released her frustration. "Okay."

Checking his watch, he tugged her toward the exit. "We should get back."

"Are you one of the Blackmirror boys?"

Hearing the question, he halted in the doorway, turning to greet her warmly. "Rem."

Jen studied his character swap. When identified, he introduced himself as Rem, and when not, as Hanjun. She wondered if he wrestled to juggle personas, or perhaps Rem existed within Hanjun and Hanjun within Rem.

Bubbling with delight, the woman's eyes lit up. "My nine-year-old daughter, Mi-Cha, loves Blackmirror! Her favorite member is Deok-Sun, and she's been begging me to pre-purchase the 'Time Machines and Dreams' album."

He broke into a smile. "I'm no Sunny, but if you'd like, we can take a photo for her."

She nodded and handed over her phone. Holding the device above their faces, Hanjun pulled Jen into the frame. The trio posed, smiling for the camera. "Say kimchi!"

With a click, he captured the moment, and the woman bowed, collecting her smartphone. "Thank you. She will cherish this."

★⁺₊★☾★⁺₊★

After the filming came to an end, the bandmates reunited on the bus. Waiting to depart, Hanso knelt on his seat, leaning over the backrest. "Hanjun, tell everyone about your dream."

He recalled how the vision remained clear in his mind. "The lead struck my shoulder, and I woke up."

"Huh. I had a strange dream, too." Soogi joined in. "I went to the kitchen and found a loaf of sweet bread on the counter. Then I spotted a buck, a doe, and a fawn on the terrace. The newborn was just born; she couldn't even stand."

Ha-Rin slid into the van, catching the tail end of Soogi's recollection while Deok-Sun turned to glare at him. "How did you know the fawn was a girl?"

Soogi shrugged. "I just knew."

Ha-Rin's inquisitive gape settled over the cabin. "Did all of you have a dream last night?"

"I dreamed of being on an island filled with pink flowers," Deok-Sun responded.

"I already told Hanjun, but I was lost in a forest until the sun came up," Hanso added.

Concealing his unrest, Jin sat in silence. His dream hadn't been as pleasant; in fact, it was more akin to a nightmare. "I dreamt we were joking around on stage when I heard a gunshot. I looked at Hanjun, thinking he was hit, but then something warm and wet seeped through my shirt, and everything went dark."

"I thought I died," he added after hearing the gasps of his teammates. "My body was cold when I woke up."

"Dreams can foretell the future." Ha-Rin examined the interior, resting his gaze on Jen. "Jenilyn, did you have any dreams?"

"Not at all. I slept like a rock."

The housemates found another parcel in the hallway. Retrieving the box, Hanjun sneered at the sentry. "Who left this?"

Head down, the guard issued an apology. "It's my fault. I went to the bathroom, and when I came back, it was there."

"Damnit." Hanjun opened the wrapping to find another image of Jen and Hanso. He snapped a picture and sent it to Ha-Rin, explaining how the guard hadn't caught the deliverer.

Soogi charged through the door. "So much for security."

Scattering as soon as he entered the home, Hanjun collapsed on the sofa while Jen went straight to bed. Jin brought her a glass of water and a tablet of melatonin to help her sleep.

"Those dreams were strange." Soogi grasped the remote, flipping through options he had no intention of watching. "Kind of reminds me of my mom's conception dream."

Hanjun propped his elbows on his knees. "Impossible."

"You haven't..." Sinking into the cushions, Jin's speech dwindled. "With Jen?"

"Hah!" Hanjun guffawed, providing a plausible excuse. "When would we have time? Besides, my dream was too detailed to be taemong."

"Maybe we should ask Mr. Yun." Deok-Sun recalled the CEO's prediction of their success. "Remember when each of us dreamed about a blue dragon soaring over Seoul? He said it was how he knew we were destined for greatness."

A skeptic of augury, Hanso scoffed. "Mr. Yun would have said anything to motivate us."

Deok-Sun urged him to consider the possibility. "You didn't think it was strange that we had the same dream?"

Hanso clung to his conviction. "There were too many variables. Jin and I dreamt of a dragon; Hanjun didn't visualize a dragon at all. And Deok-Sun, you said you saw a serpent."

Groaning, Deok-Sun rolled his eyes. "How many times do I have to explain it to you? A serpent *is* a dragon."

"Still, Hanjun imagined some blue twinkling thing."

"No," Hanjun interjected with a look of mystification. "*Indigo*, not blue. There was a distinct line of indigo in the sky, shimmering like stars in broad daylight."

Growing more frustrated, Hanso denied the anomaly as evidence. "And what about Soogi? He dreamed of Queen Heo Hwang-ok. What would a distant ancestor have to do with—"

Soogi tossed the remote aside. "The twin fish. That's what I dreamt about. Not the empress—the twin fish on her tomb."

"We're not asking Yun." Hanjun withdrew to his bedroom, stressed and strained between responsibility and desire. Pen in hand, he reached for his journal.

We each had a strange dream. It could be a coincidence, but my gut says otherwise. We raised funds for a local orphanage. Jen picked the most beautiful dress to meet my mother. I'm nervous about the meeting, but I have no doubt she'll try her hardest. Here's to hoping my mom will, too.

CHAPTER FORTY-SIX

Ae-Cha

Hanjun shook Jen awake. "We're filming today, but I'd like to visit the mall first."

Sitting up, she massaged her eyes. "I need to pick up my dress."

"Perfect." He pecked her temple and left for a shower.

She lingered until he finished and then took hers. Returning to her room, she combed her closet for a suitable outfit. Though she preferred casual dress, venturing out in public with Hanjun was risky. In the event that they were photographed, she needed to fit the part.

Smelling of his favorite dalgona milk cleanser, Hanjun stood behind her, appreciating her collection of curated clothing. Reaching for the rod, he pulled out a tank. White with delicate lace at the neckline and iridescent studs down the front. "I haven't seen this on you."

"Now you will." She seized the top and procured a pair of black-washed jeans, along with the same blazer she wore to their concert months earlier.

He sat at the end of her bed. "I remember that jacket."

She tugged the pants over her hips. "Wore it in Chicago."

"It was the moment I knew you had style." He vaunted a toothy grin.

"I don't. I wear whatever I feel comfortable wearing."

"You either have it or you don't, and you have it." Once she was dressed, he nudged her through the doorway. "Let's go. There's a driver waiting for us."

"You're in a hurry, aren't you?" Snickering, she swiped a tube of lip gloss from her vanity.

Positioning his hands on her shoulders, he guided her to the kitchen. "You know everything is fast in Korea."

"Hey guys…" Walking to the fridge, she greeted her room-mates. "I have a question."

"Yeah?" Soogi slurped from a bowl of leftover pumpkin porridge.

"I visited a shop yesterday on our break—the lady working there has a daughter who loves Blackmirror. I was hoping I could get you to sign a picture for her." It was asking a lot, as J&I didn't like the troupe signing autographs outside official events. Publicly, the agency cited the verdict to avoid favoritism, but she thought it had more to do with the fact that they'd never receive a moment of rest if they did. Without clear boundaries, they would be scribbling their stage names until their hands fell off. And some supporters would expect them to sign with the stumps of their wrists.

"I have just the thing." Hanso vacated the room and returned with a promotional single from their upcoming album release. "I saved a few of these."

"Her name is Mi-Cha." The entertainers passed the record around, penning sugary sentiments to the young fan before transferring it to Jen. "Thanks. It will be her favorite birthday for the rest of her life."

Squeezing her hand, Hanjun rushed her to the door. "We'll be back in time for the filming."

"Bye!" She screeched as he stuffed her through the entry.

Once in the hallway, she acknowledged the door sentry and held the elevator while Hanjun felt his pockets. Patting his pants and coat, he groaned. "I forgot my phone. I'll meet you downstairs."

"Okay." She pressed the ground floor button.

Watching the door close between them, he spun around, flashing an accomplished smirk at the guard. Sneaking back into the condo, he hosted a discussion in her absence. "The crew should be here soon. They've already been paid. Soogi, do you know what you're doing?"

He nodded, scrubbing his dirty bowl in the sink. "Getting the dog from the shelter."

Hanjun's attention turned to Hanso. "How about you?"

"You don't need to worry, Hyung." Jin giggled. "Hanso is wrapping the gifts, Deok-Sun is overseeing the construction, and I'm taking the dog to the spa."

"We'll be back later." Hanjun doled out hugs. "Thanks for helping me surprise her."

While waiting in the lobby, Jen sat on an unoccupied settee and took in her surroundings. The condominium was home to some of the most influential people in Korea; government officials, talk show hosts, musicians, and actors were among the occupants. Paying extra attention to their mannerisms, she had a few things to learn if she had the slightest chance of impressing Hanjun's family.

From her pocket, she produced a compact memo pad containing important reminders about the meeting. Not only her observations, but suggestions from her roommates as well.

Jin answered her inquiries straightforwardly. "Wear new socks and don't bring a speck of dirt into Umma's home."

Hanso's advice was humbling. "Remain within their line of vision; you're a thief until proven friendly. And eat whatever you're given. No matter if you like it, no matter if it's spicy. Enjoy the food, but don't enjoy it too much or my parents will think you don't know how to cook properly."

Deok-Sun didn't think she was serious when she asked what she'd need to know if she met his mother. After grasping that she was genuinely interested, he responded with the most relatable remark. "We'll sit on the sofa until Umma brings us a plate of peeled pears, and you'll have to help me eat them. If the dish is not consumed by the time we leave, she will assume you cannot eat well."

Although she took each suggestion to heart, she believed Soogi gave the best guidance. At first, she was taken aback by how candid he was, but she soon realized he was harsh because he cared. When she asked, he evaded the question by asserting he wouldn't care about his parents' wishes. Days later, she discovered a handwritten manual, complete with bullet points, on how to dazzle his mother. He never owned up to leaving the document, though he did walk by as she studied it. Despite his hardened exterior, his warm smile always gave him away.

> ○ *You will be evaluated and assessed as a marriage prospect upon entering the family home.*

○ *The fact that they must speak English with you is a negative. If Bruce Cumings can write history books about Korea, Adam Johnson can write about North Korea, or Deborah Smith can translate Korean novels into English, you can learn a few phrases to communicate. Don't be lazy.*

○ *Mind their responses as well as your own. Short, staccato answers will read as negativity. Long, flowery responses will seem self-absorbed.*

○ *Heed unsolicited advice with heated enthusiasm, especially if it pertains to health, nutrition, sleep, fans, death, aspirations, and money.*

○ *Tonal of voice matters. Bright, helium voices are good. Deep is bad.*

○ *You should possess the basic skills necessary to carry food to your bowl with chopsticks without dropping a single morsel. The moment a rogue gochugaru speck hits the pressed tablecloth, your mortal life is endangered.*

○ *All banchan on the table are to be eaten along with every portion given to you directly. Let nothing on your plate go to waste. Umma didn't wash the grains fifty times and prevent any from falling into the sink for you to be neglectful.*

○ *It doesn't matter if Umma traps you in a leg lock; you must break out of the hold and clean the dishes. If she ends up washing them, you've lost the game.*

She perused the list of instructions, her heart rate increasing with each rule. But at the bottom, in neat handwriting, he added a simple note. One that made her feel perplexed and at ease.

Don't worry too much. Being yourself is more important than being someone you're not. Hanjun loves you. We love you. You'll be fine.

Stashing the information away, she closed her eyes, praying his mother would allow her leniency. "You'll just have to try a little harder, Jen."

★⁺₊★☾★⁺₊★

The same couturier from the day before greeted Hanjun and Jen as they entered the Hanbok shop. "I hope you don't mind; I've included a gift that will be perfect with your dress."

He collected the purchase, opening the bag for Jen to peer inside. She reached in and removed a black Louis Vuitton Pochette Coussin. Inspecting the embossed fabric, she knew it was authentic by touch alone. "This is too much. Let me pay you for it."

"Please accept it as a token of my appreciation." The seamstress bowed.

Jen started to open her mouth when Hanjun interrupted. "Lesson number two: when given a gift, accept gracefully."

He bowed, setting an example. "Thank you for your generosity."

"Thank you." Bending at the waist, she appreciated the gesture, but such a grand offering made her feel indebted. As her great-grandmother always said, 'A dish should never be returned empty.'

"It's my pleasure." The dressmaker matched the gesture. "I hope you'll consider working with me in the future."

"I will. May I ask your name?"

"Ae-Cha."

"Nice to meet you, Ae-Cha." Generating the signed album from her coat, Jen passed the token to her. "I brought this for Mi-Cha. I hope she has the birthday of her dreams."

Contorting to a steep angle, Ae-Cha's eyes welled with tears. "She will be so happy!"

"Thank you for the dress. It's an honor to wear it."

★⁺₊★☾★⁺₊★

Ambling behind Hanjun, Jen contemplated why his chauffeur dropped them outside a mobile store. Entering the building, she remained at his heels; he chatted with a man behind the counter much too fast for her to keep up. She identified her name, along with Mr. Yun's and J&I Entertainment, numerous times when Hanjun turned to her. "We're getting you a phone. I had the agency send over copies of your New Residence Card, visa, and bank info for automated payments."

She released a deep, aggravated exhalation. "Hanjun—"

He gripped her hands, silencing her lips. "Jen, listen to me. Your life is going to be hell if you don't let me do this. The device the agency gave you is worthless. If it makes you feel better, you can consider it a gift to me."

She relented. "Okay."

He motioned towards a revolving display of high-priced accessories. "Pick out a protector."

She browsed through the cases, spotting one that was pink and blue galaxy themed. "This one, please."

He placed the cover on the help desk. Pulling out his phone, he sat in a waiting chair and patted the seat next to him. "Do you want to play a game? New phones take a while to set up."

"Sure." She perched at his side while he loaded a new game of Blue Marble. "I'd like to be the white piece."

Selecting the blue pawn, he passed her the phone. While her token moved six places to match her roll, a notification from Soogi popped up. "Shoog says, 'It's done.'"

Snatching the device from her hands, he tapped in a reply. "He must be talking about the dishes."

The game carried on, and she wasn't sure how long it had been—an hour, maybe two—when the employee reappeared, spouting off the order total. She didn't hear an exact figure, but she knew it was too much for a device that needed to do the bare minimum.

Finishing the transaction, Hanjun snapped a cute selfie and added himself as a contact. "I'll have the boys message you on KaTalk."

Acquiring the phone, she noticed it paralleled his, right down to the silver coloring and model. Within moments, the electronic started pinging with alerts from her roommates, who were delighted to contact her outside of work.

$\star^+{}_+\star\mathbb{C}\star^+{}_+\star$

Jen and Hanjun arrived home to find cameras set up for the day's taping. Dumping shopping bags on the kitchen counter, he led her to the living room, where she sat on the floor with her back to the cinematographers. Sitting in front of Jen, Hanjun clocked Soogi, who gave him an inconspicuous thumbs-up.

From behind the cameras, Sehoon began a countdown. "We go live in hana, dul..."

Without delay, the mates painted smiles on their faces while Hanjun addressed the lens. "Weeks ago, we bought Christmas presents and wrapped them."

The supportive crew arranged decorated boxes around Jen. Mystified, she leaned into Jin, who only smiled in return. "I didn't know I was included."

Holding a stick with a foam finger on the end, Ha-Rin elucidated guidelines. "You're going to open presents and guess who bought the item. If you guess correctly, you gain a point. The member with the least number of points at the end of the game cooks breakfast in the morning."

Hanjun initiated by unveiling a small box. Ripping open the package, he gave off a pleased grin. "Samsung earbuds? I haven't had any since I lost the last pair."

"Who do you think purchased them?" Ha-Rin jabbed the indicating stick at him.

Inspecting the room, he focused on the youngest. "I think it was Deok-Sunny."

"Ddaeng!" Ha-Rin bopped him on the crown with the rod. "It was Jin."

"What could it be?" Hanso shook his memento. Stripping away the gingerbread-themed wrapping, he glared at Jin. "A Dior day bag? This was from Deok-Sun."

"Correct."

Deok-Sun tore into his present. "Mario Party Superstars? I think this came from Jen."

"Wait a sec," Jin intervened. "Was Jen playing?"

"Assistant Jenilyn helped pick out the items, but she didn't purchase them," Ha-Rin answered.

"Let's go with Hanso," Deok-Sun surmised.

"Correct."

"My turn!" Jin ripped an oversized ribbon from his gift. "Miffy scented pens and one, two, three, four, five leatherbound journals. I bet these came from Hanu."

"Correct."

Soogi opened his gift, delicately undoing the tape without ripping the paper. Though the shape was sizeable, the unraveling didn't take him long as the offering was only taped on the folded ends. "UGG slippers? Deok-Sun."

"Ddaeng! Those were from Hanso. Soogi and Hanjun tied with zero points and will be preparing breakfast in the morning." Ha-Rin chuckled from behind the cameras. "Jenilyn, would you like to give them their presents?"

Jen sprang into action as two assistants passed her a stack of white bakery boxes. She checked the name on each package and disbursed the gifts accordingly. "I thought I'd get you something you don't have often."

Snickering, one of the assistants held a smile, transferring the last offering. "We found her in the kitchen every day."

"Is that what you were doing all last week?" Jin opened the bundle with his name, surprised by the contents. "Are these..."

She collected the delicatessen tissue falling from the box. "Your favorite: persimmon-wrapped walnuts."

"Honey cookies?!" Soogi popped a sweet into his mouth.

Hanjun unfastened his surprise, sending a rain of crinkly paper into the air. "Twisted donuts? You made these?"

"We made everything." Jen beamed a smile at the assistants, thanking them for their help. "Hanso has yakgwa and hodu-gwaja for Deok-Sun."

"Miss Jenilyn, don't forget these." An aide handed her glass jars of deep-colored liquid, and she passed the containers off to her roommates.

"This was their idea." She gestured to her colleagues. "They mentioned you like cinnamon-ginger punch."

Ha-Rin cracked up as the musicians started stuffing their cheeks with treats. "Before we close the film, would you like Jenilyn to open her gifts?"

"Yes!" Jin scrambled to her side, stacking boxes on her lap. "Open this one first."

Unwrapping the paper, her gaze fixed on Hanso. "A Bluetooth speaker? I *know* who this came from."

Stretching for an oversized gift bag, she withdrew another surprise. "A pillow? And a pet carrier? Is this so I can babysit Hanso's dog?"

Hanso had a cute chihuahua named Solo, who was an absolute baby. She loved it when he carried him around the office because he dressed the pup in high fashion similar to his own.

Soogi fathered a brown dachshund named Roly Poly. Poly captured his heart, and he was a complete simp for him, even if he didn't get to see him often.

She once overheard her housemates discussing Hanjun's beloved pet. When she inquired about the furry friend, he became dejected and stated that he didn't have one. After witnessing his countenance, she vowed to never ask again.

Deok-Sun left the living room while Jen opened the final present. A long, narrow box wrapped in glittery gold paper. Inside was a black choker with precious stones inlaid in the leather. "Is this a necklace?"

"It's a collar." Hanso burst into an embarrassed giggle. "Those are diamonds. Very expensive."

Deok-Sun rejoined with the ivory dog from the sanctuary trailing behind him. The young pup ran straight to her, assaulting her with slobbery licks. Lifting the dog into her arms, she hugged him as much as she had at the shelter. "Are we fostering him until he finds a forever home?"

"We adopted him." Hanso proclaimed.

Hanjun scowled; he wanted to be the one to break the news. "We're his forever home."

Deok-Sun nudged another item towards her: a white envelope featuring a sketched photo of the canine. She unsealed the pocket, peering around the dog to find a printed image of designer food bowls. "I wanted to order custom dishes and a tag, but I wasn't sure what you wanted to name him."

"A name—" She paused to admire the pupper. His fur was more vibrant than she remembered, and the spot over his left eye was redder, reminding her of many evenings spent watching anime. "How about Todoroki?"

"He does look like Todoroki." Soogi rubbed the dog's ears.

"Hanjun, do you want to show Jenilyn her gift?" Ha-Rin persuaded him to step forward.

Hanjun leaped from the floor and grabbed her hand, pulling her to the glass terrace doors. "I'm sorry it took so long to adopt him—I had to clear the construction with the building manager first."

Stepping out into the freezing air, she encountered a lengthy patch of simulated grass near the corner, along with dog toys and a miniature hammock for him to sleep on. Seemingly happy, the tiny dog sniffed around, wagging its tail and rubbing against their ankles.

"It's artificial for now, but we can plant real grass in the spring."

Inspecting the space, she discovered the guardrail was modified with safety paneling to ensure the canine couldn't slip through the gaps. "You did all of this?"

"I didn't do the work, but I hired the contractor. We agreed on a schedule to walk him, and the agency employs handlers, so you won't need to worry when we're at work."

"Hanjun, this is just—" She shook her head, bereft of words. "I can never thank you enough."

⋆⁺₊⋆☾⋆⁺₊⋆

Hanjun sprawled on Jen's duvet, sprinkling Todoroki with kisses. He inhaled the familiar scent of jasmine dog shampoo lingering on the pup's soft fur—the same pet cleanser Blackmirror promoted.

Lying next to him, Jen admired the pair. She hadn't known him to be much of a dog person until she witnessed the love he held for their adopted friend. "Thank you."

"For what?" He paused to give the dog a belly scratch.

She cracked into a smile, her eyes morphing more colorful than usual. "Everything you do for me. The dress, the phone, and Todoroki. You're good to me."

Resting his head on her chest, he looked up at her. "Want to watch TV like an old married couple?"

She cuddled against him. "I'd love that."

Sliding an arm around her waist, he clicked through the channels. Fifteen minutes into a cheesy romantic comedy, her breathing leveled out, and she drifted to sleep. Sighing, he untangled from her and shuffled to his room. Crawling under the covers, he reached for his journal.

I feel relieved knowing she can text me if she needs to. We now have a shared dorm dog. Todoroki.

<u>CHAPTER FORTY-SEVEN</u>

Rise of the Dragon

Chasing the scent of warm, buttery pancakes, Jen shuffled to the kitchen. The atmosphere was alive with sizzling sausages and crackling batter, and a comedic duo of culinary expertise hovered over the stove.

Yawning, she rubbed her eyes. "I forgot you had to cook..."

Startled by her voice, Hanjun nudged her into the living room. "Punishments are always filmed."

Glancing at the counter to find a tripod, she suspired. "Oh."

He caressed her upper arms and bent to examine her eyes. "I'll bring you a plate when we're done, okay?"

"Okay." Feeling deathly hungry, she retreated to her room. Deciding she wouldn't be able to fall back asleep on an empty stomach, she texted her best friend, who immediately called her on video.

Nearly in tears, Kristen rambled. "I haven't heard from you in forever! How are you? I miss your pretty face!"

She giggled. "I'm great. Really great."

"Have you heard anything about when you're coming back to the US?"

"Sometime in the new year."

"Girl! I can't wait to see you."

Crossing the room, Jen shut her bedroom door. "I have so many things to tell you, but I don't know if I can."

Kristen vented a long whine. "At least give me a hint."

She delayed, pondering if she should. "Have you been following Blackmirror on YOUniverse?"

"Ever since you left."

"Most of the rumors are false, but there is one that's true."

"HanJen?" Her friend shrieked while she nipped her lip to hide a smile. "Jeni! Have you, you know? You don't need to answer; I see it on your face. How was it?"

Incapable of hiding her enthusiasm, she exploded like a confetti cannon. "The best. No exaggeration."

"He must be special. I can't wait to meet him."

Interrupting their girl chat, Hanjun knocked on the door. "I brought breakfast."

"I-I need to go. I love you!" She dropped her phone on the bed, though her friend yelled a sprightly greeting before the transmission ended.

"Hi Hanjun!"

Slinking through the doorway, he handed her a platter. "I see you're putting your phone to good use."

"She's the only thing I miss." Peering at the dish, she found an artfully crafted heart-shaped pancake. She wondered if he possessed the skills necessary to execute such a feat or if he roped Soogi into making it. "Are you still filming?"

"They won't mind if I'm not there." He watched her stuff a bite into her mouth. "We have a meeting with Ha-Rin and a fan event this evening. I won't be home until late. I'm sorry."

Devouring the pancake, she set the plate on the nightstand. "Don't apologize. Your ethic and drive are two of the many things I love about you."

He wore a half-hearted smile. "I'd rather be with you."

Cupping his chin in her palms, she gave him a joggle. "Say it with me. Your. Career. Comes. First."

He repeated the words, looping an arm around her back. "We're announcing the tour at the fan sign. Maybe we can go for coffee after?"

"Directly after the announcement?" She held an implication of curiosity. "I thought we agreed to stay on the down low."

"If that's what you want."

"I'm asking what you want, Hanjun."

"I want to have coffee with you after the promotion."

"Then we'll have coffee after the promotion."

⋆⁺₊⋆☾⋆⁺₊⋆

Settled in the back of the escort van, Hanjun called his mom on the short ride to the office. "Hey, mom."

"Hi, son!" She returned in a high-pitched voice.

"Are you busy on the twenty-seventh?"

"I'll be home in the evening. Are you staying over?"

"Sure. I'd like to show Jen Ilsan Lake."

"Ah, you loved Lake Park even as a child."

"Yeah." Spotting droves of fans amassed outside the J&I building, he released an inaudible grunt. "I'm almost at work. I'll message you later."

"Eat plenty of vegetables and exercise at least three times a week!" She ended the call.

Marching into the office, the artists sank into their chairs. At the head of the table, Ha-Rin opened a beige portfolio. "We have a hectic day ahead of us, so we need to make this brisk. Your last two tours were swift, leading to burnout in a matter of weeks. Hanso, I know you had some concerns about that."

"I'd like a few days of rest between performances." Hanso grasped his kneecaps. "I'm not as young as I used to be."

"I wish we had more time in each city," Deok-Sun chirped.

"There's also the issue of producing while touring," Hanjun chimed in. "We'll need time to write, record, arrange—"

"2022 will be the last year we're together for a while." Jin looked over his friends.

"We'll keep this in mind when we finalize the schedule." Ha-Rin paused to skim his notes. "I received your email about possible campaigns for the tour; however, Yun PD suggested the One Love Tour. One love. One heart. One destiny."

The musicians nodded, showcasing their interest when Jin spoke. "It embraces our connection with Anti."

"And *Time Machines and Dreams* is about eternity," Hanjun offered.

Soogi leaned back in his seat. "It's fitting."

"It gives a feeling of unity," Hanso added.

Ha-Rin eyed his wristwatch. "You have an hour before you need to meet your stylists. Make the most of it."

While his bandmates decreed what they wanted to do with their unmonitored free time, Hanjun slipped out of the room and headed to the gym. Once in the elevator, he called his closest friend, Kang Tae-Gil. "Taeg, I haven't heard from you in a while."

His friend chuckled in a deep, gravelly tone. "I called. You were busy."

He nodded even though he was alone. "It hasn't been announced, but we're going on tour."

"Seems like you found a way to keep it together. I've watched your streams and read a few interesting articles."

He tittered nervously. "Yeah?"

"Yeah." Taeg matched his tone. "Are you going to tell me about her?"

Hanjun rolled his eyes. "If you watched the lives, you've seen her."

"Is it just fun?"

Wagging his head, he sighed. "I really like her."

Taeg guffawed, causing him to remove the phone from his ear. "Lots of people out there to really like."

He groaned, knowing he would respond like the bachelor rock star who viewed commitment as a death sentence to his profligate lifestyle. "Not like her."

"I hope it works out, bro. She seems good for you."

"Yeah, me too." Hanjun checked the floor number. "I'm just getting to the gym. I'll talk to you later."

"We should get together before you leave."

"Yeah." He ended the call while Taeg professed his amity.

"I love you!"

With so little time before needing to visit his stylist, Hanjun settled on a light workout. Peeling off his shirt and stepping onto a treadmill, he revisited the conversation with Taeg.

There were a lot of people out there. He met many and contemplated dating a few, but there wasn't a single person—musician or otherwise—he found to be his type. Never had he been drawn to someone like he was to Jen. He didn't even understand how she could occupy so much of his thought processing.

If falling in love was a sickness and excitement, butterflies, and daydreams were the symptoms, he understood the peculiarity as an omen of being on the right path. He wasn't controlled by passion more than any other man, even if he made choices with her in mind. In his temporary insanity, he hadn't forgotten his dreams or rearranged his end-game picture. If anything, he envisioned her standing next to him at the finish line. He hoped she would wait for him, just as the artwork in his studio did. It would be even better if she accompanied him on the journey.

Sixty minutes later, before he left the gym showers, he messaged Jen the address for the fan signing, requesting that she meet him fifteen minutes early.

⋆⁺₊⋆☾⋆⁺₊⋆

Applying copious amounts of lotion to her arms and legs, Jen moved to her closet, matching items until she found something she liked. Something Hanjun would like. The probability of being photographed together after the high-profile affair was elevated, and she needed to ensure she didn't damage his or his family's reputation. She had to exude an air of luxury, with the demeanor of a lover to a powerful artist.

After much self-debating, she selected a white collared lace dress blouse, a black sequin blazer, medium gray skinnies, and black laser-cut wedges. Slipping into the outfit, she inspected her body in the mirror, ensuring she didn't present too curvaceous or old-fashioned.

Fixing her makeup, she was nervous about attending Blackmirror's fan event. Though the agency loosened its rules about dating, she didn't want to burden Hanjun at his job. And in many ways, she didn't know who he was at work.

In the beginning of their courtship, she didn't know who Ryu Hanjun was; she only knew his public persona. After weeks of dating, she uncovered a fragment of who he was. Someone who was a bit clumsy and never failed to dribble sauce on his clothes when he ate. Someone who needed to be reminded to pack his glasses and take his vitamins. He was as nervous as he was anxious, and he often required pep talks to complete his schedule.

She had no idea who Rem of Blackmirror was and felt like she might be encountering him for the first time.

⋆⁺₊⋆☾⋆⁺₊⋆

The primped entertainers walked along the sidewalk. A layer of security thick enough to block their view of the street hid the ensemble in plain sight. Marveling at the cluster of followers gathered in a quiet part of the city, Hanjun felt accomplished. Supporters turning up for their events were tangible proof of their success.

Passing a colorful street vendor, he stopped long enough to purchase a bouquet with the assistance of a kind ajumma. Choosing festive colors of ivory and red, the florist insisted on roses and Jeju camellias.

Hanso teased him while he inspected each petal. "Hanjun buying flowers? That's unheard of."

Paying with a handful of cash, Hanjun wedged the blossoms in the crook of his arm. Adjusting the lapels of his designer suit, he snapped a selfie. "What can I say? She does it to me."

The entourage walked for another half-city block. Just as they entered the convention center through a back door, Hanjun's phone rang. "Mi Sol? Is everything alright?"

"The traffic is awful. I don't think I'll make it on time."

He glanced at the bouquet in his arms. "How long will you be?"

"I'm not sure. I might walk the rest of the way, but it'll be at least thirty minutes."

"I'll see you when you get here." Unsure what else to do, he propped the back door open and asked the security detail to keep an eye out for her.

⋆⁺₊⋆☾⋆⁺₊⋆

Jen stared out a smudged taxi window. The streetlights were starting to pop on, and traffic hadn't moved in over fifteen minutes. A quick glance at her phone proved the event started without her.

"I'll walk from here." Grabbing her possessions, she exited the vehicle.

Trampling down the pathway in shoes unsuitable for rough terrain, she noticed long lines of cars clogging the road. The jam flowed from the address Hanjun gave her and didn't show signs of ceasing. Perturbed by the blockage, enraged drivers honked and spewed profanities, waving rude gestures from open windows.

Though the occupancy of the building maxed out at three hundred, swarms of anxious supporters and reporters waited outside the establishment, swamping the surrounding blocks to catch a glimpse of the boy band. It was the kind of surge she would steer clear of under normal circumstances. The type that could cause a collapse, harming dozens, and she doubted the agency had enough security to manage the mass.

⋆⁺₊⋆☾⋆⁺₊⋆

At the front of the house, the vocalists took their seats behind a black-clothed table. Initiating the function, Ha-Rin entered center stage, clutching a microphone in his palm. "On behalf of J&I Entertainment, thank you for coming out to support Blackmirror. Before we begin, we have an extra special announcement to make."

Glancing at Hanjun, he held a delighted smile. "Rem, would you like to share the news?"

Grasping the mic, Hanjun's eyes widened. He had never seen so many people packed into one hall, and he wondered if the crowd violated occupancy regulations. Shaking off the anxiety prickling his gut, he held a pleasant tone. "Blackmirror will be touring in the new year."

"One love. One heart. One destiny. We're part of one universe." The roar of spectators drowned out his thoughts. He rotated, seeking Jen's familiar face, and found himself lost in a sea of team members.

Ha-Rin motioned for the bouncers to allow fans through one at a time. Unlike previous meets where the bandmates would spend a few minutes with each fan, Ha-Rin hurried the line, only giving them a few seconds with each devotee.

Scrawling his name thirty-something times, Hanjun considered calling Jen but remembered what she said that morning. His career came first. And he knew she meant it. She hyped him up to stay on top of his affairs, and it was something he loved about her. She never complained when he was too fatigued to spend time with her or whined when he stayed at the office. Her only concern was whether he ate and if he arrived home safe.

With too many individuals sardined into one area, the building quickly became stuffy. A handful of employees and a small group of hire-by-the-day security guards exited the back door. After a few smokes, the staff returned to the building. One of the contracted sentries secured the door, with another questioning his actions. "Didn't one of those idols ask us to leave it open?"

Wrenching the door closed, the guard sneered. "Do you think that kid would listen if I told him how to do his job?"

★⁺₊★☾★⁺₊★

The sky was midnight black when the building came into view. Plain beige, besides a neon sign affixed to the side. Approaching the back door, Jen had given up on hurrying. She was too late even before she started walking. "I can't believe I couldn't be there for him."

Her phone chimed with a delightful notification when she reached the destination. The surroundings smelled of nicotine, and the ambiance was smoky, with one streetlight flickering every few seconds. Battling strobing lights, a headache at the base of her skull crept in, and she felt for the door through the shadows. Utilizing her mobile to illuminate the way, she yanked the handle, her fingers slipping from the sealed door. "Hanjun said it would be unlocked."

Tugging on the door four more times, she considered trying to pry it open. "That won't work. It feels like there's a deadbolt."

She swept the vicinity; there wasn't much behind the building. Colored trash bins, wooden pallets, empty boxes, and a small, dilapidated shed. The rear was severely neglected and in need of a woman's touch.

Resorting to knocking, a sudden commotion erupted from inside the structure, as if the event were coming to an end. Knowing he couldn't pick up, she called Hanjun, resting her forehead on the frigid steel door. "I'm here. Jun, I'm sorry."

She terminated the call and kicked the door hard enough to set off her balance. "He shows up for you all the time, and you let him down. It's so much harder for him to make time for you and you—"

"Jenilyn?" A raspy voice questioned from behind her.

Turning to face the speaker, a chill crept up her vertebrae. "Huh?"

★⁺₊★☾★⁺₊★

Hanjun was checking his voicemail when Ha-Rin asked him to give his final words of the night. Dropping the phone into his pocket, he held the blossoms he purchased for Jen in one hand and a microphone in the other. Colorful confetti rained from the rafters, and he vibrated his lips to avoid inhaling the bits. "We will only try to make you proud, and we love you more than you could ever know."

Moving to the front of the table, the five companions held hands and bowed, flashing finger hearts to their beloved fans while a friendly announcer made a declaration over the intercom in Korean, English, and Japanese. "Please calmly move to the exit."

Disappearing behind a velvet curtain, Hanjun pulled out his phone. Just as he lifted the device to his ear, Ha-Rin summoned him over to a row of journalists. "We need photos for the press."

Posing for pictures with his bandmates, he revealed smile after smile, inching a hand into his pocket. Unfortunately, due to the publicity campaign, he was bombarded with questions from reporters who wanted to know what to expect from the upcoming tour, which songs the setlist may contain, and where they planned to travel.

$$\star^+_+\star\,\mathbb{C}\star^+_+\star$$

"Answer the question." A husky voice sneered from Jen's right side.

With her heart pounding hard enough to hear, she planted her back against the door. Furiously jiggling the knob, she whispered an anguished plea that the strangers weren't out to harm. "Please—"

A woman's voice, low and raspy, sliced through the frozen air. "You were talking to the leader of Blackmirror, right?"

Shaking her head, she refused to respond, and the woman continued with audible mirth. "That makes you Hanso's ex-girlfriend."

She turned away from the interrogation, slamming her fists on the barrier hard enough to make her palms ache. "Open the door!"

"It's the Shayo!" The man growled. "It has to be."

"Shayo?" Completely on her own, she floundered to devise a plan. Nobody was going to save her. Instead, she squared her chest, determined to face her tormentors. Though the flashing light made it difficult for her to concentrate, she captured the silhouette of the woman. Brunette, with an average build and lopsided clavicles. Her most prominent aspects were a chipped front tooth and wide-set eyes. Despite her unkempt appearance, she seemed afraid of something, and when Jen moved to assess the man, she flinched.

The man had a perverted look about him: cold, narrow eyes, an oddly slim nose, and ears sticking out far from his scalp. His neck featured a series of spider tattoos, and the prison artwork dipped into his chest cavity. He was the type of man few would allow around their children or beloved pets, yet he strived for the brunette's approval.

★⁺₊★☾★⁺₊★

After completing several impromptu interviews, Hanjun scouted for Jen. Searching every corner of the building, his leisurely walk turned into a frenzied jog, and he interrogated everyone he could find. His fingers dug into the shoulders of an audio engineer. "Have you seen Jenilyn? My girlfriend? About this tall—blonde, red underneath?"

Unable to find her, he spotted Soogi. He was changing out of his suit and into a casual jersey and baggy, utilitarian pants. "Jen should've been here by now."

He slid the slippery bottoms over his slender thighs. "I thought she stayed home for the evening."

"I asked her to join me for coffee." Hanjun seized another glimpse around the venue. Chaotic and disorganized, the squad worked to disassemble auditory equipment. "Something's wrong. It's not like her to be late."

"Yeah." Soogi pulled a zip-up hoodie over his shoulders. "She'd rather leave two hours early than show up tardy."

★⁺₊★☾★⁺₊★

"You don't understand. There was nothing going on." Jen's phone buzzed, and the screen displayed Hanjun's smiling picture. She moved to answer it, but the figure to her right lunged, knocking the device out of her grasp. Taking advantage of the distraction, she ran towards the side of the building, where the raucous enthusiasm of reporters ensured safety in numbers.

Just before she rounded the corner, powerful biceps pulled her away from the street. She thrashed, but the strobes disoriented her, overwhelming her vision with black specks. She landed several punches on her attacker until he clutched her in a chokehold. "Scream and I'll crush your windpipe."

Her sternum heaved as she struggled for air, her nails clawing into the man's forearms. It wasn't how she pictured her end—in a gloomy alley in Seoul, South Korea. She greeted death as a comforting friend throughout her life, but never at the hands of a stranger. She gouged at him, ensuring she had enough genetic material under her fingernails. If she were to perish, the agency wouldn't let the offender go easily. And even if they did, Hanjun certainly wouldn't.

She scratched hard enough to draw blood, and the man roared, firming up his grasp on her neck. "You little bitch."

"Hold her still." Snarling, the woman unsheathed a double-edged sword from her back. Light glinted off the sharp edge, catching Jen's focus. Bending to the ground, the woman grabbed a rock and hurled it into the sky, shattering the strobing light. Glass shards rained down like crashing stars, notching them with lacerations.

"If you try to run, I'll kill you." The man released his grip to solidify his hold. Cementing her to his chest, his thick fingers dug into her flesh, bruising the muscles underneath.

Desperate, she thrust forward, depleting her strength to break free, but the blade-wielding woman was prompt to counter. She stomped on her ankle, eliciting a revolting crack that sent her crumpling to the ground. While she lay on the pavement, wheezing in agony, the man tightened his hold. "I warned you!"

Unfazed by the struggle, the woman casually paced in front of them. "Do you want to die?"

"Nothing you saw was real!" Jen's arms were pinned to her sides, and the blood drained from her extremities. As she fought her restraints, the heat from her frantic movements intensified the burning on her wrists. She tried to cry for help, but her neck jerked backwards, gargling her pleas.

Snatching a chunk of her hair, the man barked. "I told you not to scream."

"Shut up." The woman moved the steel blade to her neck, spewing droplets of foul-smelling spit from her mouth. She pressed the sharp edge against her artery, biting into her skin with enough pressure to send a warning.

"Please." Whimpering, she held her breath, terrified that the slightest movement would result in a deadly gash.

"You will speak when spoken to." Removing the blade from her neck, the woman delivered a firm slap to her cheek. Head snapping to the side, she wasn't sure which throbbed worse—her limbs or her ankle. Both burned like hell, and she prayed the attackers would, at the very least, kill her humanely. "You are what is wrong in our world—quarter-breed mongrels created with little regard for purity."

"Rise of the Dragon." The woman clutched both of Jen's cheeks in one hand. "Not much of a Dragon now, are you?"

She yanked Jen's head up by her crown before letting her neck fall. "That's what I thought. You're pathetic."

"Rise of the *what?*" Jen had no idea what the crazy bitch wanted. All she knew was that she couldn't take on two assailants in her condition. The only option she had left was to stand steady in the face of evil. Maintaining eye contact, she provoked her captors. "If you're going to kill me, kill me. Don't be a snake and do it."

The woman cackled, gazing at the full moon peeking out from behind overcast clouds. "Kill you? It's not that easy. We must dismantle the movement and prove you are not the savior. Your death is only the beginning."

★⁺₊★☾★⁺₊★

With perplexed eyes, Hanjun listened to the voicemail before searching out their manager. "Have you seen Jen? She left a message saying she was here."

Ha-Rin inspected the crew. "She must be around."

Rushing through crowded hallways, sweat beaded on Hanjun's forehead. Soogi and Hanso followed behind, interrogating everyone they passed. Grabbing the wrists of a makeup artist, Soogi rattled off the same thing he asked every worker he encountered. "Jen... Have you seen her?"

"Miss Jenilyn?" The unsettled woman verified. "I haven't seen her since the filming yesterday."

"Shit." Disheartened, he thanked the beautician, noticing Hanjun rushing to the alley.

Dialing her number for the dozenth time, Hanjun sprinted to the back of the building, ramming face-first into the door. Mishandling the lock, he twisted the deadbolt and burst beyond the threshold, spewing a string of expletives. "Who the hell locked the emergency exit?"

Stepping into the vast night, he searched for her, only to find the new phone ringing on the ground near a pile of boxes. Upon retrieving the device, his heart sank into his stomach. The screen was cracked, and he knew she wouldn't have discarded the gift. "She was here."

Jogging to catch him, Soogi peered over his shoulder. "That's Jen's phone."

"Where is she?" Hanso squinted into the abyss.

"Shh!" Fixating on a distant vibration, Hanjun's breathing faded into nonexistence. "Mi Sol?"

"You don't have to do this," Jen implored one last time before accepting her fate.

"Shut the fuck up! I won't tell you again." The weaponed woman screeched. "I was chosen to cleanse the bloodline just as my ancestors did. To stop the prophecy once and for all!"

Languishing, Jen waited for a concluding blow. She couldn't withstand a slash to the throat, and her strength was drained. Her fight was over.

"Stop!" Bellowing, Hanjun rounded the corner to the dim passage. He advanced close enough to identify Jen on her knees, her arms held behind her back, while a burly man leered over her. An unattractive woman stood before them, gripping a ceremonial sword. "Don't hurt her."

"You!" Discerning a familiar voice, the woman jabbed the sharpened blade in his direction. "You brought her here!"

Hanging back in the shadows, Hanso watched as Soogi navigated the obscurity. Sneaking through the twilight, he placed a finger over his lips. Moving like a cat in the night, he went virtually unseen amidst piles of crates and pallets.

"Why would you choose to be with her?" The attacker pointed the sword at Jen. "Of all people, why her?"

"I don't see why it matters." Stepping forward, Hanjun remained calm while his torso felt as if it were collapsing. "If you don't like her, it's because you don't know her."

The woman tipped her head back, crowing into the sky. "You think you know her?"

"You don't have to do this." Facing Jen, his voice faltered. Her body drooped, and her eyes were dull. "If it's money—"

"Money?" The woman pointed the claymore at him once again. "This is about much more than money."

"The Setting Sun." The man issued a guttural growl, jerking Jen by her arms. "She's the Dragon! The bringer of Shayo!"

Hanso and Hanjun swapped glances, unsure what to make of the cryptic words. They resembled religious extremists who roamed the side streets of Seoul, only yielding an armament far more dangerous than a simple god.

"You don't know?" Scoffing, the woman rotated to face Jen. "If you can't end this, I will."

Hanjun opened his mouth to speak when Hanso positioned a palm on his chest. "You're right. Jen will sully our heritage."

Intrigued, the woman pivoted to face him. "Go on."

"What're you doing?" Hanjun's eyes skipped past the man holding Jen hostage and caught a flash of Soogi creeping around behind him. Hopping down from a heap of wooden crates, the agile performer examined the area for a weapon.

Making use of his pre-idol theatrical training, Hanso lengthened his speech, allowing Soogi time to retrieve a brick. "Jen has torn us apart from the inside. For brothers to fight over a woman is indecent. We're better than her."

Rising from a crouched position, Soogi kept his eyes on Jen. With a soundless nod, he signaled for Hanso to continue talking. Harnessing a sinister smirk, he disappeared into the shadows, waiting for the perfect moment to strike.

"We have tarnished our legacy." Performing a deep bow, he offered out his arms. "Please let me be the one to bring honor to our families once more."

"A sacrifice must be made." Returning the formality, the woman knighted him with the blade.

Swaggering across the blackened space, Hanso raised the weapon above his head. "You must not fear death, for it is only the beginning."

Jen hid her emotions in a stony disguise, but in her mind, she had already died and was awaiting the final blow. "Just do it, Ho-Young."

CHAPTER FORTY-EIGHT

The Dragon, the Keepers, and the Cake

"Soogi, now!" In a calculated maneuver, Hanso swung the sword to Jen's right side. Snapping her neck to the left, the freezing wind kissed her cheek as the blade cut through the air.

Wide-eyed, she ensured she wasn't missing an arm. "Huh?"

During the well-planned swing, Soogi popped up behind her, smashing a brick into the side of her captor's head. The man's clutch loosened, sending Jen to the ground. Discarding the bloody weapon, he scrambled to catch her before she crumbled like a tumbling tower.

"You're fine. You're going to be okay." Pulling her to his chest, he rocked her. A slow heartbeat pulsed through her arms, and her skin was cold to the touch. Fingers clenched, she clung to his collar, burying her face into his shirt. Clutching her, he focused on Hanso and Hanjun, realizing they had their own problems to deal with.

"What have you done?" Shrieking, the woman made a desperate attempt to escape, and Hanso chased her. He yanked the backpack she wore from her shoulders while Hanjun swiped at her legs, launching her nose-first onto the concrete.

Strapping her flailing arms behind her back, Hanjun pinned her to the asphalt. "Hanso, get help! Go!"

Sprinting into the building, Hanso returned with the entire crew. The commotion drew onlookers from the street, along with droves of fans who carried the group's Galabong. Ha-Rin instructed the handlers to form a circle around the area, knocking phones out of the hands of anyone who tried to document the calamity.

"What the hell happened?" Ha-Rin looked at Hanjun, who immobilized the woman. His gaze then moved to Soogi and Jen, huddled on the ground, covered in dirt and grime.

"She was attacked." Hanso took Hanjun's place to restrain the woman.

"I don't know." Shaking his head, Hanjun rubbed his forehead. "Something about The Setting Sun."

"*The Setting Sun?*" Ha-Rin glared at him. "What are you talking about?"

"They called her the Shayo." Collecting his composure, Hanjun rushed to Jen's side, explaining what he knew about the term. "Japanese novelist Osamu Dazai crafted a book of the same name. The English translation is *The Setting Sun*."

"Her heart rate is slow." Though Soogi tried to maneuver her toward her boyfriend, she didn't budge.

Hanjun ran his palms through his hair. Scowling at the man subjugated, he buried his shoe deep into his abdomen with each word he shouted. "Tell. Me. Why!"

Four security guards rushed in to divide them, issuing a curt warning. "Stop! You're going to kill him! He's not worth your career."

Fixated on settling the score, Hanjun broke free and stomped on him once more for good measure. "Piece of shit."

"You have no idea what you've done." Sprawled in a pool of his own blood, the man cackled. "We've found the Dragon!"

Hanjun made a run for him again, and the bodyguards restrained him. "I'll kill you! You're dead! You're fucking dead!"

On the opposite side of the chaos, a brigade of uniformed officers confronted the crowd with plastic riot shields, pushing eyewitnesses toward the sidewalk. Deploying high-powered water cannons, they dispersed the mob and began probing bystanders for the truth about what went down.

Within minutes, armed officers from the National Police Agency surfaced at the scene, gathering proof of the offense and obtaining footage from the CCTV cameras. The investigation started by having Hanjun and Hanso demonstrate what they witnessed, including how the attacker held Jen in a chokehold and the way Hanso swung the curtana.

Meanwhile, a sprightly emergency medical technician blocked the alleyway with their van. Running to Jen, she checked her pupils for abnormal dilation. "She's in shock. If we can't snap her out of it, she'll need to be admitted."

Soogi gave his best shot at consoling her. "Jen, the night we met, you told me you liked Drake. I had such a stupid crush on you; I listened to your favorite song all night. I don't know why I thought it would bring me closer to you."

Holding a hand on the back of her head, his lips rested on her forehead. "You're strong. You can do anything."

Rising to his full height, Hanjun stood near an interceptor while a lieutenant interrogated him. "What happened?"

Holding his head high, he made eye contact with the perpetrator. Receiving medical assistance he didn't deserve, the man held a smile, showing no amount of empathy for what he'd done. "My girlfriend was supposed to meet me here. When I couldn't find her, I came outside and found that man holding her arms while the woman tried to kill her."

The lieutenant halted his notetaking. "*Kill?* Are you sure?"

Snarking, Hanjun espied the woman. Wriggling and screaming, she resisted arrest. "She held a sword to her neck."

Drafting the report, the lieutenant blew his breath. "The man claims you assaulted him."

"I kicked him." Hanjun lowered his gaze before looking him in the eye. "A handful of times."

Rendering a cord from his gear, he wrapped Hanjun's wrists, draping a cloth over the knot. "You're innocent until proven guilty."

A few meters away, another officer briefed Hanso, who had a hard time recalling the tragedy. "Want to tell me what happened?"

Hanso arranged his arms over his torso. "They held her down, and I convinced them to give me the weapon."

"Did they say why they held her captive?"

"Something about a dragon and a prophecy. They were going to kill her; does it matter why?"

Observing his bandmates getting drilled by the law, Soogi slackened his hold on Jen. Her tight grip on his collar loosened and she pulled away. "Are you okay?"

Bowing, she solidified her response. "I'm not okay."

Acknowledging a patrolman approaching, he gave her thigh a jiggle. "Stay here. I'll be right back."

She remained on the ground where he left her, surveying the damage endured during the violence. Her ankle was distended but unbroken. Her jeans were ripped at the knees, with small rocks embedded in her skin. She identified handprints around her arms, and judging by the sharp pain around her neck, she knew she would bruise. Beyond the aches and trauma, she was alive. Her extremities were intact, and she was grateful Hanjun, Hanso, and Soogi found her when they did.

"Tell me your side of the story." A patrolman interrogated Soogi, clearly bothered by taking his statement.

"It's not a story." Growling, Soogi scowled at the man and woman. Moving his gaze to Jen, his voice softened. "I slipped around the back and took him out while Hanjun and Hanso captured the woman."

He intersected his gaze. "Are you admitting you harmed him?"

Biting his lip, Soogi positioned his arms behind his back. Holding his chin in the air, he kept his eyes on Jen while the officer escorted him to Hanjun.

Leaning against a squad, Hanjun noticed Soogi's cuffs weren't wrapped in cloth to spare his virtue. "Is she alright?"

"She was a little better when I left." Sensing how upset Hanjun was, he had no doubt that he would have killed the man had security not intervened. "You did what you could."

Unable to control his volume, Hanjun thrashed, kicking his knees against the car. "How could this happen?"

A senior officer joined Jen. Crouching to eye level, he motioned for everyone to leave the area. "I know you've experienced something awful, but I need you to tell me about it."

Rubbing along the bruising on her upper sternum, she stared at the cracked asphalt. "I was meeting my boyfriend. He asked me to go to the back door, but it was locked when I arrived. I tried calling, but he didn't answer, and they cornered me."

She hesitated, remembering her secondary education. The school was known for demonstrating disaster drills by employing people to enter the buildings and fabricate various levels of harm. Bomb threats, school shootings, drunk driver crashes—you name it. After performing the scenarios, the organizers briefed students on the events. Most couldn't recall any helpful elements, while others recollected wrong attributes. Alongside the stunt, the organization taught the students ways to remember disasters as they happened.

The most crucial attributes were in the details. While ethnicity, age, height, and weight were a good start to apprehending an evildoer, there were several factors more reliable: hair texture, hairline or lack thereof, skin condition, eye shape, pitch, speech, and gait were far better qualities to distinguish.

"You can tell me." The officer noticed her space out.

She cited everything she could remember. "The man grabbed me from behind and dragged me to the side of the building. I tried to run, but he choked me and said he'd kill me if I screamed. The woman brought a sword to my neck—"

"What did she say?"

"She was chosen to cleanse the bloodline."

"*Cleanse the bloodline.*" He made a notation on a clipboard. "Is there anything else you can remember?"

"The woman kept talking about a prophecy. And Shayo? And something about a dragon."

Completing the delineation, he seemed concerned but not at all surprised. "We'll take this to the station."

Another sheriff chatted with the assaulters. Performing an artifact search, the policemen found various images of Jen on their person, and they logged the photographs, weapon, and brick as evidence. Finishing up the investigation after nearly two hours of examination, one officer approached Ha-Rin. "We're taking your boys to the station."

Ha-Rin retrieved his phone to call the agency's team of legal advisors. "We'll send our lawyers."

Noticing the officers preparing to leave, Jen whistled to gain their attention. "Can I speak with them?"

Turning to face her, the officer's eyes moved to her scuffed shoes, surprised to find her standing. "Make it fast."

Wincing as she ran, her bones tried collapsing as she cleared the lot. Slamming into his body, she hugged Hanjun hard enough to make him wince. "I'll find a way to get you out as soon as I can."

He nuzzled into her shoulder. "I'm just glad you're okay."

She pivoted toward Soogi, clinging to his biceps. "Thank you."

Feigning a smile, he nodded. "I'll see you soon, I promise."

Witnessing them stuffed into separate sedans, she stood silently while the lights from the vehicles disappeared into the distance. The senior officer who questioned her approached her a second time. "I need you to fill out a formal complaint."

Hobbling over to Ha-Rin, she gestured to the remaining roommates, who were still processing the traumatic reality. "Take them home, and I'll meet you there."

Ha-Rin rested a hand on her shoulder. "They will do everything for you. You need to let them press charges."

"We aren't leaving." Hanso refused. "We'll wait in the cold all night if we have to."

Deok-Sun, although petrified, hid his unease. "Yeah, we're not going anywhere."

"Okay." She backtracked to the patrolman, who helped her into the vehicle.

The last strobing car left the vicinity with Jen in the back seat. Hanso picked up the bouquet Hanjun bought for her. Dusting off the dirt, he shook his head. "What the hell happened?"

"I don't know." Ha-Rin spotted the riot brigade disbanding and began to worry they'd be left vulnerable. "We need to leave. Now."

As the celebrities and their accompanying posse fled the scene, reporters tailed the entourage, demanding comments on the tragic state of affairs. Ha-Rin encouraged the group to continue walking without acknowledging the reporters. "We've just experienced a traumatic event. Please respect that."

Swatting a phone away from his face, Deok-Sun gave an attitude. "I don't know anything, okay? You saw what I saw."

Once the artists were thoroughly surrounded by security, Ha-Rin swiveled to address the flashing cameras. "J&I will release a formal statement at our discretion."

★⁺₊★☽★⁺₊★

Jen arrived at the station to find the division had separated Hanjun, Soogi, and both aggressors into isolated rooms. Handed a flimsy blanket and a cup of lukewarm coffee, she was required to fill out a stack of paperwork and provide a written statement. After she could prove her identity, that is.

Sitting alone while she waited for Ha-Rin to bring her visa, her alibi was ridiculed by the male-dominated force. Her integrity was torn to shreds, and she felt eyes preying on her, judging every part of her outfit. From her heels to her jacket, she knew they would try to find a way to blame her. Her clothes were too revealing, or she shouldn't have been out so late at night without an escort, as if she were responsible for the worst parts of humanity.

Despite the larger-than-life cartoon characters straddling the station's doors, the encounter was far worse than she could have imagined. Everything about the building was bleak. Abandoned in a damp room, she was asked to expose portions of her body that were damaged during the attack. A female photographer snapped photos of the abuse, prioritizing the bruises.

A cold room with a cold chair and a cold cup of coffee. Cold officers with cold cameras and colder apologies. Cold fingers taking cold photos of her cold skin, riddled with the marks left by cold people. Cold lighting illuminated cold faces who coldly assumed she was at fault.

She was granted the option of visiting a hospital, though she opted not to, expecting to end the inquisition in a timely fashion. The tragedy was a physical assault—not a sexual crime—and she couldn't fathom wasting resources on something captured in a few photographs.

The photographer, who spoke broken English, acted as her translator. Though the woman tried to be helpful, Jen couldn't understand why a country that spent exorbitant government funds on tourism would fail so miserably at offering fluent linguists.

Standing nearly naked, stripped of her clothing and dignity, her heart ached for the thousands of foreigners who braved worse situations. Painted as one of the safest cities in the world, Seoul went to considerable lengths to present a picturesque utopia. Foreigners were not only taken less seriously, but they were also poorly represented by translators who could only grasp the dilemma through their judgments.

For every series of portraits taken of her battered body, a male officer hung his head in, spitting off a flimsy excuse as to why he encroached on the vulnerable moment. And each time, the female photographer was horrified. Using her body to cover Jen's, her reactions proved the offensive behavior was a common occurrence within the testosterone-filled walls.

The photographs were just as dehumanizing as the violation. She was tired of explaining how she found herself in such a predicament and exhausted beyond the ability to fake a smile. She just wanted to put the terrible night behind her.

★⁺₊★☾★⁺₊★

Hanjun sat in an empty interrogation room. Wiggling his wrists, his hands tingled from the cinched rope. Under normal circumstances, he would have felt scared, but all he knew was rage. He wasn't sure how long he would be in custody, though he assumed twenty-four to forty-eight hours. The moment he retaliated was the moment he lost his right to self-defense, but he didn't care. The man deserved his foot in his gut, and he should have been thankful he wasn't beaten to a bloody pulp.

Though he did feel a degree of remorse; for every minute he was detained, Jen was left to fend for herself within the same walls. He was sure she would be fine—she was a fighter in every sense of the word—but he should have been there to support her.

An officer sauntered in, dispersing a stack of photographs on the table. "These were found on the woman who assaulted Jenilyn. Have you seen either of her attackers before?"

He studied the prints. Many of the images matched the photos from the live stream where Hanso ended the relationship with Jen. Others were snapped by paparazzo. There were even snapshots from their secluded date at the museum. His eyes landed on one; unclear and identical to the pictures they were taunted with over the previous weeks. "Over the last month, we received photos like these at our home. We were never able to figure out who left them."

"We believe they're part of an underground religious movement known as the KAIC." Tapping the tabletop, the officer sat across from him. "Koreans Against Interracial Conspiracy. There's been an uptick in violations centering around mixed races and the love interests of industry stars."

"She's not mixed—" He retracted his statement. "I guess she is."

"Your relationship with Jenilyn has attracted many eyes—some of which are willing to go to extremes for their cause." The officer scooped up the splayed photographs. "This has been the first aggression we've interpolated. She's fortunate. Had it not been for Blackmirror's prominence, the brigade wouldn't have been in the vicinity."

Hanjun lowered his head. *Fortunate.*

"There is a bright side. The assailants turned on each other as soon as they entered the station. They won't give us intelligence about the organization itself, but they did tell us about the mission. They're acting on the orders of a ringleader, but they won't tell us who."

"You're telling me a cult organized a coup against my girlfriend?"

The Chief of Police burst into the room. "The assailants confessed to their crimes. Yi Soogi has been dismissed under the Preventative Act. Ryu Hanjun has been granted an immediate release."

He derided Hanjun, taking a moment to eye him up and down. "You must have friends in high places. Keep your nose clean. I don't want to see you in here again."

"Can I go?" Hanjun held out his arms, unbothering with formalities. Barreling out of the room restraint-free, he encountered Soogi eclipsing the door. Elated to see him, he gave him a lung-squeezing hug. "I heard you got off on defense."

"Yeah. After they assessed Jen, they determined she wouldn't have made it much longer if I hadn't intervened. What about you?"

"The lawyers had me released, but I'll face a penalty, if not a lawsuit for injuries." Hanjun gave his shoulders a squeeze.

"Did they say anything to you about a cult?" Soogi headed straight for the exit.

"Yeah." Hanjun paused before opening the door. "She needs to rest before we give her something else to worry about."

The time was closer to morning than it was to night when they exited the doors. The first to notice, Jen ran to them despite her throbbing joints. "I'm so sorry!"

Soogi rubbed her back. "You have no reason to be."

Bursting into tears, she planted her face between their broad chests. "If it wasn't for me, you wouldn't have been cuffed."

Soogi and Hanjun shared an uncertain glance; it was obvious the attack hadn't sunk in. She was more preoccupied with their well-being.

"Don't worry, Mi Sol." Embracing her, he clocked his friends, unsure of what he should do.

Standing behind Jen, Hanso stepped forward, handing him the disfigured flowers. Settling the misshapen bouquet in her hands, Hanjun wanted to smile but couldn't force his muscles to move. "I promise they were beautiful earlier."

She thumbed through the broken stems. "They're perfect."

$$\star{}^{+}_{+}\star\mathbb{C}\star{}^{+}_{+}\star$$

Exiting the elevator, Jen limped along the corridor, hanging onto the wall. Soogi held a palm on her back, ensuring she didn't topple over. "Are you alright?"

"My ankle didn't hurt earlier, but I think that was the adrenaline." Catching her balance, she pulled her pant leg up to reveal a swollen, misshapen joint.

"Mi Sol, you shouldn't be walking on that." Without needing to coordinate their actions, Hanjun and Soogi lifted her from the floor. Supporting her through the condo and down the hall, they positioned her among the overstuffed pillows on her bed.

Tugging the blanket over her bosom, she closed her eyes for a long moment. "I thought I was going to die."

Soogi patted her head, stationing Todoroki by her side. "You're not leaving us that easily."

Hanjun cuddled next to her. "Can you turn the light off?"

"Sure." Flipping the switch, Soogi retreated to his room.

Climbing under the covers, he restlessly stared at a stack of notepads near his bed. It was hard for him to sleep on a normal night—nearly impossible after an evening pervaded with wrath. With a pen in his hand and anger in his heart, he pulled the pads from the shelf and finished the lyrics for the chorus Jen helped him write, making a vow to record it on his next studio visit.

Skimming through another notebook, he ran his fingers over a specific set of lyrics. The night he met Jen, he wrote a limerick about meeting her, and every time he felt jealous of Hunjun, he added to the work. Leafing through the inscriptions was a nostalgic journey of developing interest, understanding he wasn't her perfect match, and still wanting to protect her.

From the moment I met you
I knew I'd be in trouble
You were too damn cute, girl
That's why I got your number

I couldn't sleep at all that night
I could only think of ya
Pretty eyes, sexy thighs
You cast a spell I fell under

I thought I won that night
I'd take you to meet my mother
To this day, I still feel the same
Even though you chose my brother

Though I sat back and watched
I'd never enjoy the show
Hell yeah, I'm angry, but bae, you made me
I watched you fall in love with him

Knowing that he ain't me
I could never be him, even if I tried
It won't ever stop me from wishing you were mine
I'm not mad, losing to a better man

That doesn't mean I won't dream about it with every sleep I have
I'll always be here for you; I'll lift you up
You'll never know because I'll act like I don't give a fuck
You've made a fan for life, baby you're my idol

"You already have my heart; take my life. It's for you." With nowhere else to direct his fury, he scribbled a verse inspired by his inherent need to guard her.

I've never been as afraid as I was that night
Not religious, you had me thanking God
Never thought it would get this bad
Why the fuck is it so hard?

I picked up that brick without thinking
I lied, I thought about you
The situation looked to be the worst

I did what I had to do

I smashed him in the head
I would have kept going, too
But when he fell, you fell
You know I'll always catch you

I held you in my arms for the first time
Heartbeat fast, body cold
Until they put me in the cuffs
I didn't care how it would unfold

I wouldn't even change it
I would have done it the same
I'll never turn my back on you
Fuck him, fuck her, fuck fame

Finishing the last stanza, he realized he wasn't over not being chosen. He didn't know how it happened—how he could fall in love. He didn't think it would happen to him. Everyone else in the world could contract the sickness, but not him. "Love is a chemical imbalance of the brain. Self-destruction disguised as temporary insanity. Why does insanity feel so good? Why does everything I thought I knew feel so wrong? Why did she change everything?"

Lying in bed, Hanjun couldn't believe what the officer told him about the KAIC. It sounded like a dim-witted conspiracy theory. But what if there was some truth to it? How could he research further without putting Jen in danger? As much as he wanted to dismiss the idea as a ridiculous fluke, he couldn't ignore the nagging feeling that something was wrong. His girlfriend was targeted by a religious affiliation that believed they were anointed to exterminate her. But why?

After devoting an hour to scouring endless websites, he was left with little to no information. Sighing, he closed the browser and texted Soogi.

Are you awake?

Unfortunately.

> *It's hard to find information about that cult.*

Not good.

> *I'm scared for Jen.*

Me too. We can't leave her alone.

> *She's going to hate that.*

What else is there?

> *I don't know.*

Hanjun, can I tell you something?
Without you getting mad.

> *Yes, Hyung.*

I downplayed how much I liked her.

Skimming the correspondence, wishing it would change, he experienced a mix of fear and disappointment. He couldn't deny he wasn't the only one vying for her attention, but witnessing the confession made it sting even more.

Soogi coveted her while he encouraged Hanjun to pursue her. He accepted her interest in his bandmate and willingly moved aside. It pained him to admit it, but deep down, he considered Soogi a better man. If their roles were reversed and it was him who fell in love with his friend's girlfriend, he would have knowingly meddled in hopes of winning her over.

> I will never try to come between you.

> *I trust you.*

Thank you.

> *We need to have a meeting in the morning.*

Understood.

Ignoring the last notification, he placed the phone at his side. He needed to conciliate before he did something he'd regret. Instead, he reached for his journal, praying that putting ink on paper would help him sort through his inner turmoil.

A day beginning with hope ended in tragedy. The attack. The KAIC. Soogi's affection for Jen. For the first time, there aren't any answers. I don't know what to do.

Dramatis Personae

Léna
Birth mother of Jenilyn.

Pa-Goe
Birth father to Jenilyn.

Achukma
Chickasaw Great-Grandmother to Jenilyn.

Borbala
Hungarian Great-Grandmother to Jenilyn.

Ingrid
German Great-Grandmother to Jenilyn.

Ernest
German Great-Grandfather to Jenilyn.

Yu-Chi
Forgotten Great-Grandmother to Jenilyn.

Ryu Hanjun
Leader and supportive rap vocalist for Blackmirror.
Also known as Rem.

Ha-Rin
Manager of Blackmirror.

Jenilyn
Headstrong divorcee with a soft heart.

Tisho
Native childhood friend to Jenilyn.

Ha Deok-Sun
Youngest member and lead vocalist for Blackmirror. Also known as
Sunny.

Yi Soogi
Lead rapper for Blackmirror. Also known as Honey.

Kim U-Jin
Main vocals for Blackmirror. Also known as Jin.

Gan Ho-Young
Lead dancer and supportive rap vocalist for Blackmirror.
Also known as Hanso.

Kristen
Best friend and confidant of Jenilyn.

Koroleva
Elderly friend of Jenilyn.

The Base Gene
Jenilyn's favorite band.

Kyle Richmond
Lead vocalist for The Base Gene.

Mr. Yun
CEO and founder of J&I Entertainment.

Dae-Hyun
Manager of Blackmirror's Management.

Haeseong
Cutthroat celebrity stalker.

Sehoon Sohn
Lead production manager for Parallels.

Yoo Junyeong
Leader of idol group F.U.T.U.R.E.

Kim Hyun-Woo
The artist only known as J.
Renowned as Korea's 'Golden' voice.

Hopaya
Tisho's great-grandfather.

Kang Tae-Gil
Hanjun's closest friend. Also known as Taeg.

Cursory Glossary

Halmoni
[Origin: Korean] Grandmother.

Appo'si
[Origin: Chickasaw] Grandmother.

Earth Mother
Feminine deity. Responsible for gifting humanity with agricultural plants. Associated with fertility, rebirth, and renewal.

Great Spirit
[Origin: Chickasaw] Aba' Binni'li', a supreme being said to be the sole creator of warmth, light, and animal life. Believed to live within smoke, above the clouds, and in holy fire.

Holy Fire
Ritualistic fires celebrating the Great Spirit. Ungracious, unlawful, and considered the work of evil spirits to extinguish fire with water.

Blackmirror
Five-piece boy band hailing from Seoul, South Korea. The third-generation group debuted from a small agency mid-2015 with a highly curated otherworldly theme touching on topics of the unknown.

The Enantiomorphs
The massive fan-following behind Blackmirror. 'Anti' for short.

Eungwonbong
[Origin: Korean] Small handheld devices used by fans to show their support.

Galabong
[Origin: Korean] Blackmirror's official crescent-shaped cheer stick.

Alikchi
[Origin: Chickasaw] God-chosen healer.

Shawi' Iksa' (Raccoon Clan)
[Origin: Chickasaw] Highest-ranking clan of the Imosaktca (the senior moiety within the Chickasaw tribes.)

Nashoba' Iksa' (Wolf Clan)
[Origin: Chickasaw] Clan of warriors.

Hyung
[Origin: Korean] Informal honorific for older brother or close male friend to a younger male.

Maknae
[Origin: Korean] The youngest among a family or group.

heartoo
Stylized in lowercase. Up and coming monthly subscription for singles.

"Omo!"
[Origin: Korean] 'Oh my!'

KakoaTalk
Instant messaging service widely used in Korea.

J&I Entertainment
The agency responsible for the creation and distribution of Blackmirror.

ㅋㅋㅋ
[Origin: Korean] *Slang*. The Hangul letter k, representing laughter.

Aegyo-sal
[Origin: Korean] A cute, childlike appearance, referencing the roll of fat underneath the eyes sometimes displayed with a genuine smile.

Joseon
[Origin: Korean] The last dynastic kingdom of Korea, lasting just over 500 years. Founded by Yi Seong-gye in July of 1392 and replaced by the Korean Empire in October of 1897.

Windsor Heights
Wealthy district in Seoul, South Korea.

"Utpeuda!"
[Origin: Korean] *Slang*. Funny but sad.

The Multiverse

A universe of characters created by Blackmirror. Distributed internationally, the characters could be found on shelves in the form of stuffed animals, backpacks, blankets, and clothing.

Joey the kangaroo
Hanjun's Multiverse character.

Blackmirror:Parallels
Reality-based show showcasing Blackmirror's daily interactions.

-ssi
[Origin: Korean] Common polite honorific used among people of approximately equal speech levels. Attached after the full name or after the first name if the speaker is more familiar with someone.

-ie
[Origin: Korean] Diminutive suffix attached to the end of a person's name as a sign of closeness and affection.

-ah or -a
[Origin: Korean] Informal suffix attached at the end of a person's name as a sign of friendship. Less commonly used when addressing someone of equal or lesser social status.

Hoesik
[Origin: Korean] After-work gathering among colleagues.

Chikashshanompa
[Origin: Chickasaw] Mother tongue of the Chickasaw people.

"Chiholloli"
[Origin: Chickasaw] 'I love you.'

Tteokbokki
[Origin: Korean] Soft rice cakes simmered in a spicy sauce.

"Hana.. dul.. set!"
[Origin: Korean] The numbers one, two, and three.

"Gwenchanayo"
[Origin: Korean] Formal for 'I'm alright,' 'It's fine,' 'I'm OK,' or 'It's alright.'

"Bansa"
[Origin: Korean] *Slang.* A childish way to reflect jokes or insults.

Bokbunjaju
[Origin: Korean] Black raspberry wine.

F.U.T.U.R.E.
A fourth-generation group debuted under J&I Entertainment. Boasting vogue vocals, juicy jazz harmonies, and beastly, masculine sex appeal, the four members portray polished, refined billionaire sons on the rise to take over their family businesses.

The Eternals
Fandom name for F.U.T.U.R.E.

"Geukyeom!"
[Origin: Korean] *Slang.* Extreme disgust or revulsion.

Krampus
Central European legend said to be half-goat half-demon monster. Punishes misbehaving children at Christmastime.

Dokkaebi
[Origin: Korean] Mythological creatures with supernatural powers. Storied to be helpful or hurtful.

Noona
[Origin: Korean] Informal honorific for older sister or close female friend to a younger male.

Oma
[Origin: Korean] Mom. Umma and Eoma are additional English spellings.

"Ddaeng"
[Origin: Korean] Onomatopoeia for the sound of a bell. Commonly used to indicate a wrong answer.

Yakgwa
[Origin: Korean] A traditional deep-fried cookie consisting of honey, sesame oil, ginger, and soju covered in a sweet, sticky syrup.

Hodu-gwaja
[Origin: Korean] Walnut-shaped confection with red bean paste filling.

The Prophecy of the Setting Sun

A prophecy foretold before the Second War, distributed after the Korean War.

The Dragon
The Chosen One. Said to be the savior of humanity by the Prophecy Keepers.

The Shayo
The name used to refer to The Dragon by anti-believers known as the KAIC.

Prophecy Keepers
Those who trust in The Originator (the original creator of The Prophecy of the Setting Sun) and The Dragon. Carrying long-lost pieces of the prophecy, The Keepers protect the Chosen One with their lives, believing they are the only hope for humanity.

KAIC
Koreans Against Interracial Conspiracy.
Religious fanatics who believe in the prophecy, though disagree with saving the world. Their only goal is to stop The Dragon, thus ensuring the world ends as foretold.

Romanization Guide

Léna
Lee-na

Pa-Goe
Pa-Go

Achukma
A-chook-ma

Borbala
Bor-ba-la

Ingrid
Ing-grid

Halmoni
Hal-mo-nee

Yu-Chi
Yoo-chee

Enantiomorphs
En-anti-o-morphs

Anti
Ann-tie

Ryu Hanjun
Re-yoo Hahn-joon

Ha-Rin
Hah-Rin

Jenilyn
Jen-ah-lyn

Tisho
Tee-sho

Alikchi
Ah-lick-chi

Rem
Rehm

Hyung
H-yung

Ha Deok-Sun
Hah De-yuk-sun

Maknae
Mag-nae

Yi Soogi
Ee Soo-ghee

Kim U-Jin
Ghim Yoo-jin

Gan Ho-Young
Gahn Ho-yung

Heartoo
Heart-too

Koroleva
Core-o-leave-ah

Joseon
Jow-see-uhn

Mr. Yun
Mister You-n

Dae-Hyun
Deh-hy-uhn

Hoesik
Hway-shik

Tteokbokki
Tuk-bo-kee

Oma
Ohm-ma

Todoroki
Tow-dough-row-key

Taeg
Tay-g

Ajumma
Ah-joo-ma

Shayo
Sh-eye-oh

K.A.I.C.
Cake

ABOUT THE AUTHOR

J.E. Maier has been dreaming up cinematic stories since she was a girl. With exuberance, she prowled the streets of her hometown, recounting her nightly visions to friends. Soon, her fantasies turned to lyrical prose, scribbling tidbits into the pages of notebooks with no idea how to implement them. In adulthood, she utilized her artistry in the creative industry by getting her hands on any project she could. Unfortunately, Covid had a way of leveling the world, and while confined to her home, her imagination soared, leading her to what she believes is her calling.